Praise for

PACIFIC BURN

"Jim Brodie is a true 21st-century hero . . . on page after page, Barry Lancet delivers."

—Steve Berry, *New York Times* bestselling author of *The Patriot Threat*

"Just like the first two of Lancet's books, *Japantown* and *Tokyo Kill*, *Pacific Burn* is a gritty thriller . . . highly suspenseful . . . 5 stars."

—*San Francisco Book Review*

"There is really no one quite like the enigmatic Jim Brodie. . . . Lancet created a character much like Lee Child's Reacher and Michael Connelly's Bosch. It's the perfect triad."

—*Providence Journal*

"All of these stories have been outstanding, and in this new title, Jim is up against a global conspiracy that is the biggest he has ever seen, while dealing with a killer that even the underworld avoids. Barry Lancet is an incredible suspense author who has 'knocked it out of the park' yet again."

—*Suspense Magazine*

"Barry Lancet's *Pacific Burn* is a stellar detective thriller with a fast-paced, tense and complex storyline. I have been a fan of the characters in this unique series since I read/reviewed the first novel."

—*Fresh Fiction*

"I loved *Japantown* and *Tokyo Kill*, but *Pacific Burn* is Lancet's best book yet. Japan expert, art dealer, and sometimes PI, Jim Brodie makes for a character as layered and nuanced as the Japanese culture. Lancet knows art, knows Japan, and knows how to write a mystery that grabs hold and doesn't let go."

—Marc Cameron, *New York Times* bestselling author of the Jericho Quinn thrillers

"The third book in the series, *Pacific Burn*, offers a potent mix of action, atmosphere, and fascinating cultural details."

—*Los Angeles Review of Books*

"As ever, Lancet stages some good fight scenes—no one gets beaten up as well as Brodie—and keeps the action going. . . . An action-filled effort."

—*Kirkus Reviews*

Praise for

TOKYO KILL

Shamus Award Finalist for Best Mystery

"Lancet imbues *Tokyo Kill* with a vivid sense of Japan, from sections of Tokyo that only a native would know about to meticulous research into the country's history and legend. . . . Lancet hit the ground running last year with his superb debut, *Japantown,* and continues that winning streak with *Tokyo Kill.*"

—*The New York Times*

"Brodie is immediately noteworthy as one of the more interesting characters in the thriller universe. . . . A book worth reading and a series worth starting."

—*Bookreporter*

"A stellar novel of action, adventure, and intrigue. Jim Brodie is a true 21st-century hero, part of the new, gritty mythos, warts and all, but capable of turning the ordinary into the extraordinary. On page after page of *Tokyo Kill*, skeletons bang on every closet door long to be set free—and Barry Lancet delivers."

—Steve Berry

"*Tokyo Kill* is above all an excellent mystery that stands on its own for great storytelling . . . [It] also offers some nuanced understandings of the China-Japan relationship."

—Forbes.com

"Readers who enjoy fast-paced tales of intrigue are in for a treat."

—*Minneapolis Star Tribune*

"A first-rate mystery, at least as good as *Japantown*. That novel could have worked just fine as a one-off, but this second book is a clear indicator that Lancet considers Jim Brodie a series-worthy character. He'd be right, too."

—*Booklist*

Praise for

JAPANTOWN

Barry Award Winner for Best First Novel
A *Suspense Magazine* Best Thrillers of the Year

"A sophisticated international thriller. . . . Having lived and worked in Japan for more than 25 years, Lancet brings an impressive breadth of knowledge to the historical aspects of the mystery and a sharp sense of immediacy to its action."

—*The New York Times Book Review*

"The first book in what will likely be a long and successful series."

—*San Francisco* magazine

"Lancet's fluency in the Japanese language, extensive knowledge of, and empathy with, the culture from which it is inseparable, and gift for creating likable (as well as despicable) characters add depth and authenticity to this captivating thriller."

—*Washington Independent Review of Books*

"Engrossing . . . *Japantown* is full of action and surprise . . . an extremely impressive debut that is almost sure to be shortlisted for any number of awards next year. Pick it up now to see what all the excitement will be about."

—Bookreporter.com

"From gritty San Francisco to exotic Tokyo, *Japantown* is a whip-smart, razor-fast ride, and entertaining from cover to cover."

—Taylor Stevens, *New York Times* bestselling author of *The Mask*

ALSO BY BARRY LANCET

Japantown

Tokyo Kill

PACIFIC BURN

A Thriller

BARRY LANCET

SIMON & SCHUSTER PAPERBACKS
New York London Toronto Sydney New Delhi

Simon & Schuster Paperbacks
An Imprint of Simon & Schuster, Inc.
1230 Avenue of the Americas
New York, NY 10020

This book is a work of fiction. Any references to historical events, real people, real organizations, or real places are used fictitiously. Other names, characters, places, and events are products of the author's imagination, and any resemblance to actual events or places or persons, living or dead, is entirely coincidental.

First Simon & Schuster trade paperback edition February 2017

SIMON & SCHUSTER PAPERBACKS and colophon are registered trademarks of Simon & Schuster, Inc.

For information about special discounts for bulk purchases, please contact Simon & Schuster Special Sales at 1-866-506-1949 or business@simonandschuster.com.

The Simon & Schuster Speakers Bureau can bring authors to your live event. For more information or to book an event contact the Simon & Schuster Speakers Bureau at 1-866-248-3049 or visit our website at www.simonspeakers.com.

Manufactured in the United States of America

1 3 5 7 9 10 8 6 4 2

The Library of Congress has cataloged the hardcover edition as follows:

Lancet, Barry.
Pacific burn : a thriller / Barry Lancet.—First Simon & Schuster hardcover edition.
pages; cm
1. Antique dealers—California—San Francisco—Fiction. 2. Japanese—California—San Francisco—Fiction. 3. Murder—Investigation—Fiction. 4. Tokyo (Japan)—Fiction. I. Title.
PS3612.A547486P33 2016
813'.6—dc23 2015015933

ISBN 978-1-4767-9488-4
ISBN 978-1-4767-9489-1 (pbk)
ISBN 978-1-4767-9490-7 (ebook)

Three things cannot be long hidden: the sun, the moon, the truth.

—BUDDHA

DAY 1

DEATHWATCH

CHAPTER 1

SAN FRANCISCO, 7:05 A.M.

THE phone call came far too early to herald anything good.

"Feel like taking a ride?" Detective Frank Renna asked when I picked up.

"Got to get Jenny ready for school soon and I have a high-end client coming into the shop first thing today. She's eager to drop big money on an Oribe tea bowl."

Oribe is a sometimes-brilliant Japanese ceramic–style named after Furuta Oribe, a sixteenth-century tea master and samurai. I sold the distinctive green-and-white pieces and other Japanese antiques out of my shop on Lombard, west of Van Ness.

"Nice to see you making headway on the diplomatic front," Renna said, "but move it to the back burner and pack your daughter off. This is important. We're heading out to Napa."

"Are we now?"

"Yeah. There's a Japanese kid we need to see. He doesn't speak English."

"So put a phone to his ear and I'll talk to him. No reason we need to drag ourselves out to wine country."

"Kid's gone into shock and he's babbling. He's driving the local badges up a wall."

Renna was a lieutenant with the San Francisco Police Department, and a friend. He'd been instrumental in getting me a consulting job with the SFPD as their local Japan expert, which last came into play with an incident in Japantown. But I wasn't on call and received no retainer. Our arrangement was on a case-by-case basis, clearly a detail that seemed to have slipped Renna's mind.

"Isn't there a Japanese speaker closer to Napa?" I asked.

"None in their department and they don't have anyone on file. That's why they need you."

"How do they know the kid's Japanese?"

"Because that's what his father was."

"Was?"

"Yeah. There's a body, too."

Ten minutes after Renna's call, I was waiting outside in the morning fog, ungloved hands snug in the pockets of a down jacket.

I watched brief shafts of faint red light penetrate the fog. Heard the sound of a car engine approaching. Saw, finally, a boxy vehicle emerge out of the cottony whiteness and ease to the curb. Renna had arrived in a dusty unmarked SFPD car that looked exactly like a dusty unmarked SFPD car.

The passenger-side window buzzed down.

"You're doing a good imitation of something the cat *wouldn't* drag in," my friend said.

"I was up until seven talking to Tokyo," I said. "Finalizing details for the shows. Fell into bed five minutes before you woke me."

The mayor of San Francisco had launched a Pacific Rim Friendship Program to improve the city's relations with its Asian neighbors, and Japan was up first. I'd rebuffed City Hall's first two advances to be their liaison, accepting with reluctance only after the big man himself called to press me into service.

"Coffee up," Renna said, passing over a cup of Peet's dark roast as I collapsed into the front seat. "It's all downhill from here."

He urged the vehicle back onto the road. "You get Jenny off to school?"

"Neighbor upstairs will drive her."

"Client take it well?"

"Wife said her husband would be furious, but we rescheduled for later today, so I squeaked by. Listen, I get the babbling kid bit, but why are *we* on the road? It's Napa, not SF."

As was his habit, Renna rolled imaginary marbles from cheek to cheek while he considered the question. "A Napa bigwig rang our dear mayor and he rang the chief."

"So this is another favor for City Hall?" I said, wondering if they weren't pushing the boundaries.

"Not even close. The mayor hoards his political capital. He called my boss. I'm under orders. You're doing this for me. Since Japantown, everyone thinks I'm your goddamn social secretary."

"I could live with that," I said.

"You do recall we're cruising over marshlands soon, right?"

Overhead, a sign announced our approach to the Golden Gate access road. Our route took us over the bridge into Marin County. We'd pass the monied Marin communities of Mill Valley and San Rafael, cross the reedy marshes edging the upper fringe of the San Francisco Bay, then head north to Napa.

"Yeah, so?"

"You piss me off, I'll toss you into the muck and you won't be living with anything. You'll be lucky if your bones surface in a decade or two."

"Probably less painful."

The lieutenant grunted. "Hard to argue that."

I took a sip of the coffee. A hearty Italian roast rolled over my tongue. It cut through the early-morning chill, but made not the slightest dent in my exhaustion.

"I've got to close my eyes for a minute," I said. "Can you handle the drive alone?"

"Sure. One thing first, though. Napa guys sent you a present."

"Am I going to like it?"

"Wouldn't think so."

He stretched a finger toward the face of his smartphone, anchored in a dashboard cradle, but before he could tap the screen, my mobile buzzed.

An unknown number. "Hold on a sec," I said, then into my phone, "Hello?"

"Is this Jim Brodie?"

"Yes."

"Sean Navin. We haven't met yet but you're on my blacklist."

That was a first.

Before I could reply, Navin said, "You canceled on us this morning. No one does that to me."

"Sarah already rescheduled."

"I'm canceling it."

"I normally don't—"

"Save the excuses. I'm sending my wife to one of your competitors."

I closed my eyes. There goes the Oribe tea bowl commission I sorely needed. The loss was going to hurt.

"Sorry to hear that," I said. "As I explained to Sarah, it's an emergency."

"Time is money, Brodie. You play fast and loose with my time, I spend my greenbacks elsewhere."

In his voice I heard none of the goodwill I'd earned over the last couple of years. Quality art from my shop decorated his home. Some of the rarities his wife had requested I'd tracked down in distant corners of Japan.

"I regret it happened, Sean. If there was any way around canceling our appointment, believe me, I would have found it."

"You made a bad decision and it's gonna cost you."

"So you've told me. Do what you have to do," I said, and disconnected.

So much for squeaking by. His wife was a valued customer, but mind games from an overbearing husband I didn't need. Life was too short.

Renna glanced my way. He'd pieced together enough of the conversation to know that I was going to pay for this morning's excursion.

"I'd pegged you for being more diplomatic," he said.

"Husband kept twisting the knife. Got a feeling he was enjoying it."

"A lot of those types around."

"Yeah. Too bad. His wife was a regular. You were saying?"

"A present from the Napa boys." Renna punched the smartphone screen. A recording began.

"Can you tell us your name, son?" a clearly annoyed adult male voice said.

"Mondai attara Jimu Burodi-san ni denwa shite kudasai. Mondai attara Jimu Burodi-san ni denwa shite kudasai. Mondai attara Jimu Burodi-san ni denwa—"

"We hear you, kid," the man said through what sounded like gritted teeth. Then: "I'm telling you, Dick. That's all the little guy's said since we got here."

Dick gave it a shot. "Hiya, son. I'm Officer Richard Kendall. Can you give us your name? Just your name?"

"Mondai attara Jimu Burodi-san ni denwa shite kudasai. Mondai attara—"

"See? Repeat loop," the first man said.

"Considering the circumstances, can't say I blame him."

The dispatch ended and Renna said, "Still want to close your eyes?"

"Got to."

"Sweet dreams."

They were anything but.

In the recording, the babbling kid had been asking for me.

CHAPTER 2

WHEN Renna eased off the gas pedal, I woke instantly—alert and recharged. Looking out the windshield at what lay before me, I froze in midstretch and said, "You can't have the right place."

Renna had swung into the parking lot of the di Rosa, an art complex on prime vineyard land in Napa Valley.

"Afraid I do."

My heart rate kicked up a beat. An incoherent child was one thing. A crime scene linking my day job—art—to police business elevated this early-morning summons to a whole other realm. Renna, the sly bugger, had held out. The crime/art combination, as he well knew, had proved poisonous three months ago in Tokyo.

"You could have told me," I said, a rebellious rumble rising in my throat.

"And make the trip harder? No thanks."

"You didn't know for a fact that I'd refuse."

"You saying you wouldn't have?"

"This is not what I expect from my social secretary."

"So fire me."

Rene di Rosa had been the son of an Italian aristocrat and a St. Louis heiress. As a practicing journalist, he'd come west, put in a stint at the *San Francisco Chronicle*, and eventually purchased four hundred and fifty acres of neglected Napa farmland before the area became legendary for its grapes. Then he replaced free-ranging cattle and fields of barley and oats with wine varietals, explored the possibilities of California pinot noir, and eventually molded the place into the first highly respected Napa Valley winery. Later, he divested himself of his prized vines and turned to collecting Northern California art with unbridled passion.

"You understand what the kid was saying?" Renna asked.

"Sure."

"So give me a translation."

"'If there's a problem, call Jim Brodie.'"

Marbles began to roll. "The Napa cops laid down bets for and against a message along those lines. The distortion made it hard to tell if what they heard was actually your name."

"It was. The Japanese language has a second alphabet that allows speakers to render foreign words into Japanese, but it's not precise."

"Convenient."

"Eye of the beholder," I said, staring at the art preserve up ahead.

"Maybe he's not talking about you," Renna said.

"He is."

"Did you recognize the voice?"

"No," I said, "but I think I'm about to."

CHAPTER 3

RENNA guided our grime-covered rattletrap past four sheriff's vehicles before easing into a spot alongside one of two Napa city black-and-whites.

"Looks like county jurisdiction," I said, kneading the stiffness in my neck.

Renna nodded. "Napa city limit starts a few miles on. Their boys are along for support." More marbles, then: "You ever been out here?"

"A few times."

"Would the wife like it?"

I'd met Frank and his better half six years ago when the couple had strolled into the antiques shop where I was apprenticing in the Outer Sunset District. Even in plainclothes, Renna's bearing screamed cop. Hardened eyes. Penetrating look. A palpable aura of distance because in his world people were callous and calculating and lied as easily as they breathed.

"Di Rosa's focus was different but you can sense his enthusiasm for the work," I said as we stepped from the vehicle. "Your wife would like that about him."

At six-foot-four, Renna intimidated most people. Smart suspects stayed put when he confronted them. Fleeing brought down the lightning-fast hammer that was Lieutenant Frank Renna. Thick brown hair framed a large square face with a few soft edges. There was also humor at the back of his eyes if he let you past the cop deadpan.

Renna shot me a sharp look. "Did you just dish out an art world equivalent of 'she's got personality'?"

"Or 'he'? No. We're talking different tastes. Di Rosa went in for Funk Art and the Bay Area Figurative movement. Mostly loud and colorful stuff. Your wife favors quieter work."

But, to his credit, di Rosa had been a stout supporter of Northern California artists while other resident collectors looked to the East Coast and Europe for pieces. Di Rosa was beloved because he bought local—famous, and fresh-faced talent. He snapped up sculpture by Stephen De Staebler, clay pieces by Peter Voulkos, conceptual art by Bruce Nauman, ceramic murals by Jim Melchert, paintings by Elmer Bischoff, and so on, an endless string of acquisitions. He sought early efforts, before prices headed to the stars. The collection now housed more than two thousand works of art from some eight hundred artists.

Trudging uphill toward the entrance, Renna scanned the area. "Looks like a big spread. Never makes for a good crime scene."

I nodded. "Acres and acres. Gift shop and a small gallery are through the front door. The main gallery is three, four minutes up the hill by shuttle. It's ten times larger and holds the permanent collection. Then there's offices, the original home, and an outdoor sculpture garden stretching back even farther."

Renna shook his head. "Not big. *Huge* goddamn crime scene."

Two sheriff's deputies escorted us from the entrance to a waiting patrol car out back. We rolled upward toward the main gallery, which one of our guides referred to as "a queer place for an accident."

Renna's brow furrowed.

We entered the gallery and traipsed past an "art car" by self-proclaimed "junk sculptor" David Best. He'd strip down a vehicle, refashion it, then smother the surface with thousands of small objects, from toys to bits of mirror to endless salvaged knickknacks, until the car sparkled and glittered and told an American story.

A long hall peppered with sculpture and paintings and collages led us to a covered back patio and David Ireland's famous *Angel-Go-Round*—a collection of prostrate classical Greco-Roman cemetery statuary huddled in a circle. Normally, an angel—winged and pious and draped in a white robe—glided overhead in a tight circuit above the "dead."

It was present but unmoving. As lifeless as the corpse of an adult Japanese male that had fallen across the statues.

The body of someone I knew well.

Someone I had, in fact, talked to eight months ago when I visited his father's studio in Kyoto to collect pieces for my shop.

CHAPTER 4

THE angel hovered over the pallid corpse of Toru Nobuki, son of my friend and world-class artist Ken Nobuki.

Like his father, Toru is—had been—of a creative bent. He made public sculptures, which explained his presence at the di Rosa art park. But only partially. His father had mentioned sending Toru to look at the di Rosa collection once the exhibition exchange with the mayor's people was finalized. Which wasn't due to happen until next week.

So why the hell was Ken's son here now?

In Japan last spring, Toru had dropped by his father's studio with his young son for a quick chat, mostly revolving around whether I could place some of his outdoor sculptures in the States.

I'd promised to develop some leads—a promise now empty for all the wrong reasons.

Toru had collapsed on top of David Ireland's horizontal effigies. The artist lay limp and neglected, like a discarded sack of old rice. His upper body had come to rest on the lower limbs of a full-figured female, while his legs were draped over a Greco-Roman male. A concave gash behind his left eye echoed the curvature of the woman's upper thigh. His hair was matted with blood, capillary action drawing some of the body fluid up from the wound. As I took in his dead eyes and slack lips, sadness consumed me.

Ireland had gathered up the sculptures from Colma, the Bay Area's very own "City of the Dead." By the end of the 1800s, San Francisco had matured from rowdy gold-rush town to budding metropolis. Land had grown scarce, so the city passed laws prohibiting any new cemeteries. Then in 1914, officials went after the existing burial grounds, and the dead were handed their walking papers. Countless bodies were exhumed. For some reason, the pigs-and-potato outpost of Colma became the relocation spot of choice. Today, the town had more than seventeen graveyards, and a thousand horizontal residents for every inhabitant walking upright.

A stocky man stepped forward and introduced himself as Sheriff Tom Nash. He was five-ten, with bushy brown eyebrows and a paunch edging over a black cowhide belt. He followed up with the names of his deputies. Renna did the honors on our side.

I tore my eyes away from Toru's lifeless form to shake hands all around. The sheriff and his deputies wore beige shirts and olive-green pants, with copper-colored stars on their chest. The city cops had donned navy-blue tops and bottoms, with silver stars.

"Thanks for coming out," Nash said.

Renna grunted. "Thanks for holding the scene until we got here."

My gaze drifted back to the body. A good measure of Toru's blood had pooled under the statues. A small puddle of oil directly below the angel's mechanical track running along the ceiling had collected on the concrete patio. A skid mark where someone had stepped in the oil bisected the puddle. More oil glistened on the sole of Toru's right shoe.

He'd slipped in the lubricant and bashed his head in when he fell forward onto the statuary.

Nash shrugged. "Didn't want to move the father until you got a crack at the son. Especially since the big boys are plugged into this one."

A reference to the mayor and company.

"Yeah," Renna said. "Lucky us. The ME been?"

"In and out. He's thinking accident too, but won't confirm until he's got the stiff on the slab."

"Good enough. Did he mention a TOD?" Time of death.

"Already nailed down. Between six twenty-three and seven-oh-four p.m. yesterday evening."

Renna smiled. "Impressive."

"Last night?" I said.

"Yep."

Anger welled up as I asked, "How's it possible he could lie out here all night?"

Ignoring the censure in my tone, Nash said, "The dead guy wanted a look at the outdoor sculpture, even in the dark. Had a flashlight." The sheriff pointed to a black cylinder a few feet away. "The curator gave them the go-ahead. Gallery was already locked up, so they said good night to each other and our man strolled around the grounds with his son while the curator put in some overtime, then clocked out around eight, figuring father and son were long gone."

"How'd you get the times?" Renna asked.

"First time's when the father called for a taxi. Second's when the cab arrived for the seven o'clock pickup. The driver didn't see his fare waiting in the bottom lot, so after a few minutes he buzzed the cell and no one answered."

"Can't ask for much more," Renna said.

"Your tax dollars at work."

Renna nodded and I scanned the patio. Toru's son was nowhere in sight. "Was the kid out here all night too?"

"Yep."

"Where'd you stash him?"

"You mean *leave* him. We couldn't budge the little man. He's right where we found him. And all yours." Nash pointed up a grassy slope beyond the patio retaining wall.

Shu Nobuki, Ken's grandson, sat in the shadow of a giant eucalyptus tree. He was tucked up against its vast trunk, a wool coverlet draped over his shoulders. Shu rocked back and forth in a rhythm all his own, bony knees drawn to his chest, rail-thin arms wrapped around bent legs, head down. His lips moved continually, though the words weren't audible from where we stood.

"How long's he been like that?" I asked.

"I'd say most of the night. We pushed the blanket on him this morning once we saw we couldn't pry the kid loose without him going ballistic on us."

The sheriff's tone had softened and grown circumspect, as if he thought Shu might be on the brink of going over the edge.

CHAPTER 5

As I approached I heard the chant: *"Mondai attara Jimu Burodi-san ni denwa shite kudasai. Mondai attara Jimu Burodi-san ni denwa shite kudasai. Mondai attara Jimu Burodi-san ni denwa shite kudasai."*

The same refrain Renna had played for me on his phone. From a distance I deemed nonthreatening, I called out to Ken's grandson.

He continued to rock and chant.

I eased closer. "Shu-kun," I said softly, using an affectionate form of *san*, "I'm here."

The chanting and rocking continued.

"It's me, Shu-kun. Jim Brodie. You know me. You're calling my name. Look at me."

He raised his head. The chanting dropped to a low mumble, but the swaying persisted. His face was a sickly mushroom-gray. His eyes were dilated and unfocused and they wandered around a bit before they found my face. When we locked eyes, the audio ceased but his lips still mouthed the words.

Under normal circumstances, he would recognize me. Now I wasn't so sure.

I reached out to comfort him and he jerked away. A low keening escaped his lips.

I took a step back and reconsidered. I could only imagine what he'd thought of the husky deputies who had towered over him when they first arrived on the scene. Tall strangers with gruff voices. Demanding something of him in a mystifying foreign tongue. In tones that probably sounded menacing to his young ears.

From a distance of two yards, I squatted down to his level. The raw minty smell of eucalyptus was pungent. I spoke in soothing tones. In Japanese. I repeated my name. I reminded him that he knew me. That we'd last met recently at his grandfather's studio in Kyoto. Did he remember? I spoke to him as I spoke to my six-year-old daughter when she was troubled, which, with her mother gone four years ago now, was more often than I cared to admit.

I inched forward, then sat on the grassy slope with him. I continued with the soft patter, aware that comfort could be drawn from the sound alone, whether the meaning penetrated or not.

He maintained his silent incantation. I watched his lips stretch to form each syllable—*If there's a problem, call Jim Brodie.*

Well, here I was, and my arrival had accomplished nothing.

"Shu-kun," I said again, "talk to me."

I reached out again and this time he didn't pull away. The rocking continued but his mouth closed. His eyelids drooped. He rocked.

I thought about what he'd been through. In the last lingering light before the darkness swept in, Shu and his father had most likely gone out to the back acreage and viewed the outdoor sculptures. Shu-kun might have run through the grass. Maybe chased any birds that hadn't gone to roost. Tossed some rocks. Eventually, father and son had swung back toward the office, taking in the nighttime aspect of the sculptural pieces along the road then trotting downhill to look at *Angel-Go-Round.*

Which is when trouble struck. Maybe Shu-kun had seen his father slip and strike his head. Or maybe, bored with the art, Shu had wandered off to play on the nearby hill and hadn't witnessed his father's fatal accident. Or maybe he'd heard the body strike the sculpture. Heard the rattle of the statuary. It would have been dark by then, so Shu wouldn't have had to stray too far to be out of sight.

Maybe Shu had called out at the noise, and when he received no answer made his way back to the patio. Arrived to find his father fallen. No animation in his parent's face. No welcoming smile. Just a motionless form.

Shu would have tried to rouse him. Would have called to him. Over and over. Maybe tugged at his shoulder. Pulled an arm. With each negative response, Shu's panic would have risen a notch. And his confusion would have grown. He would have cast around for help. Sought another adult. But by that time, they were alone on the preserve, surrounded by acres of grapevines and grass and very little else.

Alone in the Napa countryside.

In a foreign land.

Where everyone spoke a language he couldn't understand.

Even if Shu had thought to dig out the cell phone in his father's pocket, whom would he call and what would he say? Somewhere along the line, the eight-year-old had decided to hold a vigil until help arrived, and when the sheriff appeared on the scene, he'd begun his chant.

Or maybe the chant had begun much earlier and gone on much longer.

Maybe Shu *had* slipped over the edge.

CHAPTER 6

I STUDIED him for a long moment before I said, again in Japanese, "It's okay, Shu-kun. I'm here. The men down there are friends. They won't hurt you."

He raised his head. I touched his shoulder. He sprang into my lap and flung his arms around me in a frightened, childlike hug. He shuddered. Then the tears came.

I embraced his thin, shivering frame. Even though, under the blanket, he wore a knee-length down jacket of a Japanese make known for warmth, he trembled. From the cold or the situation. Or both.

The chanting started up again.

I held him tighter. "You don't need to call me anymore, Shu-kun. I'm here and I'm not going anywhere."

The chanting faded.

"Talk to me," I said. "When you're ready."

"I'm ready," he said in Japanese.

Children can surprise you with their resilience. On the other hand, he'd been here all night, calling out for who knows how long.

"Okay. I'm listening."

"My father said ask for you if there was ever trouble." He lifted his head and ran wide bloodshot eyes up and down my face. "He told me just keep repeating your name, so I did what he said."

"You did good. I'm here."

"Can you fix him?"

"We'll have a doctor look at him."

Which, after a fashion, was true.

"Can't you wake him up?"

"Let's wait for the doctor."

Shu-kun hesitated for the first time. "Is he dead?"

The words tore at my heart. Most times I could handle such open-faced volleys. My daughter tossed them my way all the time. But this was different. My friend's son was dead and his grandson wanted a confirmation of the most terrible kind. What did you tell a young child at a time like this? And *how* did you tell him? I had no idea.

"You can say the truth," Shu said softly. "I'm eight now. I'm big. Everyone said I was old enough to come here to America with Dad. So you can tell me."

He gazed at me expectantly with the same bloodshot eyes. Then his look strayed downhill toward his father's body and the cluster of badges. His features grew somber, and his face suddenly seemed older than nature should allow. He lowered his head onto my shoulder again. There was no crying this time.

"He's dead, isn't he, Jim Brodie-san?"

It was one of the hardest things I have ever had to do, but, after some hesitation, I said yes.

I felt Shu's body wilt. He clung to me for all he was worth, his fingers as stiff as steel rods. Quietly, the crying started again. Until that moment, Shu held out a slim hope that his father could still be revived. That if he called me and I came, I could "fix" him. I wished with every scrap of my being that I had the power to grant Shu the miracle he sought.

His body seemed to melt in my arms, as if he had willed himself to disappear. I stroked his hair and we stayed that way for a long time. Salt stung the corners of my eyes.

The sheriff and his men turned their heads away. One of the Napa city cops pawed at the ground with his boot.

When the tears faded, I said, "Maybe we can head up to the office, where it's warmer."

Wiping his eyes with the back of his hands, Shu stiffened. "I don't want to go anywhere *he* might be."

I looked downhill. "Don't worry. The sheriff's on our side. I thought we could—"

Shu's head jerked up. "Not the policemen. *Him.* Do you think he's coming back?"

It was a moment before I found my voice. "Shu-kun, I'm sorry, but your father—"

"No, no, not Dad. *Him,*" he repeated in a louder voice, as if raising the decibels would clarify the matter.

"I'm sorry, Shu-kun. I don't understand. Who are you talking about?"

"The man with the gun."

My spine went rigid. "You saw a man with a weapon?"

Eyes darkening in fear, the eight-year-old boy in my arms nodded with the gravitas of a war veteran who wished to see no more firearms of any kind for the rest of his life.

"Are you sure?"

Shu nodded again. "He didn't see me. But I saw him."

CHAPTER 7

AS I staggered up the rest of the hill with Shu in my arms, he began his tale. He spoke in short bursts, clinging to me, eyes squeezed shut in a near panic, clearly afraid of what we might bump into at the top of the slope. When no gunman sprang from the shadows at the summit, the rest of the story spilled forth. Still hefting Shu's boyish bulk, I cast a come-hither head-pull at Nash and Renna and they slogged uphill in our wake.

Once I set him down, Shu headed for a giant clay sculpture of a sitting woman painted in a passionate explosion of color. He snuggled against the sculpture as he had against the eucalyptus. Large splashes of red, orange, and purple over a white undercoat brought the figure to life, highlighting features or emotions or whatever the viewer chose to make of them.

I watched Shu's mute dash for the statue in puzzled silence. Then I got it. The Viola Frey piece was reminiscent of his father's colorful abstract forms of towering metal.

Shu wasn't ready to say goodbye.

The sheriff scowled. "Damn scene was staged."

Renna rolled his marbles, dark expressionless eyes locked on me. "The kid get a good look?"

"That's what he said."

Nash's eyebrows were working. "You mind if I ask him myself?"

"No, but move slowly. He spooks easily."

The three of us strolled over and Shu's face rose to gauge our approach.

I stopped a yard short, easing my hands into my jacket pocket. "Did your father like this piece?"

Shu nodded, a smile spreading.

Sheriff Nash asked his questions, I translated, and Shu replied with impressive conviction.

We left him with the statue and pulled back to the office. The other cops gathered around.

Nash said, "I know a dynamite sketch artist over in Suisun City." He nudged his shoulder mike to life. "Dick, call Suisun PD and ask if we can borrow Cheré Copeland."

"Their forensic artist?"

"Yeah. Have her meet us at headquarters."

Renna asked Nash if Copeland was good with children.

"She's cop, artist, mother. She's good with everyone."

The sheriff's shoulder set erupted in static, then spat out a message that Copeland was on her way.

Nash's glance wandered across the yard at Shu, who was once more rocking back and forth. "If anyone can coax an image from our poor little man, Cheré can."

A slim, big-boned woman with sandy-blond hair waited for us in a large conference room at the Napa County Sheriff's Department. Her pale skin had a rosy tint from a dose of sun.

The sheriff introduced us, and Detective Cheré Copeland cast a curious eye at Shu, giving him a big smile at the same time. "Young people make great witnesses. It's only a matter of deciphering their scale. They don't understand 'thirty years old,' only 'older or younger than my uncle.' "

We shook hands, then the Suisun City sketch artist took a moment to shake hands with a couple of the deputies she didn't know. She had probing gray-green eyes, a quiet confidence, and no wedding ring, but a pale circle where one had been. *She's cop, artist, mother. She's good with everyone.* Except maybe the ex-husband.

Nash escorted us to a long table at the far end of the room.

"Is this our hero?" Copeland said, looking pointedly at Shu, her fingers skirting playfully along the edge of her belt.

Shu tracked the lively movement of her hand. When Copeland gave her fingers a final wiggle and raised them to her chin, Shu's gaze followed.

On her face was the mischievous smile of a magician. "Do you speak English?"

Shu cocked his head, waiting.

Copeland's bright gray-greens swiveled in my direction. "Should I take that as a no?"

"You should," I said.

She shrugged. "I can work with that. Now, what is it you do? You're not a cop, but you look familiar."

"Friend of the family, part-time police consultant for the SFPD, and not too long ago, I—"

Something sparked behind her eyes. "Gotcha. You're the Japantown guy."

"Guess you read the papers."

"It's my job to track *all* NoCal crime. Now, let's get to work." To the milling crowd of officers, she said, "The kid and Brodie can stay. I need everyone else gone."

A disgruntled murmur percolated up from a cluster of deputies, which had swollen to eight, one comment rising above the rest: "Who does she think she is?"

Copeland zeroed in on the culprit. "The one who's gonna toss your butt through the window if you don't gallop on out of here."

The leathery skin around Sheriff Nash's eyes bunched. "Cheré's drawings have collared more perps than some of you sad lot, so show the lady some respect."

The sheriff tipped his hat in our direction, then sauntered out, with the deputies in tow.

Cheré turned back to me with a wink. "Boys will be boys," she said. "Time to see what we can find behind those young eyes."

CHAPTER 8

THE grid came first.

Detective Copeland drew a rectangle for the head, then divided it into four smaller rectangles with lines down the center each way, horizontally and vertically. Along the horizontal axis, she drew hash marks to approximate the location of the eyes, then lightly penciled in the brows, outer borders, and irises. Two-thirds of the way down the vertical line, she sketched an average mouth, and above that a pair of linked half-loops to signify the bottom of the nose.

"Believe it or not, our eyes are about in the middle of our face along the horizontal axis," Copeland said. "I've drawn a typical pair as placeholders, and I'll adjust their position and size depending on what our little man recalls. If he saw a larger forehead, I'll redraw the top of the head, which will have the effect of shifting the eyes down. A narrower forehead will bring them up."

I translated what she said. Shu's expression turned uncertain.

Copeland addressed him directly. "You're the only one who knows what the man looks like, but we're going to do this together. You and I. Don't worry about a thing. This will be painless."

Her words in translation yielded a nod and an uptick in Shu's interest.

Copeland said to me, "What I'm going to do is jog his memory. It's easier for all of us to recognize than remember, so I'll supply him with verbal and visual clues."

"Fascinating," I said. "How much training have you had?"

"I do cop first, then the forensic art as needed. I've always painted, but after I went to the FBI forensic facial imaging class out at Quantico, I found my people. Cops *and* artists rolled into one. I'll hand any troublemaker his ass if he gets in my face, whether he's street or badge, but when I sketch, I know I'm making a contribution few others can. The whole force goes out with my drawings. That's a good feeling. The collar rate with my work is high. That's a better feeling."

I was going to like Cheré Copeland. She was feisty, confident, and shrewd. A good combination. She'd never be dull. If I wasn't set to pick up things where I'd left them with Rie Hoshino, a new lady acquaintance I'd met a couple of months back in Tokyo, I'd consider asking the detective out.

As she worked with Shu, Copeland's gentle side emerged. She touched his hand on occasion and showed him the sketch at every stage, keeping up a running commentary in soothing tones I understood were meant to set the atmosphere of the session and put him at ease. It was working. Shu followed her progress with growing, if solemn, interest.

"We're going to have fun," she told Shu as she continued to block out the drawing. "You're my first Japanese witness, and a handsome one too."

She paused to allow me to translate, and when I finished, said, "Don't translate this next bit. I've worked with Vietnamese, Koreans, Russians, and Latin Americans more times than I can count. I usually start with a questionnaire to get the basics—like type of crime, time of day, and lighting. Then I'll ask about smells and sounds and such. This part of the process takes them back to the time. Triggers memories. Refreshes them. I'll spare Shu the gruesome parts, though. Our young man here has been through enough. For the rest of what I say, don't be afraid to trot right up on the back of my words. Keep it moving."

"Got it."

She fussed over Shu a bit more, then selected a soft-leaded pencil from an impressive range of artist's gear—pencils from 9B to 2H, an electric eraser, a collection of "smudgers" for shading and tone, a T-square, a circle template, a magnifying glass, and more.

With the formalities out of the way, the process began in earnest. Copeland took Shu through a range of general questions, slowly narrowing in on the suspect's age, height, skin tone, and physique. Once she'd determined the basic framework—thirties, five-nine, slim, darker Asian—she sketched in a vague outline of the head, then added a neck with an Adam's apple.

From her bag Copeland pulled a lollipop. Shu's eyes lit up. While her subject was involved in unwrapping his unexpected windfall, Copeland leaned forward confidentially. "There's a lot of factors involved. As I ask questions, I'm spooling through a whole catalog of possibilities in my head. For example, there's age progression for older suspects because we all lose the fat in our lips as we grow older. The ears get longer. The tip of nose does too, believe it or not. If he's got the age right, it won't be a factor this time. But I'll test him with different shapes to double-check his impressions."

"I didn't know that about age progression."

"It's true. Next, we're going to go through a photo catalog of different head shapes, then hair, eyes, nose, mouth, chin, and so on. They are all photographs of actual criminals. Some of them are headline-grabbers. Even Capone's in there. They all have a look. A variation of *the* look."

"What if he can't remember everything? He's only eight."

"That's the beauty of it. He doesn't have to remember what he saw, only recognize it when he sees it again. Witnesses do it all the time without effort. The photos nudge the memory. I'll start to sketch whatever he chooses and ask him if what I've blocked out is right, or if it needs to be narrower, wider, longer, whatever. That's how we'll zero in on each feature, one by one."

And that's exactly what she did.

I watched in wonder as Copeland led Shu through the process, flipping through a catalog of features—one hundred pairs of eyes, four pages of nose shapes, and on and on with each new feature.

She stopped frequently to ask if that was how Shu remembered it. She'd have him close his eyes. Or let him toy with her equipment. Even allow him to sketch something on his own.

After the addition of each new facial feature came the refinements: Should the eyes be larger? Narrower? Closer together? Was the nose long enough? Should it be thinner or fatter? How was the mouth? Mightn't it be bigger? The lips plumper? Slimmer? Were they wet or dry?

Slowly the portrait took on a life of its own. Copeland shaded and brushed and added tones with different pencil types, brushes, smudgers, and other tools from her arsenal.

Toward the end, she tackled the headgear. Shu had mentioned a baseball cap. The Suisun City police artist questioned him about the shape of the hat, how it fell over the forehead, the curve of the bill, whether the cap portion was baggy or fit snugly. Then she penciled the outline of the hat on the drawing so we could see through it to the hair and shape of the head underneath. Despite the killer's intention to obscure the view with the ball cap, Copeland had captured the essence of his look while giving viewers impressions of the suspect with and without head covering. Very clever.

"We're almost done." She smiled brightly and I translated. "There's only two types of ears—average and Dumbo ears."

For the first time in the session, Shu laughed. *Dumbo* needed no translation.

"Average," Shu said with another boyish giggle.

After Copeland penciled in the ears, she turned the portrait around one last time for him to look at it and he nodded eagerly.

"That's him," he told me with a new enthusiasm.

The face that stared out at us had high cheekbones, a broad nose, narrow eyes, and a strong jawline. The eyes dominated. They were clear and laser focused.

Copeland leaned forward. "Now do me a favor. Give this sketch a rating between one and ten. Ten being a perfect match, just like a photo, and one meaning it looks nothing like the suspect."

Shu drew the drawing toward him and studied it for a long moment, then gave it an eight.

The detective beamed. "Good. He gave the perfect answer. A seven or eight means I've reproduced a workable facsimile we can use. A perfect ten tells me the witness has lost the image in his head and is covering up, or is lying to us. That's because reproducing a suspect's portrait with photographic accuracy is theoretically impossible. I've gotten several nines, and those scare the hell out of me because, realistically, hitting that level of accuracy should be out of reach. But the couple of times we caught an offender with a nine rating, it really was uncanny how close I got. So nines are acceptable, if a little spooky."

"Will they catch him now?" Shu asked.

"Count on it," I said.

"Ask her too."

I did, and Copeland said they would and he'd be the first to know.

Shu grinned, then in the corner penciled in his approval with an OK. The *K* was backward.

"You need that too," he told his new Suisun City friend.

Copeland blushed, abashed at his childish sign of approval. As her eyes lingered on the backward *K*, she nearly lost it.

Sheriff Nash squinted at the sketch, then at me. "You're the only non-cop in the room besides our little fella. Would you buy a car from this man?"

I gazed at Copeland's work. "Probably not."

"*Why* not?"

"I see something raw. Untrustworthy. I'd probably hesitate, or make an excuse and walk away."

"Good. We got our killer." Nash took Renna and me aside. "The ME sent up his preliminary findings. He says the skull struck the statue multiple times."

Renna looked thoughtful. "Backs up the boy's story."

"Yep. ME reckons the killer slammed the father's head against the statue's leg three or four times."

My anger flared. "Forced him down at gunpoint, then bashed his head in."

Nash nodded. "Way I see it too. Then slipped off the shoe, ran it through the oil, and put it back on. ME said the sock is bunched up a bit too much."

"Good to know," I said.

The killer was a planner, I thought.

"We got the beginnings of a pattern," Nash said. "Asian vic, Asian killer."

"But why not just shoot his target?" I asked.

"Could be a lot of reasons. Gives the killer more getaway time. Confuses things for a while. We thought we had an accident for a goodly spell. Then there's the noise factor. Gunshots carry, especially at night. Killer doesn't use his piece, it's still virgin. He's not walking around with a murder weapon."

Nash was staring at the sketch. "Cheré, what's the doodle in the corner?"

Copeland's face softened. "Sweetest thing you ever saw. After I finished, little Shu personally okayed my work."

The sheriff looked down at Shu. "Did he now?" The sheriff rummaged in his pocket and came out with a replica of his badge. "This is for you, son. Now you're one of us."

I translated and Shu accepted the badge in wonder, excitement bubbling just under the surface. While one of the deputies helped Shu pin it on, Nash turned to Copeland. "You happy with this?"

"Yeah, I got it."

"Good deal." Sheriff Nash clapped his hands together and the rest of the crew assembled. A number of new deputies had joined the pack, including three women. "Okay, boys and girls, we got ourselves a live sketch. Get copies out through the usual channels."

The room cleared out. Copeland watched Renna and Nash wander off to discuss some final details, then turned troubled gray-greens in my direction. "Just between you and me, it's accurate but there's something not right."

"Tell me."

"I've done this hundreds of times, so I know I mined everything I could from the witness. But I'm seeing something I can't put my finger on."

"So it's not as accurate as you told the sheriff?"

"No, it's functional. If the killer is still around, they'll catch him with my drawing. That's all the deputies need to know. It's just that there's an itch noodling around in my head. I tell the sheriff, he might hold back when he shouldn't."

"Okay. So what is it?"

"I guess what I'm trying to say is, if either of you run across something new, something different, call me. *Then* I'll tell the sheriff."

"You sure about this?" Renna asked.

"Not about the *what*, but I'm damn sure about the *where*." She gazed intently at her sketch. "It's in there someplace."

CHAPTER 9

FROM the Napa County Sheriff's Department, I called Japan and spoke to Ken Nobuki, Shu's grandfather. My artist friend was due to arrive next week to discuss the Kyoto–San Francisco exhibition exchange, but in the wake of his son's murder, he and his wife would catch the next flight out and pick up Shu. His spouse would take their grandson back to Kyoto while Ken would remain behind to liaise with the mayor's people and handle the details for transporting his son's body back to Japan.

After the call, I attempted to pry Shu loose, but Napa County officials saw a major lawsuit should anything go awry under my care, so Ken's grandson remained behind with social services. I left my phone number with Shu's minders, and he and I talked several times over the next two days until his grandparents arrived.

Renna and I drove back to the city and made our goodbyes. Exhausted and grieving, I drove to my antiques shop. I flipped on the shop sign, and hung up some new scroll paintings as I brooded over the deteriorating state of mind of Ken's grandchild.

In a singularly misguided thought, I figured things could only get better from here.

"Jim, let me introduce you to—"

"He bloody well *knows* who I am, Sarah," Sean Navin said, inflamed green eyes panning my way.

His wife's fractured smile served as an apology. "My husband's agreed to listen to what you have to say after all."

I studied her lesser half with skepticism. A major upside to running your own operation is you don't have to put up with anyone's bull.

Her husband said, "I still say we can do better across town."

"Door's behind you," I offered.

"Boys, boys. Play nice."

They were a curious couple. Sarah came from a well-to-do family in Palo Alto, where she'd attended the "local university," which happened to be a place called Stanford. She was smart, with sparkling gray eyes and an auburn pixie cut. Sean was a hardscrabble Irish boy who made good as a construction contractor, despite capping his education after high school.

"You're charging too much," he said. "It's crockery, for Chrissake."

His wife's brow darkened. "Darling, I explained—"

"Let me handle this, Sarah."

He was a stocky man with large bones and large shoulders. Dark-brown hair framed a pale face red from hurling a fierce stare my way.

"Fine, honey. There's some new Japanese furniture I want to look at."

"Don't get too attached to anything." She wandered off toward the back of the shop, favoring him with a breezy smile.

Sean's glare swung back toward me. "I don't hand out cash I sweated blood for without a good look-over. If we're gonna deal you're gonna have to cut me some slack on your overpriced dishware."

"Tea bowl," I said. "A Japanese Oribe tea bowl from the eighteenth century."

Sarah had taken up the tea ceremony, and her collection of bowls grew as her infatuation with the traditional Japanese ritual increased. To date, all of her pieces were contemporary and hovered in the five- to ten-thousand-dollar range. Now she wanted to add a classic Oribe work that would leave her previous price range in the dust.

"I've seen the pictures," Sean said. "It's a soup bowl with squiggles. Dropping big coin on a bloody crock pot is pure stone mad."

I shrugged. "The market sets the price, not me."

"So you say. I'm a busy man, Brodie. I got big projects all over the Bay Area need attending. When you reschedule on me you cost me money. So if we stick around, I expect a concession on your end."

"Like I told Sarah, it was something I couldn't sidestep."

There was an eight-year-old boy who sat out all night in the cold, keeping a deathwatch, I could have told him. *And a police summons*. But if I mentioned either item, Sean would feel cornered, and resent me even more.

He frowned. "Twenty grand ought to do it for baked mud, don't you think, with some wee change left over?"

"I quoted Sarah a range, which is the closest I can get without a piece in hand. Call the auction houses if you need confirmation."

"You're pretty damn sure of yourself."

"I'm sure of the art."

The ceramic ware added another dimension to the tea ceremony. Pieces made three or four centuries ago looked as fresh today as they did at conception.

"You seriously telling me you can call a bowl smaller than a piss pot 'art'?"

"The best Oribe abstracts can hold their own with Klee, Kandinsky, Rothko, take your pick."

His eyes narrowed. "You playing hardball with me?"

"If money's a problem, let's drop the lineage requirement."

"When you say *lineage*, you mean previous owners, right? Like if a house was owned by a movie star?"

"Yes, a star in the tea world."

Suspicion touched his features. "Don't they usually get the best pieces?"

"Only if they have a good eye. And many of them didn't. If we focus on quality over lineage, the price will come down. Sarah would be just as happy. Truth be told, a quality piece wins out every time. With or without a star lineage. As long as we can show provenance."

The light in Sean's look changed. "You're a talker, Brodie. Good Irish blarney. Let's see if you can deliver. I'm not throwing money away on this unless it meets Sarah's wishes *and* my needs. I've got bigger worries than a bowl of slung mud."

"Don't we all," I said, thinking of Shu.

This time tomorrow, Ken Nobuki would be arriving from Japan to take care of his grandchild and mourn his son.

Meanwhile, the Napa boys were hunting for a killer.

ONE WEEK LATER

FIRST SHOT

CHAPTER 10

SAN FRANCISCO CITY HALL, 5:15 P.M.

AMID a rolling wave of camera flashes, Ken Nobuki, the mayor, and I posed and shook hands.

Events today had unfolded with perfection—a one-on-one with Mayor Gary Hurwitz, a final run-through of the details for the Kyoto–San Francisco exhibition exchange, and a photo op for the press corps of both countries under the ornate rotunda of City Hall.

Hurwitz envisioned a series of art exhibitions with Japan, Malaysia, Taiwan, Korea, and Australia. Our no-nonsense leader had even roped in China, who had initially balked because of Taiwan's involvement until he told them to grow up. And, surprisingly, they did. With similar forthrightness, the mayor had convinced me to act as his emissary to Japan, a nod, he said, to my help with the city's Japantown problem. In turn, I'd brought in Ken to handle the Japanese side.

Initially, I'd been leery of mixing politics and art, but this afternoon the mayor's crew had created magic, and it appeared we would all benefit greatly. My years of struggling to raise myself up in the art world might be over.

Then the first shot blew it all apart.

Exiting City Hall, Ken and I had started down the granite steps toward a limousine waiting to whisk him away to his hotel.

He never made it.

We had no reason to suspect trouble, but after what had happened to Ken's son in Napa the week before, I was on edge. So when the glint off the shooter's scope revealed his position I didn't hesitate.

I shoved my artist friend sideways.

Jostled without warning, Ken got tangled up in his own feet, which delayed the full lateral shift I'd intended. A bullet found him—and etched a line along his scalp, shearing off the top of the left ear in the process. A fine spray of blood misted the air.

Ken hit the ground hard, and so did I.

A second bullet kicked up stone dust three yards behind where the two of us had stood a second earlier, the speeding metal ricocheting off the granite walkway, then off the City Hall façade we had left behind only a moment ago.

My friend lay bleeding on an unforgiving city street, and I hugged the pavement alongside him, wondering if a bullet would find me next.

Ken's eyes flickered and closed.

The limo afforded some cover and was only a few yards away. Scrambling forward on my stomach, I dragged my stricken companion by the scruff of his shirt toward the safety of the gleaming black vehicle. From behind its front fender, the young driver watched me inch in his direction. His eyes radiated fear.

"What's happening?" he whispered, as if the gunman some three hundred yards away might overhear him.

"Sniper on the roof of the Asian Art."

"Why's he firing at us?"

"I've no idea."

Once sheltered behind the limo, I peered back at City Hall. The sheriff's deputies who manned the security checkpoint inside were scrambling. They ran for cover, shielding themselves behind the massive stone walls of the domed municipal monolith as they drew their pieces and took flash-peeks through the glass doors, scanning the area for the triggerman.

"Top of the museum," I shouted.

One of them nodded and spoke into a radio.

I stripped off my shirt.

A third round took out the front tire on the driver's side, and the car rocked. The shooter hoped to flush us out, but I had no plans to budge. However, before I could stop him, the chauffeur raised his head.

"Get down," I said. "Now! And change position!"

The driver ducked and shifted about six inches before a fourth bullet clipped the fender, pierced his shoulder, and spun him around. This time the round drew pulverized bone with the spray of blood.

I knotted my shirt around Ken's head, then turned my attention to the driver. Behind closed eyes, my friend groaned.

We'd had no time to run. And nowhere to run *to*. City Hall opened onto Polk Street and a spacious central plaza with a promenade and groomed gardens but no protection. No barriers. No obstructions. No place to seek refuge. The Asian Art Museum lay directly across the plaza, giving our attacker an unobstructed shot.

Had the hired vehicle not been parked curbside, we'd be bleeding out on the pavement.

I was sure of that and three other things:

We were trapped.

This was the second assault on Ken Nobuki's family in as many weeks.

And the father of three—two, after the attack in Napa—might not make it.

CHAPTER 11

"HANG in there," I said.

The driver gritted his teeth. He'd regained focus once I'd wound my undershirt around his shoulder to stem the blood flow. I was now topless in San Francisco on a breezy December afternoon, fearing for my friend's life and aware that four rounds from a sniper's rifle had shattered months of planning. Had that been the shooter's intention? Or was he operating under a different agenda?

For a brief moment in time, all had been right with my world. As the point man for the first joint exhibitions in the mayor's Pacific Rim Friendship Program, I was on the cusp of a breakthrough. Ken and I had lined up a pair of eye-opening shows. An assemblage of brilliant Oribe ceramics spanning the ages culled from Kyoto museums was set to open here, while a sister exhibition focusing on cutting-edge San Francisco painting over the last three decades would travel to the Japanese cultural hub.

The international art swap would benefit both cities, both mayors, and both liaisons. It would burnish Ken's international reputation and stood ready to catapult my career to the next level. A win-win on all sides.

But those dreams had just imploded.

I glanced at my motionless friend. He'd slipped down a black hole. I wasn't sure if the wound or the spill had sent him under.

What I did know was that—for the moment—he was still among the living.

We were tucked behind the front tire of the limo. For the sniper to connect a third time, he would have to thread a round through both the engine block and the wheel assembly.

Ken's breathing was shallow, his chest movement minimal.

"Stay with me, Nobuki-san," I said.

A nerve flickered on his right cheek, but his eyes did not open. Maybe he'd heard me; maybe he hadn't.

Twenty minutes had passed since the first shot. We'd been saved by a glimmer of sunlight bouncing off the scope of the rifle, but since then the SFPD had left us stranded in the chilly afternoon sun.

Where was the all-clear? Had the sheriff's deputy in City Hall really heard me through the protective glass when I shouted out the shooter's location? Was the gunman still drawing down on us?

I called Renna on speed dial.

He picked up swiftly and immediately moved to disconnect. "Brodie, can't talk now. I'm rolling on a call."

"City Hall?"

"Yeah, how'd you—? Shit. Tell me you're not there."

"Wish I could."

I practically heard Renna's mind clicking into gear. "The visiting VIP who's down? Ken Nobuki?"

"You're two for two."

"Damn. What do you need?"

"Tell me you guys know the triggerman's on the roof of the Asian Art Museum."

"We know and we're on it."

"What's taking so long?"

"There's some sort of booby trap. A bomb or a very good facsimile of one."

"Clever."

"Good until the last shot. You'll have to stay put until we can confirm he's gone."

"I can do that, but Ken's fading."

"Give me an update and I'll pass it on to the medics. They're right around the corner, out of the line of fire."

I fed him the conditions of both men, and on the other end I heard Renna scribbling.

"You hit?" he asked as I wound up.

"No."

"Okay. Then get to work on the question of the hour."

"Which is?"

"Who might want to put a serious dent in the Nobuki family line?"

CHAPTER 12

ONCE the all-clear was raised, a pair of ambulances rolled up within seconds. I was now pacing the hall outside the hospital emergency room in dusty jeans and a teal-green scrubs top a harried intern had tossed in my direction.

Renna came barreling through the hospital an hour later, his six-foot-four frame scattering people like a charging bull at Pamplona.

He stared at my scrubs. "You changing careers or making a fashion statement?"

"Career. Be safer."

"Wise move."

"Anything on the rooftop?" I asked.

He shook his head, imaginary marbles tumbling from cheek to cheek in silent frustration. "Sniper did an Elvis long before the first man got there."

Left the building.

"Find *anything* useful?"

He lobbed a cynical grimace my way. "Forensics is poking around, but a sharpshooter smart enough to rig a fake bomb won't be dumb enough to leave evidence. How are the patients?"

"Driver's wound is clean, and minor. He's talking to your people now. Ken's still out, with a neurosurgeon set to put in an appearance shortly."

"Neurosurgeon? That doesn't sound good."

"Disaster is what it is."

"But why the Nobukis?"

"I've no idea," I found myself saying for the second time today.

The Pacific Rim Friendship Program had been shaping up to be favorable to all involved—cities, artists, the mayor, and me. Being low man on the totem pole, I had the most to gain.

Turned out I also had the most to lose.

Mayor Hurwitz arrived ten minutes later with a pulsing retinue of city officials and press hounds. I recognized a few television reporters, as well as the new deputy mayor and Hurwitz's one-woman brain trust, Gail Wong, strategist and attack shark par excellence.

Hurwitz came straight at me, his face crumpled in apology. "Brodie, I don't know what to say. Shot leaving City Hall? I'm stunned. I've asked the police chief to put you on as a consultant."

"Thank you, Mr. Mayor. I'd be working this one anyway."

"I know you would. But now you're official."

He also informed me that the SFPD and all other city resources were at my disposal. If Lieutenant Renna couldn't set it up, I was to call Gail. Further, the city would cover all medical expenses for both victims. And so, did I know who had done this and why?

"Not yet. But I will."

"Of course you will," he said, nodding to himself. "You won't disappoint me."

I nodded, my lips compressing of their own accord. I had a lot of skin in the game already. I didn't need political pressure applied with a personal touch.

Behind us, a door swung open and a pair of nurses turned to stare at a doctor in surgical scrubs. He made a beeline for us with his hand outstretched. His fingers were long and slim and well turned. The man himself was tall and slim and well groomed.

"Dr. Lance Samuels, Mr. Mayor," he said. "How can I help?"

"How's our patient, Doctor?"

"Receiving the best care possible, Mr. Mayor."

"Glad to hear it. What can you tell us?"

"The patient is hanging on. The bullet gouged a trough along the left side of the cranium. I can see brain tissue in the wound. We're dealing with a very serious brain injury. I'm taking him to surgery right now. I've got to go scrub, but I wanted to pass on the basics."

The mayor said, "He'll live?"

The doctor searched the ceiling before meeting Hurwitz's intense gaze. "The immediate problem is the scope of the brain injury. Normally, I would explain the risks and complications, but there isn't time for that now. I will do what I have to do depending on what we find."

"You'll keep my office informed?"

"I'll call personally."

"Thank you, Doctor."

Watching the physician retreat, the mayor's face tightened. "This does not happen in my city without a response." His stern countenance swung our way, taking in Renna's bulk and my pained expression. "I'm counting on you two."

Hurwitz's exit was as sudden as his arrival. Support staff wedged an opening through the crowd of reporters, who trailed after our fearless city leader with an onslaught of questions.

"Well, look at that," Renna said. "A useful pol. Drew off the newshounds."

My phone rang, the touch screen indicating an undisclosed number from Japan. I hit the connect icon and said hello.

"I just heard," Rie Hoshino said in Japanese. Outside of *thank you*, she spoke not a word of English. "Are you all right?"

Officer Rie Hoshino and I had met when a client for Brodie Security—the detective firm founded by my father in the Japanese capital, and now run partially by me since his death—saw his old World War II buddies dropping of blatantly unnatural causes in a series of home invasions three months ago in Tokyo. She was one of three reasons I had tickets back to Tokyo in a couple of days' time.

"I'm fine," I said. "How could you already know?"

"I carry a badge for the Tokyo police, remember?" She cleared her throat. "Besides, my phone is ringing off the hook."

"So much for secrets."

"*That* secret is still safe," she said, referring to our nascent relationship. "Everyone knows we both worked the home invasion case. They think I have an inside track with you."

And she did—more than anyone could or should know. For personal and professional reasons, we both preferred that our budding liaison remain discreet.

"Is Ken Nobuki okay?" Rie asked.

"Hard to tell yet."

"Who did this?"

"Hard to tell yet."

She drank in the broader implications. "You're in the middle of a big international incident that's only going to get bigger—at least as far as Japan and the United States are concerned. I'll understand if you need to put our next date on hold."

"Not going to happen," I said.

From a huddle across the room with one of his detectives, Renna darted a look in my direction.

"I'll find the time. Even if it kills me."

Hesitation arrived from the far side of the Pacific. "There are some things you mustn't joke about, Brodie."

Renna's look grew insistent.

"I've got to go, but you'll hear from me soon."

"I would like that. Remember, you have an out if you want it. But if you find the time, I have a surprise."

"What might that be?"

"*Fugu*," she said. "My treat."

Blowfish, a Japanese delicacy, and poisonous if prepared incorrectly.

"You do know there are two ways I could take that, right?"

She laughed. "Of course. You'll have to show up to find out my intentions."

"Count on it. Really have to go, sorry."

We disconnected and I approached Renna, who said, "Sheriff Nash out of Napa just rang my office. He's recirculating the police sketch along with an updated APB."

"Good."

"He also raised a killer question."

"I take it your phrasing is not accidental."

"Not a chance. We all agree everyone in the family should lie low. What the sheriff asked me was if there were any more Nobukis floating around. I said I'd ask the oracle."

"Afraid the oracle's got some bad news for you, then," I said. "Ken Nobuki's daughter is in the US. I just don't know where."

"Find out."

"The call's already in."

"Let's hope it's not too late."

CHAPTER 13

As soon as we'd arrived at the hospital, I'd sent an email about the shooting to Naomi, Ken's daughter, a Japanese reporter of some acclaim. Earlier today Ken had mentioned that Naomi was in the States—on the East Coast—and I was hoping to get to her before she saw the shooting on the news. I'd known Naomi nearly as long as I'd known her father. We'd dined together in Tokyo and San Francisco, and I'd introduced her to American sources for some of her stories.

Now my phone was buzzing with a call from her.

"Hi, Naomi," I said.

"Brodie, are you at the hospital?" she asked in Japanese.

"Yes."

"Thank heavens. Is Dad okay? I can't get anything out of the nurses there."

That was Naomi's journalistic instincts. She'd tried on her own first before asking for assistance, even though her English was limited to a collection of serviceable phrases. Naomi was only slightly less vulnerable than Shu had been that first morning under the eucalyptus tree.

"He's in the operating theater as we speak."

"Have you heard from a doctor yet?"

"Yes, but only in the vaguest terms. He said there might be some brain swelling."

"I don't know what that means but it sounds awful."

A sort of coded message came over the hospital PA system with Dr. Samuels's name attached. Two nurses abandoned their posts and rushed through the emergency doors.

Another bad sign.

"Will you call me as soon as you have an update?" Naomi asked, vulnerability seeping through her usually impenetrable journalistic veneer.

"Of course. How is your mother taking it?"

"I haven't spoken to her yet. With the time difference, I didn't want to wake her. And I just got off a plane. I called you first."

A chill crawled up the back of my neck. "Naomi, wait—you've been traveling? Where are you now?"

Renna was deep in conversation with a detective buddy but had one ear attuned to my conversation. Now he had both.

"I flew to Washington this morning. Why?"

My voice took on a forceful edge. "Listen, you need to stay put. Somewhere indoors we can control. If you have a flight out, cancel it."

Naomi stammered, "W–w–hy would you say that?"

I grew confused in turn. She was smarter than this.

Tentatively, I said, "Well, considering all that has happened . . ."

"*All?* You mean there's more?"

"You haven't heard?"

"Tad and I have been at a retreat in upstate New York until this morning."

Right. Ken had mentioned that Naomi and her husband were together on the East Coast. I was momentarily relieved to know she wasn't alone.

"And you guys are in DC now?"

"Yes. I mean, no, it's just me. Tad's about to board a plane back to Japan. It was a bear to get him to come out here at all. What about—"

"Give me the name of your hotel."

She did and I said, "When you get there, stay in your room. Lock yourself in and under no circumstances go out or even open the door."

"You're scaring me, Brodie. What's going on?"

As gently as I could, I broke the news about her brother's death, then about the trip her mother had made to pick up Shu in Napa.

A piercing shriek blasted down the line. "My brother too? This can't be happening."

I tried to calm Naomi while she explained, through her sobs, that the retreat she and her husband had been on forbade access to phones and Wi-Fi. Attendees had to commit to being fully unplugged. Seeking to prolong his peace, her husband had extended his offline time until he returned to his law firm in Tokyo the following day.

I let her cry her way through the first round of shock, pain, and denial. All of which would strike deeper notes once she hung up, but my immediate goal was to secure her safety.

I said, "Listen, we'll get through this together, okay? I'll handle as much as I can."

"I'm sorry, Brodie. I can't—"

"I understand this is difficult, so just listen, okay? I'll have someone from my office in Tokyo contact your mother and your husband after he lands. That will take care of your immediate family for the moment. You can ring her later, when you're up to it. More important is your situation. I need you to do exactly as I say."

My words were intended to act as a verbal slap in the face.

"Brodie, now you're really scaring me."

"Sorry. But this is important. You have to follow my instructions to the letter."

I told her that under no circumstances could she tell anyone else where she was. She could not send any emails after we hung up. Nor make any calls. Once we finished, she needed to disable her phone—meaning power it down and remove the battery but keep both on her person. The fact that she hadn't contacted anyone in the last week might be the only thing keeping her alive.

Next, as soon as we hung up I would be sending some men to protect her. They'd be there inside of thirty minutes with a password that could only have come from me. Under no circumstances was she to open her door to anyone else. She must remain in her room. If the drapes were open, she should close them and stay away from the windows. I needed her alert, with none of her senses impaired. That meant no headphones or television or shower or bath until my men arrived.

They would be on their way in minutes. If the unthinkable happened and someone tried to force his or her way in, she was to lock herself in the bathroom, reconnect her phone, and call me. Doors in the better hotels were stout and would hold off any initial attempts.

"Okay, but—"

"Before I answer any questions, I need you to repeat my instructions."

Reporter that she was, she did so without missing a point. Then a timid note of optimism crept into her voice. "Brodie, don't you think you're being just a bit too paranoid?"

"Yesterday, maybe. Today, nowhere near enough."

CHAPTER 14

WHEN my father left me half of Brodie Security in Tokyo, I'd also inherited a list of affiliates I could reach out to at any time of the day or night.

Which is what I did as soon as I hung up—I raced to set up protection for Naomi.

Not trusting my own phone, I culled the name of our DC affiliate from my address book, bought a disposable cell at a convenience store on the next block, then hailed a taxi.

I told the driver to head west toward the ocean and tell me when we'd traveled a mile. I made him turn several times. No cars followed. When the cabbie called out the mile mark, I rang DC and put Naomi under twenty-four-hour guard until further notice. The password to entry was the name of the gallery where her father held his first exhibition.

I knew it, and she would too.

I told the taxi driver to take me to the hospital.

He caught my eye in his rearview mirror. "We've been going in the wrong direction."

"No," I said. "We haven't."

Once again I was getting sucked into the machine. Into the world of crime and violence that had been my father's line of work, not mine.

He'd arrived in Japan to head up an MP command post on an American base in the greater Tokyo area, where he met my mother, a volunteer in the Red Cross, but an art curator by trade.

Brodie Security was the third of my father's postmilitary efforts, following a short stint in the LAPD and the first incarnation of Brodie Security in Los Angeles, which opened and closed without fanfare. Falling back on the resilience of his connections in Japan, my father resurrected the agency in Tokyo, in the process establishing the first Western-style PI/security firm in the Japanese capital.

Then I came along, born in Japan to American parents—both Caucasian, as my fair skin, black hair, and blue eyes testified. My parents enrolled me in the local public school, where I learned the culture, the language, and the mindset of the Japanese. At the age of six, my father signed me up for judo and karate under the tutelage of two Tokyo masters in his inner circle. At twelve, I'd started working at Brodie Security after school and soon found myself enthralled with the gritty tales of the in-house operatives—stories involving con games, blackmail, robberies, assaults, kidnappings, and even murder. Culprits ran the gambit from errant spouses, slippery executives, and crafty government officials to local street punks, grifters, hardened criminals, yakuza, and a dozen other types of lowlife. I accompanied operatives on so-called no-risk outings, though once or twice I'd found myself in unexpectedly dicey situations.

At his death fourteen months ago, my father shifted half of Brodie Security to me. My friends considered it a windfall. But they couldn't have been more wrong. The firm came with strings of the highest order. First, I knew many of the employees, so I couldn't in good conscience unload the place and pocket the cash, as most of those around me advised.

Second, the agency was the only thing my father left me. We'd been estranged since my parents' divorce, when I was seventeen. The separation flung my mother and me back to a toxic Los Angeles neighborhood, where I shut down the curiosity of the local gang with a few swift martial arts moves. After the third episode, they left me alone, making my daily passage through the neighborhood at least marginally safer.

I also shut down all communication with my father and we never spoke again. In the intervening years, I kept up my martial arts; added some street-fighting moves learned during local skirmishes; discovered that, like my mother, I had an eye for art; took some college courses at a local community college in LA; struggled to find a way forward after my mom died far too young of intestinal cancer around my twenty-first birthday; moved to San Francisco for a fresh start; spent a few rough years on the scrappy side of the Mission District; stumbled into an apprenticeship with a local antiques dealer; married at twenty-five to Mieko, a Japanese woman I'd met in LA when we were both teenagers; had a daughter, Jenny; opened my own place out on Lombard Street; then lost Mieko. Three years later, my father died and punted half of Brodie Security in my direction. That was my first thirty-two years in a nutshell.

For now, I carry the weight despite the risk. Despite the wear and tear my father's occupation entails. Despite the tension bubbling up at home with my daughter whenever she senses danger.

I can handle the work most times, as some of my father's DNA seems to have trickled down, but my first love is still art. The searching, the acquiring, the coddling, the placing of pieces in good homes. Artistic activities nurture. A new find inspires. And along the way, a spiritual appetite is sated—until the next hunt begins. Sarah Navin's commission for the Oribe tea bowl is one such instance; it is the kind of quest I live for, even when it comes with an abrasive husband attached.

Detective work sits at the other end of the spectrum. It draws me down different trails. Darker trails. In the danger that bubbles up around a case, art holds out a promise that there is still something right with the world when all else looks so wrong.

And given what happened next, I would need that promise more than ever.

CHAPTER 15

AFTER disabling the convenience store phone, I rejoined Renna and filled him in on Naomi's whereabouts.

He shook his head. "Got to wonder about this family's luck. But you did the right thing. She's a sitting duck out there. Did she give you anything useful?"

"Saw to her safety first. I'll get back to her with questions after she's calmed down."

Renna only grunted. Dr. Samuels pushed through the swing doors leading to the back rooms. Once more, the nurses' station jumped to attention at the handsome doctor's approach.

He glanced around. "The mayor still here?"

"No," I said.

The surgeon tried unsuccessfully to hide his disappointment. Blood spatter stained his smock.

Renna stepped forward. "What have you got for us, Doc?"

With some reluctance, Samuels refocused on us. "Your friend is out of surgery. It was as we feared. The brain was badly bruised. The brain swelling will cause an increase in the intracranial pressure."

"Which means you need to relieve pressure in the brain. But how?" I asked.

"We have to give the brain someplace to go. The only way to do that and prevent more brain damage is to perform a large craniectomy, which means removing a large portion of the skull. We're dealing with massive cerebral edema."

I stared at the doctor. "You *removed* part of his skull?"

"Yes."

"How much?"

"Wait," Renna said, looking like he wanted to draw his gun and shoot Samuels. "What is a cerebral endema?"

"Excess fluid in the brain."

"Okay, Doc, onward. How much of our guy's skull did you cut away?"

The doctor cleared his throat. "We removed the bone from above his left eye back to his ear on the left side." If he does well, we can replace the bone in several months."

Poor Ken. What had I gotten my friend into?

"When can I talk to him?" I asked.

"Not for at least a week." Samuels grew defensive. "We have given him medication to decrease the pressure and keep him in a deep coma."

This was a nightmare. "What happens after a week?"

"If and when the pressures normalize, we slowly decrease the medications and see if he wakes up."

Shooting his hand sideways to silence me, Renna posed the next question. "What do you mean, *see if* he wakes up?" There was an intimidating growl behind his words.

"We are unable to determine the degree of brain impairment while he is on the medication. We hope for the best."

"So there's no guarantee . . . ?" I began.

"I'm afraid not. We don't even know if he will wake up. We've done the best we can for now. We support him and wait for the swelling to go down."

I'd never felt more helpless in my life. There was not a single thing I could do to help my friend. And his whole family could be under attack.

With apprehensive eyes locked on Renna, Samuels produced one last surprise. "Mr. Nobuki regained consciousness before we put him under for the operation and left a message for you, Mr. Brodie."

Surprise flooded through me. "Really? What did he say?"

"His English was broken, but essentially he said, 'Ask Brodie to find my daughter and keep her safe.' Does that mean anything to you? Can you do that?"

"Yes to both questions," I said, exchanging a look with Renna.

Looked like I was heading to DC.

DAY 3

TUESDAY

DEEPER WATERS

CHAPTER 16

WASHINGTON, DC

THE red-eye flight to Washington's Reagan National Airport was long and easy and I slept the whole way, dreaming of my daughter. We'd spent the last few hours before my departure together.

"I'm sorry I have to go away so much," I'd said, prepping her for my back-to-back trips, first to DC, then to Tokyo, with only a sliver of time in the Bay Area in between.

"It's okay, Daddy. Just remember, my birthday is only two weeks away."

My girl was turning seven.

"How could I forget?"

"You'll be home?" she said, her eyes wide and watching and yearning. Jenny had big eyes and long black hair, usually braided, but today we'd pulled it back in a ponytail.

"I'll be back in plenty of time."

"You know what I want for my birthday, right?"

"Jenny, I don't think a year's supply of gelato is a reasonable request."

"But Daddy—"

"You'll blow up like a balloon."

"I will *not.* I play soccer every day. We run so much even the mascot dog stopped chasing us. I want gelato, Daddy."

"As the guardian of your health, I'm registering an official protest."

"Daddy, it's my birthday."

"We'll, see, okay?"

She pouted.

I said, "I promise it will be a great birthday. I've got a *lot* of surprises planned."

Jenny settled down after that. I hugged her, kissed her forehead, then carried my giggling six-year-old upstairs on my shoulders to her friend's apartment, where she would spend the night.

That was a good moment. And the last one I would have on the home and the work fronts for a long time to come.

After grabbing my duffel bag from the overhead bin, I shuffled forward to the front of the aircraft with the rest of the deboarding passengers, then stepped out onto the enclosed jetway that would take us the last thirty yards to the terminal.

A suited man stood immediately outside the vessel door to my left. Another suit was planted to the right. Sunglasses masked their eyes. Neutral expressions masked their intentions. Their presence, however, was brassy in-your-face Big Government making a statement.

They expected to be noticed.

Which made me wonder. Were there VIPs on the flight to escort? A rowdy they planned to interrogate? A criminal in transport they needed to cart away?

As passengers shuffled past, neither man showed any outward preference for any departing traveler. I moved down the tunnel. When the jet bridge doglegged right, I snuck a swift backward glance. The suits had joined the slipstream.

I shifted my duffel bag to my weaker hand and walked on. Between the suits and myself were a retired couple and a clutch of high school girls. Directly in front of me were more schoolgirls and a solitary California surfer. None of them looked threatening. None of them seemed likely points of interest for the suit-and-shades set.

In the terminal, two larger men of a different cut hovered. Black jackets and pants, dark-olive knit shirts, callous unforgiving faces. No sunglasses. They were bigger and bulkier and had the outward-curving arms of weightlifters.

The pair fell in step alongside me, one on each flank.

I had traveled solo. No one was meeting me on this end until I arrived at Naomi's hotel. For another few moments, we would traverse a heavily trafficked public terminal. My upside would disappear once we reached the exit. Clearly, I would not be allowed to hail a taxi.

"Gentlemen," I said. "Can I help you?"

"We'd like you to come with us, Mr. Brodie," the smaller of the behemoths said. He was older, with a full head of silver bristles. A burning fever behind his eyes told me I was their target—and the enemy. The man topped out at six-three and two hundred forty pounds, specs exceeding my six-one, one-hundred-ninety-pound frame by a respectable margin.

"Who's asking?" I said.

"Your government."

Federal agents. Not good.

"I'll take a rain check."

Scorn darkened his features. "We're not offering one."

I said, "I've got a previous engagement and I never keep a lady waiting."

The second, larger man grabbed my upper arm and squeezed. My fingers went numb. Larger tipped the scale at sixty pounds over my weight, and towered five inches above me.

"Take the hand off," I said.

The troglodyte glared. "We ask nice once, Brodie. And only once."

"I was raised better, so I'm asking a second time. The hand."

Larger tightened his grip. Instead of resisting, I shoved aggressively into his space and caught him by surprise. I forced him back, then stomped on his instep, shot a sharp elbow into his ribs, and pivoted away and out of range. With each blow, the oversize thug grunted from behind compressed lips, his body stiffening as he swallowed the burn.

Then he pounced, a steaming mass of muscle. He took two quick check-steps, his fists rising. He attacked with a sharp right jab. I brushed the punch aside with my left arm, a right of my own following quickly for a strike that glanced off his jaw. His second jab slammed home, clipping my chin and rocking me. We both staggered back, then he charged in a second time, pelting me with a pair of hammering blows to my midriff.

I backpedaled, raising my arms and circling away. He followed. I feinted, which stalled his advance, then I dropped back farther, opening up some space between us. As he pressed forward again, I struck out with a straight snap kick to his kneecap, a blow that would have ended the fight in an instant had it connected.

It didn't.

He dodged the thrust, spun away, and leveled a roundhouse kick in return. I swept inside the wide arc of the kick and pinned his leg against the side of my chest with my left arm, then jammed the heel of my right hand into his eye. He grunted and fell away. I released his leg. His hand snaked under his jacket for a holstered SIG Sauer I'd seen earlier. As he brought out the gun, I grabbed his wrist with my right hand, his forearm with my left, then forced the gun up and away. We wrestled for control of the weapon, our bodies slamming against the back wall of a kiosk, bouncing off, then knocking over a rack of souvenirs.

Miniatures of the White House and the Capitol Building and the Pentagon clattered across the tile floor like a fleet of tiny wind-up toys set suddenly loose. Deboarding passengers screamed and leapt aside. I smashed Larger's arm against a sharp corner of the kiosk and the handgun flew from his grasp. I scrambled after it.

I was reaching for the SIG when the agent with the silver hair yelled, "Touch it, I shoot."

I froze, half bent, hand outstretched, my fingers twelve inches from the pistol. Out of the corner of my eye, I saw the man had his own metal trained on my chest. He was ten feet away. A no-brainer of a shot.

Moving only my head, I locked eyes with him. "Call off your man."

"One more inch, Brodie—"

"Enough!" the first suit from the jetway said with authority. "Put it away, Swelley. Now."

I craned my neck to catch a glimpse of the new speaker. His gun was pointed at Silver Hair. Swelley. Not a name I'd forget in this century.

With his free hand, the suit peeled off his shades. "I said stand down." His voice projected unmistakable menace. And something more.

"We don't answer to you," Swelley hissed, squaring his shoulders, a fiery strength rippling through him.

"I'd like to stand," I said. "I have no weapon. And we have an audience. A *large* audience."

No response was forthcoming, so I didn't move.

Around the terminal, there were easily fifty witnesses. A few had cell phones raised and rolling in what I suspected was recording mode, but I kept my gaze focused on Swelley. The feverish glint in his eyes told me I was in grave danger. Told me I was dealing with a fury disengaged from the man. A nearly independent force that could act on its own—to my detriment. If I wanted to get out of this alive, I needed Swelley to reel in more than his weapon.

I kept my eyes on him. I waited for my words to penetrate. It was a long, tense moment, but finally I saw Swelley blink with deliberation. His expression clarified. The unanchored animosity retreated. My words had broken through. Out of the corner of my eye, I caught sight of the fourth agent. He held his weapon unobtrusively at his side—ready to go either way.

"I'm going to move away from the gun," I said.

Very slowly, in nonthreatening increments, I retracted my outstretched hand. Then I straightened.

Swelley's gun tracked my withdrawal. "Step away from the weapon," he said.

I complied and he retrieved the errant firearm, pocketed it with blazing eyes still on me, then holstered his own piece. The remaining two weapons disappeared.

The peacemaker palmed a cell phone and tapped the touch screen without removing his glance from the other players.

The four men had clustered together in a crescent, just out of range. The stream of disembarking passengers—frozen in place as the drama unfolded—began to flow once more. Nervous glances darted my way.

A voice on the other end of the phone said, "Yes?" and the unknown mediator raised the mobile to his ear, eyes shifting to me. "Tom, we've got Brodie. Talk to him." Navigating around Larger, the man advanced two steps in my direction and extended the phone.

I accepted the instrument and said, "Stockton?"

"Yeah. You have unfriendlies all around?"

"You guessed it."

"We're under siege here too, but I told them no one's coming in until we hear from you."

Tom Stockton was one of the men I'd sent to guard Ken's daughter.

I said, "You were able to keep them out?"

"This is the Willard. Charging in here would make them look bad. We're not criminals. Yet."

Yet.

"Tell me what I'm looking at."

The man who'd passed the phone listened to me but kept a watchful eye on the two aggressors. Swelley had gone still. Larger was fuming. He rocked on the balls of his feet, partly to relieve the pain, partly to prepare himself to spring if the wind changed. As dangerous as the lug I'd locked heads with was, Swelley would be the more formidable of the two. The flinty stillness in the older man's expression told me he was calculating maneuvers broader in scope than any physical assault.

"The man with the phone is Agent Dan Kastor of the FBI. I've known him for years. A straight shooter."

"The others?"

"Alphabet soup. FBI, CIA, DHS. Don't know the mix that's braced you, though."

The usual suspects, plus the Department of Homeland Security.

"What do they want?"

"The Nobuki woman. The deal I made with Kastor is we open up only in your presence. Your client agreed. Said she wouldn't talk otherwise. They knew of your arrival. Homeland tried to force the issue, but Kastor's boss held them off. Didn't hurt that we're hunkered down at the Willard."

"All right. Be seeing you soon, I imagine."

"There'll be cars waiting. Stick close to Kastor. Part of the deal."

Stockton was hinting at something.

I waited and the Brodie Security affiliate filled in the blank. "Guy called Swelley is leading the Homeland team. He's ex–Special Forces and a ruthless son of a bitch. Big with silver hair. He or his people might brace you. Also, he's got connections to the White House he flaunts. If he makes a play, try to disengage diplomatically. But if you can't, get away at all costs. Fast. They snatch you, you could disappear for a long time, especially if they feel insulted."

"We're already past that point."

Stockton exhaled audibly. "The Brodie gene pool rarely disappoints."

The DC detective had worked with my father back in the day. We'd met for the first time in Tokyo when he attended my father's funeral, and again a few months later when Stockton swung by San Francisco to say hello while on an unrelated job.

"What can I say?"

"No need. Like I said, glue yourself to Kastor. I got him to watch your flank."

I hung up and said to Kastor, "I'm all yours."

"For now," Swelley said.

The FBI man shot him a sharp look before turning back to me. "Luggage?"

"Just what you see."

Kastor nodded. "Vehicle's outside."

We moved off, Larger limping noticeably. He and the other suits hovered about two feet behind, while Kastor stayed at my elbow.

Meanwhile, my brain was miles away. First Napa. Then San Francisco City Hall. Now DC. Was anywhere safe for the Nobuki family?

Or me?

CHAPTER 17

As we proceeded toward the exit, two more men emerged from the crowd, trailing after us three yards back.

"CIA?" I asked Kastor in a low voice, with a discreet eye-roll at our new shadows.

He nodded without enthusiasm. "Your popularity precedes you."

With Swelley and his ape now out of earshot, I said, "Why is Homeland Security here?"

Disgust formed itself into a frown. "Never-ending power play. They stick their nose everywhere."

The *something more* I'd heard earlier.

"For?"

"Control and all-you-can-eat government funds."

"And the FBI doesn't care who knows it?"

"The more the merrier."

Finding themselves out of listening range, the DHS men eased closer, and Kastor and I covered the remaining ground in silence.

Transportation turned out to be three cars, all black, each a different model. Predictably, Swelley made a move to herd me into their windowless SUV, but I shoved him away and saw at once that by laying hands on him I'd made an enemy for life. I followed Kastor into a sedan with darkened windows, while his partner swung around the far side and got behind the wheel.

Once we were rolling, Kastor said, "You been to DC before?"

"Half a dozen times."

"Why?"

"Work."

"Which kind?"

Kastor had done his homework.

"The art kind."

The FBI agent nodded, whipped out his phone, and punched in a number. "Enjoy the scenery," he said. "It's a nice ride in."

It was my turn to nod. We eased onto the main egress road. Overhead, a jet roared by for a landing, surprisingly low, the runway stretching out just on the other side of our causeway.

In the distance, the needle-shaped monolith that was the Washington Monument split the sky. Joggers ran on a wide sidewalk alongside us. A moment later, the Potomac River, blue-green and glittering, showed itself on the left, then extended its reach to the right.

With Kastor occupied, I took a minute to consider my unexpected reception—and near abduction.

What did it mean?

What did I know?

I knew a sniper had tried to take out Ken Nobuki and me yesterday. I knew my arrival in DC had drawn dark men from the shadows, and Naomi Nobuki was the connecting link. What I didn't know was why. I expected a hired gun might come after Naomi—but not three branches of Uncle Sam's finest and most brutal. What had she done to draw the government down on us?

I knew Naomi had become an antinuclear-power crusader since the Fukushima nuclear plant had melted down in the aftermath of the disastrous earthquake and tsunami of 2011. I knew most of her long and ongoing campaign was—as were those of other protesters—directed at TEPCO, aka the Tokyo Electric Power Company, and sections of the government in collusion with the firm. The utility company's mishandling of the power plant made daily headlines immediately following the meltdown and grabbed headlines to this day as the outfit continued to deceive the Japanese public. Even four years after the incident, they were caught red-handed yet again, this time allowing contaminated water to flow into the Pacific unchecked.

TEPCO and its allies were a formidable foe. Naomi's outspoken ways had made her a target, and behind-the-scenes pressure by the utility forced her from her cherished position as a news anchor. TEPCO was a major sponsor of most big media in Japan, so journalists critical of the utility did not fare well.

Yet Naomi hadn't stopped. A network of friends had come to her aid. Then a number of grassroots antinuclear-power groups rallied around. Her reputation surged. Next, a forward-thinking Japanese women's magazine offered Naomi a full-time berth and she found herself plugged back into the media grid, with an expanding platform, this time predominantly female, many of them mothers and grandmothers who held strong antinuclear sentiments because of the adverse effects of radiation on young children, who were more susceptible.

As I considered various political avenues that would bring the United States into play, the FBI vehicle glided smoothly onto Highway 1. From our newly elevated perch, the Capitol Building reared up in the distance, its distinctive dome white and gleaming.

In Japan, the pro camp was represented by what was dubbed the "nuclear mafia" or "nuclear village," a collection of energy companies, politicians, ministry officials, scholars, and media—many of which are beneficiaries of funds liberally spread around by TEPCO.

The nuclear mafia would not be pleased with Naomi's visit to Washington.

However, the question of the hour was this: Had the Japanese pro-nuke gang started this ball rolling with a roundabout hit on Naomi's brother back in Napa? Or was someone else set on knocking the Nobuki family off its pedestal?

Five minutes on, we raced over the Fourteenth Street Bridge. The Potomac River flowed high against the banks, brimming with a recent onslaught of winter rain and early snow flurries.

We dropped down off the bridge onto Fourteenth Street proper and crossed the National Mall, with its stout trees and long stroll paths. The sun was out and bright, and soon tourists and clusters of visiting schoolchildren would be prancing up and down the concourse, which was, today, crusted with patches of snow. I'd love to bring Jenny here one day. Maybe in spring, when the cherry trees were in bloom.

It was six in the morning on the East Coast, which meant three o'clock back in San Francisco. Jenny would be asleep in the apartment above ours, next to her best friend, Lisa Meyers. Lisa's mother and I had a long-standing babysitting arrangement. As two single parents, we pooled our resources. Each of us watched the other's daughter when asked, a fair fee accompanying multiday absences on either side.

I dragged my thoughts back to the matter at hand. What else did I know?

I knew that Naomi's father had supported her protests against the nuclear-power combine, as had I. But there the trail forked yet again. Had his activities spilled over into her life, or hers into his? Or Mayor Hurwitz's into both of theirs? Both father and daughter lived high-profile lives. I imagined Naomi's antinuke exertions held more sway with the feds than any endeavors of her talented artist father.

But I could be wrong. Stranger things had sandbagged me. With Mayor Hurwitz's reach across the Pacific and Ken Nobuki's skyrocketing art career part of the mix, I realized all I really knew was that I was facing a nightmarish mix of motives and suspects.

Kastor's telephone conversation had turned cryptic from the outset, so I'd tuned him out. When he finally signed off, I said, "You want to tell me what the fuss is all about?"

"Your lady friend took a room two doors down from the White House. That sent everyone scrambling."

"It's a free country."

The FBI agent fired me a look that said don't even go there. "You want to fill me in on your connection?"

"Like you don't already know?"

His eyes narrowed and he waited for my reply. Some procedures were etched in stone.

I said, "Today, I'm here as a friend to Ms. Nobuki and as consultant to the SFPD. I'm also connected to the Tokyo outfit that hired Tom Stockton."

"Quite a nexus you got going there."

"Not nearly as impressive as your world-class vocabulary. Are you really with the Bureau?"

His lips quivered with the beginnings of a smile. "Time to time, I have to check my badge to make sure. Heard you sidestepped a bullet outside City Hall. Saved the father's life."

"Did do a bit of a fast shuffle."

Kastor nodded. "Commendable."

"There's that vocabulary again. What's your interest in Naomi Nobuki?"

The budding smile vanished. "That can wait until we're in the same room with her."

"Give me something."

He took my measure with a sideways glance. "Let's just say her communication style tripped some alarms."

CHAPTER 18

NAOMI had been setting off alarms in Japan for a while now, but I never imagined her activities would lead to a confrontation in Washington.

About a year ago, a good four years after the tragic earthquake and tsunami, she had called me for a favor.

The disaster had been cataclysmic on multiple levels. A colossal quake registering a bone-rattling 9.0 on the Richter scale was followed by a devastating wall of water. Along the northeastern coast of Japan, giant waves thirty-five to fifty feet high rolled over a handful of breakwaters as easily as a sixteen-wheeler semi over a twig. One after another, the massive tsunamis smothered shorelines for two hundred miles. And in places where the land was flat, the water swarmed as far as six miles inland.

Only those people who reached high ground survived.

The invading swells swamped dozens of towns and villages and wiped out more than three hundred fishing ports. At the first stage, the ocean surge turned to kindling nearly every house, school, office building, and apartment block in its path, then in retreat dragged the bodies of its victims out to sea and a watery grave.

Next, before anyone could find time to mourn the dead, the third leg of the disaster struck: the Fukushima nuclear power plant began to come apart.

Cracks in the pipes.
Leaking coolant.
Escaping radiation.
Explosions.

I'd been at my antiques shop on Lombard Street with my daughter when Naomi called. There were no customers, so Jenny and I were playing hide-and-seek in the "safe" area of my cavernous store filled with Japanese traditional wooden chests, display cases of Asian artifacts, and an endless maze of classic lacquer ware, ceramics, hanging scrolls, and more. My daughter knew to be cautious, and not to touch anything.

When the phone rang, I was pretending not to know she was hiding behind the eighteenth-century Japanese stairway chest.

"Time out," I called. "I have to take this call."

"Okay," she said from her hiding place, immediately giving away her location. Then: "Oops."

I chuckled and said hello into the receiver.

"Hello, Brodie-san. It's Naomi Nobuki. Can you talk?"

"Sure. How are you? Are you in Tokyo or are you out in Fukushima?"

"I go back and forth. I'm still reporting on the nuclear plant disaster every chance I get. And gathering information."

The last comment gave me pause. "You're a brave lady."

"I need your help, Brodie."

"For what?"

"For *gaiatsu*. When the time comes."

"Of course. But how?"

Gaiatsu translates as "outside pressure." To crack open the closed world that often defines certain segments of Japanese society, reformers try to leverage overseas assets—an outside "voice," usually coupled with foreign media or a foreign institution of some renown.

"I'm working that out now," Naomi said. "But I wanted to ask your permission in advance. I'm angry, Brodie-san. So angry."

"I don't blame you."

"I'm a reporter, but it's become personal. Too many people have been permanently displaced. There are reports of radiation exposure and sickness among the children. The bureaucrats and the utility people have done so little about any of it. They are taking us all for idiots. Dad is also disgusted. He suggested I contact you."

"Fine by me. Just call when you're ready."

"I will, once I get a handle on the direction. Right now I am focused on the meltdown and the fact that there was no backup plan should all the emergency power systems fail."

Which is exactly what happened.

Neither the utility in charge of the nuclear power plant nor Japan's Nuclear and Industrial Safety Agency had made contingency plans.

"It was incompetence on a criminal scale," Naomi said.

My industrious friend was referring to the decision to put the main backup power system for the plant in a basement *without bothering to waterproof the room.* The tsunami rendered the system useless in seconds. Which meant that vital coolant couldn't be pumped into the reactors. Which caused them to heat up beyond control. Meltdown and extensive radiation leakage followed. The end result was the spread of radiation that nearly reached Tokyo and beyond, and in the end caused the permanent evacuation of more than 160,000 people. They lost their land, their homes, their way of life.

"Isn't the utility claiming that they couldn't possibly have known that such a big quake and tsunami could hit Japan? This in the land of tremors and tsunamis?"

"Yes. Corruption, of course. They are covering themselves by saying there wasn't enough *accurate* information, even though according to experts *outside* Japan who cannot be influenced, there was overwhelming evidence."

"I can't tell you what to do, Naomi. But if you follow your conscience, you'll get a good night's sleep."

I heard a small gasp at the other end of the line. "How'd you know?"

"It's in your voice," I said. I found myself biting my lip before adding, "If you choose to move against Big Energy, be careful. They and their cronies aren't called the 'nuclear mafia' for nothing."

And here we were more than five years after the calamity, her brother dead, her father shot, and Naomi in hiding, with three of the most powerful US agencies about to knock her door down.

CHAPTER 19

WHAT had Naomi done to bring out the FBI, CIA, and DHS?

We eased up to the front of the Willard, a stately hotel perched on a street corner a block from the White House grounds.

A uniformed porter opened the car door.

"We going in the front?" I asked in some surprise.

"Why not?" Kastor said. "We're practically neighbors."

A reference to the FBI's center of operations a mere five blocks away.

"You been here before?" Kastor asked.

"Once for drinks."

As had countless world leaders and VIPs before us, we strolled up the red carpet leading to the entrance. The Willard was one of the capital's legendary lodgings and meeting places. Aside from seeing nearly every president grace its halls since the mid-1800s, its gilded and colonnaded lobby was said to be the birthplace of the word *lobbyist.*

Outside, I spotted no additional watchers, but inside, they had taken up discreet observation posts. True to form, the foyer swarmed with lobbyists huddled in sequestered alcoves. Their aides hovered either over their shoulders or in secondary positions farther removed but still within sight, urgently working their phones.

Despite the crowd, I was able to pick out three additional agents. A suited woman stood unobtrusively at the bellhop's station off to the right, with a newspaper in hand as if waiting for her luggage. A second, in casual clothing, was stationed alongside the front counter to the left, trying to blend in with the clientele. A third sat on a bench near the elevators, leafing through a newsmagazine.

"Your people?" I asked Kastor, nodding toward one of the watchdogs.

The FBI man frowned and said nothing.

All six of the airport contingent boarded the elevator in my wake, then trod the plush hall to Naomi's door, where Swelley knocked and said they had me in tow.

Tom Stockton called out from behind two inches of solid oak. "Brodie?"

"Here, and still vertical," I said.

The door swung open.

Under the hostile stares of a roomful of federal agents, Tom Stockton and I shook hands. He had a pale complexion and hair the color of mahogany. He was tall, slim, and as accurate with a gun as he was fast, which is why I'd specifically asked for him to guard Naomi.

My friend's daughter exhibited speed of another order. Without hesitation she approached me with a question in Japanese, "Are any of these gentlemen responsible for what happened to my father and brother?"

Naomi occupied a richly appointed room spilling over with majestic dark-wood furnishings and splashes of old-world royal red throughout: red pillows, red lampshades, and swatches of red in the carpet. It also spilled over with alphabet boys, and a scattering of their female counterparts. The agencies matched one another body for body. Attendance had risen to four people per outfit. Two on each end of the operation, exclusive of those lingering in the lobby. An alarming number.

Swelley stepped forward. "Ms. Nobuki. You'll address your comments to us, not Mr. Brodie. Do you understand?"

He pointed a finger at a woman with straight auburn hair and tortoiseshell glasses, who translated the demand.

Naomi blinked rapidly, surprised at the gruffness of the senior DHS agent's words. "Yes, but—"

Swelley cut her off. "*After* we've finished, if your answers are acceptable, we'll consider questions."

He motioned to a protégé, who stuffed a file into his outstretched hand. Extracting a clipped sheaf of papers, he turned it around so Naomi could read the top sheet, saying, "Did you write this?"

The interpreter immediately repeated the question in a cadence that echoed Swelley's severity.

The document had what looked like five lines of text on it, photocopied and enlarged and shaded in places. Naomi read the material with studied determination, her lips moving faintly, and said yes when she'd finished.

"And this?"

She looked at a second page. "Yes, that's mine."

"This?"

A third sheet. Her lips traced the words.

"This was a return message."

"These are why we've detained you, Ms. Nobuki. Pretty damning. Who is TK?"

"Toshio Kawaguchi, a Japanese-American man living in Los Angeles."

I scowled. "Let me see those."

Swelley had angled the documents away from me so that I couldn't read them.

He said, "They're classified."

"How about I classify you upside the head?"

For the briefest instant, his eyes flared with unbridled contempt. Then they grew dismissive and he turned away. Kastor cleared his throat. Swelley flashed the FBI man a look of disgust, then thrust the papers at me.

I shuffled through them quickly. Each sheet contained a short email message. Across the upper edge of the pages ran a continuous refrain of TOP SECRET. Underneath was a line of coded gibberish.

I read the first one.

ECRET—TOP SECRET—TOP SECRET—TOP SECRET—TOP SECRET—TOP S
eck2ap59,s**qc83a40f naowppp20sbfper92[anbit[**sao1-94ns-4sa;udd

Dear NRC,

Please my last week email about nuclear explosion in Japan and America respond.

Sincerely,

Naomi Nobuki

Then the next two.

OP SECRET—TOP SECRET—TOP SECRET—TOP SECRET—TOP SECRET—T
k294*$sad wp&@fu&-sob toshen eoth!#aos shoq wotoxqqp-45624$^^a

TK,

Answer not come from NRC about nuke problem.

NN

RET—TOP SECRET—TOP SECRET—TOP SECRET—TOP SECRET—TOP SEC
Ppp3918^^doensa;302bgosown%%#skeua;aksbt =!!!!)!)4akooquanbe;e

NN,

This is not surprising. The American govt is always secretive about its nuclear program.

Yours,

TK

Naomi's independent streak had surfaced. She'd tried to enlist the Nuclear Regulatory Commission to her cause. Or at least bring them into the loop. This was an attempt at *gaiatsu*—outside pressure—of the highest order. To be waved in the face of the authorities back home, if she could catch the NRC's eye.

But she'd approached them on her own. And in a clumsy manner, without an introduction or someone more versed in English to clarify her intent. I admired her tenacity. It was how I handled most things. But nuclear power issues were political hot potatoes. Perhaps she thought her status in her home territory would be enough of an entry ticket. It wasn't. Her lone outreach had raised red flags, and her awkward English phrasing raised them higher.

I glanced at Naomi and drank in her open expression and trusting eyes. Her cute button nose. Clearly, she was anyone's definition of devious.

"Did the NRC reply?" I asked my journalist friend.

"No. I started with phone calls but my calls were never returned so I tried email."

I faced Swelley. "Ms. Nobuki's attached her name to these. She's hardly hiding."

"It triggered a midlevel security alert," he snapped back.

"After which you did your due diligence, right?"

"How we proceed is classified."

"Let me tell you, then. You didn't. I'd bet good money you didn't even make the effort because this low-hanging fruit was too tempting. But guess what? What you have in these emails is standard English usage in Japan. Grammatically incorrect but typical of their speech patterns. The level is remedial and doesn't mean the writer can actually speak English. At this level, most times they can't. Your analysts should know this, or would have dug it out if someone had bothered to put them on it."

In our post-9/11 world, hunting for a disaster-in-the-making was fine and as it should be, but Naomi wasn't hiding. She wasn't a threat.

In calling out the troops, Swelley had done the country a disservice, if anything. Wasting major resources on a minor lead. He should have checked up on the person behind the potential threat first. He hadn't—and Naomi had nuked him with bad grammar.

I said, "Did *any* of you check on Ms. Nobuki before you charged over here?" I looked around.

In a monotone, Kastor said, "We let our Homeland colleagues run with it."

But his FBI superiors still wanted a piece of the action. Maybe that was the problem. There had been a stampede to corral a potential culprit and collect the credit.

I inhaled deeply and breathed out slowly. *Steady, Brodie.*

I said, "Ms. Nobuki has a lengthy track record of antinuclear-power activity after the Fukushima disaster in Japan. That is *nuclear* as in *nuclear power plant*, not *nuke*, the bomb."

"We don't know that for sure," Swelley said.

I shook my head, annoyed. "But you should. There are dozens of her articles online. Plus video clips of her work as a news anchor. She's a public figure. A newscaster and reporter. She's not running below the radar."

"All her work is in Japanese."

"Because that's the language she speaks. The *only* language she speaks."

Swelley remained intractable. "It's another kind of cover, isn't it? We thought a preemptive strike while she was in our bailiwick was in order."

"You nailed her. Hiding out at the Willard."

"A hundred and fifty yards from the White House."

"A hundred and fifty yards of ferroconcrete hotel, shopping mall, and office space."

Swelley stared at me for a long moment, then nodded at his minions, who trailed out after him into the hall for a huddle, the last of the group dragging the door closed.

In the room, we all waited in silence. Kastor tipped his chair back against the wall and closed his eyes.

Five minutes later Homeland Security returned, Swelley reading something on his cell phone screen. "We wait for Tokyo," he said. "They should be calling in shortly."

"Better this century than next," I said. Then in Japanese to Naomi: "We need to get some protection for your family in Japan, too. Immediately."

Ken and his wife had three children: Toru, Naomi, and Akihiro. Toru had died in Napa. With Naomi safely under our watch that left three family members unattended—Ken's wife, grandson, and his other son, Akihiro.

"Oh, yes. Please. Dad would want that."

I pulled out my phone and began a text message in Japanese to Kunio Noda, the chief detective at Brodie Security and my best man in Tokyo.

Larger looked at his boss. "What's he doing?"

"Naomi's family is under siege," I said. "I'm getting them protection."

"We can't have that," Swelley said.

Larger moved forward, eyes set on confiscating my phone and inflicting damage in the process.

I rose and faced the Homeland hothead, terse words directed at his controller. "Give me one good reason why an American citizen can't handle private business not related to national security in your presence. Another inch and I'm going at it again with your pet."

Kastor's glance rolled lazily in Swelley's direction. "Well?"

"Well what?" the DHS man said.

"Do you have an answer for Brodie?"

"I don't answer to him."

"I'd like to hear it, though. For the record."

A dark shadow passed over Swelley's face. "Make it short."

CHAPTER 20

WHILE I was messaging Tokyo, Naomi excused herself to freshen up, which meant restoring both her makeup and her composure. By the time I finished, she had yet to return so I let my curiosity off its leash.

I said to one of the two CIA agents who'd followed from the airport, "Worked with a guy called Luke a little while back."

Luke had appeared quite mysteriously during the Japantown case when I'd asked a Japanese shadow powerbroker to help muster some additional manpower in the States. Luke had arrived, lent a hand, then disappeared as inexplicably as he had appeared.

My comment elicited a pair of cryptic smiles. "The agency's a big place. A lot of people work there."

"Thousands," the second guy said. "The exact number's classified."

I nodded. "That's all right. Most of them are probably in this room."

The first guy said, "This Luke have a last name?"

"He never said."

The two men exchanged a glance.

"On the other hand," the first guy said, "some people everybody knows."

So Luke was a known entity inside the CIA. Despite a cast of thousands. Which said a boatload about his status.

I said, "You run into him, say hello."

Something clicked for the first man and a startled look surfaced briefly in his gaze before he smothered it. "You wouldn't happen to be the Long Island Brodie, would you?" he said, referencing the endgame from the Japantown case.

I cocked my head. "That's one way to put it."

"Should have said so right out of the gate."

"Nobody asked."

He put out a hand. We shook. "I'm Brown, this is Green. You mention us in that combination it'll get back to us." Not real names, but the gesture was significant.

Naomi returned from the bathroom, and immediately tuned in to the ongoing tension in the room. In her makeshift English she said, "We are done, are we not, yes? No?"

Several voices from the DHS contingent said no.

Naomi bowed politely. Switching to Japanese, she said, "I am sorry to have caused such a big inconvenience. Please accept my humble apology for my clumsiness."

After the translation, there were several mumbled responses, none of which merited translation.

Naomi swung troubled eyes in my direction. "Brodie, while we are waiting can we talk about my father?"

"Sure. What is it?"

"Just, there was this strange message for me to stop or I would regret it."

"Stop what?"

"They never said. It came in five days ago, but I only saw it yesterday because of the retreat. It said, 'Stop or there will be more of the same.' " She looked at me with fresh tears pooling in her eyes.

Five days would put it soon after her brother's murder in Napa.

"Was this the only threat?" I asked gently.

"Recently, yes." Her lower lip quivered. "But in Japan, I receive many threats, Brodie-san. They are routine. They come from right-wing crazies who support the government and TEPCO." She glanced around at all the agents' faces while she waited for the interpreter to finish, then her eyes swung back my way. "I traveled with others and took care not to get caught somewhere alone. The threats have always turned out to be empty, so I learned to ignore them. But this time is different and I can't understand why."

"Was there ever any specific threat against your family?"

"No, never. Will you look into this for me?"

"Of course. Is there anything else you know that might help?"

She shook her head, which is exactly the response I most feared. It left the field wide open.

Suppressing a growing frustration, I said, "Okay, we need to get you to a safe place."

She bowed slightly. "Thank you. If possible, I prefer to stay in Washington because my work is not done."

Since traveling is always risky, the idea was not a bad one.

"Staying put's fine for now, but no more poking the bear until we find out who's behind all this."

"Of course."

I cast a sharp eye around, addressing the room in English. "And I presume, gentlemen and ladies, once the DHS hears from its Tokyo branch we'll be done here."

"*If* they clear her," Swelley said.

DAYS 4 & 5

WEDNESDAY & THURSDAY

KILL ORDER

CHAPTER 21

SAN FRANCISCO

DESPITE their threats, in the end Homeland Security gave Naomi a clean ticket, the alphabet crowd cleared out, and I boarded another red-eye back to the West Coast and arrived Wednesday morning.

Since Jenny had already left for school, I retrieved my classic maroon Cutlass from long-term airport parking and headed straight to intensive care. Ken was in the third day of a medical netherworld. He slept on with chemical assistance, a section of his skull surgically removed.

Induced coma.

I sat with my friend in his hospital room for fifteen minutes. The room was worn but spotless, and smelled of disinfectant. Machines ticked and beeped and hummed and flickered at regular intervals. They were connected to Ken via a clutch of wires and sensors. Through tubes, fluids ran in and out of him. His head had been shaved. A turban of bandages was coiled around his skull.

I spoke to him as I always had.

He lay on his back. Eyes closed. Chest rising and falling in an even cadence. There was a whiff of the withered about him. The fumes of decay. The spark of energy that had always infused his speech and action was not in attendance.

But I was certain he was in there somewhere, so I continued to talk. I told him I'd seen Naomi and she was fine. I told him the rest of his family was being looked after, and that I'd personally see to their safety. I would see them when I left for Japan later tonight, and follow up in Tokyo on the rest of this—and go wherever it led me.

I nodded to the SFPD guard outside Ken's door, then headed to the nurses' station. I wanted a firsthand report from Dr. Samuels if the surgeon was around.

As usual, the hospital was busy. Attending to their rounds, nurses and doctors and other staff moved in and out of rooms with purpose. Since it was visiting hours, families and friends traipsed down the corridors as well, fixing their bedside faces in place.

The potent smell of disinfectant carried over from Ken's room into the public areas, occasionally interrupted by more personal scents—perfumes, colognes, hair sprays. As I headed toward the nurses' post, I automatically pinned names on two perfumes and an aftershave. A classic Versace perfume my mother used to wear. Then some lighter, floral scent favored by several women in my building. And a Nivea aftershave sitting on my shelf at home, a gift from an old girlfriend.

At the busy nurses' station, I asked for Samuels and waited while a candy striper checked to see if the doctor was in attendance.

I leaned forward and rested my forearms on the counter.

On the stroll to the front desk, my nerves had started to jump. I'd attributed the response to the unsettling visit with Ken, but now that I had a free moment, another thought tugged at my consciousness. The hair at the back of my neck rose.

Something wasn't right.

I jumped up and looked around.

Nothing.

But there was something.

My early-warning system had kicked in but I'd been too distracted to notice.

I scanned the halls and the nurses' station. Still nothing. I backtracked to the intersection of two extended hallways, each going off in two directions. Four corridors. I looked down each one. Nothing clicked. I glanced once more at the nurses' area. More nothing. Where was it? And what was it?

I headed back toward Ken's room at a fast clip. My feet urged me on. I picked up the pace to a trot.

Then I was running.

The hall was long. I was fifty yards from the T-section where the passage ended then branched out to the right and the left. Ken's room was to the right, thirty yards beyond the turn.

A fragrance. It was a fragrance.

One of them had triggered my alarm.

Was it either of the perfumes? The aftershave?

No.

I'd logged two other scents as I strode down the sterilized hallways to the nurses' station, each noteworthy because it interrupted the pungency of the disinfectant. A cologne and a hair oil, both on men. Neither of which I could identify.

I was reacting to one of them.

The hair oil. That was it. I didn't know the name but I knew the scent because it was familiar. And common. Not here, *but in Japan.*

It was the odd smell out and had triggered my subconscious. The chances of running across a Japanese hair product in a San Francisco hospital were rare to nonexistent. But I had. The scent had come off an Asian man in blue scrubs. Thick hair, low on the forehead, a sanitary mask smothering the bottom two-thirds of his face.

He'd been pushing a cart. His head had been turned away as I approached.

Damn.

I rounded the corner.

Thirty yards ahead, the guard on Ken's room stood, reacting to something inside, as if he'd been called. In he went.

I raced on. I was still twenty yards away.

Then ten. Then five.

Straight-arming the door, I charged into the room.

The guard was sprawled across the floor, unconscious or dead. The male nurse was approaching Ken's bed, with a switchblade drawn. The mask was on, all but the eyes still concealed.

He turned as I entered, and for the briefest moment recognition lit his gaze. The look vanished as quickly as it appeared—then the knife swung my way.

CHAPTER 22

WITHOUT a second thought, I ripped off my jacket and whipped it around my left arm, gathering up one end in my left fist and tucking the loose end in at the bottom. Counting the thick winter lining and overlapping cloth, my arm was now swathed in four layers of protective material.

Three seconds had elapsed.

I circled to the left, away from the fallen guard, opening up an opportunity for a quick exit should the faux nurse be so inclined. He wasn't.

I hated knives. More often than not, street scum carried them. Sneaks or thugs or gangbangers flashed metal at the slightest insult. I'd contended with more than my fair share of knife attacks in the dicey neighborhoods of Los Angeles and San Francisco where I'd lived for some seven years.

But this was no street slug. He was a professional. He wielded the weapon as if it were an extension of his arm. Friction tape circled the handle to eliminate slippage and fingerprints.

The intruder approached with assurance, gauging my potential as an opponent. He was in no hurry. His knife arm began to move in a languid crisscross motion. Top right to bottom left, then looping up. Top left to bottom right, then up again. Repeat. He started slowly, priming his muscular memory. The rhythm accelerated. I followed the pattern.

He built momentum. I clocked the speed. He picked up the pace.

Then he surged forward, the cutter carving up the space between us like a large whirling blade.

I tracked his advance and the continuous cross-loop. When the dagger reached the bottom of a downward sweep at my left, I dove in, batting his rising knife arm away with my left forearm and simultaneously attacking with my right hand, sending an open-handed karate jab at his eyes. Which he slapped aside with his free hand.

We both backed away.

The would-be nurse was brandishing an eleven-inch Italian stiletto. Easy to conceal when retracted; long enough to do the job when opened. Light and deadly, it was an intimidating span of steel that added seven inches to his immediate effective range.

On the surface, my six-one height gave me seven inches on him, but the steel effectively lent him a reach as long—or longer—than mine. With it, he could slice through my arm as if it were a stick of butter. But that would only be a means to a deadlier endgame. He sought more lethal targets—arteries or organs. Or the neck, abdomen, or a half dozen other places meant to cripple or maim or cause me to bleed out.

The killer lunged again, this time going for a straight-line attack to the solar plexus. I backed away then veered left. When his knife arm swung around to follow, I swatted it away, following up with a quick fist to his throat. Again, he blocked my counterpunch without effort. He was as fast as a whip. And maybe faster than me.

Once more we separated and circled.

I'd been lucky on two fronts. First, timing. Another thirty seconds and Ken would have been dead. Second, I'd seen the blade beforehand. Professionals use knives for stealth. They want to get in and out quickly and quietly. A gangbanger or a street thug will wave his steel to intimidate. A pro doesn't bother with theatrics. His tool appears at the last second after he's penetrated your personal space, then the edge slides in and out swiftly—once, twice, three times and he's done and gone. His victims rarely see the weapon until it's too late.

We continued to circle. Out in the hall, there was a yelp followed by a loud crash. My adversary's eyes shifted involuntarily. For the briefest instant his body language slackened. I sluiced in, knocked his knife arm aside yet again, and clubbed him on the side of the head with my free hand. He blasted his other hand into my ribs, then the weapon returned before I could retreat and slashed my arm. Four layers of coat material parted to expose a thin red line of blood across my forearm. The wound was shallow but stung. He'd tagged me on the backswing.

Still inside, I ate the pain, released the jacket to free up my fingers, and pinned his weapon arm at the wrist. I hurled him against the wall and grabbed his other arm. He pushed off the backdrop and punched his knee up toward my groin. I twisted my hips into the blow and muted its thrust, then in a continuation of the defensive move slung my foot backward to hook his leg—hoping to trip him—but he twirled away, dragging me with him.

With both our arms occupied, our knees and legs came into play. But the space between us was tight and our strikes proved ineffective and easily blocked. We tugged each other one way, then the other. We slammed into the end of Ken's bed. We caromed off a wall.

Then I stepped in a growing pool of the guard's blood. My leg slipped out from under me, collided with my opponent, and we both began to fall. Our natural momentum carried us across the floor. Our hips hit the ground together. Our shoulders followed. Feetfirst, we continued to slide. The switchblade came loose and spun away. Our feet plowed into a set of hospital lockers. They rocked, clearly top heavy, and before either of us could react two hundred pounds of steel came crashing down.

I was taller and bulkier and took the brunt of the impact—as well as a glancing blow to the head. A black pool opened up behind my eyes. I was dizzy and disoriented. My grip faltered and broke. I tried to rise but the force behind two hundred pounds of falling furniture had left me momentarily stunned and breathless.

My smaller adversary wormed his way out, staggered upright, then slithered after the steel. He retrieved the knife and had swung back my way when shouts from the hallway reached our ears. Footfalls cascaded in our direction.

With great reluctance, my assailant flicked the stiletto shut and let it drop into his pocket. Gliding toward the door, he met the onslaught of concerned faces with soft cooing sounds of gratitude while pointing at me.

As a wave of hospital workers swarmed past him to come to my aid, the assassin slipped away.

CHAPTER 23

A FLURRY of last-minute activity occupied my final hours before departure.

After Renna doubled the security around Ken Nobuki, I replayed the scrimmage in the hospital room for him and his SFPD crew but had nothing concrete to offer other than a comment on the fighter's skills.

Superb.

And maybe unbeatable.

They flung dozens of questions my way. No, I hadn't seen his face. No, he didn't speak. Did I think he was Japanese? Yes. Could I prove it? No. Was the hair oil proof? Not definitive but a good indicator. Did I think the man might have been the suspect in the Napa killing? Possibly. Then I recalled the fleeting look of recognition and said he could have been the sniper. Anything more specific than an impression? No.

After the debriefing, I plunged into a huddle with Renna in a secluded corner of the hospital, where we informed each other of our next moves. Renna's squad was following up on a number of leads and I had people moving in Japan.

The airline had called with a special offer of a storm-delayed flight leaving at midnight, twelve hours earlier, so I grabbed it. The sooner I could get to Tokyo, the better. I dashed off two more research requests to Brodie Security's chief detective in Tokyo, flung some clothes into a duffel bag, and then spent every last second I could salvage with Jenny.

I took my daughter out for an early dinner and gelato, and we talked about plans for her birthday and her soccer camp over winter vacation, which started next Monday. Her birthday was the day after the camp ended.

After a hug and a large smile I'd carry with me across the Pacific, I escorted Jenny upstairs to her friend's apartment, where she'd spend the next few nights, then I drove out to the airport and boarded a new Airbus jet.

Six hours later I crossed the international dateline into Thursday, touched down in Tokyo, and smacked into what appeared to be headwinds of the yakuza kind.

DAY 5, SHIBUYA DISTRICT, TOKYO, JAPAN, 9:30 A.M.

Once I cleared customs at Haneda—the in-town airport tucked up against a reed-filled waterfowl habitat of Tokyo Bay—I caught a cab straight north to Brodie Security in Shibuya.

As usual, when I emerged from the narrow box of an elevator into the fourth-floor office, I was met with an active, bustling agency, the staff engaged with the phones or computers. In an impossibly narrow space, twenty desks had been divided into four workstations. A string of glassed-in offices lined the far wall. All desks had been assigned, so an empty perch signified a detective or staffer out in the field.

The office of Kunio Noda, the head detective handling all of my stateside inquiries, was vacant.

I circled around the half-counter that functioned as Reception and exchanged greetings with those closest to the front of the office. One of the staff rang Mari, our computer wizard, who doubled as my assistant when I came to town.

"Welcome back, Brodie-san," someone called out. "Noda's out for soba. He said to ring him when you're ready. Are you?"

The chief detective was a soba fanatic and sought out the Japanese pasta at its freshest—buckwheat flour just ground, dough just rolled.

"Give me half an hour to get settled."

"Okay."

"One more thing," someone else called out. "There's a strange message on your desk."

I nodded. Brodie Security received a lot of crank calls. Any high-profile case drew a heated response. Protocol required that the messages be jotted down. They were reviewed, mostly dismissed, then filed away. Just in case.

From the start, the firm my father founded offered personal security and investigative services, the former taking up the bulk of the workload. Protection details involved guarding foreign CEOs, visiting dignitaries, and incoming movie or rock stars of all ranks. We also coordinated overseas bodyguard services for traveling Japanese VIPs. For the most part, investigations encompassed blackmail, missing persons, and recovery of stolen goods. But we handled any situation a criminal mind might imagine, or to which a client could succumb. And in Japan the variations were endless, unique, and invariably tangled.

Inside the office and out, things never waxed dull.

"Hi," Mari said, trotting out of a back room with a smile. "So you made good time from the airport."

Mari Kawasaki was a twenty-three-year-old who, like most Japanese women, looked years younger than her actual age. Unlike most of them, when she entered the workforce she continued to dress for her crowd.

We indulged her because she was a bona-fide genius on the computer and also happened to be plugged into Japan's counterculture, talents Brodie Security coveted. Her interests expressed themselves not only at the keyboard but also in her wardrobe. Mari was as likely to show up at work sporting Hello Kitty overalls as a subdued homage to Lady Gaga. Today's outfit was a flamboyant purple tuxedo jacket coupled with snow-white pants and cummerbund. The plum-colored tuxedo was cut away below the ribs at the front but stretched in the back to luminous tails that hung down to her ankles. A violet hairpiece with tendrils falling to her hips completed the costume.

"Haven't seen this one," I said. "New?"

"Finished it over the weekend."

I nodded. Mari was debuting a fresh ensemble in her growing cosplay collection. *Cosplay* is a mash-up of "costume" and "play," referring to a popular dress-up activity of the anime-and-manga crowd in Japan and, increasingly, in the United States, Europe, and elsewhere.

"Should I ask?"

She smiled. The purple hairpiece bracketed a small face, a small nose, and a slim body. Her walnut-brown eyes had green flecks and were shimmering and watchful and caring. There was mischief there, too.

"Kamui Gakupo. He's like the coolest vocaloid."

"Got it."

Originally synthetic voice programs, vocaloids soon morphed into holographic rock stars. With a live band of actual musicians backing them, these fictitious bundles of light gyrated onstage to sophisticated choreographic dance moves for hordes of adoring fans. The young crowd paid good money to see a headliner that was nothing more than a projected cartoon image in human form, albeit a very convincing one. Vocaloids sang and pranced and were backed up by million-watt light shows and fireworks displays. At the end of a tune, they disappeared in a burst of stardust or some other flashy display and reappeared seconds later in a new costume, ready to charge into the next song. The live performances of these make-believe music stars posted on YouTube were as hypnotizing as those of their flesh-and-blood counterparts.

"Looks like a male character with crossover appeal," I said.

"Yes, I'm stretching out. This is for a big cosplay event in Kyoto tonight."

Mari did a little shuffle and syncopated body wave.

I smiled. "Impressive. What does your boyfriend think?"

She blushed. "He likes it a lot." Regaining her composure, she added, "By the way, I was very sorry to hear about Nobuki-san. The shooting's all over the news. Is it as bad as they say?"

We have to give the brain someplace to go. The only way to do that and prevent more brain damage is to perform a large craniectomy, which means removing a large portion of the skull.

"Worse," I said. "But thanks."

I nodded goodbye and threaded my way through the maze of desks to my office, offering more greetings as I passed.

Closing the door behind me, I sat in what had once been my father's office, behind what had once been his desk, and looked at the token items he'd left behind—a Japanese short sword, an Old Bizen saké flask, and his LAPD marksmanship award. To this collection, I'd added a large framed photograph of Jenny and a certificate for "exemplary services rendered" from the Japanese government.

In this room was a slice of my family's history. And the firm's. Each of the items had a story. The walls held the secrets about the decades of PI work my father had overseen. The desk might be worn, the chair wobbly, but they'd seen things too, as had the people manning the desks out front. The sense of time's passage, of people's problems mended, of desperate situations salvaged—all seeped from the walls.

To this secret history would be added, today, the launch of an investigation involving the Nobuki family.

An urgent inquiry.

Who had shot Ken Nobuki and killed his son, and why? Who had sent the gunman to Napa and put the sniper on a San Francisco rooftop? These were heady matters to be treated with care. I felt the weight descend.

As it always did.

Then the phone memo caught my attention. The time stamp told me the call had come during my ride in from the airport. From a man. He'd neglected to give his name, and our system had captured no caller ID. But he'd left a succinct message:

"Tell Brodie to stay put until I call again."

We have to give the brain someplace to go. The only way to do that and prevent more brain damage is to perform a large craniectomy, which means removing a large portion of the skull.

CHAPTER 24

BEFORE I could put possible names to the call, my office phone buzzed. I glanced at the phone panel, which in Japanese read *Undisclosed source.*

"Yeah?" I said, my nerves on edge.

A gruff voice forever imprinted in my memory rumbled across the wire. "You got big problems."

"How could you already know?"

"I always 'already know.' "

Who was I to argue? He usually did. It was a talent that explained why he knew I'd just arrived on a rescheduled flight. On the other end of the line was one of the deadliest men in Japan—Big Haga, aka Tokyo no Tekken. TNT for short. He was the top lieutenant of a local branch of Japan's most powerful yakuza group. Half of his job was to know more than the other guy; the other half was to dispose of anyone who crossed his boss.

"So tell me what's happening to my clients."

A pause. "Not *that* problem."

"Which you don't know about?"

"Might be related. Other than that, don't know, don't need to know, so don't care."

"Right. Forget what I said. What have you got for me?"

I had more than a passing acquaintance with Big Haga, whose

moniker, Tokyo no Tekken, translated as the "Iron Fists of Tokyo," and was a tribute to his sledgehammer mitts, which, if rumor were to be believed, had put any number of men in the ground. He was arguably the best bagman in the land.

"Had drinks with a guy. We need to talk."

"Why?"

"Because the guy's a friend and jabbers more than he should. You've got a bigger problem than what's happening to your clients."

"Do I?"

"Yeah, but maybe not for long."

"Why's that?"

"Once you're dead it ain't a problem no more."

"So talk," I said.

"Not over the phone."

He gave me an address.

"Can this wait?"

"Till the end of time, all I care," the yakuza enforcer said. "You got maybe a week, maybe a couple of days. After that you're a dead man. Take all the time you need."

I inhaled deeply to steady the chorus of nerve endings now popping and tingling in every part of my body. "Okay. You gonna give me a hint to hold me over until I get there?"

"You got anyone watching your back yet?"

"No."

"Bring someone but leave 'em outside. And try not to get aced on the way over."

CHAPTER 25

JINBOCHO DISTRICT, CENTRAL TOKYO, 10:45 A.M.

TWO soldiers had died at his hand before I arrived. A third bottle of Kirin Lager was on its last leg.

Quart bottles.

At ten-plus in the morning.

I pushed open the door of a coffee shop down an alleyway in Jinbocho, where Haga's gang held "interests." At the closest table, a pair of construction workers were unwinding from the graveyard shift. Each had a five o'clock shadow. A scattering of empty plates and beer bottles littered the table between them.

The proprietor motioned me into the back room, where behind a curtain I found TNT waiting alone at one of four small tables. The yaki enforcer was the only customer in the room. He held up three fingers and the owner, a stooped silver-headed old man in his seventies, dove through a second curtain into what I imagined was the pantry.

I took a seat and our server reappeared with three more bottles.

While we waited for him to set down the beer and pop the caps, Haga stared at me with his gangland deadpan and I stared back with an equally neutral expression. Neither stare was hostile. What lay between us, despite any edgy banter, was a mutual respect.

Our eyes locked and stayed that way. Mine were blue, with a few flecks of green, or hazel in a certain light, I'd been told. His were obsidian, under hooded eyelids, and stark and cold. They gave away nothing. Neither did his six-foot-four, two-hundred-forty-pound bulk. Big Haga was stillness itself, but any experienced fighter understood his muscular frame could fly out of the chair in a flash if irritated. I'd experienced his quickness on one singular occasion. The Iron Fists had played a role. His nickname, though cheesy, was no exaggeration.

The old man uncapped the final bottle then turned to my silent tablemate and said, "You need me gone?"

The big man nodded.

"The guests out front?"

He nodded again.

"Your tab?"

A third nod.

The shopkeeper bowed and shuffled through the curtain to the front of the store, keys jangling in his hand. He stopped at the occupied table and spoke softly to the two men with the five o'clock shadows. I bent back in my chair and peered through a breach in the curtain. The two guests stood, pivoted toward the rear of the shop, then bowed in our direction and departed. They couldn't see Haga, but when TNT requests you leave *and* picks up your tab, you pay your respects and exit in haste, no questions asked.

I heard the shop buzzer in the kitchen announce their departure, then the owner's. His keys rattled as he locked up. He flipped the sign on the door to CLOSED.

I was impressed. Throughout the whole process the aged owner expressed no curiosity about my presence. His gaze remained on the floor or the bottles, with tentative birdlike glances at TNT when necessary. Never did his eyes stray in my direction or linger on the yakuza hitman.

There was a reason the proprietor had lived to seventy among the clientele in this neighborhood.

I looked at the beer. I looked at the clock on the wall. Ten fifty-one.

"Guess there's no coffee brewing."

"This late, we're gonna drink."

I knew that was coming. The Japanese mafia were nocturnal creatures.

"Fair enough."

He poured my drink into one of the complimentary glasses the Japanese beer companies spread everywhere, then refilled his own. We bumped glasses and drank. TNT drained his in one long gulp. I did the same.

My taste buds got an unwelcome wakeup call. As did my stomach. This early in the a.m. the beer tasted brassy and sour, but my yakuza associate was doing me a favor, so drinking with him as he closed down his day seemed the least I could do.

Haga downed the next cup in one swallow. I drained mine at a slower pace but that did not prevent my host from pouring yet another round, which he made disappear before slapping down his glass, his thirst finally sated.

"I'm hearing things," he said.

"What sort of things?"

"You working those killings in California? The art guy out of Kyoto?"

"Yeah."

"Why?"

"I'm a good friend of the artist and his family."

"Tough luck. Papers say Brodie Security is involved too."

"That's right."

TNT drank, I drank, and he splashed more beer into our glasses. The morning booze got easier.

"Tell me about Napa and San Francisco."

It wasn't a request. TNT's stare grew more disbelieving with each new twist in my tale. The end of the story found him shaking his head as he topped off our drinks.

Big Haga said, “You’re in another mess. How’s that happen so often?”

“Nature of the work.”

“Naw, that ain’t it. You got some negative karma thing going.”

“Thanks a lot.”

He snorted, then his black eyes narrowed. “ ’Bout thirty seconds from now you ain’t gonna be thanking me any which way.”

The big man held the third bottle up to the light. It was empty. He stood and glided into the back room for fresh supplies.

CHAPTER 26

TNT retook his seat and poured another round. "You got a problem I never want to have."

His comment startled me and my heart bucked in protest. The yaki lieutenant before me was shrewd and fearless, and had once fought on the professional boxing circuit in Asia. After that, he'd handled any kind of problem that came down the pike for his mafia boss. Big Haga had been so successful that the Tokyo PD started a file cabinet dedicated solely to his work. All of it suspected, none proven.

The dark eyes zeroed in on me. They remained distant and unreadable, but no longer cold.

"I owe you for two lives," Haga said.

I grew still.

He didn't move.

I said, "You saying what I think you're saying?"

Eleven months ago I'd been in the position to spare his life, and that of his younger brother, and I had. What TNT seemed to be offering was information of such value that it would clear a major portion of his debt.

He nodded.

I reached for my glass and drained it. "Let's have it."

"You got people watching your back now?"

"Right outside."

"Keep 'em there."

"You going to tell me why?"

"You working with Noda again?"

"Yeah."

"Keep him close. He's the best you got."

"I'm not liking this."

"Ain't gonna get better. You ever hear of the Steam Walker?"

"No."

"Guy's a ghost."

"What kind of ghost?"

"The kind nobody's heard of or seen. The kind that kills and disappears."

I thought of the fight in Ken's hospital room. If it hadn't been for the scented hair oil, the killer would have slipped in and out of the medical complex without notice and my friend would be dead.

"Know what he looks like?" I asked.

The yaki enforcer shook his head. "Nope. Nobody's ever seen him long enough to talk about it."

A coldness crept into my veins. I braced myself against his next words.

"What exactly do you have?" I asked.

"Only thing that matters. The Steam Walker's next kill order. And as far as I know, he's never left a kill order unfilled."

"So who's his next job?"

"I'm having a beer with him."

I had just settled in behind my desk when Noda plowed through the door without knocking. He collapsed into the guest chair and targeted me with shrewd brown eyes that gave away nothing.

Brodie Security's head detective was a bulldog of a man. A thick waist, barrel chest, and broad shoulders blocked out a stocky five-foot-six frame. Knowing eyes looked out from under bushy eyebrows, one of them long ago bisected by a yakuza's blade. After the ensuing scrimmage, Noda was still standing. Reports on the knife-wielding thug's condition all came back negative.

"Give me everything," Noda said. "San Francisco first."

Straight to it. No hello. No welcome back. But there was no questioning his loyalty—to me, or to my father before me.

After I'd brought the man of few words up to date about Napa and City Hall, he said, "You have a takeaway?"

The detective had few tells, but chief among them was the scar. When he was angered, it flared. Now it was neutral.

"Too early. Only laid out direction. Is the Nobuki family covered?"

"Of course."

"Anything on who might be out to get them yet?"

In my follow-up message from San Francisco, I'd asked Noda to root out any possible enemies Ken or the family might have, public or private, old or new, in the art world or otherwise. A tall order.

"Going to take some time," he said.

"Tell me you have at least one name."

The most obvious lead usually turned out to be the best—and often the guilty party.

He shook his head. "Nothing from sources. Even less from the wife."

"She should know something, even if they're only shadow threats. You get his financial worth?"

"Wife didn't know that either."

But Noda would.

I said, "And?"

"One-point-four billion yen."

Fourteen million dollars. Ken had set himself apart with his distinctive Oribe ceramics, and risen to even greater prominence when he'd made a strategic decision to move from his native Gifu, the home of Oribe ceramics, to the outskirts of Kyoto. His work now fetched top prices. No "crock pots" here.

During my preflight huddle with Renna, we'd narrowed the search for suspects to three areas—a personal assault on the Nobuki family, a backlash for Naomi's inflammatory activities on the Fukushima nuclear front, or a political response at home or abroad to Mayor Hurwitz's Pacific Rim cultural exchange.

Narrowed suggests we'd blocked out a manageable range. In fact, the potential scope of the investigation threatened to cross so many borders, Renna had grown alarmed.

"Would I be in the right ballpark," he had said, "if I assumed that whatever crawled out of the woodwork could be confined to Japan?"

"Can you rule out enemies of the mayor's? Personal or professional?"

The homicide lieutenant's concession was reluctant. "Not yet. So two ballparks. I can cover the Bay Area. Can you handle the overseas contenders?"

"I can handle Japan, with Brodie Security. Our Asian affiliates will take the rest."

"Send the bill to the mayor. How wide a net?"

"It's too early to rule any parties out, so I'll start with the five other countries in the Pacific Rim program."

Renna winced. "Start?"

"We'll need a roving investigator or two to sniff around for a disgruntled sleeper elsewhere in the Pacific Rim. Say, for anyone who might have been offended by being left out of the mayor's program."

"Christ, forget ballparks. We're talking a whole league. Maybe a couple of them."

Now, seated behind my desk at Brodie Security, I said to Noda, "Where are you with the rest of Asia?"

"Affiliates in each country are moving."

"You find a rover?"

He nodded. "Severson out of Singapore, and his group. He can handle five languages. *Kao ga hiroi.*"

The phrase literally translated as "His face is wide." Noda was implying that Severson's group had an abundance of connections.

"Good," I said. "We're going to need every last one of them."

Mari knocked, entered, and set down green tea, which I accepted gratefully. The cup of coffee I'd guzzled to combat TNT's early morning booze after I returned to Brodie Security had been an inadequate first step.

She glanced my way. "You all right, Brodie-san? You left so suddenly."

And with backup went unsaid.

"Fine," I said.

The chief detective ignored her. "TNT give you something good?"

"*Good*'s a matter of opinion."

Mari's eyes widened. "You *know* TNT?"

"Yeah, for a while now," I said. "We had a chat. And more beer than my system likes to confront this early in the day."

Noda scowled. "You and Mari can socialize later. What he give you?"

Mari blushed and excused herself, closing the door behind her. The gruff detective wasn't known for his social skills.

"Ever hear of the Steam Walker?" I said.

"Whispers, yeah."

"Is that all?"

"Got a pile of useless ghost stories too. How good was the guy in the hospital room?"

"As good as they come. I kept him at bay, but I was losing. It could have gone very badly."

The chief detective dropped into thought. I could tell he was running through a catalog of culprits. A few moments later his expression told me he'd unearthed no contenders.

I said, "TNT gave me a story, too."

Noda frowned. "Never a good sign. Let's hear it."

CHAPTER 27

IT began long before recorded history.

The Japanese archipelago had risen from the sea through a chain of volcanic eruptions. When humans came to the islands, as far back as twenty thousand years ago, active volcanoes existed in great numbers. There were frequent lava flows and massive ash clouds and scalding geysers. During cataclysmic times, casualties were high. Sometimes whole tribes perished.

I'd lived in Japan for the first seventeen years of my life. After that, I'd been in and out of the country more times than I could remember. I'd heard a lot about nearly everything. The people. The culture. The art. The history. I'd heard whispers about things swept under the proverbial tatami mat. The secrets. The shame. Events best forgotten. I'd heard rumors and ghost stories and tall tales. About things that might have been. Or could be. Or never were. Most likely.

But a tale about a living legend was a first.

Japan's history is extensive and convoluted, with large gaps of missing knowledge. There are the emperors and empresses to consider—all one hundred and twenty-five of them, starting from the current one and tailing back to the head of the imperial line that is traditionally said to begin in the seventh century BC. *Traditionally* because the first fourteen rulers might or might not have existed. Most likely not.

More legend.

Among the legends percolating up through the folkloric ether is the mythos of the Steam Walkers, a tribe that lived near the volcanoes and walked the dangerous mountain byways. They built modest thatch-roofed huts on the edge of the active volcano clusters, just shy of the danger zone into which most people dared not venture. But near the hot zone the soil was rich, and the mineral-laden hot spring waters restorative.

Even so, the hinterlands kept sensible people at bay.

In these natural minefields there were blowholes that shot scalding steam into the air without warning. There were covered sinkholes where the earth dropped the unwary into dark, inescapable crevices. There was gas belching from craters and fissures. At least one type was odorless and colorless and asphyxiated any creature within its reach. Flocks of birds plummeted from the sky and herds of grazing animals staggered and fell, never to rise.

The Steam Walkers were watchful and clever, and over time learned to navigate the volcanic badlands. When ruthless warlords or cutthroat marauders galloped down on them, the Steam Walkers fled *into* the fiery foothills with their families. Confident in their might, the armies followed—and died horrible deaths. Their spears and arrows and swords could not protect them from being boiled alive by the angry breath of the mountain spirits. Or swallowed by hungry demons. Or strangled by invisible goblins. Invading armies quickly came to understand that certain villages were protected by the spirit-gods, and best left alone.

The Steam Walkers' secret art deepened and evolved and was passed down. Eventually, volcanic activity lessened. The killing gases lessened. The steam spouts lessened. The talk of those who could walk among the steaming lands faded, then turned to rumor, then dissolved into myth.

But in the middle of the twentieth century, after a defeated Japan was plunged into poverty and starvation at the end of World War II, the rumors returned. In the harsh new reality of postwar life, work in the outlying areas was scarce, and the provincial bosses wielded uncontested control. The generous rural leaders saw their communities flourish. The greedy ones leveraged their power and prospered themselves. They monopolized trade routes in and out of their region and undercut the wholesale price of the rice and nectarines and cabbages the farmers brought them.

The villagers were trapped. They had no choice. In increments, they grew poorer. When an unexpected storm hit, their losses mounted. The overlords lent them money against their homes and their land, then paid them even less for their crops and eventually assumed ownership of their property and houses and rented both back to the impoverished farmers. Next, the newly rich village heads cast their eyes on the young daughters of the neediest families. Fresh-faced girls fetched good money in the red-light districts of the big cities.

One day, a simple yet desperate request found its way to a Steam Walker's door. For the few meager coins the villagers managed to gather, the community pleaded with the Steam Walker to trick the unscrupulous headman into "following him into the mountain" as his ancestors had once done with bandits and hostile samurai soldiers. There were, after all, still plumes of steam, still the occasional eruption, still dangerous gas emissions. The Steam Walker, a victim along with the rest of the villagers, agreed.

So one night the crooked village boss disappeared. Word spread and the Walkers found themselves once more traversing their old haunts, this time on a champion's mission.

They became folk heroes.

Until, over time, the corrupt taskmasters had been vanquished.

But by then, others had begun to come to the Steam Walkers for "disposal." Aside from the neighborly commissions charged those early farmers and villagers deep in the countryside, their service never came cheap.

But it was effective.

CHAPTER 28

AFTER I finished, Noda said, "Lucky the yaki brute owes you. Still a goddamn ghost story, though."

"I know."

"TNT give you an address?"

"No."

"A home base?"

"No."

"Go-between?"

"No."

"Any way to find him?"

I shook my head. "None. What I really want to know is, how the hell do you guard against a legend?"

SHIBUYA DISTRICT, TOKYO, 7:30 P.M.

I met Rie Hoshino at an upscale *izakaya* pub restaurant north of Brodie Security and a few steps down a side street across from the main Tokyu Department Store. My watchdogs set up camp outside, one on each end of the narrow lane leading to our eatery.

Rie arrived in a beige blouse and brown skirt that complemented her cocoa-brown eyes, which were bright and inquisitive. Her black hair was cropped fashionably short, her complexion clean and bracing.

Uoshin specialized in exactingly fresh fish. On the street, a large glass front welcomed us, as did several strategically stacked empty crates from the Tokyo fish market. Inside was all wood and white surfaces and cheerful pale-yellow light.

"I don't come here that often," Rie confided, "because it chews up my paycheck, but the fish is *so* good I can't stay away for long."

"This is on me," I said, as we were led to a table under an interior awning across from a counter, behind which a parade of cooks sliced, diced, and tossed foods for salad, frying, or sashimi.

"I can't allow that," she said, her brown eyes steady on mine.

Tonight was our second date. The first, a hastily conceived dinner at an elegant Franco-Japanese restaurant, had gone extremely well. The date took place *after* the home invasion case we'd worked together had wound up about three months ago. The next day, I'd flown home to San Francisco, returning to Jenny and the demands of my antiques shop. We'd hit the pause button until I could find my way back to Tokyo.

Which was tonight.

Maybe the pieces would fall into place, or maybe they wouldn't. Rie had rules. As did I. She did not date anyone in the department, or anyone involved in an ongoing case. Both were about survival as a public servant. Mine revolved around women whom Jenny might find admirable, because it was likely she would emulate anyone I chose.

"Sure you can," I said. "It'll even things out since you're taking me for fugu next time. Besides, this may be your only chance. Who knows if I'll survive the blowfish."

"True enough."

We shared a knowing smile. Death by fugu was rare these days. The stories—plentiful and vivid—were overinflated. In truth, nine out of ten poisoning cases involving blowfish arose when a weekend fisherman found the delicacy on the end of his line and filleted the unexpected bounty himself to circumvent the high costs of a meal in a certified restaurant. But there were reasons for the price tag and the Japanese culinary laws that mandated chefs receive a license before serving the rotund fish—the same reason the species was outlawed in the EU: cut it badly, people die.

We selected our food from a handwritten menu, ordered a light Japanese beer to wash away the dust of the day, then Rie said, "So tell me about the Nobuki case."

I gave her an insider's overview, after which she shook her head. "What a mess. Lucky you weren't shot or knifed. Do you have any idea in which direction you need to go from here?"

"All of them."

"Don't you hate that?" she said.

Through courses of sashimi, a seafood-and-tofu salad, sautéed greens, and a lightly grilled whole fish that may or may not have had an English name, we wound up the discussion about the case, after which Rie guided the conversation in the direction of my work with Japanese antiques.

"You sure you want to hear about that?" I asked.

"Are you kidding? After dealing with police business all day, stepping out of the gutter is a refreshing change."

I indulged her probing, which was only slightly subtler than an interrogation. She queried me about my art trips to Japan and how I unearthed rare pieces. I told her about the scattering of like-minded dealers I knew across Japan and Europe, and how we tracked down pieces for each other when necessary. She expressed curiosity about high-end clients, and I told her about Sarah Navin's commission for a classic Oribe tea bowl. I didn't tell her that my roster of top-tier collectors wouldn't fill out the starting lineup for a beach volleyball game. Last, we talked about some of the other types of art I handled: scroll paintings, lacquer pieces, furniture, and a whole range of quality ceramics, which are a major art form in Japan.

At the end, she took a last sip of her beer and said, "Art's an expensive hobby."

"It doesn't have to be if you have a good eye and you're patient."

"Do you collect?"

"No. I have a daughter and bills. But I have the privilege of living with the pieces until they sell. I take some of them home for a few weeks."

"To study?"

"To learn their secrets."

Rie eye's drifted skyward as she repeated the phrase. "*To learn their secrets*. I like that."

The drinks flowed. I paced myself but still managed to consume twice as much as my dinner companion, who sipped at her beer in a ladylike manner, then treated her next choice, plum wine and soda, with equal delicacy. I switched from beer to Kurose, a smooth brand of *shochu*, a Japanese spirit. I ordered it *oyu-wari*, which meant several parts hot water to one part alcohol. It was a mellow accompaniment to our fish-based meal, and warming on a cold December evening.

While I drank the shochu, Rie nursed her plum drink and asked after Jenny.

"She's fine," I said. "And studying judo now."

"Really?"

"Yes, an indirect tribute to you, I believe."

Jenny had spent time with Rie during our last visit to Tokyo, and they had meshed.

"I'm honored." Her eyes sparkled and she did a little bunny hop in her seat.

"Did you just do a seated bunny hop?"

She pushed her lips out in a mock pout. "I suppose so."

"I didn't know that was physically possible. Your hands were in your lap."

"I am a superbly trained athlete. Many women on the force are."

Rie's reference to her conditioning sent my mind wandering down a wayward avenue. Trained observer that she was, the off-duty policewoman divined the direction of my thoughts.

"I think we should consider dessert," she said with an amused smile.

Her phrasing only served to heighten my "roaming," which I managed to hide with more skill the second time around.

Rie signaled for a menu, we ordered a final culinary flourish, and as the waiter carried our request to the kitchen, Noda rang.

"Bad news," the chief detective said by way of greeting, a phrase I'd come to dread coming from him.

"What happened?"

My dining companion's smile fell victim to concern.

"I'm heading to Tokyo Station," he said. "Need you there too."

"Why?"

"*Shinkansen* to Kyoto."

Japan's high-speed bullet trains—*shinkansen*—were a phenomenon. The fastest version covered the three-hundred-mile stretch between Tokyo and Kyoto in about two hours and twenty minutes. With runs on the Tokyo–Kyoto line departing every five to ten minutes during the busiest times, the system was convenient, clean, swift, and eliminated all the messiness of catching a commuter flight (as in no security checks).

"Again, why?"

"Akihiro's gone missing."

Damn. Ken's youngest son.

"How could that happen? Our men were watching the whole family."

"Tell you on the train. The nine twenty Nozomi."

Currently, the Nozomi was the fastest bullet available. While slower trains on the high-speed system paused en route to allow the speedier runs to pass, the Nozomi waited for no man or mechanical beast.

Looking at my watch, I said, "It's too tight. Let's catch the next one."

"It's the last of the day. Say goodbye to the girl and grab a cab."

"How did you—?"

"No time. Double the cab fare."

"What?"

"Only way you'll make it. Get a move on."

The line went dead.

CHAPTER 29

THE fourth driver was my man.

The Japanese are law-abiding to a fault. Which meant finding a wheelman willing to tear across town on a kamikaze drive would be difficult.

I'd let three necktied cabbies roll by before I spied a likely candidate. The image fit, but would he? He was in his midtwenties, with slicked-back hair, no tie, and a cigarette dangling.

While I stood alongside his vehicle, he vetted my proposal with a broad, nicotine-stained grin and shards of pidgin English. "You same like me. You make challenges in life."

"You could say that."

"What if cop catch me?" Flakes of ash drizzled onto his lap.

"The money's good and you're a pro, so the risk is yours," I said, switching to Japanese so there could be no misunderstanding. "But I'll still double the fare. You in or out?"

He considered the proposal for another beat, then gave me the nod. I vaulted into the backseat, my bodyguards dove in behind me, and we tore across town. My chosen wheel jockey pushed every yellow light, an eye to approaching traffic on each side in case a driver jumped early. He wove in and around slower vehicles and took more than one corner with screeching tires.

Once his cigarette had burned to a stub, he tamped it out and didn't replace it. The grin, however, never faded.

We rolled into the taxi entry to Tokyo Station and the young cabbie pulled up short. The final approach was jammed bumper to bumper with arriving cabs.

An eye at the dashboard clock, he said, "Two minutes, mister. Now your turn to make fast."

I dropped twice the meter's total on the front seat and ran the last eighty yards, the footfalls of my guard detail pounding the pavement at my heels.

Waiting inside the ticket gate, Noda pointed at me and yelled "That guy" to a nearby attendant as soon as I turned the corner, then the chief detective showed me his back.

With an alacrity that defied his bulldog bulk, the head detective barreled up a short stack of steps, disappearing from sight. I nodded goodbye to my watchdogs and sprinted for the gate. The gatekeeper waved me on without a ticket and I bolted through the gate, up the short stack, then scaled a long set of thirty-odd stairs three at a time, all the while conscious of the earsplitting trill of the one-minute warning bell.

I hit the platform, then lunged through the doors as the bullet train's panels slid shut with a pneumatic hiss. My chest heaved. I glanced into the closest carriage. The car was full.

"Good thing the seats are reserved," I said to Noda, who stood to the side.

Noda waved a pair of tickets. "Last two."

Which had been the same phrase the waiter had mumbled when Rie and I ordered matcha custard for dessert seconds before the head detective yanked me away from a promising evening.

"A work emergency. I'm really sorry, but—" I'd told her after finishing the call with Noda.

She shunted my apology aside with a warm smile. "Just go. I'm third-generation, remember?"

Her father and grandfather had joined the force before her, not to mention two older brothers. Rie carried the distinction of being the first woman in the family to wear a badge.

"How could I forget?" I'd said, racing for the door after dropping some bills on the table to cover the meal and a dessert I'd never see.

TOKYO STATION, 9:20 P.M.

TWO HOURS AND TWENTY MINUTES FROM KYOTO

We wove our way down the aisles of five cars, past other passengers and a food cart, before finding our seats.

Noda slid into his high-backed chair, pressed the recline button, and eased his seat backward.

"So tell me why I'm here?" I said.

"Youngest ran off to the big cosplay event in Kyoto."

"That's where Mari is planning—"

"I know."

"Did you—"

"She's on it."

Noda didn't disappoint. He'd moved the pieces forward. Now it was my turn.

I'd called Mrs. Nobuki twice since my arrival—once after settling in at Brodie Security and again before I headed off to meet Rie—but she had been napping both times. With medicinal assistance. I'd told the guards not to wake her. I took a deep breath and dialed.

Ken's wife picked up on the first ring. "Hello?"

"Nobuki-san? Brodie."

"Brodie-san, thank you for calling. I apologize for all the trouble we've caused."

"It's been no trouble," I said, reciting the ritual answer to her ritual opening. If all of this turned out to be linked to Mayor Hurwitz's program, I'd owe her a lot more than a ritual response. The idea that I might have indirectly been the catalyst curdled something down deep.

"Naomi gave me the latest news from the hospital. She says Ken is in good hands. Is that true?"

"The mayor himself is overseeing Ken's treatment, and we have our best man in Washington watching your daughter."

A mother's sigh of relief expressed her gratitude, and some of the weight lifted. "We'd never know where to start without you," she said.

Without me you might not have had to start.

I inhaled deeply, clearing away the darker thoughts. "I'm here to help in any way I can."

"Do you know why all this is happening?"

"We're working on it. Tell me why Aki-kun skipped out."

Her next sigh boiled over with exasperation. "Akihiro's nineteen and believes he's king of the world. I couldn't stop him from leaving. He has a new girl and they have been looking forward to this event for months. I don't even know what cosplay is. Do you?"

I explained it to her, and a melancholy sigh reached my ear this time, suggestive of a wilting from within. I didn't like what I heard.

"We'll find him," I told her, instantly regretting the pledge but loath to retract it.

"Thank you. I'm so sorry for the inconvenience."

"Is there anything else you can tell me?"

"I forgot to mention to the man from your office who called earlier that Akihiro wants to be a *manga-ka*."

A Japanese comic artist.

"That's good to know. Is there anything else you can tell us?"

"Their costumes have a lot of red. They paraded around here yesterday."

My gaze strayed to the stream of city lights flashing by outside our window. We were rocketing toward Shin Yokohama Station, the last stop in the greater Tokyo area before we hit Nagoya, some two hundred miles down the tracks.

A lot of red. We needed more than that if we were going to pluck her son from the crowd.

"Do you know which characters they're going as?" I asked.

"No."

"Do you know if the costumes were store-bought or handmade?"

Many cosplayers fashioned their own outfits. Zealous fans made as many as two or three a month, twenty or thirty a year, in exactingly accurate detail. Mari would be able to spot the difference.

"I don't know. My son couldn't have made them, but the girl might have, I suppose."

Nothing but dead ends. Think, Brodie. *New girl . . . paraded.* A romantic angle? "Were they wearing matching costumes by any chance?"

"Yes, but tailored differently, boy and girl styles."

"That's something." *Though minor.* There would be dozens, maybe hundreds, of couples with paired outfits.

"I'm so worried, Brodie. I can't concentrate."

"You're doing fine. Did you notice anything else? Any extras?"

"Like what?"

"Accessories. Maybe a sack or a sword or a crown?"

"Masks. They were wearing masks."

"Great," I said. "That'll help a lot."

Or a little.

Attendance was expected to surpass seven hundred.

KYOTO

Mari was glowing.

She was in her element. Well, one of them. Her professional world revolved around everything digital—computers and software and hacking. Much of her personal life touched the same chords, since her circle of friends were keyboard jockeys like her. Many of them were into cosplay too, which offered distraction, release, fantasy, playacting, and new friendships.

Tonight's gathering was magnificent. Hundreds of people *just like her* in costume. She'd always been different. Even after she discovered her talent for computers.

Even after her IQ tested off the charts.

And earlier tonight, Brodie Security had called with her first field assignment ever. Brodie-san had promised her it would happen one day. He'd pushed against the prevailing office opinion to keep her chained to the computer because she was the best they had. She craved a change and Brodie had come through.

But there was still no sign of Akihiro Nobuki.

Mari stood in the middle of a circle of friends and new acquaintances, some of the latter gravitating naturally toward her group because they too had dressed as vocaloids. Their conversation rose above the thrum of the crowd, loud and enthusiastic. Mari joined in, even as she scanned the immediate area for Akihiro and his girlfriend.

As she looked about, the amended description sent by Brodie from the bullet train played over and over in her head: *male and female in matching costume; mostly red; wearing masks*. And occasionally, to refresh her memory, she glanced at the photo of the youngest Nobuki sibling on her mobile.

Although in Mari's mind she had reached the upper age limit for prancing about in costume, she reveled in tonight's festivities. The event was chaotic and glorious. Raucous and mad and liberating. When she slipped into a costume, she could escape the stifling suffocation of society. She could show another side of herself—any side she chose: playful, wise, exotic, sexy, dangerous, noble, or her own unique mix of those.

With cosplay, everyone was transformed.

Colored lights flickered everywhere, dropping the crowd into shadow or darkness, and then spotlighting them with a rainbow of hues. It was a frenzied and fantastic escape. Only now, in this maddening, ever-growing, swirling, prancing, posing throng, she needed to find a man-boy and his girlfriend.

Quickly.

For their own good.

CHAPTER 30

YOKOHAMA, 9:38 P.M.

ONE HOUR AND 54 MINUTES FROM KYOTO

AS soon as the bullet train left Shin Yokohama Station behind, Noda said, "We better fast-track this case."

With people dying, he'd get no argument from me.

"You have a plan?" I asked.

"Your mayor's program first. Tag any disgruntled parties yet?"

"No, but there could well be. On either side. Those opposed to their country's participation, or those left out."

"Any similar program in other countries?"

"Not that anyone's heard of, but that's what we have our rovers working on, right?"

Noda nodded. "The Asian side. That's one."

One line of inquiry, he meant.

Noda swung his eyes in my direction. "Art's your field. Enemies?"

"Professional jealousy's an occupational hazard when this much money is involved, but we're talking about artists. The petty ones can be vicious. Gossips and backstabbers, but I can't see that extending to rooftop snipers."

"Nobuki's tops in contemporary Oribe?"

"Top three."

"Slot opens up, what's it worth?"

"If Ken were to die, people would begin to think in terms of the next Oribe artist 'in line.' Once there was a consensus, the 'chosen one's' profile and prices would rise."

"Can the consensus be influenced?"

"You know it can."

He grunted. "What's an opening worth?"

"Millions," I said.

Noda nodded. "To dealers and collectors too?"

"Yeah."

I'd had to explain the dynamic to Renna because, like Sean Navin, the SFPD detective had veered off in the wrong direction.

"Your friend's a potter," Renna had said. "I guess we can strike greed from the motive list."

I shook my head. "He's a successful *potter. In Japan, the best potters approach clay as an art form. They get art prices. Very respectable prices."*

"What neighborhood of respectable are we talking about?"

"Ken's net worth could be anywhere between five and twenty million."

"Dollars?"

"Yeah."

"Good neighborhood. And maybe deadly."

Now, in Tokyo, six thousand miles west of San Francisco, Noda underscored the sentiment: "So businesspeople *around* the artist could also profit?"

"If they're clever about it," I said. "God knows there's plenty of them who stockpile works by anyone they think could be the next Living National Treasure."

"Big money?"

"Very."

"That's two," the chief detective said.

KYOTO

There was music now.

Loud, pounding, vibrant music. The lights flickered faster. And whipped about. Shadows deepened. People swayed to the beat. They wanted to dance but the crowd had grown too dense.

Mari's enjoyment levels had plummeted. Finding Akihiro had become urgent. With each passing minute, their chances grew worse. She envisioned him being hauled off by some faceless undesirables.

Mari moved through the crowd now, swaying to the rhythm of the music, acting out a distinctive move of her character when a space opened briefly in front of her. After all, this was cosplay and she should stay in character.

Tension mounted in her throat and chest. She wanted to locate the man-boy. Not that she was much older. She was twenty-three to his nineteen, but his features were soft. A pudgy boyish face. The wide eyes of an innocent. A spoiled pout edging the corners of his mouth.

Mari circled clockwise through the cavernous hall; her boyfriend circled counterclockwise. Brodie Security had hired two floaters from a Kyoto affiliate. They circulated too, outside, where the overflow congregated. The event was sold-out. Rumor had it that a couple hundred cosplayers had crashed the gates before reinforcements arrived. A second rumor claimed the arrivals outside outnumbered the paying customers inside. All in costume.

Compounding the problem, the Kyoto affiliate had sent the wrong kind of people. They were middle-aged and without costume.

A colossal blunder in this world.

Mari had seen one of them from a distance earlier in the evening. A sharp-chinned, angry woman, who resembled nothing if not a furious mother looking to drag her kid home—which wasn't winning her any friends.

Passive rancor, at first. People moved aside with languid disregard. Turned their backs and continued to chat with friends, holding their ground. In growing frustration, the Kyoto operative started elbowing people aside. People shoved back. Where they might have been more reserved toward an elder during daylight hours, in costume they were different people. This was *their* world.

Even the man-boy would shirk away from the two Kyoto ops if he saw them first. He would guess they were looking for him.

Mari's phone chirped with a text message. The Kyoto woman was being taken to the emergency room with injuries. Mari was not surprised. The clueless operative must have jostled the wrong person. Or the wrong *character*. A cosplayer in character might jab an offender with a sword. Or one of the many sharp-edged fantasy weapons. Granted, cosplayers wore fake weapons, but they were serious reproductions for fanatics, filled with detail work and molded from high-quality plastic.

Hard high-quality plastic.

Clueless or not, we're down to three people, Mari thought. In a crowd approaching two thousand.

With the clock ticking.

CHAPTER 31

NAGOYA, 10:57 P.M.

35 MINUTES FROM KYOTO

ON the train, we slept and woke in starts. I was battling jet lag. Noda habitually slept whenever he could because, in this job, a case might keep you running thirty hours straight.

As the train stormed out of Nagoya, a fresh thought occurred to me. "You know," I said when Noda opened his eyes, "a rooftop sniper is a stretch for a family motive, too."

"Unless . . ."

The detective's voice faded as he turned to watch the city lights streak by in luminous streams of color. Long straight avenues flashed by outside our window. Like many of Japan's urban areas, this coastal city had felt the brunt of the World War II firebombings. From the ashes of thousands of wooden houses along mostly narrow, often twisting passageways, the city leaders devised a plan of wide avenues and buildings of brick and ferroconcrete. Progress or a step backward? Arguments had ranged on both sides, but Japan had moved on.

"What?" I asked.

"Any of the Nobukis have reach?"

"Toru was a sculptor, Naomi's a local reporter, her husband's a domestic lawyer, and Akihiro is a wannabe manga artist. They're all homebodies. I had to drag Ken to San Francisco."

"Naomi travels."

"When she can, which is infrequent because her husband hates overseas trips."

We reached the edge of the city. Nagoya was small by Japanese standards.

"How good's her English?"

"It's one step above nonexistent. Which doesn't stop her, as we know."

Noda's glance lingered on the changing scenery. Away from the city, moonlight painted the night a brooding silver-blue. The orange glow of farmhouse windows shimmered in the distance.

Noda's head lolled back toward me, dark eyes on mine, the scar bisecting his eyebrow neutral in tone. "Anything stop her?"

"Now that you mention it, no."

"Which makes enemies," the chief detective said. "That's three."

KYOTO

Mari was exhausted.

Her feet ached. Her throat was parched. Her eyes burned.

Young Akihiro Nobuki was nowhere to be seen.

She needed her first field assignment for Brodie Security to be a success. Otherwise, why would they offer her more?

She rubbed both eyes with her palms.

Blinked.

And then he was there.

She saw the couple first, their matching costumes streaked with blue and red and white, then the masks. Her fourth potential target of the night. *Not* predominantly red getups but streaked with three colors, red being the brightest among them.

Which could give the impression of a red ensemble.

Staying in character, she pranced in their direction.

"Nice costumes," she shouted over the music, her eyes going to matching shoulder sashes they'd fashioned on their own.

"Thank you," they both said.

The girl looked at Mari's long purple locks streaming to her waist. "I love your wig. Where'd you get it?"

"Nakano Broadway. I got help with the costume from a shop on Asagaya Anime Street."

"Oh, the new place! How is it?"

"Wonderful. Small but growing, and their heart's in the right place."

Mari smiled at them both, trying to see behind the masks. Then she just went for it. "You're Akihiro Nobuki, aren't you?"

He froze. The girl blinked in surprise. The couple backed away.

"Wait. Don't." Mari reached out and touched the girl's wrist.

"Who are you?" Akihiro asked.

"I'm a friend of Jim Brodie. I work for Brodie Security."

The boy's mouth gaped open. "They sent people *in disguise*?"

Mari was insulted. "I signed up last spring. They only asked me to help after you disappeared."

He relaxed. "That's different. So you know Brodie-san?"

"Of course."

He exchanged a look with his girlfriend. "Well, tell him I appreciate what he is doing for my family, but I don't need looking after."

The pride of a man-boy. Grandstanding for his girl.

"Of course you don't." She cast her eyes down, hesitating. "It's just that against real weapons it's hard for anyone . . . alone."

He frowned at her, fingering the plastic saber at his belt. "I know the difference. And I can take care of myself and my girl."

"Why don't you tell Brodie that yourself?"

Akihiro looked around in panic. "He's here?"

"He'll be here in thirty minutes."

Relief washed over both faces.

He said, "We're planning to get engaged as soon as my father returns, you know."

She hadn't known. Not that their intention justified his irresponsible run from their protection.

"Congratulations," Mari said.

"Thank you," they both said, again in unison, before Akihiro added, "so we have some alone time planned for tonight."

He gave the girl a meaningful look and she flushed.

Mari said, "After the ball is over, right? So you'll have time to talk to Brodie-san. Your mother would be very relieved to know you're okay."

"I *am* okay. Tell her that. Tell Brodie too."

He took a step back.

"Please, don't go."

Mari sent him a pleading look she hoped would seem needy and sisterly and anything but motherly. The look bounced off him without effect, but the girl hesitated.

Mari offered an engaging smile. "What could it hurt?"

Akihiro's smile was sly. "Nice try. If Brodie wants to meet up, tell him to stop by the Manga Museum tomorrow afternoon at three."

"Just a little longer and you—"

"Sorry, but tonight's our night," he said, linking his hand in the girl's and melting back into the crowd.

Watching the couple's retreat, Mari shuddered as she recalled Noda's last words when dishing out the assignment: "He's nineteen and full of himself," the chief detective had told her. "He'll resist. Try the girl."

"What'll happen if we can't bring him in?"

Noda's features had darkened. "A killer like the Steam Walker won't miss the chance."

DAY 6

FRIDAY

FULL-FORCE PURSUIT

CHAPTER 32

AKIHIRO'S vanishing act had us all on edge.

Every moment Ken's son was out from under our protection increased the level of danger, so we dragged a fresh crop of five affiliate operatives from their futons and continued the search through the night. We weren't going to risk waiting until the next afternoon.

If you knew where to look, Kyoto wasn't that big, especially when hunting for an errant couple in heat. We targeted Kyoto's hotels, hotspots, and hideaways. None of us slept. None of us stopped. But despite herculean efforts and insider knowledge of the city, we couldn't unearth Akihiro's love nest.

Calling off the search at noon the next day, we grabbed some sleep, then hailed a taxi to the Manga Museum thirty minutes before the appointed time. In the cab, Noda mentioned that our Asian affiliates had tagged three potential suspects: an Indonesian rebel group of ill-defined origin, a Taiwanese mob faction who supported the president's opponent, and a Muslim fundamentalist group in Malaysia receiving surreptitious funding from the Middle East.

At the museum, Noda took up a post in the café fronting the property. Mari and I headed indoors and paid the entrance fee.

"Maybe he's already here," Mari said.

"Have you ever known a teenager to be on time?"

"Responsible ones, yes. Man-boys, no."

We strolled the halls to get a feel for the place. Originally a public school, the large, three-story, L-shaped building had fallen into disuse as families abandoned pricey properties in the city center. The conversion was minimal but effective, with a gift shop, exhibition halls, and endless shelves of manga comics to peruse.

I said, "He's picked a lousy time to rebel."

On the first floor, we glided past the gift shop, a Hall of History, an auditorium, and a children's playroom.

There was no sign of Akihiro or his girlfriend.

Climbing the stairs to the next level, we found another large exhibition hall. A forest of two-panel screens had been set out, wings spread. They stood five feet tall and eight feet wide. Each had been covered with multicolored manga illustrations from a different artist.

"This is wonderful," Mari said, watching manga fans wander freely in and around the works in stunned silence. "These are all from famous cartoonists."

Outside the exhibition space we found more bookshelves, and alcoves with benches and chairs in which visitors could curl up with a comic book of choice. But no sign of the youngest Nobuki sibling or his girlfriend.

We mounted a staircase to the third floor and crossed a skywalk over an atrium. From our perch, we looked out on an Astroturf-covered courtyard and had a close-up view of a giant phoenix, the main character from pioneering cartoonist Osamu Tezuka's story of the same name. The sculpture was resplendent in yellow plumage, sky-blue eyes, and a sparkling red cockscomb.

We turned a corner.

Ten feet away a woman in her early twenties had settled on a cushioned chair with a manga. Luxurious reddish-brown hair cascaded over her shoulders. She looked up as we approached. Her eyes alighted on Mari and she smiled.

Mari started.

"Someone you know?" I asked, instantly alert, glancing first at the woman, then back the way we had come, then into every corner and the hall beyond.

No unfriendlies. No one advancing on us.

"Akihiro's girlfriend."

"Ah," I said.

Ken's son was not as naive as I had hoped. He'd sent an emissary.

CHAPTER 33

AKIHIRO'S girlfriend introduced herself as Yumiko Watanabe. She was slim, with quick chestnut eyes bracketed by long, tastefully colored reddish-brown hair.

"You know," she said, "Akihiro's smarter than you think."

"I'm relieved to hear that," I said.

"His family's worried," Mari added.

"He knows there's danger. But he's staying off the streets. And we were in costume most of the evening, remember?"

"The key word being *most*," I said.

"The rest of the time we've been . . ." She blushed and looked down.

I thought of my interrupted date with Rie and almost sympathized.

"Mari tells me you're engaged."

"Nearly," Yumiko said, her head bobbing up with a refreshed smile. "We're waiting to tell the family when Akihiro's father returns."

It was my turn to look away, plagued by what had gone down on my watch. But she'd given me an idea. A workable solution loomed. If Mrs. Nobuki knew about the couple's plans, she might not be averse to the two of them staying under her roof.

I gave Yumiko a verbal nudge. "Sounds like another reason Akihiro should go home. Comfort his mother. Besides, it's dangerous. For both of you."

Yumiko stiffened. "He's not coming in."

"You're looking at this all wrong," I said. "He's not a criminal."

Her look was triumphant. "Akihiro calls it 'house arrest.' "

"Wordplay distorts the idea. He's taking a huge risk bypassing our protection. Protection his parents requested."

"We can take care of ourselves."

"Like his brother and father?"

She gave me a chastening look. "We're dug in where no one can find us. Don't try to follow me when I leave."

"If you care for him," I said, "you should convince him to go home."

Yumiko twisted her hands in her lap.

"Or at least," I added, "let me send some men to guard the both of you. They'd stay out of the way. You'd never see them."

She popped out of her chair, alarmed, her face flushed. "I . . . we . . . can't . . . couldn't . . . have that. That would be . . . no, no, sorry, I have to go."

She bowed hurriedly, the strands of her long hair billowing out, then snapping back, and she scuttled off at a fast clip. The young lady's modesty was acute.

"That went well," I said.

"Did you expect it would?"

"Not really."

In fact, I had a backup plan in place. As soon as Yumiko was out of sight, I phoned Noda with her description. Dragging Akihiro home seemed an unlikely outcome, but we could guard his love nest without him knowing, despite his girlfriend's reluctance. Noda would tail Yumiko, then ring me with the location and we'd put a team on the lovebirds.

Noda called seven minutes later.

I picked up on the first ring. "That was quick. They must be close."

"She hasn't showed."

"*What*? There's only one way out of this place."

"Check the halls, the restrooms."

Mari and I did a quick canvass of all the floors and restrooms, but Yumiko was nowhere to be found. When I queried an employee about a rear exit, he confirmed a second way out for employees and VIPs.

Damn. Duped by a pair of kids.

I rang Noda.

"Bad break," he said when he heard.

Words that would prove prophetic sooner than any of us could have imagined.

CHAPTER 34

THE EASTERN FOOTHILLS OF KYOTO, 11:00 P.M.

YUMIKO gasped.

She'd never seen such a thing. When Akihiro had removed the blindfold, she found the whole of Kyoto spread out below her. The ancient capital was awash in a luminous moonlight and a sprinkling of city lights that stretched below her like a vast, glittering carpet.

"Oh, Akihiro. It's magical."

In her heart of hearts, she was still a simple country girl from a little hamlet two hundred miles west of Kyoto. She'd taken up cosplay and all the city affectations only after she'd met Akihiro.

"Didn't I tell you I knew a special place?"

"You did."

He'd hailed a taxi, and with her permission blindfolded her as soon as they were settled. Then he'd directed the driver through the streets to an access road that ran up the side of the hill along the Kiyomizu-dera compound, one of the city's most beloved temples. He had mentioned no names, so Yumiko had not the slightest clue as to their final destination other than their slow ascent into the foothills.

"Tonight is for you," Akihiro said.

"It's wonderful," she said, awe edging her voice. "We're alone. How did you manage it?"

Famously, the four-hundred-year-old temple building rose up five stories into the air on an open-air crosshatch of interlinking pillars and beams without the use of a single nail—only intricate Japanese joinery techniques. Thousands of tourists flocked to the "pure water" temple compound every day, crowding its walkways and lookouts. But this evening the two of them had the well-trampled veranda of the Innermost Temple—acclaimed for its panoramic view—all to themselves.

"One of my buddies tends the grounds," Akihiro said. "I asked him for a onetime favor."

When the taxi had arrived, he'd led her, still blindfolded, along a paved walkway, then to a gate. She heard him insert a key. Secretly, her heart thrilled. Yumiko expected something special, but not this special. Her Akihiro was such a romantic.

"It's spectacular," she said. "I couldn't think of a better birthday present." Her eyes drank in the whole of the sparkling cityscape below.

"Couldn't you?" he said.

The tenor of his voice drew her gaze from the glittering city lights to his gleaming dark eyes, then followed them as they dropped to his palm, where she saw an open ring box.

Yumiko gasped for the second time that night.

"Would you marry me?" he asked with what was the silliest, most adorable grin she had ever seen.

Her upbringing impressing itself on her, she began to bow. Then she hesitated.

"Is something wrong?" Akihiro asked.

"No. Everything's perfect."

She flung her arms around him. It was a gesture far too intimate for a public place, but they were, after all, alone.

Akihiro clutched the jewelry box in a panic, almost losing the ring over the side. He did not relish the idea of searching for the ring case in the dark after a sixty-foot drop. With an embarrassed laugh at his girl's impulsiveness, Akihiro slipped his arms around her waist.

Yumiko pulled herself away. "I thought we were going to ask your father first?"

"I couldn't wait. Do you mind?"

"Oh no, no. Never!"

"I have another surprise. I just sold my first manga story to Shokusha. The money's small, but it's a start. With that and some savings we can go on a honeymoon. I was thinking Thailand."

A voice neither of them recognized said, "You'll be going on a trip a lot sooner than that. Shorter too."

A man in a leather jacket and a baseball cap stepped from the shadows.

Akihiro straightened to his full height. "You're not supposed to—"

The man charged, bending low and ramming Akihiro with his shoulder. When Akihiro doubled over in pain onto the attacker's back, the stranger accepted the weight, wrapped his arms around the boy's waist, straightened suddenly, and flipped the slight youth up and over the four-foot guardrail.

Akihiro's earsplitting scream cut through the night as he plunged into the darkness. Three stories down, tree branches snapped. Two stories farther, his body smacked into a fern-covered slope with a stomach-turning thump.

Yumiko's scream rose in tandem with her fiancé's, then faded when the assailant produced a knife. Her eyes locked on the weapon. She backed against the rail. Tears streaked her face.

"You want to live, do you not?" he asked in an unearthly whisper.

Petrified, she nodded and found she couldn't stop nodding.

"Your boyfriend had to die. But you can live if you want. Do you want to?"

"Yes," Yumiko said.

The killer's whisper was soft and soothing.

"Then I need you to calm down," he said. "Can you do that for me?"

Yumiko continued to nod, frozen in place. She wanted to believe him. She *needed* to believe him. Seeing Akihiro fly over the rail was devastating, but a desire to live surged through her.

The man smiled. He slipped the weapon into a pocket. "Good. Now I'm going to walk away, but before I do—"

Without warning he drove a fist into her stomach. When she doubled over, her attacker threaded his arms into the hook of her body and hoisted her up and over the rail. The girl was thin and petite and offered no resistance.

Yumiko's mouth opened in a scream. But, breathless from the blow, her lips could form only a silent circle of horror. In midair, she flailed her arms and lashed out with her feet.

Her body crashed through tree branches, then hit the fern-covered earth sixty feet below with the same nauseating thud.

In death, as in life, the two young lovers were aligned side by side.

DAY 7

SATURDAY

THE BLACKNESS BEYOND

CHAPTER 35

AT five thirty in the morning, Noda pounded on my door. The Kyoto PD had promised to keep him in the loop.

"Bad news," he said. "The police found Akihiro."

Exhausted and frustrated, we'd returned to our hotels only an hour earlier.

"How bad is it?" I called back, tearing off my *yukata* sleepwear and slipping into a pair of jeans.

"Took a one-way dive," Noda said.

We'll find him, I'd told Mrs. Nobuki.

We'd found him, but couldn't hold him. Then he'd outfoxed us and now he was dead. I had no idea how I would face my friend once he woke from his coma, but in the meantime I had to break the news to a mother about the death of her youngest child just two weeks after the death of her eldest.

Minutes after hearing the news, I'd phoned our Kyoto affiliate to double the guard on the Nobukis. That made four men on duty each shift, twelve hours on, twelve hours off. Then I woke someone at our Tokyo office and asked him to relay the news to Naomi in Washington.

The pros at Brodie Security also recommended the highest level of containment, which I'd implemented as well. Over and above all the standard restrictions, the family members were now to remain indoors twenty-four/seven. No more brief excursions to the store, even with bodyguards. Any necessities—food, toiletries, medicine, whatever—would be brought to the house.

In short, total lockdown.

Noda pried loose one of the affiliates' cars and the three of us drove out to the Nobuki homestead and studio workshop at top speed—in hopes of beating the Kyoto police.

"Oh, Brodie," Mari said more than once during the drive.

Which said it all.

We'd signed on to protect the family, not hunt down a rogue member. Even so, we all felt miserable. Wanting to release Brodie Security's newest field operative from the ordeal, I'd suggested that Mari wait back at the hotel, but Noda vetoed the idea.

"She comes with us," he said shortly.

"Can't we spare her the—"

"No baby steps." The chief detective glared at the roadway without another word.

"Brodie, it's okay," Mari said.

"No, it's not."

I hadn't been able to save the young Akihiro, but maybe I could ease the pain of another starling among us. But Noda was having none of it: "Either she's part of the team or she bows out."

For Mari, it was to be trial by fire.

One of the guards let us in. The Kyoto police had yet to arrive but they wouldn't be far behind.

Mrs. Nobuki stood alone at the far end of the family room, in front of a beige couch with matching chairs. She wore a one-piece sleeveless housedress. Her arms were crossed and hugging her chest.

I'd asked the watchmen to be subtle. If any questions came up, they were to stall until I showed up, since I felt duty-bound to relay the news myself. One look at Ken's wife told me that all subtlety had left by the back door the moment reinforcements had arrived at the front. She had only two words for us, spoken with uncharacteristic abruptness: "Tell me."

I hesitated and Mari stepped into the void. "Nobuki-san, perhaps you should take a seat. We—"

"Tell me," she repeated, a faint tremor rippling her lower lip. "Security has tightened. They got to Akihiro, didn't they?"

Her husband's calligraphy graced a pair of hanging scrolls on the left wall. His pottery lined a three-tiered shelf on the right. One of Shu's toy cars nudged the chair leg near her right foot, but her grandson was nowhere in sight.

Mari said, "Mrs. Nobuki, please . . ."

"No more." She raised a hand to stop all conversation. "Brodie, tell me."

My friend's wife stood before us, rigid and demanding and as fragile as porcelain.

I opened my mouth to speak, but Noda got there first.

"He's dead," the bulldog detective said. Simple, abrupt, no punches pulled.

I winced and expected Mrs. Nobuki to shatter. Her eyelids drooped, then closed. She swayed on her feet.

Mari rushed forward, then paused halfway across the room. Mrs. Nobuki's body stiffened. The swaying ceased. A shiver shook her frame. Another tremor rippled across her lips. She pursed them. The Nobuki matriarch was struggling. Reaching for some inner strength.

We waited. We didn't speak. Neither Noda nor Mari nor I exchanged glances. Our attention was on our client as she grappled with yet another casualty.

It is too much for one person, I thought. *Especially for a mother.*

And yet she held on. She hadn't fainted or fallen. Color began to return to her features. We were witnessing a shattered heart recycling. A rebirth. A matriarchal phoenix rising.

Her eyes opened.

I said, "I'm sorry. So sorry."

Unable to find her voice, she simply nodded. A tear trickled down her left cheek. With dignity, she lowered herself onto the couch. I eased into the neighboring chair and clasped her hand lightly in mine. She did not pull away. Her eyes eased shut once more.

I'd done everything the Brodie Security staff and I could think of, and the effort had fallen gravely short. She knew it. I knew it. Noda knew it. And Mari was learning it.

There was nothing more to be said.

Mari disappeared into the kitchen and a moment later reappeared with a pot of green tea. She poured a cup and set it in front of Mrs. Nobuki without a sound.

The silence lengthened. We waited some more. Steam from the hot beverage rose from the cup.

When Mrs. Nobuki finally opened her eyes, she greeted us with a weak smile, then her eyes dropped to the tea. "Thank you," she said.

My friend's wife sipped the beverage gratefully. A little more color returned to her cheeks. She said, "Tell me the rest," so I did.

"That was our Akihiro," she said when I'd finished. "Rebellious, impulsive, sensitive, romantic. He wanted his girl to see the city, but he should have stayed hidden."

I nodded but said nothing.

"He might have had a chance then," she said more to herself than to me.

Maybe, I thought, *or maybe not.*

CHAPTER 36

WHILE Noda and Mari headed back up to Tokyo to continue working the case, I needed one more night in town in order to check on Sarah's Oribe tea bowls.

Two watchdogs from our affiliate trailed me back to my hotel, a small hideaway in the Pontocho district near the canal with the weeping cherries. Under normal conditions, I liked to stroll along the channeled stream in the evenings and enjoy the glow of the streetlamps on the backstreets. During the day, I usually lingered over the way the cherry trees reflected off the water, whether in bloom or drooping with greenery.

December offered only bare branches, yet the quarter still displayed all the classic touches of the ancient Japanese capital. Elegantly fashioned wooden homes. Traditional sweets shops. Delicately woven bamboo vases in display windows. At night, people meandered along the shaded lanes under lamplight. A muted hum of excitement hung in the air. All was dignified and respectful.

But on this trip, for me, there would be no casual strolls—day or night. Not with the Steam Walker on the prowl. I could still take in the ambiance, but only from the safety of a moving vehicle with bodyguards in attendance.

Once I unlocked the hotel door, the senior of my two watchers nodded me aside, then entered. I waited in the hall while the duo cleared the room.

They didn't return immediately.

After the third minute, I began to worry.

After the fourth, the younger of my minders poked his head out the door and motioned me inside. His partner greeted me with a frown. "Someone's been here."

He pointed to an envelope with my name in Japanese, leaning against the bedside lamp.

"Anything else?"

He shook his head. "No bodies, no bugs, just the letter. We called down to the front desk. They don't deliver to the room. They keep everything downstairs, and turn on the message light."

The envelope was not hotel stationery.

"Recognize the handwriting?" the senior bodyguard asked.

"No."

He nodded. "Go ahead and open it. Outside's clean. Inside looks okay. But by the edges. We'll still want to check for prints."

I lifted the missive by its edge, pushed open the flap with the pointed end of a hotel pen, and shook out the quarter sheet of paper inside.

It fluttered from its casing, falling faceup on the bed, its message in Japanese succinct and ominous:

> *Tonight. Alone. Nine o'clock. Takemori no Komichi.*
> *Start down the path.*

A mandatory meet at a bamboo forest on the outskirts of Kyoto. The Steam Walker had found me. Just as he'd found Akihiro.

I had three things to do.

Urgently and in a specific order.

First, I called the lead man on the Nobuki family, told him I had contact, and put the team on high alert. Whoever had left the communiqué had slipped in and out of my room without a trace. Next, I turned to my backup, both Kyotoites, and asked for their take on the meeting spot.

"It's a classic Arashiyama bamboo grove," the older one said. "Illuminated for tourists and lovebirds. Civilians will be all around. Smart choice."

"They'll spot backup?"

"Yeah. Alone is your only bet."

"Could we end up alone *in public*?"

He considered the question. "Maybe. But they can't know in advance."

"So it's public enough."

He nodded. "We could put a few random strollers behind you, but they wouldn't be hard to pick out."

"Got it," I said. "Not an option."

Last, I contacted Noda and brought him up-to-date.

"Know the area," he said from the bullet train. "You'll have to go it alone, unless you don't go at all."

"I'm going."

"Advantage is all theirs."

"No way around it."

I heard a low growl of protest at the back of his throat. "Best we abort. We'll get the Walker another day."

"There's no *we* this time. I'm heading out there."

"Listen, Brodie—"

"Forget it, Noda-san. Akihiro and his girlfriend are dead. Toru's dead. Ken's in a coma. I've got to get a handle on this."

The chief detective fell silent. If he hadn't been on a train rocketing to Tokyo at one hundred and eighty miles an hour, I had the sense he would have tackled me and strapped me to a chair until I cooled down. As it was, he mumbled to himself under his breath, then said, "You've got your father's talent."

"So you told me a few months back."

"Instincts on target."

A chill bloomed at the back of my neck. The gruff detective was reaching for diplomatic. This conversation would not end well.

"Heard that before too."

"Take it slow," he said. "Don't rile whoever shows up."

"You mean the Steam Walker. He's been untouchable. We've got to change that."

"But not tonight. Not alone."

"It's settled. I'm going."

Shifting in his seat, Noda acquiesced with a growl. "Okay, then try not to get yourself killed."

CHAPTER 37

I BREATHED in the rarefied air of Kazuo Takahashi's antiques shop. The brisk clean smell of the interior cleared my head. The faint mustiness spoke of centuries past, and instantly lifted my spirits.

"Brodie-san, welcome back," he said, with a slight bow. "It's been too long. You should visit us more often."

With the meet in the bamboo grove hanging over my head, I'd debated whether to view the tea bowls today or postpone my visit until tomorrow. But as soon as I stepped through the door, I knew I'd made the right choice.

I said, "I know, I know."

My art dealer friend was small, quiet, self-effacing, and well groomed. His blue wool suit was tasteful and modest. He wore a freshly starched white dress shirt and a red necktie, smartly knotted. Every hair knew its place. There were millions of men in Japan who were as particular about their presentation as Takahashi, but none of them had his perfect eye.

He led me to the rear of the shop. With a diffident sweep of his hand, he said, "Here they are."

A pair of Oribe bowls lined a back counter. One in the green-and-white mode, the other black-over-white.

"They both look excellent," I said.

Takahashi smiled. His intelligence was palpable. So was the lively glint in his look.

"Take your time," he said.

I stepped up to the counter. My gaze swept over the bowls. I lifted one, then the other. Both were enchanting. Both had the signature Oribe look—charming abstract designs on fields of white, alternating with wide swatches of green or black glaze. One had interlocking circles, the other stylized plum blossoms and geometric shapes.

"Impressive," I said.

"Ah, but which to choose?" The glint in his eyes grew brighter.

The art of the tea bowl was elusive, and the ornamentation of the Oribe bowl equally complex. There needed to be balance and perfect placement and open space that allowed the decoration to breathe. There needed to be a dynamic yet serene profile.

I pointed at the black bowl. "Great shape and decoration. Superb lip."

Takahashi nodded. "The bowl seems to dance, does it not?"

"It does."

And there needed to be a good depth to the glaze and to the interior "scenery." Again the black was superior, its glaze luxuriant yet subdued. The interior walls swept downward in a dramatic touch. The bottom had a full, luscious curve that finished with a subtle indentation at the center.

"Breathtaking," I said, pulling my eyes away with reluctance.

"Don't forget the underside."

The finishing touches. "Of course not."

I lifted the bowls to view the bottoms, and again the black won out. "Brilliant. Wonderfully textured clay and a nicely turned foot. Very natural."

Takahashi was pleased. "The best of the two, of course, and of the twelve I looked at in five shops."

"You've worked hard. Thank you."

He smiled. "You told me it was for an important client, and we have to keep you in rice. My only complaint is that you always walk away with the finest pieces."

"And yet you continue to test me."

"Amusement is the price I must extract for my exertions."

"My client will love the black bowl."

"I'm glad."

Takahashi's voice fluttered with suppressed excitement.

I eyed him with mock suspicion. "You have a line on something else, don't you?"

He chuckled. "How do you always know?"

"Trade secret," I said.

"Then you should keep it. But you are correct. An absolutely stunning piece I sold ten years ago may come back on the market any day now, if you can wait. It's pricier than either of these, but it's a minor masterpiece."

"Nothing's wrong with it?"

"Only that its owner needs to raise some quick cash. Interested?"

"Yes."

The Japanese tea bowl is the spiritual center of the tea ceremony, so the demands on the artist-potter are immense. To bring together the lip, profile, inner surface, and concluding foot with the right feel takes the artistry of a master. To consistently bring them together with an aesthetically pleasing balance of clay, glaze, and firing as well requires the touch of a genius. The black Oribe was a prime example. What Takahashi was offering was a step above it—and why I accepted his proposal of the second piece sight unseen.

"It's yours, then."

"That's extremely generous. What can I do for you?"

"There is one thing," my art dealer friend said.

"Name it."

In exchange for supplying me with Japanese art, I helped Takahashi secure the Western pieces his clients demanded, sometimes bidding in his place at Sotheby's or Christie's.

Takahashi prefaced his answer with a nod toward my bodyguards, who waited at the front of the shop, out of earshot. "Give up your father's work. Focus on art."

"Anything but that."

Takahashi clasped his hands tightly behind him. "Every moment you spend away from the art world is a loss. You have a first-rate eye, and you can teach people so much of what Japanese art has to offer. And art in general. You are also a good conduit for our country. There are so few and we are a shy people."

"I am hardly all of that, but I'm sure I can handle both jobs."

A sadness darkened his usually cheerful aspect. "I beg you to reconsider. There is so much menace in your *other* line of work. And the life expectancy, I fear, is—how should I put it—so very tenuous."

CHAPTER 38

THE WESTERN EDGE OF KYOTO, 9 P.M.

HE fell in step a half a pace behind and ordered me not to look back.

"Glad you could make it, Jim Brodie."

The words were relayed in a whisper reminiscent of steam pushing itself loose from a covered pot. A low brooding hiss of a sound that was hot and moist on the back of my neck.

"The pleasure is all yours," I said.

A breathy chuckle. "I like a good tourist attraction, don't you?" No one was nearby, but still he whispered.

"Not particularly."

"It suits our needs," my unseen host said.

We were ambling down a walkway that cut through a forest of giant Japanese bamboo. A low thatch fence framed the trail on both sides and prevented visitors from penetrating the grove. Fifty-foot stalks shot into the night sky, their leafy green tops curving inward and enveloping us in a tunnel of darkness. Dim amber floodlights behind the thatch illuminated the base of the bamboo and rose to meet a second line of vivid blue-and-green illumination, brightening the sides of the living tunnel while keeping the viewers in semidarkness. All of which allowed the man behind me to hide in plain sight.

"Our?" I said.

"I am a messenger. You will see me once. If you ignore the message, the next time, *he* will visit, and you will not see anything—ever again." A hiss seemed to linger long after the last two words had been uttered.

I wondered what was behind the whisper. A medical problem or an old battle wound perhaps. Maybe a partially crushed throat. Not enough to kill but enough to maim and distort.

"He?"

The sneer in my host's voice was evident. "Spare me your amateur fishing expeditions, Jim Brodie. For clarity, let me lay out the ground rules. People are stationed along the route, behind and ahead."

And, I thought, *in the bamboo.* Twice I'd heard a faint rustle of leaves to the left. Human, not animal movement.

Aloud I said, "Noted."

"If you try anything, they will extract me and finish you."

Don't rile whoever shows up.

With a thick cloudbank smothering the moonlight, my host and his crew had plenty of cover from which to work. The bamboo shimmered. The illumination was dramatic, dark, and indirect. Ahead and behind us, couples drifted languidly along. Paired silhouettes with hands interlocked. Occasionally bumping shoulders like two anchored boats nudged by the tide.

"Maybe I'll grab you as a shield," I said.

"Then you will die."

We walked in silence for a dozen paces. At our feet, Japanese lanterns dotted the edge of the path, their glowing patches of soft yellow light hovering around our ankles. More contained light. Hoping to catch a glimpse of my host, I started to turn my head.

"Do not look back, Jim Brodie," he said.

I returned my eyes front and center. I wondered what was behind the stilted syntax. Social awkwardness, or something else.

I said, "Why didn't you kill the child in Napa?"

"Why did not *he*? He has rules. He will not touch children. If you wish to know more, you may ask him in person should you ever have the chance. But if he shows himself, I doubt there will be time for talk."

I shrugged. "Why am I talking to a flunky?"

"Insults do not help your cause."

"Fine. So talk."

"There are many young couples out tonight. They remind me of a pair of lovers who are no longer among us."

My anger flared. "You don't want to make me mad."

We were coming up on the first turn in the path. There was a graveyard up ahead. A watcher hovered in the layered shadows of the tombstones.

The whisper grew heated. "Threats are unwise for a man in your position. I am simply displaying our bona fides. Tonight is a courtesy call, the last one you will be paid. You are an amateur who has had some luck. But you are sentimental, Jim Brodie. You are easily played. You are also easy to find. Focus on what is important."

"Which is?"

"You should be afraid."

In actual fact, I was. I wouldn't let it show, but fear tripped along my spine. It was primordial and life giving. I'd known too many men who had lost their sense of danger to overconfidence, then lost their lives. Fear is instinctual. It is natural. Paying attention to it was the smart move. It was about survival. When it surfaced, I lived with the knife-edged emotion as I would with a snarling, unlovable watchdog in my yard: I might not find the companionship endearing but I knew it guarded my flank.

"You've made your point," I said. "Why am I here?"

The path swung to the right where it abutted the graveyard. The farther in we went, the darker our surroundings grew.

"You have interfered twice, Jim Brodie."

Meaning at City Hall and in Ken's room.

"Was that you at the hospital?"

"Your question strays from the point we wish you to understand.

We are in control. Everything you think you know, we will know beforehand."

"So?"

"You are to stop interfering. You are to stop looking for *him*. You and your people."

"And if we don't?"

"Listen only to the message, Jim Brodie. Nothing else counts. You want to think about the Nobuki family."

"Already doing that."

"Think about them *more*. They are nearly extinct and you are not helping. You will be next."

"But not now?"

"Your kill order has been conditionally suspended."

"Depending on?"

"Tonight's outcome."

"I see."

"We hope you do. It is only a matter of finances. Our client was not expecting the additional charge for Akihiro's fiancée. Now he is hoping to dissuade you with a warning, which costs much less."

A high-paid killer. That could be useful. High fees require a rep, and reputations were something we could track. The path forked up ahead. The right branch squired visitors to some sort of shrine or monument, maybe both. The left fork led farther into the forest.

"To the left, Jim Brodie."

I made the turn. "And if I choose to ignore your advice?"

"Then I am certain the client will pay to finish the job."

"Maybe I'm not so easily killed."

"True, you have friends, but so do we."

"Who is this *we*?"

I heard a low rumble of disapproval. "Wrong question. Last warning. I found you in one day. Slipped in and out of your hotel room. If *he* has to look you up, he will not be leaving you a love letter."

I made no reply.

A low outbuilding belonging to a local temple reared up on the left. There was a small clearing and narrow driveway. Any person trailing us on that side would have to detour around the structure.

We approached the drive. On the opposite side, a gap in the thatch opened up and a trail ran into the gloom of the bamboo. We passed the temple building and the trailhead.

My walking companion's presence behind me weakened.

Then it was gone.

I turned. I saw the outline of a shortish figure twenty feet back, edging into the bamboo.

He turned back and stared at me. My eyes adjusted immediately to the extra layers of shadow. The features that sprang out at me sent shock waves down my spine. His face matched the image in the Napa police sketch. The same high cheekbones, sharp chin, and broad nose.

Down to the generic baseball cap.

This was no flunky. This was the killer himself.

Son of a bitch.

I took a step in his direction—and from the darkness behind me a silenced gun spat out a bullet. It pinged off the pavement at my feet and disappeared forever into the foliage.

I pulled up and raised my hands to my waist. Not enough to attract attention from strolling couples but more than adequate to make my intentions understood: I wasn't advancing any farther.

White teeth appeared in a dark face as lips spread, then the Napa killer disappeared into the blackness beyond.

DAYS 8 AND 9

SUNDAY AND MONDAY

FUGU

CHAPTER 39

EN ROUTE FROM KYOTO, EARLY MORNING

MY sleep was fitful, and I woke up frustrated and groping for direction. Today I had a meeting with an expert on TEPCO and the nuclear mafia. I needed to learn more about Naomi's situation and the danger she faced.

I caught the 6:00 a.m. bullet train to Tokyo, immersed in the nuances of the case, not to mention the threat hanging over me. Outside my window, rolling hills and fallow rice paddies flashed past in a blur of inattention.

Don't rile whoever shows up.

Last night, I'd met the Napa assassin. The man who'd executed Ken's two sons, put my friend in the hospital, and nearly succeeded in completing the job while Ken lay in a comatose state. I'd held the killer off in San Francisco and would have taken him down in Kyoto if I hadn't been convinced I was dealing with a messenger boy. Which, in retrospect, was what Noda was afraid I'd do. He knew me well. Or knew the Brodie gene pool. I'd pushed the Steam Walker and witnessed an immediate reprisal.

Clearly, he'd come prepared. He'd controlled every aspect of the meet. His answers were swift and assured. He was a quiet yet formidable force.

Try not to get yourself killed.

How close had I come?

CENTRAL TOKYO, 9 A.M.

"They don't usually kill people," Dr. Morikazu Ohashi said.

"Usually?" I said.

"They don't kill people," he said, dropping the qualifier, his tone unamused.

I sat in a conference room of the ISEAJ, and flung a worst-case scenario at the doctor. The Institute for the Socio-Economic Advancement of Japan was a think tank with a long name that did everything but roll easily off the tongue. I'd come straight from Tokyo Station via taxi, with duffel bag and Oribe tea bowl in tow.

And a new team of bodyguards fresh from Brodie Security. Even though the Steam Walker had declared a reprieve, none of us would be banking on a killer's word.

"Fair enough," I said. "So if they don't kill people, how does the nuclear mafia peddle their influence?"

Dr. Ohashi resembled a praying mantis in nerd form, all stick-thin limbs and a bony diamond-shaped head. With black glasses and a pocket protector. His movements were awkward, and he kept his hands together more than apart. The proud possessor of three PhDs, Ohashi was also blessed with impeccable manners, which made him proper, intelligent, and creepy all at once.

"They attack the foundations of those whose lives they wish to influence. Status, livelihood, reputation."

The three-legged pedestal on which people built their lives. In Japan, losing those three condemns a person to a living death. There is no bouncing back. Even the loss of one of them could cripple a career and a lifestyle. My apparent repugnance raised a flicker of a frown from Dr. Ohashi.

"We don't judge here, Mr. Brodie. We are objective. We offer observations based on measured, unbiased perception."

"Don't you find it distasteful?"

He cleared his throat. "Any decent citizen would. But our charter is clear. We proceed without judgment."

"Do you believe that?"

"On the job, I am not in the position to believe or disbelieve. I am a researcher and an observer. If you wish candor from me, you will need to rein in your condemnation."

Despite the buggy look, Dr. Ohashi came highly recommended. He was a man of science, I was told. A believer of facts. Not a spin doctor. He'd verify or refute or qualify a truth without offering an opinion. The perfect person to fill me in on the long arm of TEPCO, and the rest of the nuclear mafia.

"Sure. Fine. I apologize."

"No need for apology, I assure you. Most of our Japanese guests arrive with the same attitude. Ideally, think tanks are meant to be neutral, although many function as propaganda machines. We suspend judgment. We illuminate. It behooves others to . . . to . . . act accordingly, if they so choose. I was given to understand you and your firm might be among 'the others.' Have I been misinformed?"

"Far from it."

"Then consider our research a tool to be utilized should you find items of value. And personally, outside of office hours, let me assure you I welcome any corrective measures."

There it was. We understood each other. Boundaries had been staked out. It was a matter of shading and subtlety and phrasing.

I said, "When you say 'they attack foundations,' can I interpret that as meaning they, in essence, crush their targets?"

I thought of Naomi. Her family's money had broken her fall.

But such safety nets were rare. More often, sometimes tragically, the tumble from the narrow path of career building—no matter the level—was swift, merciless, and irreversible, regardless of the rung reached.

Ohashi raised tented hands to his chin. "Obviously, you understand our ways. I trust, then, that the statement has made itself sufficiently clear for your purposes."

I took his answer to mean yes. He had a line to toe. I wondered if there was a microphone and perhaps an unseen camera to be catered to as well.

"Can you give me specifics?" I asked.

Ohashi flipped through a file on the table, contemplating one page, then the next. "Their pattern is generally predictable. They go after the job first. They're plugged into the top levels of most, if not all, institutions, meaning the ministries and the political mechanisms, all connected directly or indirectly to the nuclear mafia. Any of these can bring huge pressure from above."

"Meaning someone's boss?"

"At the very least, but more often their boss's boss or higher, adding more layers of separation and deniability. The average employee is usually overwhelmed. Submission follows quickly."

"Relentless," I said.

A half-nod. "I would not dispute that conclusion."

"What about someone who won't stop even then? Or on whom such techniques won't work?" I said, thinking of Naomi, who managed to skirt the nuclear mafia's usual ploy.

He flinched. "I don't know."

"Will they go . . . further?"

"There is no proof of such actions."

"How about an educated guess?"

For the first time since the interview began, Ohashi fidgeted. A nerve in his cheek twitched. "You know, Mr. Brodie, I am unsure of how to proceed from this juncture. I work from facts and data and

CHAPTER 40

I RETURNED to Brodie Security and nearly crashed into Noda making a mad dash for the exit.

"What the—?"

"Later," he said, and was out the door.

Something else was heating up.

I took the respite to catch up on incoming news.

Out of Washington, Tom Stockton had reported the arrival of Naomi's lawyer-husband, Tad. It had occurred to me that her continued presence there could be interpreted by whoever was sending the threatening messages as an extension of her activities, so I'd suggested she leave, with an escort of course. She'd refused, insisting anyone could see she'd ceased working. So Tad, who hated air travel, flew in to make an impassioned plea for his wife to return home.

Out of Asia, our affiliate had confirmed that Malaysian opposition to Mayor Hurwitz's Pacific Rim Friendship Program was strong. The Muslim fundamentalist group leading the protest had set off a car bomb two blocks from the prime minister's home. In Taiwan, the local mob had gunned down the president's brother-in-law as an expression of their displeasure with the country's participation. There were also vague reports of stirrings by Indonesian rebels.

Stateside, there was a memo on my desk from Renna back in Cali-

research. You're asking me to step into the realm of pure conjecture. It is beyond our mandate."

"Not *pure*. Educated speculation, which has its value."

As in, would the nuclear mafia send a sniper to San Francisco?

Ohashi fiddled with the pens in his pocket protector. He stared down at the open file on the tabletop before him. "I still have nothing concrete to offer you but a piece of advice."

Maybe a camera, without audio, monitored our session.

"I'm listening."

"I would tell you to be extremely careful. We examine both honeybees and cockroaches because both have roles to play. But we tend to study cockroaches *more* than honeybees. After all, the very name *honeybee* defines its nature."

So much for *they don't kill people.* The nuclear mafia had just risen a notch on the suspect list.

fornia. He'd checked in yesterday evening with a message dictated to the staff.

> This is only a preliminary report. No need to call back. My squad has zeroed in on eight potential suspects. Three of the most likely are a political rival in the mayor's own party, a Tea Party candidate desperate for attention, and an old business partner who is backing a new challenger. We're collecting big noise and small. No other serious prospects on the horizon but we expect the list to grow. Gail Wong from the mayor's office dumped a stack of hate mail on us. We've got twenty-three names on that list, including one former soldier whose letter mentions a gunman. Be in touch soon.

Alone in my office, I exhaled loudly. Not unexpectedly, Renna's list was lengthy. Candidates were many, solutions elusive.

Elusive? Make that nonexistent.

ELSEWHERE IN TOKYO

Jun Tasaki waited for the Steam Walker's call with growing irritation.

He got that the legendary assassin worked with only the best. He got that the guy demanded precision. But Jun's brain was buzzing from all the hoops the Walker wanted him to leap through.

He'd rung the yakuza middleman to complain.

"Just do what the man says," the go-between said. "You can't knock the paycheck."

"Guy's a control freak. Maybe he won't pay if he don't like how I handle the setup."

On the other end of the line, the fixer paused for a long moment before he next spoke. "Jun, *listen* to me. You wanna show him *big* respect. The Walker always pays, only sometimes it's to the next of kin."

Jun bristled. "You know me. You know my skills."

"You're thinking on it too much. It's a hustle like any other. No delays, no screw-ups, you'll be hearing a loud *ka-ching*. Just check the attitude. And don't ever mess with the Walker."

"Have you met him?"

"You shitting me? Never done, and never want to. You in or out?"

The money was too good. "I'm in."

That was a few days ago.

Now Jun looked at his watch. Five more minutes.

I checked the time, and saw a window open to ring Jenny. My daughter's camp allowed phone calls between certain hours, and it was hard for me to match their time frame from this side of the Pacific.

"Daddy!" she said, picking up on the first ring.

"Hi, Jen. How's camp?"

"Great! They made me team captain!"

"That *is* great. Are you playing games or still practicing?"

"Playing games. Actually both. And a tournament," she said, the breathlessness in her voice growing more acute with each additional phrase. "That's why they made me captain. Can you come watch?"

There was so much need, and so much genuine desire, in the question it tore a piece out of me. Since her mother's death, my daughter wanted me close. She tracked my every move. I wanted to be close, but I also needed to earn a living. Which took me away from her when it involved Brodie Security.

"If I finish up early in Tokyo, you'll see me there."

"Can't you come?"

I pursed my lips. Ever attentive, my daughter picked up on the faintest nuance. "I want to come. I'm just not sure I can make it."

But for a reason I'd never reveal to her. The Steam Walker had threatened me, and the last thing I was going to do was lead him back across the Pacific *toward* my daughter.

"Okay, Daddy. Just don't forget my birthday. And all my gelato."

"I won't. Still not promising you a whole mountain of gelato, though."

I heard her stamp her foot. "Daddy, it's my birthday."

"I know, kid. I love you. We'll talk again soon."

Late in the afternoon, Noda barreled into my office. He paced the narrow open space fronting my desk. The scar was a dark crimson.

Trouble was brewing.

"What is it?" I said.

Noda glared. "Nobuki's will has disappeared."

"*What?* You sure?"

"Called the lawyer."

"He tell you what was in it?"

"Couldn't recall. Needs the document."

"Wife know?"

"No."

"Got an opinion on what happened?"

"Not yet," he said, and stormed out. A moment later I heard him in his office, tackling the phone.

I closed my eyes and inhaled deeply. From Taiwanese gangsters and the Japanese nuclear mafia in Asia to political rivals and ex–military personnel in San Francisco, the case was spinning out of control. We weren't saddled with a widening list of suspects. We were dealing with a population explosion.

I looked at the clock. Time to meet Rie. I washed up, changed into beige chinos and a brown shirt, then left Brodie Security with my shadows trailing close behind.

Jun and the Steam Walker had talked three times. With game on for today, the final setup call was coming through any second now.

And there it was. Jun answered on the first ring.

Without even a hello, the Walker asked in his unsettling whisper, "Did you confirm placement, Jun Tasaki?"

Did you confirm placement, Jun Tasaki? Who friggin' talks like that?

"He's in," Jun said. "At the higher price."

"Acceptable."

"You need his name?"

"No. Just execution as promised."

"Guy'll give it his best."

"Acceptable. Keep me informed at every step."

"What if he can't find the moment?"

"Just keep me informed, otherwise it's a deal breaker."

Jun felt his whole body go cold. *The Walker always pays, only sometimes it's to the next of kin.*

"I'll relay the message."

"You do that, Jun Tasaki."

CHAPTER 41

ASAKUSA DISTRICT, TOKYO, 7:00 P.M.

WE were about to dine on fugu—the first or second most poisonous fish in the world, depending on which expert you believed—aka blowfish, cowfish, boxfish, porcupine fish, balloon fish, globefish, and sea squab, among others.

Miura-ya was tucked away down a backstreet in Asakusa, an old-town district in northeast Tokyo. The quarter was also home to the renowned Senso-ji temple, a large complex founded in the seventh century and dedicated to the Buddhist deity Kannon, who is esteemed for her compassion toward human suffering and weakness.

The hostess guided us to a table on the second floor.

"Why are we here again?" I asked in a low voice, as we ascended the stairs.

"Because I'm returning a favor."

When we'd found ourselves working together three months ago, I'd put Rie front and center in a takedown of a crooked art dealer. She had performed admirably and received kudos back at police HQ.

"Not that. This particular place."

"Oh, Miura-ya was my favorite uncle's favorite haunt, so I like to come here when I have a cause to celebrate. It reminds me of him. But it has to be during the season."

Blowfish is served from October to March, with the tastiest period being from December to February, when ocean waters are coldest.

Once seated, she said, "I was thinking we could take a stroll after dinner. With the pagoda and other buildings lit up, Senso-ji temple's quite charming."

I thought about my late-night walk in the bamboo forest. And I thought about how well the Steam Walker and his people worked the shadows.

"We'll see," I said.

Picking up on my lackluster response, Rie gave me a curious look.

The Steam Walker was cold and displeased and stoically bearing up against the chilly December evening while waiting for a long-overdue phone call. What part of *keep me informed at every step* had the hired hand not understood?

One finger hit the speed dial, and when Jun picked up, the Steam Walker said, "Where do we stand, Jun Tasaki?"

"Not sure yet."

"I need information at every step. That's what I pay you for."

Something in the assassin's voice put Jun on edge. He recalled the job broker's warning: *No delays, no screw-ups.* Even so, Jun hit back with a jab of his own. "You sound nervous. Is your fallback in place? Just let me know if you need a hand."

"You sure you want to talk to me that way?"

The ice-cold downward slide of the killer's whispered words funneled from Jun's ear to the pit of his stomach, ending in an involuntary shiver.

"No, no. Just a joke. Please accept my apology."

"This time only," the Steam Walker said, and disconnected.

The mafia fixer had also mentioned that the Walker had no sense of humor whatsoever and cautioned Jun about the danger of a stray comment, even a light ribbing. Jun hadn't believed him. Now he did. Believed it to his core. *Felt* it there. What's more, the fixer had mentioned that people who disappointed the Walker simply vanished. Jun hadn't believed that either.

Now he did.

CHAPTER 42

AFTER we ordered, Rie excused herself to freshen up. I buzzed my shadows, Ito and Sasaki. They had arrived behind us in a second taxi and lingered nearby, one downstairs in the first-floor dining area, the other on watch outside.

"How's it look?" I asked.

"No sign of the Walker."

In Ito's voice I heard a calm watchfulness.

"Okay," I said. "You have the sketch and my description."

We'd briefly discussed canceling my date, but in the end decided we could use it to draw the Steam Walker out into the open. The fact that Rie was a trained police officer tipped the scale in favor of our acting tonight.

Sasaki said, "Have you told Hoshino-san?"

"Not yet."

"Be sure and do it, Brodie. If our man shows, a delay on her part could be dangerous for all of us."

Rie rounded the corner and was making her way to the table. I gave her a brief smile, then returned to the phone. "She's on her way back now. Bet you'd like to be a fly on the wall for that conversation."

Rie wore a navy cashmere sweater, which she'd paired with a thin gold necklace and black slacks. A tasteful and modest ensemble.

"Will be if you wait a few minutes. See the table they're clearing on your floor?"

"Yeah."

"I'm moving there any second."

"So many eyes. Fun times."

"Lucky you."

He hung up and I apologized to Rie.

"That sounded like business. Anything important?"

"You may not want to know."

"Are you serious? 'So many eyes'? 'Fun times'? Tell me everything."

Jun rang the Steam Walker. "We're on," he said.

"Haven't seen an ambulance, Jun Tasaki."

"They've started with drinks and appetizers. The doctored fish goes out with the main course, the fugu stew. Heard the poison is painful. Paralyzes you wide awake and you feel yourself dying inside. That true?"

"That's what they say. Is placement confirmed?"

"Better. The head chef is out today. My friend says getting the bad fish past the second chef is no problem."

"Good to hear," the Steam Walker said.

"We caught a break."

You make your own breaks in this world, Jun Tasaki. That's the difference between you and me. I have no time for amateurs.

Our appetizers and drinks arrived with a briny freshness.

Uni sashimi, aka raw sea urchin, and *fugu tataki*, flash-grilled blowfish of sashimi quality, the flavor of the fish coaxed forth by a light touch of the flame.

Rie said, "Now spill. The story, not your drink."

"First things first," I said, removing the lids from the capped porcelain cups of hot saké spiced with a toasted fugu fin. "*Kanpai.*" Cheers.

We touched glasses and drank. The saké was warm and smooth and infused with a smoky flavor. A sweet, woody aroma rose up from the cup, a browned fin floating on the surface.

"Well?" Rie said.

"Right. Did you notice the new diner who just came in?"

"Of course. Short Japanese male in a blue suit and striped tie. Eating alone. What about him?"

"One of ours."

Rie's eyebrows rose. "So something's going on. Unless that's your way of telling me we're on a double date."

"Worse," I said, and laid out the story.

By the time I wound up, an agitated excitement had pooled in her eyes. "Brodie, you should be in a safe house, under guard like the Nobuki family."

"Better this way. If we keep the window of opportunity small and tempting, we have a chance to catch him."

"And get your first solid lead?"

"Exactly."

Her excitement flickered as she reconsidered. "It's not an ideal date, but I'm pleased you included me."

"Anyone else and we would have gone in a different direction."

I nabbed a piece of the grilled blowfish with my chopsticks. The flesh was succulent and chewy, with a hint of honey.

"I'm flattered," she said. "On the other hand, I missed the tail. How embarrassing."

"It's beyond your training. No one threatens the police department."

My dining companion's thoughts had already skipped ahead. "It's only natural Brodie Security would protect one of its own, especially their *shacho*."

Their president.

"It's a title of convenience," I said, taking another sip of my drink.

Fugu-fin saké leaned toward a lowbrow brew but that did not make it any less addicting.

Rie's protest was immediate. "It's more than convenience, and you know it. Brodie Security has a certain expertise in the field *because* of its American background, so they need you alive and healthy."

"Yes, but—"

"No *buts*. You are a second-generation American PI in Tokyo, even if the job is inherited. Lineage is vital in Japan. If something *happens* to you, Brodie Security loses all credibility. Clients will think, rightly, that if your firm can't protect its shacho, how can it protect them and theirs? If you get yourself killed, your staff loses their livelihood."

I nodded unhappily. My personal rock-and-a-hard-place. I'd always been aware of this quirk in the way we practiced the trade, but I'd never taken the time to articulate it in terms of my own life and death. A hefty price tag had been attached to my carcass. Consciously, I'd managed to sidestep the issue. But no more. Aside from a daughter I had to raise single-handedly, I needed to stay alive for Brodie Security employees and their families.

The burden grew heavier.

My date watched me closely. "Don't put too much pressure on yourself."

"I'll survive."

She searched my face. "You're doing more than surviving. With your last two cases, you've brought them honor and distinction. It's not the Japanese way to say these things aloud, but I'm certain they feel that way."

Before I could reply the main course arrived. Fugu stew.

"Do you know how to cook the meal?" our server asked.

"Yes, thank you," Rie said.

Our waitress bowed and retreated, leaving behind two platters brimming with food. On the first was an elegant spread of Napa cabbage, Japanese leeks, tofu, and clear noodles; on the second, succulent chunks of filleted blowfish. We were to add the ingredients to a deep pot of lightly boiling water set on a tabletop burner, then scoop out the cooked foods and dip them in a seasoned sauce.

"Looks promising," I said. "Is it safe?"

"No promises," Rie said, with a mischievous smile.

Licensed chefs in Japan study for two years before being allowed to serve fugu to the public. They learn to fillet the fish and gingerly remove the toxic sections *without* accidentally puncturing, slicing, or otherwise damaging them and releasing the poison onto the flesh.

I said, "Maybe I should ask the server to prepare the meal."

"Maybe you *should*."

A part of fugu's popularity is a fascination with what might be: the ultimate penalty versus a sublime dining experience. The story about the famous kabuki actor who couldn't resist the call of the fish's delectable but poisonous liver because he believed he'd built up an immunity is true. His name was Mitsugoro Bando VIII, and his headline-grabbing death occurred in 1975.

"Are you scared yet?" Rie asked.

"Quivering all over."

"About time."

Although the danger is nearly nonexistent these days, on rare occasion a Japanese urbanite still ends up in the hospital or the morgue. Death by fugu is not pretty. Victims endure an agonizingly slow death as the toxin paralyzes the body in stages—while the stricken person remains fully conscious of the pain. A single blowfish carries enough tetrodotoxin—the poison in question—to kill thirty people.

"*Itadakimasu*," I said, the Japanese equivalent of *bon appétit*, with an additional nod to the host or cook for providing the meal.

Rie and I dug in.

When she screamed, the blood in my veins froze.

CHAPTER 43

A WOMAN two tables down watched in horror as her male dining companion grabbed his throat.

"I can't breathe," he wheezed.

His companion jumped up, intent on coming to his aid, but managed only a single step before collapsing to the floor, her body thrown into convulsions.

"I can't feel my legs," she said.

"Call an ambulance," one of the servers shouted.

The head waitress reached for the phone, and a man in chef's whites rushed from the kitchen area with a first-aid kit.

Ito and I traded glances.

This was no coincidence.

The Steam Walker was here.

Jun called the Walker. "The poison was delivered to the wrong table. They had the same order."

The Walker frowned. Most everyone ordered the dish. If two orders happened to come up at the same time, an accidental switch was a mishap Jun or his inside man should have prevented.

"That complicates things."

"This is not my fault."

"No blame will be assigned," the Steam Walker said, on the move even before they disconnected, thinking, *You did not make the cut, Jun Tasaki.*

I scanned the room, then the exits. "We've got to go, Rie."

Ito appeared at our side.

Rie took a step toward the stricken diners. "We should help," she said, her sense of duty as a public servant surfacing.

I touched her arm. "Another time."

The tone in my voice gave her the information she needed.

"You think it's *him*?"

Ito and I nodded.

She looked from us to the couple and back. "But—"

I said, "Leave the staff to handle it. They've been trained for this situation."

"That makes sense, but I still feel I should help."

"I can't stay," I said, "but if you really want to, I suppose you could."

Ito's urgent protest betrayed the danger. "She can't. She's been seen with you. We all need to go *now*."

Understanding flooded Rie's features. "You think he might come after me?"

"Yes," Ito said, "or he could use you in some way against us. We're wasting time."

"All right."

Rie's glance, sorrowful and reluctant, swung one last time in the direction of the afflicted couple, who had been turned on their sides to facilitate breathing.

Ito had a phone to his ear. "Yeah, me. There's been a poisoning and we're on our way out. Coming down from the second floor. Evac plan two." Ito listened to the response, then hung up.

To us he said, "Follow me," then dove through the split curtain hanging over the doorway of the kitchen.

"Different exit?" I asked.

"Yes, prearranged. Back way out."

"Good idea."

We moved swiftly through the preparation area. A spotless stainless steel tabletop dominated the center of the kitchen. Sparkling utensils hung on the walls. Two blowfish, washed and glistening, lay in a tray next to a cutting board, ready for filleting. Every item in the room had a place. Everything was meticulously arranged. There would be no accidental poisonings in this establishment.

"You see it?" I said to Ito.

"Yeah," he said.

The Steam Walker removed a long coat and dropped it in a trash bin, then glided out from between two buildings.

"Sir," the Walker called to the man at the back of the fugu shop. "We need you to move away from the rear of the restaurant."

The man was ten yards away. The Walker advanced.

Nine, eight . . .

"I'm on duty with a surveillance team. My name's Sasaki. Let me get my card."

Seven, six . . .

"Did you inform the precinct?" the Walker asked.

"No."

Five, four . . .

"Then do *not* reach for anything in your coat."

Three, two . . .

Sasaki said, "I can assure—"

The Steam Walker's hand whipped out. A lightning jab crushed the man's throat. He spoke not another word. Nor would he ever. He was gasping for breath as the assassin dragged him behind the line of trash cans.

In the distance the Walker heard the first of the sirens—from an ambulance, then a police car. Followed by a third and fourth.

Anyone watching would have seen a smile brighten the killer's features.

We descended a spiral staircase that brought us to a serving pantry on the edge of the first-floor dining area.

Ito held up his hand. We stopped. He spoke into his phone to Sasaki. "Status?"

"Clear."

"This way," Ito said, pocketing his mobile and leading us to a door at the rear of the restaurant.

When we reached the exit, Ito motioned for us to pause.

"This opens to a back alley," he said. "A secondary attack from inside the restaurant is still possible, so I'll go last. My partner has the alley area secured, so Brodie, you exit first and he'll cover you. Hoshino-san will leave next. Move quickly out and off to the right. Don't stop unless I say so. Got it?"

We both nodded.

"Good." Ito looked behind us one last time, then tapped the door lightly, heard a confirming tap on the other end, then said, "Now."

CHAPTER 44

A POLICEMAN waited on the other side of the door.

"This way," he said, and Rie smiled and scooted sideways around me.

"I'm so glad—" she began, going to her purse for her badge.

I blanched. "Rie, no."

I reached out to pull her back but was too late. A crack to the side of her head swept her aside. Her body slammed into a lamppost and crumpled. She was down and cleared away. Not dead but unconscious. No longer a threat.

By none other than the Steam Walker. The Napa killer. Mr. Bamboo Forest. His visage peeked out at me from under the visor of a policeman's cap.

My recognition had not been instantaneous. He'd applied makeup to change his appearance. The shape of his face, its angles, the size of his eyes—all had been transformed. My warning to Rie had been instinctual, based solely on seeing a uniform at the rear entrance instead of Sasaki-san, the second Brodie Security guard.

Had Rie not slipped by me, the advantage would have fallen to the Walker. The few extra seconds his disguise bought him might have been enough to finish the job.

But brooding over spilled milk was not in his constitution. He attacked swiftly, targeting my throat with a sharp karate thrust meant to crush the larynx, with suffocation and death to follow in short order. I was trapped in the narrow confines of the restaurant's exit corridor, Ito penned in behind me by my bulk. I ducked my head and took the hit on the jaw. My head snapped back. My neck muscles shrieked.

But my counterattack was already in progress.

I'd begun a beat earlier and the Steam Walker reacted a beat later. From cocked hips, I delivered a retaliatory side kick that clipped his pelvis and spun him around.

I rushed after him, but he twirled all the way around and sluiced forward to truncate my charge, recapturing his territory. He was determined to keep Ito out of the picture. As long as the Walker stalled my advance, our encounter would be one-on-one. Unlike Rie, Ito was too big to squeeze past me.

My jaw throbbed. Rie groaned but didn't stir.

The Walker feinted with a head bob, then threw another karate punch, changing up midstream and striking out with a leg snap. In the confines of the corridor, I leaned away from the kick, nullifying most of its effect, but absorbing a jarring blow to my right thigh.

Swallowing the pain, I sprang before he could regroup. But my injured thigh caved against the weight and I was forced to retreat.

I'd gained a yard, which allowed me to cover Rie if the need arose. I wasn't going to give any ground but neither was the Steam Walker. Ito was still trapped.

Distant sirens grew louder. They sounded close. The ambulance maybe two blocks out, police vehicles four. Still plenty of time for the Walker's purpose. In his disguise he could linger until the last second.

Seeing me stagger, the Walker swarmed in. Thirst for the kill glittered in his eyes. I shifted my weight to my good leg, then swung my sore limb around in a tae kwon do hook kick. Most people favor an injured appendage and take it out of play, which hampers their options. I went the other way.

Startled by the counterintuitive move, the Steam Walker backpedaled. As I finished the arc of the sweep, I dropped to the ground, pushing both hands palm out to break my fall, then flipped on my side. Supported by my forearm and strong leg and leveraging the momentum of my leg sweep, I "walked" my free hand in a rapid circle, and as the Walker regrouped and swooped in again, I helicoptered my legs around and knocked him off his feet.

He rolled away and rose a moment after I pulled myself upright. We glared at each other. Freed at last, Ito dashed forward.

Out front, a police car gave a last electronic whoop as it pulled up to the restaurant. Even with our two-on-one advantage, the Walker considered another advance. Which telegraphed just how hard-core his training was.

Then Ito reached under his jacket for a weapon and the Walker eased back a step, then another, then faded into the night.

We watched his retreat in silence.

Eventually, I said, "Have anything under there?"

"Nope. Sasaki has the gun. But next time we'll *both* be carrying."

Ito went in search of his partner and I turned to attend to Rie.

I bent down alongside my motionless date. Her face was relaxed, her breathing steady. Both good signs.

"How's Sasaki?" I called.

"Found him," Ito said, and stepped behind a line of trash bins.

Rie had a strong pulse. I shook her gently. She groaned. Her eyes opened.

"That was some trick," she said with a weak smile. "Embarrassed twice in one night."

Coherent. Good recall. Cracking a joke. I'd seen my share of post-fight recoveries, and this was as good as it got.

A minor miracle against someone of the Steam Walker's caliber. Maybe we squeezed by.

"Hoshino's okay," I said. "How's Sasaki?"

Ito's voice cracked. "He's gone."

We made a brief detour to the emergency room on the way to my hotel.

Rie glided through without damage, other than a slight swelling where her head had met the lamppost. I was another story.

Rie was tough and knew how to take a blow. Years of judo and kendo had given her exceptional muscle tone, balance, and combat instincts. By the time help arrived, she was steady on her feet and perky, if slightly abashed. I limped into the hospital. I could feel my jawline and cheek swelling up. But bloating and bruises were special effects that a high pain threshold allowed me to ignore. Aside from a limited soreness, I felt fine. I walked out of the trauma center with a stack of heat plasters for the soreness and pills for the pain.

Rie accompanied me to the hotel, as did a fresh guard detail, who took a room across the hall. Rie ran a bath. I thanked her, and she made to leave. At the door, I bent over to kiss her and found myself knocked sideways by an invisible force.

Rie stepped back inside. "What was that about?"

I found my balance. "I think the medical cocktail the doctor fed me kicked in. I'll be fine."

Rie studied me for a moment, then trained her gaze on the king-size bed, large sitting area, and oversize flat-screen TV.

"Don't you normally stay at your old family home?"

Although the firm held the paperwork to my father's place, I usually bunked there when I came to town.

"Yes, but we've got a client who needs to hide for a while."

"That doesn't explain the deluxe room. Someone in your office overcompensated." Then her eyes narrowed. "Or was this part of a grand seduction scheme?"

Even in my drugged state, I was lucid enough to know we'd just treaded out onto a shaky ledge. Shades of nuance emerged with the question. One suggested she might feel manipulated depending on my answer, while another hinted that I could hurt her feelings because I *hadn't* cared enough to arrange an elegant setting, even if she had no intention of staying.

"Aside from wanting to see you again, there was no grand plan, though if there was to be, this would be a good way to go. The clerk at the front desk upgraded me when he matched my name to the Brodie Security corporate account."

"I see." Rie cracked open the drapes with a finger and peered out. "VIP treatment. Great scene out there. Too bad you can't enjoy the view."

In light of the sniper action in San Francisco, my shadows had drawn the curtains after clearing the room.

"No complaints about the other amenities, though," she added. "There's a large-screen TV, a stereo system, and a phone in the bathroom. In the very large marble-floored bathroom."

"Yes, but did you notice the cushioned lounge chair?"

"Of course. Now off with the cell phone and the clothes."

"What?"

"With you, I'm beginning to think there's never going to be a right time and I don't like my men scratched and dirty."

"You only want me for my fancy room. Or are you fishing for an apology because I got called away to Kyoto in the middle of our last date?"

She leaned forward and kissed me. "Still charming after all we've been through. No fishing. Kyoto only proves my point. That's why I want your mobile turned off. You need a bath and we need some private time."

CHAPTER 45

DAY 9, SHIBUYA DISTRICT, TOKYO, 12:15 A.M.

I HIT the shower, soaped up, scrubbed, rinsed, then stepped clean and suds-free into the deep, steaming Japanese bath and allowed fingers of heat to work their way through my body. Muscles were soothed. Nerves were calmed. Serenity surfaced. Several centuries back the Japanese had found the ideal way to lift the weight of the day, and in all my travels I'd yet to find a better solution.

When I emerged five minutes after the soak in the blue-and-white *yukata* sleeping garment provided by the hotel, Rie had the television tuned to a news program.

"Nothing about poisoning yet," she told me, "or our back-door skirmish."

"Only a matter of time."

Rie grimaced. "My people will question Brodie Security first, then get to you eventually."

"But not tonight?"

She shook her head. "We're thorough but slow. I'll leave first thing."

"I'm thinking I should keep your name out of it."

"I'd be grateful."

With Rie in earshot, I rang the guards across the hall. We contrived a common but believable fictional name for my date. It would lead nowhere. I'd start out insisting my dining companion was incidental to the scene as the attack was directed at me. If pressed, I would relinquish the name. If pushed further, I'd dig in my heels.

Once I rang off, Rie headed for the bath, smiling back at me over her shoulder. I heard her disrobe, then the sound of the shower left the rest to my imagination. I glanced at the clock. It was nearly one in the morning. I slipped between the sheets for a moment of shut-eye.

I lost consciousness.

Some time later, Rie joined me. I felt a gentle kiss on my good cheek, then my neck.

Consciousness returned. I took it from there.

Much later Rie said, "You held up quite well, considering."

"I aim to please. The meds dulled the pain."

"Remind me to thank the doctor."

"How about we turn this into a double feature, then you'll really have something to thank him for?"

We were sitting up in bed, sipping complimentary hotel coffee.

Rie set her cup down. With her finger, she traced the scar near my collarbone, where a bullet had nipped at the muscle tissue along the ridge of my shoulder. "You are damaged goods. Tell me about this."

We'd woken early, had a morning tussle, then slipped back into the blue-and-white sleeping robes we'd discarded during the night and never recovered. We washed up in turn, brushing teeth and such. Rie discovered a K-cup coffee machine in a cabinet near the desk and brewed an impressive French roast with the touch of a button.

"A small round clipped me."

"In LA or San Francisco?"

"Right here in Tokyo."

"That's unusual. Was it yakuza?"

Unusual because Japan's rigid antigun laws were strictly enforced. Criminals or anyone who momentarily slipped over the edge could be forgiven a lot as long as they didn't wield a firearm. Bring a loaded weapon to the party and the whole of the police force would hunt the offender down with fierce doggedness, then bury him for a long long time. She guessed yakuza because they were the ones who most often flaunted the gun law.

"Another PI, actually. He had some resentment to work out."

"You get payback?"

"A friend nailed him for me."

Rie's finger circled the pearly scar tissue, then dropped down to a wound just below my ribs. "This is one of the sword injuries, isn't it? They made a big deal of it in the police report a few months ago. You have another one on your thigh, right?"

"Yes. Never do anything by half. That's my motto."

"I thought the wounds were supposed to heal without scarring because the cuts were shallow."

"I suspect the doc was wearing rather large rose-colored shades when he gave the prognosis. On the other hand, it's only been three months."

Rie reached for my arm and looked at a horizontal slash across my forearm, then a matching one on the other arm. Then a thin diagonal scab line. My newest trophy, from the knife fight in Ken's hospital room.

"The knife cut must have hurt, but these other two look worse."

"They went to the bone," I admitted.

And through all the muscle and nerves to get there. At one time, I'd known the names of the injured body tissues, but in the end I relegated the whole basket of medical jargon to an echo chamber of discarded memories.

My companion winced. "What could do this?"

"A garrote," I said.

Rie stifled a gasp but couldn't dampen the surprise that flashed across her features. "Was that when—"

"Yes. Have you finished your cataloging of my imperfections?"

"Hold on. Last night, in the dark, I thought I felt *two* scars on your thigh, not one. Also a starburst on your back."

"Interesting, isn't it, where police training comes in useful?"

"Shut up and turn over."

"I'd like to finish my coffee."

Rie favored me with an indulgent smile that said *not a chance*, gently relieved me of my cup, set it on the side table, and nudged me. I rolled over and this time was rewarded with a clearly delineated gasp.

"Is that a knife wound?"

"It is."

"I thought you collected only art."

"Only one collection is intentional."

"I certainly hope so."

"And only one has any value."

I heard a throaty giggle. "Oh, I wouldn't say that." She gave the starburst a friendly peck, flipped me over, and kissed each of the other scars, then my nose, both cheeks, my lips. She lingered over the last destination.

"Very affectionate for a hardened cop," I said when she raised her head.

"Shut up. See if you can keep up this time."

Despite the tough words, Rie mixed eagerness with a becoming modesty. Her pale-beige skin glowed with a translucence I'd once seen in a European painting, the name of which, in my distracted state, escaped me.

Afterward, we settled in for some bedroom talk. Some personal, some professional, all of it memorable.

But not as memorable as a stray comment of hers later on that sent the case in an entirely new direction.

CHAPTER 46

WHEN I emerged from my shower squeaky clean and with a hotel towel tight at my waist, I found Rie fully dressed and glancing through the papers on the Nobuki case I'd spread out on the coffee table in the sitting area.

She'd showered before me and had filled the wait by flipping through the paperwork. Now she waved the police composite of the Napa Valley killer in the air. "I hope you don't mind."

"All in the family," I said.

"This is the Steam Walker, right?"

Rie had been knocked aside before she could catch a good glimpse of her attacker.

"Yes. Everything started with that."

"You gave me the overview, but how about more details? Maybe I can help."

More eyes on the case couldn't hurt, so as I dressed I laid out the events once more, inclusive of the finer points. I told her about the "accidental" death of the first son in Napa; Shu's eyewitness account that turned the supposed mishap into murder and garnered us the sketch; the City Hall sniper attack that sent the father to the hospital with brain damage; the mayor's Pacific Rim Friendship Program; Naomi's antinuclear-power activities and her DC dance with a record-breaking three federal agencies; my fight in Ken's hospital room after my return from Washington; TNT's narration of the Steam Walker legend and the yakuza enforcer's warning about the contract out on me; our desperate attempt to track down Akihiro at the cosplay event in Kyoto; the follow-up meeting at the manga museum with his girlfriend; their sixty-foot death plunge off the veranda of Kiyomizu Temple; my encounter in the bamboo forest; and finally, the consultation with a researcher at a think tank whose comments put the nuclear mafia front and center on the suspect list. A hell of a lot had happened.

When I'd finished, I looked up to find her flush with astonishment.

"What's wrong?"

"You *know* Big Haga?" Rie asked.

The same detail Mari had tripped over, expressed with the same sense of amazement.

"I know a lot of people, and a lot of criminals. But that's not the point."

"You're right. I'm sorry. Tell me who you're looking at for this."

I concluded the review with a full list of the suspects, the recital of which elicited a fresh round of disbelief. "That's an unmanageable number for a single case," she said. "How can you possibly narrow the field?"

I reached for a slate-blue shirt. "We poke and prod and dig, and when we hit a nerve, we press it."

"And hope you don't get yourself killed."

"That too," I admitted, recalling my art dealer friend's plea that I give up my father's old work. "Not a word to any of your police friends."

"Of course not." She pointed at Shu-kun's sign of approval at the bottom of the Napa portrait. "I'm sure you followed up on this, right?"

I raised an eyebrow. "Shu Nobuki scribbled that *OK* after the police artist finished her work. What's to follow? He's eight and got the *K* backward."

Rie shook her head. "No, *you've* got it backward. It's Komeki's."

My fingers stalled over the last button of my shirt. "What or who is that?"

"It's a Japanese women's fashion brand. Very exclusive, very expensive."

"How come I've never heard of it?"

"They don't advertise. They only have a handful of shops. There's nothing in their boutiques I could buy for less than two months' salary. Even the small stuff. This is their logo—KO with a little curlicue in the O."

I looked closer. Turning the letters upside down had transformed what we'd presumed was an awkward sign of approval into a company emblem.

Son of a bitch.

An insignia could lead places. To an office, a shop, a person.

To the Steam Walker—and his client.

CHAPTER 47

I CAUGHT Cheré Copeland, the police artist from Suisun City, in her unmarked patrol car. We'd exchanged mobile numbers in case the unexpected came up.

California was seventeen hours behind Tokyo, so it was four in the afternoon there. And probably about fifty-five degrees, with a crisp winter sun lording over clear blue skies.

"Hi, Cheré. Brodie. I'm in Tokyo. They keeping you in the loop?"

"Sheriff Nash does. He talks to Renna."

I switched her to speakerphone, and Rie listened attentively to our English conversation, for all the good it would do her.

"Perfect," I said. "You remember you said something bothered you about the sketch? Did you ever figure out what it was?"

"And here I thought you were calling to finally ask me out. I didn't figure you for the shy type."

"Normally, I would have, believe me."

"Aww," she purred. "A lady needs to hear that on occasion. I also heard a catch in your voice. Do you have a current lady fair?"

I looked across the room. "You could say that."

"So close, yet so far. Keep me in mind should your progress stall."

"Top of the list," I said.

"About your question. I never did pin down what bothered me. Then I got busy with other cases."

"Could it have to do with the sex of the suspect?"

Copeland mulled over the idea. "You mean sexual orientation? An LGBT angle?"

"Maybe. Or even more direct, like a woman in disguise."

"A female perp? You know, I think that's what it was. How'd you come up with that?"

I told her about the logo.

"Really? Damn. That's a letdown. That darn little scribble was the cutest thing to come my way in ages. How is my little Japanese cowboy, by the way?"

I cringed at the question. The guards watching the Nobukis had reported that Shu had withdrawn completely and wasn't talking to anyone. "Struggling with his father's death. He never knew his mother."

"That's terrible," Copeland said. "He's such a sweetie. Say hello for me. A woman perp, huh?"

"Just an idea we're playing with. Jog anything loose?"

"Little Shu's selections did come from the softer side of the characteristic charts—the eyes, the cheeks, the mouth—so I must have had a flicker of a thought along those lines, but if I did I dismissed it, because it happens more often than you'd think."

"Why?"

"Because hormones are fickle. They play tricks. They can soften features on men or harden them on women," Copeland said. "And family genes contribute. A lot of women have very masculine features just under the surface. Look beyond the makeup and the long hair and you'll see what I'm talking about. Didn't you ever do a double take at a woman and think that if her hair was shorter she'd look exactly like her brother? Or uncle or father?"

"Sure."

"And it can go the opposite way with men."

"True, now that you mention it."

"Have you asked little Shu about it yet?"

"He's next up."

"Give me an update if you uncover anything new and I'll rethink things here."

After we disconnected, I noticed Rie regarding me with narrowed eyes. I saw uneasiness there, not curiosity about what I'd learned. I asked if something was bothering her.

"The woman cop likes you."

"She's a detective and forensic artist."

"That's worse."

So much for dancing around the issue. "How can you know that? You don't understand English."

"I understand tone and I understand women. It was in the *current* running through her voice."

Current. Dating a policewoman could try the nerves.

"She did drop a hint or two."

"Were you flirting with her?"

"No, I was letting her down easy."

Rie nodded, still vexed. "Good thing."

"Why's that?"

"Because otherwise I'd have to shoot her."

I sent a photograph of Shu's doodle to his grandmother's phone. When I called to ask my questions, I noticed a new coolness in her voice.

"Did you get the photo I sent?"

"Yes." Cooler still. "What about it?"

"I need to talk to Shu."

I heard a heavy intake of air. "I wish you wouldn't. It's bad enough we have guards around all the time. He thinks the whole thing is his fault because he didn't stop it."

My heart went out to Shu-kun. He'd never known his mother and now, at eight, his father was gone too. If I feared one thing for my daughter, it was life without family, which at this point consisted of me—and only me.

I had no fear of death myself. I'd die a thousand times to protect Jenny. But she needed me around, at times desperately. I did everything I could think of for her. But there were places I couldn't reach. What remained of her mother were faint memories—feathery impressions muffled by the imprecise mechanism of a toddler's brain. Whenever a mother picked up one of Jenny's friends at school, her sense of loss surfaced. Or when she went to a classmate's house to play. No matter how attentive I tried to be, I couldn't compensate for maternal loss.

In losing his father, Shu had lost more than a second parent—he'd lost his male role model, and all the future father-and-son moments. He was too young to think in those terms, but he felt the hole in his life instinctively. An immense, irreparable hole, compounded in his case by guilt.

My reply was muted. "If it will help, why don't you ask him for me? That way he won't have to hear my voice."

Since when had I become an ogre?

"That would be better."

I wondered if Shu knew, as yet, what had happened to Akihiro, his uncle. And if our failed effort had been linked, in his mind, to his father's death. I could hardly bear the idea.

Mrs. Nobuki said, "What do you want me to ask him?" The coolness rose another notch.

"Could you remind him where he drew it, then ask *why* he drew it?"

I gave her the details and she set down her phone. Even though it contained the photo. Even though it was a mobile. I got the message.

In the distance, I heard her voice, then Shu's. The exchange lasted several minutes, then footsteps approached and she lifted the phone.

"Brodie, sorry to keep you waiting. I hope you understand."

"I do."

"It isn't you," she added.

But it is, I thought.

Mrs. Nobuki cleared her throat. "Shu said he was copying what he saw for the police lady. He liked her."

A worthy consolation prize for Cheré. "And she likes him. If you think it a good idea, you could tell him she says hello. I just got off the phone with her."

"I'll need to think about that."

"Of course. What exactly was he copying?"

"A logo he saw under the man's shirt. Well, actually, along the hem of another shirt sticking out from under his shirt. Sorting that out is what took me so long."

"Thank you. It's the Komeki logo."

"I know. They always put them on the hem. You usually don't see it. It gets tucked in."

"Do you have any Komeki there?"

"No."

"Is there any place Shu might have seen the insignia before?"

"Would you like me to ask him?"

"Please."

Again, I waited. When she returned, Nobuki's wife said, "He told me he's never seen it anywhere else. He didn't know what it was."

"Thank you, Mrs. Nobuki."

"I told Shu-kun what the police lady said. He smiled a very small smile. The first one I've seen in three days."

The image of that very small smile tore at my heart.

"I wished there was something I could do."

"Don't we all. Do you think this will help your investigation?"

"I do," I said.

But I had no idea how.

CHAPTER 48

FIREWORKS erupted at Brodie Security when I showed up, limping and bruised.

If something happens to you, Brodie Security loses all credibility . . . and your staff loses their livelihood.

"I'm all right," I said, trying to assuage the wave of concern flooding the office. "This isn't the first time I've taken a few."

My words spread little comfort. I stuck my head in Noda's office and we agreed to meet in the conference room in twenty minutes. Which was how much more time Mari needed to fill the request I'd made earlier in the day.

Mari hummed softly as she pulled together the report.

Brodie had called from his hotel first thing this morning. He wanted her to dig up everything she could on the fashion company.

"And I mean everything," he had said. "The Steam Walker plans down to the last detail. No one laid eyes on him at Napa or City Hall or Kyoto. It was only by chance that I caught him in the hospital. Even then, I didn't see his face. The Komeki logo on the hem slipped out *by mistake*. I'm sure of it. From a guy who doesn't make mistakes. So, if it means something, we've *got* to find it."

This was her first case, and she wouldn't let Brodie down. She'd scanned every digital signpost of any worth and found a connection. It was tenuous and weird. But it was there.

It took her ninety minutes to compile the data and twenty-five more to assemble the report. After the first thirty minutes, she uncovered no major new revelations, just endless repeats of the Komeki story with the occasional fresh tidbit, all of which she gathered up with care.

The basics were simple. The company was a petite boutique chain run by designer-owner Kiyomi Komeki. According to her official biography, the characters for her first name meant "pure beauty," which is what she pursued with a "single-minded passion." Yuck.

What was not in her personal profile—but became apparent to Mari ten minutes into her research—was that Kiyomi avoided the limelight with more expertise than *hikikomori*, the Japanese introverts who hide behind closed doors and rarely come out.

There were no pictures of her on the company site, and she was absent from her own fashion shows. She didn't exhibit overseas, despite numerous invitations, so there was no passport photograph to be pilfered from the authorities by enterprising newshounds or computer wizards. Mari had scoured every corner of the Net and discovered not a single image of the reclusive designer, and Mari knew how to look *every*where. Finding nothing was weird.

Komeki goods were confined to seven retail outlets. One each in Osaka, Kyoto, Karuizawa, Sendai, and Sapporo. Two in Tokyo—Ginza and Aoyama. Each boutique was located in an upscale neighborhood filled with rows of other opulent brand-name boutiques. Komeki garments were expertly designed, "made in Japan from concept to the last stitch," and produced in quality cashmere, silk, linen, or whatever material Kiyomi chose to feature for the season.

Komeki, the brand, did not advertise. It did not solicit. It did not encourage media coverage of any kind.

Which brought the fashion line more coverage than most.

Mari could not determine if this was a calculated strategy or an offshoot of the owner's determination to sidestep the spotlight.

Japanese paparazzi had tried unsuccessfully to catch a snapshot of the designer-owner, but she gave no interviews. Neither did her staff. You either knew of the apparel line or you didn't.

Was this shrewd marketing or something else?

The reason for Kiyomi Komeki's withdrawal from public life was thought to originate with the place of her birth, the village of Kanbara, which has the distinction of being Japan's Pompeii. More than four hundred people had been buried alive in the devastating eruption of Mount Asama in 1793, when molten lava gushed from the volcano. The red-hot outpouring created a gigantic avalanche of magma, steaming mud, and debris. One arm of the torrent entombed Kanbara, a few miles to the north. The scalding flow smothered all in its path and is said to have outpaced fleeing rabbits and galloping horses. It deluged marshes and rivers, morphed into a massive mudflow, and continued to surge through the countryside for some one hundred twenty-five miles.

There was speculation about a "Kanbara type" personality, of which Kiyomi Komeki was a prime example. Those residing in the shadow of Mount Asama were brought up with the tragic stories of their ancestors. Humbled by their village history and still living "under the eyes" of the volcano, they approached life with trepidation, every action with caution, and strangers with suspicion. A doctor in a neighboring village who treated many of the Kanbara natives noted that "severe shyness was endemic among the residents."

Reporters latched on to the doctor's comment to explain the fashion designer's retiring nature, but Mari thought it more likely that the novelty of Kiyomi Komeki's birthplace gave news scribes a colorful sideshow to serve as a frame for what was otherwise a skeleton of a story.

Still, her eyes glittered with anticipation. Obscure though it was, the volcano angle tied in with the Steam Walker myth. And Mount Asama was active. On the other hand, you could hardly toss a rock anywhere in Japan without hitting a volcano.

Remove the Kanbara episode and the fashion writers had nothing.

Which left Brodie Security with even less.

I didn't follow the fashion world, but what Mari had gathered was intriguing, if shallow.

Komeki catered to the rich and the famous. Thousands of people strolled through the designer's luxurious boutiques to marvel at the latest offerings, but only a select few bought. Or could afford to buy. As the Japanese love nothing better than scarcity, a Komeki garment or accessory more than made the grade as a status symbol.

"Does any of this help?" Mari asked.

"Yes," I said. "You found a second connection. We've got the Steam Walker wearing a Komeki, and now we've got volcanic activity, so to speak, on both sides."

Mari frowned. "But what does it mean?"

"Don't know. Noda?"

The man of few words shook his head.

Mari said, "Do you think Kiyomi Komeki *is* the Steam Walker?"

"I can't see it."

"It would explain why she's so secretive."

Noda said, "Can't rule it out yet."

I remained skeptical. "Mari, see if you can track Komeki's movements on the days when the attacks went down. Napa, San Francisco, Kyoto, and Tokyo. Include the bamboo forest time as well."

Our IT pro frowned. "I can try, but she's really really private."

All very convenient if she were working in the shadows.

I said, "What if we go the other way with this? If the Steam Walker *knows* Komeki, he might wear one of her items as a memento."

Mari nodded enthusiastically. "As a keepsake of the woman he loves? Very romantic."

"Not unheard of," I said. "Or maybe he's superstitious. Like a ballplayer wearing his lucky high school jersey under his pro uniform."

I shot a look at Noda and he shrugged.

"Any of the apparel unisex?" I asked.

"Not intentionally."

"Could it be? With imagination?"

Mari hit some keys. A catalog of Komeki sweaters and blouses scrolled up the screen and she studied each one. She pointed out four tops she thought could swing both ways. "What do you think?"

I frowned. "All the killers I've ever met were hard men. But there's a couple that could work."

Mari slumped in her seat. "So we're back to a man."

"Who knows?" I said. "But don't look so glum. You laid new tracks. Let's see if they go anywhere."

CHAPTER 49

TOM Stockton, the guard on Naomi, called to report that her husband had finally prevailed. Naomi was leaving Washington, though not heading back to Japan.

I thought about this twist in the itinerary. "That could actually work in our favor. Where do they want to go?"

"A hideaway in Singapore."

"Ah, the Palm Springs of Asia."

Singapore was a well-integrated country that worked. In an area about a third of the size of Maui, nearly six million ethnic Chinese, Malays, Indians, and a scattering of American, European, and other expats lived side by side. They were Buddhist, Catholic, Muslim, Taoists, and Hindu, among others, and they got along. The people were pleasant. They smiled often. The crime rate was lower than Japan's.

For visitors, the Asian city-state was all about eating, shopping, and lounging around in the heat. Only wet heat instead of dry. Land was at a premium in Singapore, so there was far less golf than in the California desert resort, which had more golf courses than Vermeer had paintings. Singapore offered other entertainment, including dining on the quay, night markets for the adventurous, and high-end casinos—all just a short, air-conditioned taxi ride away.

"You with them now?" I asked.

"Yes."

"Put the husband on, would you?"

"Sure thing."

A minute later the phone was picked up. "Hi, Brodie," Tad Sato said in Japanese.

"Hey, Tad," I said in the same language. 'You holding up?"

I'd met Tad twice since he and Naomi married, once at a show opening of her father's and once when I visited the Nobuki home in Kyoto. Tad was short for Tadao. He shared the same enthusiasm for Japanese ceramics as Naomi's father, which was a source of bonding between Ken and his son-in-law. It gave the two of us plenty to talk about as well.

"You know me and flying," he said.

"I know you'd rather shoot yourself in the foot. What changed your mind?"

"My mother-in-law. She's lost both her sons and wants her daughter with her in Kyoto until this thing's over."

"How'd Singapore enter the picture?"

"Naomi's too embarrassed to go home empty-handed."

"That doesn't help your mother-in-law."

Tad's voice dropped to a whisper. "Japan's only a short hop from Singapore. Once we get there, I'll work on Naomi some more."

"Can I talk to her?"

"You got it."

His wife came on next. "Hi, Brodie."

"Hi, Naomi. I'm glad you're leaving DC. Under the circumstances it's the right thing to do."

"Yes, of course. I appreciate everything you're doing for us."

"Don't mention it." *Because I failed with your brother. Abominably.*

Naomi said, "I know Akihiro must have been impossible. He's been that way since his early teens."

Somewhere in the darker reaches of my being, a lightness stirred. Not much. But a fraction.

"Thank you for that," I said.

"You needed to hear it from one of us. Here's Stockton-san again."

She passed me over to the security man. "You want me to send someone with them?" he asked.

"Absolutely. I'll set up a changing of the guard on the other end. Your man can pass them on to our affiliate in Singapore. Until then, make sure he stays close."

"Consider it a done deal," Stockton said.

Which it was. Until it wasn't.

DAYS 10 TO 12

TUESDAY TO THURSDAY

WHAT THE DEVIL PUSHED OUT

CHAPTER 50

THE Singapore affiliate called right on schedule.

"Brodie, is that you?"

"Yes. All's well, I presume."

"Only if you like magic tricks."

Goosebumps peppered the back of my neck. "What have you got for me?"

"Nothing. And *that*, my good friend, is the problem. Your people didn't get off the plane."

My heart lurched. "That can't be."

A disconcerted sigh reached my ear. "You've just answered my next question. They really were supposed to be on the aircraft?"

This couldn't be happening. "Yes. Is everyone off?"

"My people are confirming as we speak. Are you absolutely certain someone along your chain of command did not make any changes in the schedule at the last second? Some additional precaution not passed along to you, what with the time difference and all? Say, while you were asleep."

"I'm sure."

A second sigh escaped his lips. "Then *I'm* sure we have trouble. We've had binocs on since deboarding. They did not slip by us. They were not ushered through a VIP entrance. No one has been whisked away by a preemptive police escort."

"When will you have confirmation on remaining passengers?"

"Five minutes, tops. You want to wait or should I call you back?"

"Call me back."

We hung up and I thought, *Let this be a mix-up*. Maybe someone *did* call and pass on a change in itinerary I'd yet to receive. Which was a wild idea I clung to but into which I funneled no hope. All I knew was that I *could not* lose Ken's last living offspring.

I had Mari get Stockton on the line. What our Washington affiliate told me only heightened my apprehension. He had personally watched Naomi, her husband, and his own operative step onto the plane, his firm's status allowing him security access into the boarding area.

"When was the next planned contact?" I asked.

Stockton's man had confirmed arrival at Los Angeles International Airport, where they were to change planes, and sent a text message just before takeoff from LAX. The final communiqué was set to occur as soon as the airplane touched the tarmac in Singapore. Which was now, if not earlier.

"And you have nothing?"

"Nada," Stockton said.

"Deboarding looks to be over."

"Then we're screwed. Jeremy should have called or texted on touch-down in Singapore while the jet was taxiing to the gate, and long before he and the clients left the craft. No one else here has heard from him."

"Okay. Double-check to make sure nothing's been missed on your end and get back to me ASAP."

Clearly, something had gone down along the way. If there was no sighting in Singapore, that left Southern California.

Napa. San Francisco. Kyoto. Tokyo. And now LA.

Nowhere was safe from the Steam Walker.

CHAPTER 51

THE Singapore affiliate had rung me twice while I was on the phone with Stockton. When I called back, he confirmed that all passengers had disembarked.

It was official. Naomi and Tad had vanished. If the last of the Nobukis' three children ended up dead on my watch, I'd probably have to throw myself under a bullet train.

Stockton had promised to start working his end immediately, but I held little hope of an answer emerging from his side.

"What does it mean that you haven't heard from your man?" I'd asked him.

"Nothing good."

"How bad?"

"This long? He's either restrained or dead."

"Your guess?"

"Dead."

"Why?"

"Jeremy has three black belts. Real ones. He's fast, and very aware. There's only one way to stop him."

I was afraid of that.

And it was unlikely Naomi and Tad would fare any better.

Noda, Mari, and the auxiliary players on the case crammed into my office.

After informing them of the situation, I was rewarded with half a dozen possible scenarios, from kidnapping to murder, and an equal number of routes to explore. The upshot was, we sent a half a dozen detectives in a half a dozen directions in three different cities in a frantic attempt to track down the missing couple.

Soon only Noda, Mari, and I remained. Noda fumed in his seat, his scar blazing. Then he sprang up, grumbling something Mari and I couldn't decipher, and disappeared out the door.

Mari turned a worried look in my direction. "We can't let anything happen to Naomi Nobuki and her husband. She's the *last* one."

"I know."

"The papers will get hold of the story and that will be the end of Brodie Security."

"I know."

An invisible hand clutched at my throat. Mari's eyes dropped to her lap. Sitting in my father's old office, I gazed at his mementoes. Next, my eyes tracked to Jenny's photograph. She looked out from the frame with her broad, gap-toothed smile. I found her unabashed grin endearing, all the more so because it was less than perfect. It would fill in soon. Brodie Security might not be around when it did.

Mari looked up. "So I need to leave for a while. Is that okay?"

"Sure."

"To make some calls."

"Sure."

She had a germ of an idea she wasn't yet willing to share. Everyone else involved in the case was scrambling. None of us expected anything from Brodie Security's newest and youngest field agent, but at least she was giving it the good fight.

Mari trotted out the door in Noda's wake.

Naomi and her husband had fallen down a black hole. The Steam Walker had been on these shores, so either he had an accomplice or the puppetmaster pulling the Walker's strings had another operative on the line.

Where had Naomi and Tad gone? And were they alive or dead?

CHAPTER 52

RENNA called from San Francisco with tidings.

"Man, I'm sorry to hear about the daughter and her husband. Snatched right out from under."

"I know. If I lose Ken's third kid . . ."

"Don't do that to yourself, Brodie. This case is off-the-charts insane. We have how many countries involved now? Eight?"

"Including Indonesia and the US, yeah."

"We're both slammed, so let me give you the latest on my end, then we can get back to the hunt."

Renna's summary was brief. They'd eliminated the Tea Party politico only because he could barely organize a sit-down lunch for two, let alone an operation involving a professional assassin. And that was without bothering to consider his campaign platform, which revolved around ridding San Francisco of all tech workers since they were secretly creating a robot race to commandeer the city, starting with the mayor's office.

As for the others, Renna's squad was tracking three priority suspects, nine other primary leads, and one new target courtesy of Gail Wong, the mayor's attack shark.

The three chief contenders were the mayor's former business partner, who, out of spite, was funding a third-party challenger and had the connections to pull off the sniper attack; Mayor Hurwitz's main political rival, whom many considered an anything-goes slime bucket; and the former soldier who had written a hate letter. The fighting man, it turned out, was ex–Special Forces, with access to dark connections. He also struggled with mental issues that either put him in or out of the running, depending on which expert the SFPD consulted. The most recent addition was a popular city assemblyman with mayoral ambitions Gail Wong wanted investigated.

"Plus," my police lieutenant friend said, "the number of suspects is on the rise."

I stifled a groan. "How seriously should I take your list?"

"Very. Except for the last one, which is Gail playing gutter politics, we can't discount any of them."

"This investigation is going in the wrong direction."

Renna's grunt embraced the frustration we both felt. "Problem is, there's too many vampires on my end. I'd kill to narrow the field."

"So would I. Let's hope we don't have to."

I underestimated our newest field agent. She came through with a message as startling as it was brief:

Naomi and her husband
passed through passport
control at Narita Airport
fifteen minutes ago.

I had Mari on the phone thirty seconds later. She was sitting with a hacker friend who had access to the Japanese immigration and passport-control computers. I could not mention the fact to anyone else at the office other than Noda.

I said fine.

Mari's energy level plunged with her next words. "But it's too late, right? They'll be gone by the time we get out there."

"Not necessarily. They still have to pick up luggage, clear Customs, and find transportation into town or make a connecting flight. A company near the airport we deal with may be able to intercept them."

"What do you want me to do?"

"I'll move on Narita and fill in Noda. See if there's a connecting flight. I bet there is. That's top priority. Then get back to the office. I'm here now."

"Okay," she said.

"And Mari?"

"Yes?"

"Great find."

We disconnected. Sometimes I forgot how well plugged in our keyboard jockey-slash-cosplayer with the face of a teenager was.

I put the Narita affiliate on the missing couple, then leaned back in my chair and tried to work out how the hell Naomi and husband had ended up back in Japan.

An hour later, Mari showed up dressed in Goth black, perhaps a reflection of her mood. She'd discovered that our charges had flown into Tokyo on a JAL flight from Los Angeles, holding a connecting voucher for a shuttle to the Osaka-Kyoto area. The tickets had been purchased at LAX.

I assembled the Brodie Security brain trust in the conference room. We brought them up-to-date, then coordinated with my expanding team of watchers, which now numbered six, in eight-hour shifts. If this kept up, I'd have a whole army trailing behind me.

We whipped through old business, then swung urgently into new.

Which focused exclusively on the Steam Walker.

One after another, detectives and researchers submitted the names of hired killers and known bagmen they'd run across. Each was disqualified by one or more members of our in-house conclave. Next we went through the roster of local crime syndicates, then national, then known independent gangs who might employ the Walker. We perused the police wanted list and sifted rumors of any new professionals we'd heard of with the skill set displayed in Napa, San Francisco, and Kyoto. We arrived at the end of our inquiry empty-handed.

Not a single match.

Not a single contender.

Which confirmed what Noda and I suspected. We had ourselves an assassin flying so far below the radar he might as well be on another planet. Among law enforcement ops on all levels, he was a nonentity. A true ghost. The legend from which even Japan's top mafia enforcer insisted on keeping his distance.

We were up against a killer far more cunning than any of us could have imagined. The attempted poisoning was only the latest example of his work—Rie and I had been saved because of a kitchen mix-up. Naomi and Tad's disappearance in transit reeked of the Steam Walker's touch, even if he had orchestrated the vanishing act from these shores. Nearly every day brought a startling new gambit. If we couldn't stop him coming for me, all was over.

For me. For Brodie Security. For everyone at the office.

The mood in the conference room nosedived. No one moved or spoke or looked at his or her neighbor. The stillness grew alarming. My breath caught in my throat.

It was as if I were previewing my own wake.

Finally, Hiroshi "Tako" Kawabata, a veteran detective with a good solve-rate, broke the silence.

CHAPTER 53

TEN years ago I followed a lead out to the Japan Sea coast."

Groans rose up around the room. Kawabata was a good detective, with one major fault. He was a notorious babbler. His nickname, Tako, means "octopus," because he'd entangle you in his stories and never let go.

"Not now, Tako," someone said.

"This is the first I'm hearing of all this," he fired back, which only served to increase the grumbling because no one believed he had anything meaningful to add. "I've been in Hawaii for two weeks. But even after taking so much time off, I'm ahead of all of you. I've actually heard of the Steam Walker before, out in Niigata City."

As swiftly as the griping had erupted, it ceased. Niigata is a port town on the other side of the country. The Japan Sea side. Distant and isolated. Which meant fresh territory. Which meant a fresh source. Which meant, possibly, a fresh direction.

Rubbing his belly, the elderly detective said, "This is slim and only a rumor, but since we've got nothing else I thought I'd mention it. One evening me and a Niigata detective killed three bottles of saké in a back room of HQ, comparing notes on the ones that got away. He had a case where a local couple disappeared. Never found a clue. Never recovered the bodies. He attributed it to someone called the Steam Walker. You want more?"

"Yeah," I said, "but make it quick."

Tako's nod was solemn. "The detective passed away five years ago but he told me one memorable thing about the Steam Walker. The name of a place. Tsumagoi."

I sat up, startled. "Are you sure?"

"Yes."

"What is it, Brodie?" Mari asked.

I could barely get the words out. "Kiyomi Komeki again. The fashion designer."

"What about her?" someone asked.

My heart racing, I said, "Tsumagoi is a township spread over a large area near Mount Asama. Most of it is open land. It's a cluster of farms and villages. Kanbara—where Komeki was born—is *right there*. It's one of the villages."

The logo was pointing the way. I didn't yet know what it meant, but the Steam Walker had definitely slipped up.

We ran with it.

CHAPTER 54

MOST Japanese have never heard of Kanbara—Japan's Pompeii—nor of Tsumagoi.

I knew of both because they had appeared in the caption of an old *ukiyo-e*, aka Japanese woodblock print, depicting the eruption of Mount Asama.

We set to work. Joining Noda and myself, a handpicked team combed through the earlier report Mari had assembled on Komeki. At the far end of the conference table, Mari listened to our chatter but focused on her screen—and a new assignment, which she tackled with great reluctance.

There were ten pages of material, some typed, some downloaded. Ten pages sounded like a lot, but it wasn't. I'd read through them a half a dozen times on the first go-round. Now I simply stared at the file after skimming the pages once more. Most of the facts had been rattling around in my head since Mari first pulled the information together. I found nothing new. But one item floated to the top.

Seven retail outlets. One each in Osaka, Kyoto, Karuizawa, Sendai, and Sapporo. Two in Tokyo—Ginza and Aoyama.

The list of locations had bothered me from the outset, but I hadn't been able to pinpoint why.

Now I zeroed in on them. One of the shops, the Karuizawa branch, was *near* Tsumagoi.

"You know," I said, "Karuizawa is an oddball location. It doesn't fit."

"The owner comes from the area," one of the staff pointed out.

"Yeah, but every other store is in a district known for its high-end boutiques. Extreme high-end. The Karuizawa site sits in an outlet mall."

"The town's a vacation spot for the rich and famous," another staff member chimed in. "The emperor met his future wife there."

"I'm not denying the prestige of the place," I said. "Or that it's a resort town. Only that no one does any serious shopping there. The mall caters to bargain hunters from Tokyo."

I knew all about the buying habits of the Karuizawa gentry because several years back I'd explored the idea of selling American and European antiques through a local gallery, but they stocked only commercial pieces that were little more than pricey souvenirs. The rest of the shops toed the same line. The moneyed crowd dropped big money in Tokyo or elsewhere closer to home.

"But the Karuizawa outlets have Gucci, Bulgari, Ferragamo, Armani, Bottega Veneta, and others."

"Except they are *still* outlets," I said. "Everything in Mari's report puts the Komeki label leagues above the standard luxury brands. The outlet location breaks the pattern."

"It allows the owner an excuse to visit home a lot."

"Does she need one?" I asked.

The conversation dried up.

I pondered the problem. "Has anyone been to the mall? Is it elegant?"

"Well, the interiors are as nice as each store chooses to make them, but the site itself is a series of strip malls with some trees and a pond."

"So we have a mismatch," I said.

"Or," a new voice ventured, "it's an aberration for the owner's convenience. She still has a home in Kanbara. She works out there. She can certainly afford to indulge her whims."

All of which, unfortunately, was true.

Stalemate. We were back where we started.

Then Mari broke the standoff: "So, like, I've done what you asked, Brodie-san." Everyone looked her way. "I hacked their back-office network."

"And?" I asked.

"It's a supertight system and a little scary. I didn't want to risk it before. But now's different, so I got a couple of friends to watch my back. Then I checked for recent activity. They've got a GPS mapping system. It tracks truck routes in real time. The Karuizawa truck made a pickup at Narita Airport two hours ago."

Where Naomi and her husband had recently landed.

"They shouldn't be sending a truck to the airport," I said.

"I know, right? So I looked around some more. Komeki has these supercool software graphics. Run your curser over the truck icon and images of the items it's carrying pop up. You can see all the blouses, sweaters, wallets, purses being shipped. On the truck heading to Karuizawa it's got all of those, but some cargo comes up blank."

"What about the other trucks?"

"No blanks."

A murmur of excitement rose up. From Mari's report, we knew Komeki's clothing was hand-stitched in Japan. The material was from the finest Japanese textile houses. They didn't import product or material. They didn't export. The designer didn't show overseas.

There would be no reason to pick up cargo at the international airport.

Unless it were human cargo.

CHAPTER 55

"YOU'RE closing the gap," Mari said, by phone.

Noda sluiced into the well-guarded fast lane to zip around a dawdler before easing back into the slower artery without dropping his speed. In this case, 240 kilometers per hour. In miles, 150.

"Gonna be tight," the chief detective said.

Noda and I were chasing the Komeki truck in a company car. Mari manned the computer back at Brodie Security, where she could monitor the truck's movements without losing its location due to poor reception.

Once we broke loose of the traffic on the expressway, Noda's foot hit the floor and stayed there. The highway leading out to Karuizawa varied from two to four lanes, so the chief detective continued to weave in and around plodding clusters of traffic, avoiding at all costs the cameras trained to catch speed demons tearing up rubber in the fast lane. The illegal black box that alerted practiced speeders to a hidden camera or radar gun sat on our dashboard.

"After the expressway we take Route Forty-Three to Eighteen," I said, double-checking the car's built-in navigation system against a printed map. "Somewhere along the way that becomes Prince Road. We drive by a couple of prestigious golf courses and past one of the Prince hotels."

Echoes of royalty.

Noda nodded but said nothing.

After a closer examination of the outlet map, I said, "The mall complex is huge. There looks to be three or four groups of stores."

Noda flashed a lightning glance my way. "Is Komeki on its own?"

"No. It's with a bunch of other shops."

"Then we'd better start looking elsewhere."

Son of a bitch. He was right. Outlet operations were streamlined by definition. Everything beyond the backrooms of the stores unfolded in the public eye. Including shipment arrivals. In most outlets, trucks pulled up to the stores and unloaded in plain sight. Whether at the front or back or from a shared loading dock.

Hard to transfer a body in plain sight, even when disguised.

Mari picked up on the first ring, her voice tense. "Something happen?"

"We may have a problem. Can you see if Komeki has any other buildings in the area? A location more secluded than the outlet?"

"Give me a minute . . . searching . . . searching . . . yeah, they have a warehouse . . . but . . . let's see . . . it's a long ways away, up Route One Forty-Six . . . hold on . . . I'm looking at a local map . . . now a satellite image . . . it's a weird location."

"Why?"

"It's on the other side of Mount Asama . . . in . . . Tsumagoi . . . Kanbara . . . of all places."

Kiyomi Komeki's hometown.

Noda grunted. "That's our spot."

Mari's voice turned tentative. "Brodie-san, maybe she really is the Steam Walker."

"Hate to admit it, but it's looking more likely," I said. "Were you able to check on her movements like I asked yesterday?"

"I did and I couldn't find anything that gave her an alibi during any of the attacks. But she's way off the grid, so I can't really track her either way. I also can't find her personal email account. Wherever it is, it's well hidden. There's no personal correspondence on her company email." Excitement edged into Mari's voice. "If she is the Steam Walker, it would tie up all the connections perfectly, including the Komeki logo at Napa."

"It would," I said, not to mention the police artist's impressions about the suspect's features leaning toward the feminine side.

My phone buzzed immediately after we made our goodbyes, this time with an incoming call from our affiliate at Narita Airport.

"Been trying to get you for the last couple of minutes," he said.

"Sorry. I was on the phone with the office."

"Tried Noda's phone but it went straight to voice mail."

I turned to the chief detective. "Your phone off?"

"At these speeds, yeah."

I checked the speedometer. We'd edged up to the 280 mark. Around 170.

"Sorry," I said to the caller. "What have you got?"

"A living, breathing body."

"Naomi?"

"No, her husband."

CHAPTER 56

"CAN he talk?" I asked.

"He's bashed up pretty bad."

Tad had been beaten unconscious, then pumped full of narcotics and shut in a toilet stall. When the drugs wore off, he'd stumbled out into the terminal, blood splattered all over his clothing. The airport police pounced on him and were all set to arrest him before our affiliate stepped forward.

"So where are you now?" I asked.

"Outside the airport first aid station. . . . Hold on. The nurse is waving me over."

He kept the line open, but the sound was muffled. I took the opportunity to bring Noda up-to-date.

"Get what you can," the chief detective said, "then get off. I need your eyes."

Meaning for cop lookout and tracking the route, in that order.

"Right."

"Brodie, you still there?" our Narita contact said.

"Yeah. What's the story?"

"Sato can talk. In fact, he insists on it."

"What are they saying about his condition?"

"The attending physician wants to keep him for observation. He's got a gash on his head that took ten stitches. There's a suspicion that the 'happy cocktail' the thugs injected him with was a gray market item and could have harmful side effects. So after he talks to you, they're carting him off to a hospital, where they'll hold him for at least two days, maybe three. Here's Sato-san now. I'm going to put it on speaker so I can follow."

I heard shuffling sounds as the phone was passed, then: "Brodie, is that you?"

"Yes, Tad. You okay?"

An erratic panting erupted over the line. ". . . dizzy and nauseated, but so what? Can you tell me about Naomi? Nobody here's saying anything. Have they found her?"

"Not yet."

"Oh, God," Tad said, the tenor of his voice leaping to hysterical in two beats. "It's happening to her too. You've go to stop this, Brodie. You've got to."

"I will, but I need you to fill me in first."

"Anything. How can I help?"

"Tell me why you disappeared in Los Angeles, then ended up back here in Japan instead of Singapore?"

"What do you mean disappeared?"

"We lost track of you."

"No, you didn't. Your man was on our flight."

"*What?*" The comment ran in the face of everything Stockton had told me. "All right, start from the beginning. With your landing in LA."

"Naomi couldn't stop worrying about her mother," he said, his breathing loud in my ear. "By the time we got to Los Angeles for our connection to Singapore, Naomi was feeling so guilty we traded in our Singapore tickets for ones to Japan. There was nothing going to the Kyoto area soon enough, so we settled for Tokyo."

"Is that when you dumped your protection?"

"I told you, he was on our plane. And if anything, he deserted *us*."

"That's not possible."

"I don't know, Brodie. One minute he was two steps behind us, the next he was gone. We waited. We started to worry. Then we got a text from him. We gave him our new departure information. He said he'd be on the plane but we wouldn't be able to spot him and we shouldn't try."

"Did you see him after that?"

"No."

"Not even on board? In passing?"

"No. But it was a jumbo Airbus. More than five hundred passengers on two levels."

"Why didn't you give me a heads-up?"

The heavy breathing kicked up a notch. "What do you mean? We thought he was in touch with you."

I had no answer to that. The Steam Walker had found a weakness in our plan and exploited it.

Tad plowed on. "Are you close to finding Naomi?"

"We've got a lead. We're heading to the Karuizawa area and a place called Tsumagoi."

With brisk verbal strokes, I apprised him of our progress, and how we were closing the gap.

"Can you stop by and pick me up?" Tad asked. "I want to be there when you find her. I want to help."

"We're way beyond your position. The truck left Narita hours ago."

"Really? I was only out ten or fifteen minutes."

"You were attacked some three or four hours ago. You need to rest, Tad. You do that and we'll go after Naomi. What can you tell me about the people who mugged you?"

I heard him shuffle around. "Almost nothing, I'm embarrassed to say. We arrived in Narita and had time to kill before boarding our flight for Tokyo, so we ate. Then we split up to go to the restrooms. The women's was right next to the men's. I was soaping my hands when they hit me from behind and kept hitting me. I heard two, maybe three voices. Then I felt a needle prick. I never saw any faces. When I came to, I went looking for Naomi, but airport security nabbed me. I was covered in blood. I was so worried about Naomi, I never bothered to look at myself in the mirror."

What I understood from the few tidbits Tad had just supplied was that the attack had unfolded in two stages. First, the Steam Walker's team had breached our security in LA, where they stripped away the bodyguard. Second, the message Stockton had received just before take-off from Southern California had not mentioned a change in itinerary, so it had been a decoy.

I said, "And there's still no sign of your wife over there?"

"Your man here's shaking his head."

The Steam Walker had Naomi.

CHAPTER 57

I CALLED Mari. "Where are they?"

"Three hundred yards from the exit. You're only twenty kilometers behind."

A little more than twelve miles back. At this speed, only four minutes away. *If* they weren't about to leave the expressway.

"Let's keep an open line from here," I said. "I'm putting you on speaker. If you have nothing to report, just continue tracking."

"Okay."

I set my mobile in the dashboard cradle. Around the next bend, we entered extreme terrain. Taller mountains with abrupt upheavals of rock filled our windshield. The new peaks were high and dramatic. Evergreens ran up leaf-covered slopes until towering reddish-brown stacks of volcanic stone interrupted their progress, jutting into the sky, mighty and proud, demanding and dominant. No evergreens could tackle them.

With each turn in the expressway, a new stony butte swung into view, shooting skyward with authority. These weren't volcanoes themselves, but rather hardened beds of lava rock shoved upward at a later time with the tumultuous buckling and thrusts of the earth's crust. It was as if we'd jetted back through time and entered some long-lost terrain.

This was the world of the Steam Walkers.

"The truck just exited the expressway," Mari said. "You're coming up on the same turnoff."

Noda nodded but stayed focused on the road. He maintained his speed until the last two hundred yards, then decelerated swiftly and swung into the sharp turn of the ramp far too fast.

The car drifted sideways. Burning rubber reached my nostrils. The back tire edged onto the shoulder and caught the lip of the embankment, a forty-foot drop beyond. Noda flicked the steering wheel, and the rear of the vehicle whipped back onto the roadway, swinging into position.

I kept my eyes straight ahead, and my mouth shut. Working with Noda was never dull.

Mari's voice broke the silence. "Okay, you're on Route Forty-Three. They're on Route Eighteen, just passing the last golf course."

"How far back are we?"

"Eight kilometers."

Damn. Still five miles behind. In a flash we'd lost ground.

No, not *ground*, *time*. At the expressway exit, we'd narrowed the gap to within three minutes, but now, on surface streets, at lower speeds, while our physical distance jelled at five miles, the time to traverse the distance ballooned from three to twelve minutes.

Which was why Noda had held the highway speed until the last possible second, milking the road for every inch he could manage.

"They've hit the edge of the outlets," Mari announced. "They're three hundred yards from the intersection . . . they've turned . . . heading toward the outlet entrance . . . closer . . . closer . . . oh no!"

"What?"

"As expected, they've driven past the outlet, but they're headed *away* from the warehouse."

I checked the map. She was right. Was there a *third* location? Hidden and not on the company books?

Noda and I swapped a look.

Mari came back on with an update: "There's no third building. The driver took a detour to avoid construction."

Mari guided us through the alternate route, then said, "They've turned back toward the warehouse access road."

Noda saw an opening in the traffic, zipped in and out between three cars, then ran two red lights. We hit the access road, Route 146, and soon after began our ascent toward Mount Asama. Kyu-Karuizawa, where the emperor met his future bride, was a few miles to the east. Mount Asama, which had buried the hamlet of Kanbara, was somewhere directly ahead.

As was the Steam Walker's home ground.

Had Mari pegged the Walker's identity? Were we actually chasing a fashion designer–assassin? One, moreover, who moved like a ghost in and out of Japan, killing at will?

Route 146 snaked up the mountain, its curves long and lazy. Lush forest bordered the roadway. The trappings of the resort town yielded to pristine woodland with low grasses and shrubs underfoot. Pines. Birches. Elms. Then they, too, began to thin, and small stacks of lava rock poked through the groundcover.

Without warning, Mount Asama sprang into view, tall and brooding, its peak shrouded in cloud cover. The sky darkened. A heavy downpour pummeled our vehicle. The volcano commanded its own mini-climate, and it was dismal.

We raced onward. Off to the left I glimpsed Onioshidashi. The name translated as What the Devil Pushed Out—awkward in English but in Japanese a perfect summation of the nightmarish landscape streaming by outside our window.

More than two hundred years ago, around the time the volcano buried the people of Kanbara, it had also loosed a monstrous lava outpouring that buckled and cracked and built towers of rock ten, twenty, and thirty feet high. The outcroppings sprawled as far as the eye could see, wild and desolate and alien and unknowable.

We rolled on.

"You're close," Mari said. "Another three-quarters of a mile, on your right."

By degrees, nature reversed itself. The gruesome volcanic pilings gave way to shrubbery, then virgin woodlands, then plebeian roadside attractions—Japanese diners offering tempura, noodles, and fresh-baked pastries. Not civilization as it was meant to be practiced but at least no longer primeval.

I glanced at the map. "Isn't there a turnoff for Kanbara coming up?"

Mari said yes, and seconds later we saw a sign for the village, then a turnout, then the warehouse—low and long and the length of two houses stacked back to back. A fourteen-foot semitrailer truck with a discreet Komeki logo on its side panel had backed into a small loading bay.

"That's got to be it," I said.

Noda slammed on the brakes.

CHAPTER 58

We barreled through the warehouse door.

In a small office directly behind the reception area, the driver and a seventy-year-old caretaker huddled around a kerosene room heater, sipping green tea.

They both looked our way, startled.

"Open the truck," Noda called as we charged into the room.

"You can't come back here," the caretaker said.

He wore a standard workman's uniform of matching gray pants, shirt, and cap. The uniform that spelled conformity throughout the country. The other man had on a long-distance driver's vest bristling with energy bars, cigarette packs, and his mobile phone, all stuffed into the various pockets.

"We're detectives. Open the truck."

The trucker eyed us doubtfully. Squaring his shoulders, Noda stepped closer and the driver said, "Okay, okay, you can look, but don't touch nothing."

His face was sallow, and his body sagged as if he'd logged a million miles and was burdened with a million more yet to go. He circled around to the loading bay, slid back a double bolt on heavy metal doors, and pulled open the left-hand door.

"You look," Noda said to me. "I'll stay out here and watch things."

Meaning he'd keep an eye out for the sudden appearance of weapons, reinforcements, or a move to lock me in.

"You got a badge?" I heard the driver ask Noda as I stepped into the cavernous truck bed.

Stacks of boxes with the Komeki logo were secured along the front and sides of the trailer. They were all small and manageable and of the type no doubt shipped to Komeki shops around the nation.

Nothing large enough to hold a body. Unless . . .

I shook my head, refusing to go there. I returned to the loading dock, saying, "Nothing here."

Eyebrows diving, Noda scowled at the anemic driver. "You drop anything off on the way here?"

The two men were inspecting Noda's business card.

"You're private cops," the trucker said, ignoring the chief detective's question. "We don't need to answer you."

I pushed into the man's personal space. "You're absolutely right. We're dealing with assault, kidnapping, and multiple murders on an international level. Maybe we get the local police involved. And Komeki, Inc. Maybe you played a role. Maybe you both get suspended while they investigate."

In Japan, official investigations stretched on for months. The men fidgeted where they stood, and caved.

Noda repeated his query about an earlier delivery and the long-hauler replied in the negative.

"Anyone make a pickup here?"

"Yeah. A couple minutes before you arrived."

"Komeki goods?"

"No, his own. He subcontracts delivery with the head office. We haul stuff out here for him sometimes."

Tad had mentioned voices, plural, which made sense. The Steam Walker couldn't be everywhere. Sounded like others had accosted Tad and Naomi, then sent Naomi—all bundled up—straight into the Walker's hands.

"What's the guy's name?" Noda asked.

"Don't know. I'm not local."

Noda's stormy features swung in the caretaker's direction. The old man quickly shook his head. "I don't know him, either."

"You're local."

"But he's not. Only see him when he comes in for a pickup."

"Ever talk to him about anything?"

The Komeki warehouseman shrugged. "The fellow don't encourage talk. Picks up his package and scats."

"What kind of truck?"

"White delivery van. Looks like all the other ones on the road."

"Make? Year?"

"It's white."

We'd hit a dead end.

I said, "Did the guy wear a hat?"

"Baseball cap." The old man thought for a moment. "*Always* has a hat, but not always the same one. Always covers a lot of his face, though."

"Talk in a low voice? Sometimes a whisper?"

"That's the guy."

We had a lock.

The Steam Walker had been and gone. And we'd missed him by minutes.

"You help him carry the package?"

"No." The driver stretched his hands as wide as they would go. "Too long. Guy wheeled them away on a furniture dolly."

"Them?"

"Yeah. There were two this time."

Noda and I exchanged puzzled looks.

Two packages meant two bodies. Who was the second one? Perhaps Stockton's missing bodyguard had made it to this side of the Pacific after all.

CHAPTER 59

OUR window for finding Naomi was rapidly closing.

"Nearly had him," I said.

Nodding, Noda drew in a mouthful of chilled soba noodles. "Matter of minutes."

Back at the warehouse, we'd gone through the motions of eyeballing the paperwork for the delivery. The client section of the form listed a company called Asama Industries, a PO box fifty miles away, and a telephone number that went straight to voice mail. A typical professional cover—and dead end.

I snagged some cold noodles with my chopsticks and dipped them into the accompanying sauce. Hunger pangs had forced us to stop for food. True to form, Noda had sought out the nearest purveyor of buckwheat noodles. Like any soba fiend, he was on a perpetual prowl for the next perfect eighty-twenty noodle—eight parts buckwheat flower to two parts wheat. We'd passed a pair of soba shops on the way down Mount Asama, so hit the more promising one on the way back.

I said, "Got any ideas after we eat?"

"None. You?"

"Not a one."

I glanced at my phone for the tenth time. Nothing new from our digital whiz kid. I'd asked her to dive deeper into Komeki's computers, but neither of us expected Mari to find anything useful within our time frame.

Noda took in another mouthful of noodles. Outside, gravel crunched as a vehicle pulled into the lot and drove through to the rear.

"We've got to get back on the road," I said. "Thoughts?"

"Outlet shop's our only choice."

"Afraid you'd say that."

It was a last-ditch effort unlikely to lead anywhere.

"Time's running out," I said.

Noda frowned into his food. "Might already be dead."

As we gulped down the last of our meal, the server emerged from the back room.

"Here's your *soba-yu*," she said.

She set down a rectangular red-lacquer pitcher with a lid and pour spout unique to soba cuisine. It held hot cooking water, or *soba-yu*, into which many of the nutrients from the buckwheat noodles had seeped. Diners poured the steaming liquid into their remaining dipping sauce and spiced the mix with leftover condiments to make a savory soup that, today, in the rain and the gloom, would provide a welcome warmth.

"Thank you," I said.

At the back of the shop a spring-loaded screen door creaked open and slapped shut, followed by the sound of a lot of weight on old floorboards.

"Delivery?" I asked the waitress.

"I suppose," she said, confusion muddling her expression. "But most of them come in the morning before we start the noodle-making."

A moment later, the cook called from the kitchen in the back: "*Oi*. You forgot something."

Our server gave us a fractured smile, bowed, and retreated.

As she shuffled unhurriedly toward the kitchen, I glanced over the tabletop. The soba-yu was the last of our order. The check was on the table. Our teacups were nearly full. We were the only customers.

There was nothing to forget.

Noda came to the same conclusion at the same instant.

We rose together and followed silently in the server's wake. We moved quickly into the back dining room. As soon as she parted the doorway curtain and disappeared into the rear, we closed the distance and took up positions against the walls on either side of the curtain.

I flashed a look in the head detective's direction and saw we were on the same wavelength: *the trucker or the caretaker had tagged us.*

The next instant four men charged through the doorway, their eyes forward, rushing right by us into the front dining area, where we'd eaten our meal.

"They're not here," the point man said. "Must have just gone out the door."

"That ain't right, you dumb ass. The bill's still on the table," a second one said. "Higuchi, check the front. The rest of us—"

He never finished because a moment later they all *knew*. It was instinctual. Primal.

They turned in unison.

The second speaker was clearly the man in charge—and the one to target. But we had to get through the others first. We hurtled toward them as they turned. I slammed the heel of my hand into the solar plexus of the man nearest me. Air burst from his lungs. As he doubled over, I brought clasped hands down on the back of his neck and he crumpled. The assailant closest to Noda was five inches taller than the beefy detective, so my partner kicked him in the crotch, then followed with one of his knockout punches, a merciless uppercut that met a plunging chin. The assailant's eyes rolled up into his head and he toppled over backward, into oblivion.

The remaining two lunged at us. They were bigger and faster and moved like they knew their way around a fight. Noda's man landed the first blow and I saw my partner fly back against the wall. Then I was consumed by my own problems.

My opponent—the leader—attacked with his right fist already in play. He snarled as I swept his looping roundhouse aside, then rammed my free hand into the soft joint of the jaw, just under the ear. It was a combination judo-street move that used his own momentum to slam him into a side wall. He bounced off the paneling, unfazed and furious, and scrambled back at me.

I looked for an entry to put him down, but he was an experienced street fighter with speed and power, which made him dangerous. We traded blows, each blocking the other, each seeking an opening. After several ineffectual exchanges, I backed away and circled.

Out of the corner of my eye I saw Noda still engaged. My opponent raced in yet again. I circled away. When he advanced the next time, I threw a pair of staccato jabs with my left to keep him at bay, then launched a slow circular body blow with my right that I let him block. Which he did, his snarl turning into a smirk of superiority. In his new-found confidence, he missed the closed-fist thrust headed his way. It exploded into his chest and he flew across a tabletop before smashing headfirst into another wall and slipping to the floor.

Thoroughly pissed off, and still unfazed, he started to rise, fumbling under his jacket for something.

I was already rounding the corner of the table when what looked like a Smith & Wesson cleared his jacket. As his hand emerged, I kicked the weapon away.

Five things happened at once. His finger—caught in the trigger guard—snapped. The pistol discharged. He howled. The shot punched a hole in the ceiling. The gun flew from his grasp.

I rammed my knee into his stomach. He collapsed and this time stayed down.

I pivoted around in time to see Noda land another of his classic jawbreakers. His second target went down.

And out.

CHAPTER 60

WE had the leader's wallet. His name was Toshiaki Baba.

"You *will* tell us," I said.

Baba turned evasive. "Ya want Higuchi. But he's out cold as a snapper."

Two of the men were unconscious and Noda stood guard over the third. Baba was a bulky tree stump of a man in overalls, with a large head and intelligent, shifty eyes. A tough country thug who would be wily, loyal, and hard to break. He'd already put the broken finger behind him.

"Nice try," I said. "It's you we want and it's you we're going to put holes in if we don't get answers we like."

"I'm telling ya—"

I cut him off with a wave of the gun. "We're not buying. Take us to the woman."

In the brief tableau we'd witnessed before the fight, the other men had hung on Baba's words. Shrewdly, he'd let them take the lead and only spoke up when he thought they were alone. Before he realized we were behind him. The remaining three were underlings, or pickup players hired for the day's outing. The group hadn't moved like a practiced unit.

Our captive sneered. "I ain't who ya want. But even if I was, what you're asking ain't gonna happen."

"You are and it is."

When the dust had settled, the owner poked his head through the split curtain, flustered, ready to call the police. We waved the equivalent of two hundred dollars in his face, and persuaded him and his server to take a slow stroll down the road, assuring them we'd be gone by the time they returned. When they did circle back, they'd find another two hundred on our table.

He expressed concern about additional damage to the shop, so we topped off our offer and commandeered a battered shed behind the restaurant.

"You sure you'll be gone?" the soba chef asked, even as he accepted the money.

"Count on it," I said.

We'd better be. Our window was getting narrower by the minute.

"Take us to Naomi Nobuki," I said again.

"Who?"

"The woman the Steam Walker grabbed."

"Can't."

"Last chance," I said.

He gave me a bored look.

I shot him in the leg and he bellowed. We let him. There were no neighbors to hear his howls of pain.

Noda squinted at our hostage. "He's more afraid of the Steam Walker."

"That true?" I asked.

"You'd be too, if ya knew as much as I do."

"I might. I've met him a couple of times. And I'm extremely glad to hear you know so much."

He reddened. "Didn't mean it that way."

"Too late."

"No one meets the Walker more'n once and lives."

"It was close," I admitted, thinking of the poisoned meal that was most likely meant for me. "But I'm here, so keep that in mind. You give us what we want and *you* live."

"I'm not saying a word about the Walker."

"I'll shoot you again."

"Yeah, but he'll *kill* me."

"Your choice," I said, and shot him a second time.

His outcry redoubled. Both times, I'd aimed for the meatier edges of his substantial calves, avoiding the major arteries. Maimed, our prisoner thrashed around on the floor like a wounded feral beast. His breathing came in snorts between waves of pain. His eyes teared up.

Something nebulous and undefined inside of me stirred in vague protest. I hated being forced to inflict serious pain, but time was short and words had no effect.

When his breathing evened out, the mulish leader said, "You can keep shooting till all the bullets are gone but I ain't taking ya there."

I smiled. The pain had clouded his thoughts. He'd dropped the pretense of *not knowing*.

I stared down at him with a hardened look of need. What I sought was leverage greater than the terror instilled by the Steam Walker's formidable reputation.

"There's three bullets left," I said. "I could put one in each arm, which would send you to the hospital and then a wheelchair for a spell. Or I could put a round through your spine and you'd be glued to a wheelchair for life."

No reaction. No fear. The Steam Walker's hold was stronger. But I had a backup plan that relied on an aversion so alarming and so primitive it was hot-wired into every male on the planet.

"Or maybe," I said, "I could take out your third leg."

I watched as my meaning slowly took hold. Baba's gaze moved from my face to the gun. A light sweat appeared at his hairline. I edged the gun a few inches toward the intended target and a primitive dread seeped into his expression. He turned pale. He shook his head weakly. He said no but his protest was faint.

I moved the weapon a few inches more and he told us what we needed to know.

CHAPTER 61

WE loaded our captive into the backseat of our car, his legs wrapped in makeshift tourniquets.

He directed us back to Mount Asama, then onto a narrow back road used only by rangers, researchers, and, apparently, the Steam Walker. The road began to climb, then fed into a series of switchbacks edging up the mountain.

Our involuntary guide said, "You can't follow the Walker. Not when he goes to the volcano."

"Don't bet on it," I said.

"Don't have to."

After the eighth switchback, the access road came to an abrupt end. Above us towered Mount Asama. Gray-black clouds clustered around the peak and long, ghostly cloud fingers streaked its slopes. The mountain rose gradually, then jutted up dramatically as it neared the edge of the crater.

I wondered how the Steam Walker "goes to the volcano."

There was a pullout at the end of the road. Beyond that, a shed. A covered pickup with an extra-long bed and a high roof rested in the pullout, its tailgate open, a ramp leading down to the ground set in place.

"That's his?" I asked, and Baba nodded.

Smart. The Walker had changed vehicles. And unloaded something big.

"What was in it?"

Our guide pointed up the slope.

"Don't see anything," Noda said.

"You will."

Noda cut the engine. Quiet swept over us. We listened and waited and focused. A noise echoed in the distance. The sound of a motor. A faint, grinding hum.

A black spot emerged at the top edge of the closest cloud band. It was some kind of all-terrain vehicle, small and boxy, like a dune buggy but with a black roof and glassed in on all sides. Grated tank treads circling the wheels pulled the vehicle upward.

"That's the Walker," Baba said with a sneer. "You'll never catch him."

I looked at Noda. Then at the Walker's pickup. Then at the shed.

"What's in the shack?" I asked.

Baba gave an indifferent shrug. "Research vehicle the scientists use. You don't wanna touch that. It's government."

I headed for the storage unit at a trot. A hefty padlock secured a large door. Noda strutted up with massive bolt cutters he'd pulled from the trunk and snipped the lock shaft with ease. Our company cars were stocked with provisions for the road.

"Good thing we didn't have to shoot it off," I said.

Noda agreed. "Need the bullets."

Our captive had carried no spare rounds on his person or in his car. I looked up the mountain. "*If* we get close enough."

I yanked the lock from its perch and swung back the doors. Inside, climbing gear and monitoring equipment for tracking volcanic activity lined the walls. In the middle was an industrial-size version of the all-terrain vehicle taking the Steam Walker to the top of the volcano. It had a bright-red fiberglass roof and tank treads three feet wide and four feet high.

I climbed into the cab but could find no keys. I searched the glove compartment, under the seats, the door pocket, and in the console between the front seats.

Nothing.

"You see a key anywhere?" I called to Noda, who scanned the walls and a workbench and said no.

I ran my hands down the steering wheel shaft and into the shadows. Near its base I found a starter button. Right. I pushed it and the machine rumbled to life.

"Got it," I said. "Pull it out. I'll be right back."

I raced back to the car and grabbed the keys from the ignition. I drew the gun and waved the barrel loosely at the mountain. "Explain it to me."

Behind us I heard a roar of steel tracks grinding up stone as Noda brought the monstrous machine out of its cave.

"The Steam Walker knows the volcano inside and out," Baba shouted over the thunderous clamor of the machine. "Knows when the gas will come. Knows how to spot them hidden drop holes. Because the other Walkers taught him. He used to play around the edges of the no-go area, then started camping out on the mountain when the beatings got too bad."

"What beatings?" I shouted back.

Noda pulled the transport alongside.

"They say his old man whipped the wife and kid. The Walker fled into the mountains. Stayed till the father cooled off. Only he wasn't the Walker then. The beatings got worse, so the Walker stayed out longer. There were other Walkers on the mountain, they say. They took him in."

"His father wasn't a Steam Walker?"

Baba's sneer was dismissive. "The only thing his father was was dead, after the mother was killed 'falling down some steps.' Beaten to death, of course, but no charges were ever brought 'cause nothing could be proved. A few years later, the father disappeared on his way to work.

Never seen no more. A policeman went to the mountain to chase down the Walker. Never came back."

"I see."

His look was smug. "You two ain't coming back, neither. The mountain'll get you if the Steam Walker don't finish you first."

CHAPTER 62

WE plowed ahead up the mountain, the tank tracks grinding away and pulling us upward. We were gaining.

The Steam Walker had seen us as soon as we rose above the first line of cloud cover, and he'd jacked up his speed. We saw his vehicle pop forward, then strain and buck and drop back down to its previous pace. A white smoke trail curled from his tailpipe. Our tank of a mountain vehicle had already topped out, but we continued to gain.

"Can you see if Naomi is with him?" I asked.

"Can't."

Then I remembered a pair of binoculars I'd seen in the oversize glove compartment and yanked them out. I zoomed in on our target. The back window was a clear wall of Plexiglas.

"See anything?" Noda called over the noise of the engine.

I scanned the interior and my heartbeat ticked up. "There's a bundle in the back. In a blanket. It could be her."

"Any movement?"

"Can't see any . . . wait . . . I got the back of a head. A woman's. Got to be her."

"See a second 'package'?"

"No."

We stormed on. Noda maneuvered like a master, detouring expertly around outcroppings and steep slopes, fighting for each stretch of ground.

"You see the smoke coming out of his vehicle?" I said.

"Yeah."

"Bet he doesn't know about it."

With our larger transport, we'd cut the distance in half. The rim of the crater loomed overhead, ragged and sharp against a brooding sky. I scanned the final approach with the binoculars. If that's where the Walker was heading, the last span could be accomplished only on foot.

"I'm thinking we should get the doc moving," I said.

Noda nodded. "Do it."

I pulled out my cell phone. Reception was weak but extant. Baba needed to be treated for his injuries, but any medical clinic would report the bullet wounds, and the national police would descend on all of us. Brodie Security had an ex–US Army doctor on call for the occasional delicate situation. We knew Baba wouldn't talk on his own, but the police could legally hold him for months and chip away at his resistance.

I hung up and said, "He's on his way. He'll call when he arrives in Karuizawa."

Next I rang Mari and her concern surfaced immediately. "Where have you been? Are you okay?"

"Fine. Just busy. We're on the mountain and going after the Steam Walker."

"*The* mountain?"

"Yes."

"Brodie, that's not good at all. Mount Asama's like one of Japan's most active volcanoes." She pounded the keyboard. "Let me read this to you—'from one to seven eruptions in every decade for the last century, some continuous for months or years.' "

"Didn't know it was *that* active."

"Lots of eruptions, but lava not so much. Other kinds. Says the mountain can rain down boulders as big as cars."

"What about the gas?"

She tapped some keys. "Volcanic gas warnings happen like *all the time*. There's one in effect now."

"Right now?"

"Yes. They won't let hikers within three miles of the top."

My throat went dry. We were well past that point.

"Tell me more about that."

She tickled the board and relayed what she found. The community was in the middle of a "noxious gas episode," a period when the mountain spews out gases at irregular intervals. The crater might expel carbon dioxide, hydrogen chloride, or sulfur dioxide. People most often fall prey to the first one, which is odorless and colorless and kills by asphyxiation. As a precaution, locals carry gas masks in their cars, which works for some gases but not carbon dioxide.

After we hung up, I mentioned the gas to Noda, and he pointed to a strip on the visor above his head. I leaned over and read the Japanese notation. The band changed color when gas emissions were detected, at which time we were supposed to slip on gas masks and leave the area. I peered in the backseat. No masks. I raised myself up and scanned the rear storage bed.

Nothing.

We'd closed the gap to within one hundred yards.

I moved my binoculars between the Steam Walker and the human bundle he was carting up the mountain. Occasionally, he tossed a backward glance our way. There was no panic in his look. No excitability. No loss of nerve. Just a curious calm I knew we had to disrupt to take him down.

He had a plan, and even with our arrival he had not wavered.

I took out the Smith & Wesson. The gun had a maximum effective range of fifty yards, give or take. Not a hundred. But *effective* was a physical limitation, not a psychological one.

I aimed. Our vehicle bounced up and down, rocked left and right.

"Got a smooth patch coming up soon?" I said.

"Yeah."

"Call it."

Forty-five seconds later, Noda said, "Twenty yards . . . ten . . . five . . . *now.*"

I fired high. The sound echoed across the terrain. The next instant the Steam Walker's head jerked around. A fine crackle spread across the upper corner of his rear window.

"Nice shot," Noda said.

Our prey popped the gas again and his machine bucked. Black smoke poured out the back, then a flame.

"I like that," I said.

The Steam Walker's vehicle sputtered and bucked again but it continued to shuttle forward. Smoke was billowing out now. The Walker wrestled with the steering wheel. The body in the back bounced around. Shifted. The blanket slipped down. I saw the face.

It was Naomi.

Alive or dead, I couldn't tell.

We heard rattling sounds, then the frame of his car shuddered and went still. The volume of smoke had redoubled.

The Steam Walker hopped lightly from the driver's seat, grabbed a daypack, and trotted uphill, lobbing a look our way with the same calm assurance.

He had left Naomi behind.

We raced on.

CHAPTER 63

WE'D separated the Steam Walker from his victim.

Our quarry continued to trot uphill, which spoke volumes about his conditioning. Occasionally, when he hit a steep section, his upward jog transformed itself into a series of mini-switchbacks, three strides one way, then three back.

Noda pulled up inches short of the Steam Walker's stalled machine and I leapt out. Naomi was in the back, a motionless log.

Please, not Ken's last child.

"Naomi," I called.

There was no response.

Her forehead was warm to the touch. When I ran a finger under her nose, I felt a warm exhale, shallow but steady.

There was still a chance.

"Naomi," I called again. Gently, I shook her shoulders, and her eyes opened with lethargic ease.

"Brodie," she said with a sleepy smile.

"Naomi, how do you feel?"

"Like I'm floating on cotton. Where am I?"

"Mount Asama. Near Karuizawa."

Startled, she tried to pull herself upright, then gave up when her body wouldn't obey. "Last I remember I was in Narita, heading for the woman's powder room."

She'd been driven across three prefectures and up a mountain. The Steam Walker seemed to possess a whole arsenal of potent pharmaceuticals.

From a distance, Noda said, "She looks okay. We should go."

I checked Naomi's pulse. Her eyes strayed toward the second voice but they had trouble locating the source. When she finally did, she stared with alarm at the rough bulldog bulk, with its bisected eyebrow.

"He's a friend," I said. "We work together at Brodie Security. Will you be all right here for a while?"

"It's comfy."

"Uh-huh. Any pain? Numbness? Strange feeling anywhere?"

"Oh no. I'm just kinda happy." She giggled.

I'd been so focused on Naomi, I hadn't noticed a second body on the floor, cloaked head to toe with another blanket.

"Looks like we found Stockton's guy," I called.

"He alive?"

I pulled back the cover, felt for a pulse on his neck, and found a slow, rhythmic beat. I nudged him lightly, then harder, but he slept on. He looked Japanese. I extracted a wallet from his back pocket. This was not Stockton's man.

"The name Jun Tasaki mean anything to you?" I asked Noda.

"No. We got to go."

I nodded at the smoke snaking from the tailpipe. "We better move them away. The thing could blow."

"Okay, but quick."

We carried Naomi and Tasaki from the stalled vehicle, set them down, and covered them once more with blankets. In the front seat, I found a custom-made body harness. It echoed designs for baby carriers but was enlarged and reinforced to hold an adult. It had thick, padded shoulder straps for hauling a heavy load, a series of horizontal belt loops with buckles, plus a crotch strap to separate the legs and lock the body in place. That's how the Walker conveyed his victims the last stretch to the rim of the volcano and beyond.

"We'll come back soon," I said to Naomi, then Noda and I hopped back into our tank and headed after our prey once more.

The research vehicle gained on the Steam Walker.

"Why'd he leave them alive?" I asked.

"Because he's experienced."

"Meaning what?"

"You ever carry a dead body?"

A hint of nausea ruffled the edge of my stomach. "No."

"Dead weight is harder to manage."

The nausea rose. "Drugged is easier?"

"Much."

I focused on the chase. Three hundred yards on, the upward grade became too steep. Our motorized transport had reached its limit.

"Got to hoof it," Noda said.

"Wait," I said, and reached over and peeled the warning strip from the visor and slapped it to the sleeve of my jacket.

The Steam Walker's jog had slowed to a fast walk, which was still faster than the pace Noda and I managed. I kicked it up a gear and felt the thin air burn my lungs.

But I pressed on. Noda kept pace. The surface of the volcano was dark and grainy with volcanic sand and pebbles. Elsewhere it was covered with cascades of rocks the size of cantaloupes. Boulders too large to climb appeared in odd clusters. Low-lying mountain scrub staked out protected crevices.

Our man was thirty yards from the rim of the crater, and we were twice that distance from him. We trooped on. It was a slog. I checked the gas patch on my arm. No change. The slope steepened for the Steam Walker. His pace slowed while ours did not. We closed the gap further. His daypack bobbed with each step.

When he was ten yards from the rim, we'd narrowed the distance to twenty. I drew the gun and yelled for him to stop. Normally, I could hit a target from this range, but the uphill grade complicated the shot.

CHAPTER 64

WE caught up a minute later. Our breathing came in spurts. My lungs were on fire. I wondered if it was the gas, but the Steam Walker looked to have no such concern, so I let the thought pass.

Our new captive stared at us. I did the same, inspecting him for bulges suggestive of hidden weapons. I saw none. The Steam Walker wore baggy mountain gear in browns and grays. Concealed weaponry was possible but unlikely. Why would he be carrying? He had expected no interference today. He'd planned to ascend the volcano alone and dispose of the bodies as he'd done who knew how many times before.

At five-six, he was not a big man, but I knew from experience that he was swift and agile. His face was still largely hidden in the shadow of his cap, but even so I could see that this was not the visage I'd seen in the bamboo forest or that Shu had described for the Napa County Sheriff's Department. Nor was it the one I'd seen behind the blowfish restaurant. This was a third face, and I presumed his real one. For those confrontations, he'd applied makeup with a deft touch to disguise his features. Today, he'd expected no face-off, only a routine retrieval at the warehouse from a worn-out trucker and an old caretaker, so he'd opted for a simpler disguise. His nose was slim, not broad. His cheekbones were prominent but not the exaggerated height of the police sketch. The eyes, however, were the same. Piercing and predatory. He ran them up and down Noda, then me.

The Walker moved on without bothering to look back, so I put a slug in his vicinity and a cloud of volcanic dust bloomed a yard to his right. Accuracy was not a problem. He stopped and turned.

"Come down here," I said.

"No."

I didn't shoot and he smiled. Noda and I advanced. The Steam Walker moved to resume his ascent and I said, "Do that and I'll empty the gun. One slug ought to connect."

One slug was all I had left, but he didn't know that.

He turned to face us.

"Got any more bullets in that gun?" the Walker said in his characteristic whisper.

"Enough."

He nodded lazily, then called my bluff. He feinted left, and moved right.

I shifted with him, then corrected as he changed direction. The earth underfoot was pumice and pebble. It was loose and unstable. Which made maintaining traction hard, especially in street shoes. We had not come prepared to climb a mountain. The Walker had. I began to slide downhill. I flapped my arms and recaptured my stability.

Noda was not so lucky. Succumbing to the same feint, the chief detective, in black loafers with soft rubber-foam soles and even less traction than my black-on-black sneakers, watched helplessly as his feet drifted downhill. He windmilled his arms, overcorrected, and frowned as he flopped over onto his stomach and was dragged downhill. He raked the ground with bent fingers to stall his downward momentum, but succeeded only in drawing trails of loose fragments after him.

I was suddenly one-on-one with the Steam Walker.

On his home ground.

And all but rooted to where I stood.

Clearly, the fine volcanic rubble had worked its way into our shoe treads during the short hike to the top, neutralizing any purchase our footwear might have possessed. Well aware of the mountain's attributes, the Walker had knocked Noda out of commission with the simplest of moves.

Now he advanced on me.

I scrambled to secure a footing, but there was none to be found. I could plant my feet on the shifting volcanic debris beneath my shoes, but no foothold would support a sudden move. If I took a swing at the Steam Walker, I'd lose my balance and go tumbling downhill in Noda's wake.

I stood helplessly by as the Walker charged in for a body blow with shoulders lowered. When he rammed into me, I latched on to him, the soles of my shoes skating backward. He pinned my gun arm with one hand and slung the other around my waist. The muzzle pointed between our feet. I tried to angle it up, but my shoes slithered around under me. The Walker's hand glided down my forearm to my wrist. Then he applied pressure to my trigger finger. The firearm discharged. A cloud of dust geysered between our feet. The struggle continued. My shoes slid over pumice and pebble, captive to the Steam Walker's thrusts. He struck my trigger finger again and we both heard an empty click. My last advantage disappeared.

I managed to find a tentative balance and took my free hand off the Walker, but before I could strike out, he drew up short. And released my gun arm. That's all he had to do. I tilted back, floating away over the rubble underfoot. Arms flailing, I clawed the air. In one last desperate attempt, I snatched at the Walker and came away with his ball cap—and a handful of hair.

The movement whisked my feet out from under me. I flopped over on my back and slid headfirst down the slope, but not before I lifted my eyes and caught a glimpse of shoulder-length brown hair.

I stared down at the wad in my hand.

A hat—and a wig.

Then I glanced back at my assailant. The Steam Walker was a woman. An attractive one at that.

My downward slide continued unabated. I dropped the hat and hair and snatched at the earth, but like Noda before me, I had no success. Thirty yards down, the slope flattened for about ten yards before continuing its descent. Noda had come to rest on the shelf. My downward momentum stalled in the same stretch and I found myself lying alongside the chief detective. A film of volcanic dust had turned him a ghostly white.

"You see that?" I said.

He nodded. "Another reason for the body harness."

We looked back up the slope. The Steam Walker had reached the edge of the crater.

He—she—planned to escape downward, into the volcano.

CHAPTER 65

WE discovered what the Steam Walker was carrying in the daypack.

From our lower perch, we watched helplessly as she retrieved a lightweight harness with dangling parts attached—what I imagined were belay devices and pulleys and quickdraws.

She came fully prepared to descend into the mouth of the volcano.

Only this time without her prey.

"*Naruhodo*," Noda said. It figures.

The Steam Walker fastened the harness around her waist, then slipped into the leg loops. Her movements were assured and economical.

I said, "Wish we could make another run at her."

We couldn't reclaim the lost ground in time. Even if we could catch her, we were ill equipped to take her down.

Noda grunted unhappily. "Clever lady."

"She goes in, she has to come out."

"Eventually."

Gloves and a climbing rope appeared next. Once the gloves went on, the Walker straddled the lip of the volcano and wedged what must have been a camming device in the rock. Cams are clips with a miniature lever system that expand to lock themselves in place. The climber's own downward pull anchors its position in a crack. They come in a series of sizes to accommodate a range of crack and crevice sizes and have mostly replaced the pitons of decades past, which were hammered into the cracks and fissures. Pitons tore up the rock and became permanent fixtures on a mountain trail. Cams could be retrieved and used again and again and left few if any visible marks of the climber's passing.

The Walker looped the rope through a cord attached to the cam in the lead stone, fired a grin our way, and disappeared into the crater.

It took three long, painful minutes for us to hike back up to the rim of the crater. Both of us had shred some skin on the slide down.

We grappled with the last upward sweep and peered over the rim.

The crater dropped straight down for two hundred feet, then became a curved slope, which ended in a narrow footpath. Beyond the path was a further drop of incalculable depth.

Before us lay an off-planet scenario. There was rock and sand and pumice. There were deposits of ash. There were cragged striations etched into the sides by fire and steam and hot expulsions of lava. In places, the rock exhibited vivid coloring, some no doubt courtesy of the irregular cycles of gas vapor. The rugged downward sweep before me was unlike anything I'd ever seen before. Photographs of extreme terrain on the moon came to mind.

Elsewhere around the rim, the drop began as a crescent-shaped slope rather than a sheer plunge. But even the curved sides of the crater would require a rope and climbing gear. No person could walk down unsecured.

Which gave me an idea. I gazed over at the rock to which the Steam Walker had anchored her line. On which her life had hung, and which she'd need to climb back out of the crater. What if we cut it? Severed her lifeline? Not a nice idea, but eminently practical.

But the Steam Walker was way ahead of me.

She had secured the rope to a second cam thirty feet down, then severed the rope above it, leaving the beginning length dangling from the first cam.

I stared at the abandoned stretch of line. It signaled that she planned to exit the volcano the same way she'd entered. Which couldn't be. It was too simple. The assassin I'd been tracking would not be so careless. The strand left behind was meant to be a decoy.

On all levels, the Walker was a master. As we watched, she navigated the foreign terrain of the crater like a natural. She scampered along an impossibly slim footpath. The trail was no wider than two feet, and at times narrowed to half that width. To her left was the ascending slope of the cone. To her right was an unfathomable drop. At a large, craggy outcropping, she retrieved a second line and attached it to another cam and rappelled farther into the interior.

"You want to follow or should I?" I asked Noda.

The head detective growled. Which said it all. We were both angry and frustrated. We could not go any farther unless we had a death wish.

I said, "We've got to find her again. Ideas?"

"Working on it."

"She won't stop, will she?"

"Not that one. Unless the contract's canceled."

Fifty yards down, the Walker halted. Hanging from the rope over the central pit of the crater, she glanced at her sleeve, then delved into her pack and pulled out a gas mask, tugged it into place, and continued her descent.

I cast a look at my own patch. It had begun to flicker, its earlier neutral color of pale beige giving way to a brightening orange-red.

Then the mountain began to talk. It gurgled and groaned and grumbled, as if it were waking, or turning over in its sleep, or about to belch. A blast of air brushed our hair aside. The strip turned darker.

I said, "We have to get out of here."

CHAPTER 66

WITH very un-Japanese exuberance, Naomi flew into the arms of her husband. There were tears on both sides, as well as enough bows and other expressions of gratitude directed our way to last a lifetime.

Relief at Naomi's safe return was rewarding on several levels, yet I remained on edge. We'd rescued Ken's third child from the brink—literally. His daughter was once more on safe ground, but the Steam Walker was still loose, and the kill order on Naomi—and me, for that matter—was still in effect. Hoping to mine some additional fragments of information that might point toward the assassin, Noda and I questioned the couple closely, but unearthed no new nuggets. Disappointed, we left the reunited pair alone.

Outside in the hall, Noda instructed the guards to stay alert. We'd added a second man to each shift. I gave them an updated description of the Walker, telling them that she could appear in male or female dress. Brodie Security had set up a camera in Tad's room that broadcast straight to the nurses' station, keeping him under the eyes of the staff twenty-four/seven. A second feed went to our office. In addition, we installed a lock on the door, which was to stay engaged at all times, and set up a procedure by which doctors and nurses could attend Tad only in numbers of two or more. The approach of any solitary figure would trigger an immediate alert.

Even with the upgraded security, I was not reassured. The Steam Walker was that good.

During the Q&A session, my phone had buzzed with an incoming call from Stockton in Washington. I'd let it go to voice mail, but now I listened to his message. It was a curt *Call me*. Which I did.

Without preamble, our DC affiliate said, "Dust off your magic carpet."

"You found something."

"Oh, yeah. A big something."

DAY 11, WEDNESDAY, WASHINGTON, DC, 9 A.M.

Noda and I disembarked at Reagan National Airport, the second time for me in less than two weeks. Stockton met us outside of security. I scanned the terminal behind him. No alphabet boys in sight.

But they would be along shortly. This time, at my urging. I'd already called on the services of one, and anticipated the possible need for two more.

Stockton led us to a black Pontiac Grand Prix. On the drive into town, as the Washington Monument and then the Capitol dome swung into view, he filled us in on the details.

"Guy's name is Noakes. He's a local fixer. A lowlife the law suspects is doing quite well for himself without their interference, thank you very much. He's smart. Lives quietly. Guards his secrets. Most of them, anyway."

I nodded. I knew how to pry secrets loose. "You have him solid on this?"

"Very. He's part of a telephone chain. The last link before the killer, is our guess."

"You're talking a chain to protect both ends—the Steam Walker and whoever is issuing the kill orders?"

"Precisely," Stockton said. "Each person knows only the name and number directly before and after. Noakes made a call from the same disposable cell phone two to three days before you or your clients took a hit. Every time. To a pair of different numbers, but that's the killer changing phones or countries or both."

"That fits."

Stockton smiled. "'Course it does. We're using superb new software able to leap tall databases in a single bound. It made the connection after the fact. Napa, San Francisco, Kyoto, your warning in Kyoto, the hit on you, Naomi's kidnapping. Each call narrowed the field. Pinpointed Noakes's number on the fifth call, but we couldn't nail down the name."

"Were you able to nab a name earlier in the chain?"

Stockton's brow crumbled. "Nope. But that's why you're here."

"How'd you get him?"

"After the last transaction, he got sloppy. He made three personal calls from the same phone. Probably forgot his real phone that day and got lazy. Those calls were enough for the software to isolate him."

"No sign of his skipping since we rattled the Steam Walker?"

"None."

"I like the sound of this."

"You should. Doesn't get much better. We're a go whenever you two are ready."

"Sooner the better," I said.

Later in the afternoon, I managed to catch the window for calling my daughter.

"Hi, Daddy!" she said before I could say hello.

"Hi, Jen. How's camp?"

"Best ever. I'm scoring every day."

"Great."

"Which means I should get more gelato on my birthday."

"It means you're learning at camp."

"Daaddddy."

I thought, *cavities, obesity, no compromise*. I wanted to say no. Instead I said, "I'll think about it, okay?" My daughter was hard to refuse.

"Guess what else? I braided my own hair for the very first time. Without your help. It was better than you do."

"I bet it was," I said, and inhaled deeply, at once proud of her accomplishment and sad to have missed it.

CHINATOWN, 6:30 P.M.

Noda and I slid onto barstools of a faux British pub called the House & Hill. Stockton was hunkered down in his car around the back, ready to tackle any escapees, or come off the bench if we needed him.

We ordered two pints of Black Sheep Ale on tap, an English brew rare on these shores. The barkeep set us up. We drank. The beer was nutty, with a slight caramel tail.

"Good choice," Noda said.

"Outside of protecting Ken's family, once in a while I get something right."

Noda nodded absently. I looked straight ahead into a mirror that ran across the back wall of the bar. The mirror allowed me to watch everything behind our backs without appearing to do so. Every booth and table was filled with tourists enjoying an evening out after a hard day of sightseeing. A lot of Europeans. A scattering of Asians. A few Americans from the heartland. Not a single local in sight.

I said, "Stockton's right. Our man's got gray matter to go with the muscle. This is the perfect front."

"Explain," the chief detective said, hoisting his beer.

Everyone but the tourists knew DC's Chinatown now existed in name only. Echoes of its former life lingered in the stray eatery and the Chinese ideographs edging the signs of the newer chain restaurants and coffee bars. Noakes had figured out that frustrated travelers would settle for a touch of the Union Jack once their visions of a tasty Chinese meal evaporated. He was cleaning up by simply dishing out pints and shepherd's pie with a splash of atmosphere.

I added this to what Stockton had told us earlier: The fixer's full name was Trevor Noakes. British by nationality. "He's a thug and brawler who slipped past the Immigration watchdogs," Stockton had said. "Did muscle work in the beginning, moved up to bookie, then parlayed his connections among his better clientele to become a fixer to the K Street lobbyists and other political scumbags. To elevate his image, he channeled some of his gains into the pub."

After listening to my assessment, Noda said, "Okay. We go in harder and faster."

"Thinking the same thing."

Halfway through our brews, a young punk in a classic bomber jacket strolled in the front door with a proprietary attitude. He headed straight for the back rooms. We bided our time. No one else came or went, so Noda and I stood, stretched, and followed Bomber Jacket through the door marked PRIVATE. We heard the bartender shout after us, but we kept going and found ourselves in a long hall with half a dozen doors.

Noda grabbed my arm. We stopped and listened. A phone rang behind the third door on the left.

"That one," the chief detective said.

The bartender calling to warn the boss.

We plowed through the door at top speed. First me, then Noda. Sitting at a desk five paces into the room was Bomber Jacket. He held a tumbler with ice and whiskey in his hand. At his elbow stood an open bottle of Johnny Walker Blue, extracted from the top case of a nearby stack of five.

Bomber Jacket flung the glass at my head. I batted it away with my left hand and sidestepped his grasping arms as he surged up out of his chair.

I left him for Noda and dashed toward his boss, who sat at a desk farther into the room. The surveillance photos were accurate: Noakes had mean eyes, a large head, close-cropped black hair, and a round, hard body. He dropped the phone that had been pressed to his ear, and sprang from his chair with fists cocked, fury rippling across his features.

Eyes locked on the big prize, I didn't notice the punk push his leg out. I tripped and flew across the room. My momentum carried me into the side of Noakes's desk, both head and shoulder slamming into a wall of taut gunmetal. I slid to the floor with a groan.

"Bollocks to you mate," Noakes said, and kicked me in the ribs.

As he withdrew his foot, I rolled toward him, wrapping my arms around his ankles and wrenching them together. He tottered, then his burly frame tumbled over. I spun away and lifted myself up, wincing at the flicker of pain electrifying my ribs. My head ached. My shoulder throbbed. I took a moment to collect myself, and glanced back at Noda. He'd contained the punk but had yet to put him down.

Noakes took advantage of the second I'd let my gaze wander. Up on his knees, he yanked open a side drawer. He groped blindly for something neither of us could see. I kicked the drawer shut just as he started to retract his arm. Howling, he jerked his hand free, jumped up, then barreled into my chest. He forced me against the wall and began pounding my ribs as fast as he could manage with his meaty fists.

In boxing, this is where the referee steps in to separate the fighters. But there was no referee. My consciousness began to ebb.

I brought clasped hands down on the back of Noakes's thick neck. My signature move had no effect. Toughened muscle shifted but didn't give. The man was a bull. I felt my legs begin to melt. I clubbed him on both ears. More nothing.

With my remaining strength, I dug my fingers into Noakes's shoulders and shoved him sideways. He'd been listing to the right as he pummeled my midsection. He stumbled away, needing two large steps to recover his equilibrium. I brought my knee to my chest and snapped my foot up and out, striking him in the solar plexus.

The kick should have put him down, breathless and gasping. It didn't. Instead, it slung him back. He bounced off a far wall, staggered forward two paces, and was readying to rush at me again before sinking to his knees. Delayed reaction. He sucked in air. His chest moved in and out like a giant bellows. Color returned to his face. He began to rise. The man was a machine. Mule-solid.

I disabused him of any further advance with a roundhouse kick angling in from his blind side. It crashed into the side of his head. He went down, and stayed down. But not out.

"What the hell you want?" he said, hauling himself into a sitting position on the floor.

"I'm Brodie," I said.

Understanding flooded his eyes. "Screw you."

"Actually, tonight it's the other way around."

I jerked open the desk drawer and fished out a Glock. I examined the weapon and smiled.

"A full clip," I said. "You're too kind, Noakes. Time to answer some questions."

When he heard his name, my prey deflated. If we knew his name, we knew all. The fixer stared morosely, but didn't speak.

"Let's start at the beginning. You sent the Steam Walker after me."

"Who?"

"The hit man in Japan."

Who was not a man but that is information I have no reason to share.

"We just passed on names. We had no idea why."

"You were paid too well not to know why."

I got the morose look again.

I glanced at his desktop. There were no business papers or files or any of the flotsam of a flourishing bar business. I looked at the punk's desk. More of the same nothing. Noakes did have a red Washington Nationals cap, a small leather-bound journal that looked suspiciously like a bookie's notebook, and a tumbler with an inch of booze neat. Any of the actual paperwork needed to keep a robust pub running was nowhere in sight. The true back office was elsewhere.

I said, "You've got a nice front out there."

Some more air leaked out of him, but he kept his mouth shut.

"You're clearly a sharp businessman."

His eyes narrowed.

"Let's see if your smarts extend to survival. Give me the person who called you with my name."

Not a single word. But no denial.

"I don't have a lot of time, so last parlay, Noakes. I'll lay it out once. We can reason together and you don't get hurt, or I can hurt you and then we can reason together."

His mouth stayed shut.

"As a signing bonus," I said, "I'll leave you and your business standing. I have no use for you. Only the guy who passed on the kill orders." I waved the Glock at him. "Again. Full clip and I don't mind using it."

We got the next link in the chain.

CHAPTER 67

NOAKES spit out the names of two high-powered DC lobbyists. Extremely well-connected wheelers and dealers, he assured me. I didn't want to mess with them, he said. I assured him I did and would.

Then I cautioned the bar-owning middleman about passing on a warning. If I detected even a hint of his meddling, I'd come down on him with my own big sluggers. No matter what the status of his so-called hotshot lobbyists in this town, they would not be able to protect him. Further, they would tell me everything I wanted to know, and if Noakes passed on a heads-up, not only would I find out but I'd also come back and bust up everything in the House & Hill, starting with him.

"You don't look like you got that kind of clout in this town," Noakes said.

"Have your gofer pull up the FBI's number."

With a cocky mix of wariness and bravado, Noakes nodded and Bomber Jacket called up the listing on his phone. He was nursing a sore jaw courtesy of Noda.

"Now," I said, "have him ring them. When the operator comes on, ask for Dan Kastor."

Noakes nodded for his protégé to proceed. Bomber Jacket did as instructed, and when I held out my hand the punk tossed me the phone.

I hit the speaker function a second before my new FBI acquaintance came on the line: "Dan Kastor, Special Agent in Charge."

"In charge of what, I've always wanted to know."

"More than you'll ever find out, Brodie. You at the pub?"

"Yeah."

"Noakes there?"

"Yeah."

I pointed the face of the phone at the fixer and Kastor said, "Do what the man tells you, Noakes."

"Like I have a choice," Noakes said.

"Smart man. You might live to cheat another day. Call me later, Brodie," Kastor said, and was gone.

"So there you have it," I said, lobbing the mobile back at Noakes's underling.

Then I plugged the rest of the loopholes.

I stood over the thickset British transplant and told him that if his clients skipped town and I couldn't find them, I would come back and break things. If they were not *exactly* where they should be when we rang them, I would do the same. Then the FBI would hound him until he left DC. He'd lose everything.

On the other hand, if his clients were where they should be, I'd forget I'd ever heard of the House & Hill.

Would he continue to exhibit the survival instincts we all suspected he possessed?

He assured me he would. And apparently he had.

We had an appointment with the next link in the chain.

DAY 12, THURSDAY, 11 A.M.

We were quite a welcoming committee.

When Stockton ushered Thomas C. Correll and James Henry Barrett of Correll & Barrett into the second-story room of what was billed as a town hall mansion, the two men got an unexpected eyeful.

The expected attendees were Stockton, Noda, and myself. The ringers were Dan Kastor of the FBI and the inimitable duo of Brown and Green from the CIA. The three men sat together on a couch along the back wall.

Stockton cast a curious eye around the room. "Don't know why my people chose this place. I think it used to be a bordello."

"You're joking," I said.

He shook his head. "If this was ever a town hall, I'm Tinkerbell."

"You don't look that sprightly."

Correll and Barrett didn't know what to make of our chatter. Neither did they know who the three additional men were, but they knew at a glance *what* they were. The pair edged toward the door, but Stockton stepped forward and blocked their retreat.

"Make yourselves comfortable, gentlemen," he said, gesturing to a table in the center of the room.

"I think we'll stay right here."

Both men were blond. Correll was trim and tanned. Barrett had bulk.

Stockton shrugged. "Suit yourself." He turned the lock on the door and pocketed an old skeleton key.

Correll had been a behind-the-scenes powerbroker in the Republican Party, and Barrett was the son of a senator who sat on the Energy Commission. Inclusive of its founders, C & B had six employees—three support staff and one aspiring lobbyist it had taken under its greasy wings. Stockton had requested they leave the fledgling in the nest, and they had.

I jumped right in. "My three friends are only here to observe. You don't need to know who we are."

Correll recovered first. "We can work that way."

He wore a high-end blue designer pinstripe with an embedded silk thread. A pale-yellow handkerchief peeked from the breast pocket of his suit. It, too, was silk.

"Absolutely," Barrett said, taking a cue from his partner's newfound cheerfulness. Barrett was an aspiring blueblood who, Stockton had informed me, was piling up money and looking to marry for lineage.

"Good to hear," I said.

Then I told them what they would be supplying.

CHAPTER 68

"SOMETIMES, cases require mopping up," my father had once told me at the dinner table.

I was three years into my apprenticeship at Brodie Security. At fifteen, you pretend to understand everything, don't let on that you understood only a fraction, and commit all rarefied dialogues to memory until a point in time when meaning reveals itself. Many such conversations with my father, not to mention with Brodie Security operatives back in the day, were seared into my brain.

"You mean sweeping things under the rug," my mother said with a wry smile.

They were two years away from a vicious divorce, and already at each other's throats, but the threads of what had once been a full-fledged love, though frayed, still held.

My father gave her comment some thought. "No, not *under*, but *up*. Sewer scum can be tricky. You can't always bring them into a proper court of law, so you have two choices. Either let them loose or dish out the medicine yourself."

"Are you teaching our son vigilantism?"

"I'm teaching him how to kick maggots out of Dodge."

"I wish you wouldn't use such language at the dinner table," my mother said.

She was an art curator by profession. *Maggots* tested her sensibilities.

"As you wish. But make no mistake, son, their type are out there. And when there's no other way, you'll have to clean house yourself, or live with the mess. And if you don't kick them hard enough, they'll come back at you."

"Our hands are clean."

Correll reshaped his silk kerchief as he spoke. He was working on regaining his confidence. Under the blond hair were green eyes and a dimpled chin.

"Hardly," I said.

"We didn't lift a finger," Barrett added, echoing his partner's sentiment, as if the repetition would magically persuade us. His five-thousand-dollar suit seemed to underpin his confidence.

"Ah, but you picked up a phone," I said. "You *caused* it to happen."

Kantor, Brown, and Green watched with amusement. The untrained eye might interpret their practiced looks as contrite, which would be a mistake.

And yet it was a mistake C & B made. It also did not escape the pair's attention that the total cost of the three government men's suits wouldn't cover half of Barrett's outfit. Disdain flickered at the corners of their mouths, and they missed the bigger picture. Or, more likely, considered such concerns beneath them.

"Which you can't prove," Correll said, in a sudden shift in strategies. "Try anything and we'll squash you like a bug. We own this town. We know everybody in it. After we send you home with your tail between your legs, we'll find out where you live and—"

"—drink your blood for breakfast. Then, I, personally will—" Barrett paused in puzzlement, sensing a change he could not pinpoint.

A moment earlier, during Correll's rant, Luke, my old friend from Japantown, had slipped into the room through a back door hidden behind floor-to-ceiling blue velvet curtains. He stood in the corner deepest into the room. His hands were in his pockets. He wore a tailored gray suit. Like he always did.

Luke had listened politely to Correll, then the beginning of Barrett's follow-up. He didn't say a word, but a chill crept into the air. Then the faint wintry smell of his cologne permeated the chamber.

Eyes scanning the spacious suite, Barrett sensed Luke's presence without seeing him, his tirade collapsing in midsentence once he found the CIA freelancer, alone in a distant corner of the apartment.

Luke exuded a faintly frigid Nordic air. His cool slate-colored eyes did nothing to dispel the eeriness of his unannounced arrival.

Barrett stared, confused.

The dynamic of the meeting had shifted. Neither Correll nor Barrett understood how or why, only that it had.

CHAPTER 69

CORRELL, the powerbroker, found his voice first. "Who the hell is *this* guy? Aren't there enough of you people already? You think your new friend's going to stop us from gouging the eyeballs from your skull?"

"I didn't say he was a friend. In fact, he's not even here." I turned to Brown, who had helped me corral Luke on short notice. "Where is he exactly?"

"Wolfsberg, a small town one hundred and fifty miles southwest of Vienna."

Barrett, the congressman's son, looked nervously from me to Luke. "What are you doing, Brodie?"

Luke took a step forward.

"I'm not going to lift a finger," I said.

"Damn right you're not," Correll said, regrouping.

He reached for a phone on a side table. I slapped his arm away with my right hand, and with my left yanked the phone cord from its socket.

"What was *that*?"

"I misspoke. Sue me."

"We'll do more than that. We'll—"

Luke took another step forward.

Barrett's eyes went rabbit. "Keep him away from us."

"Who?" I said.

"The guy in the gray suit, you idiot."

"He's not here."

Correll turned to Luke. "And you, when we're done with you, you'll be wearing prison orange. We'll . . ."

As the wheeler and dealer spoke, Luke cocked his head an inch to the left and stared at him. His eyes, without any overt movement on his part, seemed to grow fainter and icier. Correll stopped speaking, and his own eyes became dark tunnels of fear.

Luke shook his head in the mildest of rebukes, as if scolding a child.

Once more taking his cue from his partner's verbal assault, Barrett stepped into the void. He was confident of his physicality. He worked out. At six-two, he was also three inches taller and fifty pounds heavier than Luke.

Barrett faced the new arrival. "Listen, I don't care who the hell you are or where you come from or how good your schoolyard stare is. Screw you and the dumb-ass donkey you rode in on."

Something changed in the clarity of Luke's pale-gray orbs. A gun glided out from behind the left lapel of his jacket without a ripple and he shot the verbal offender in the fleshy part of his hip above the bone. The bullet grazed the silk and nipped the flesh.

Barrett slapped his hand over the wound in disbelief.

The weapon disappeared back behind Luke's lapel.

A silencer had been attached.

Barrett sunk into panic mode. "What the fuck? *What the fuck? Whaaat the fuucccck?* You bastard, I'll sue you for everything you're worth and everything your parents are worth and everything—"

Luke eased the gun out once more and Barrett said, "You wouldn't dare. You wouldn't—"

Luke raised the weapon until Barrett could look directly down the barrel. The lobbyist shut up. Finally. For a guy with an expensive Ivy League education Barrett took an awful long time to connect the dots.

Luke panned his weapon in Correll's direction, and cocked his head as if miming a question.

Correll raised his palms. “No need for that. I’m listening.”

Luke said, “Both of you on your knees.”

Correll complied, a shaky smile on his lips. “No need to get violent. Just tell me what you want. I’ll fix it. That’s what we do best.”

Luke’s gun disappeared a second time. He stepped between the two men, grabbed a fistful of each lawyer’s hair, and, bending down, pulled their heads toward him until they looked like a cluster of three bushy coconuts.

Then he began whispering. It went on for five minutes in a soft steady hum. Neither lawyer spoke, which in itself was a miracle. I don’t know what Luke told them, but several times I heard key phrases like *your career* and *your family*. Motionless, the lobbyists listened. Barrett dripped only the occasional drop of blood on the carpet, testimony to the precision of Luke’s shooting.

After a time, the CIA ace straightened and stepped away from the two men.

“Brodie,” he said, giving a two-finger salute, then making to go. “Always a pleasure.”

“Anything I need to do on this end?”

Luke turned his cold gray eyes toward the pair and they both shook their heads.

“Ask your questions,” Luke said. He turned toward Noda, nodded, and walked out the front door.

We heard the two men’s confession.

Dan Kastor taped it.

A week later, the pair turned themselves in to the authorities, accompanied by a pair of DC’s highest-priced lawyers. Knowledgeable sources said they’d most likely lose their law licenses, receive three- to five-year sentences in a country-club prison, serve a token amount of time before they were released, and be back on the lobbyist circuit in half a blink, but several notches lower in the pecking order.

Correll and Barrett provided a single name.

Another link in the chain.

And it was a shocker.

A lawyer-on-lawyer connection. It made no sense whatsoever, but the lead was solid. The fear Luke had injected into the proceedings assured the point, even if lobbyists as a breed were among the slipperiest of DC's creatures.

The name?

Tad Sato, Naomi's husband.

DAY 13

FRIDAY

WITHOUT WARNING

CHAPTER 70

NARITA, JAPAN, 5:30 P.M.

THE moment Noda and I cleared Customs, we snagged a taxi to Tad's hospital, a ten-minute ride from the airport.

I rang Naomi from the cab and asked her to meet us in the cafeteria, then requested she keep our pending arrival a secret from her spouse. As a result, when the two of us strolled into an uninviting lunchroom with yellowed linoleum flooring and frayed tablecloths, we faced an apprehensive wife braced for bad news.

"I ordered you coffee," she said, gesturing for us to sit. "After flights to DC and back, I'm sure you could use some."

"Thank you," I said for the both of us.

A boomerang run was a fact of life when you dealt with Western countries from this side of the Pacific.

"How bad is it?" Ken's daughter asked.

"Bad," I said.

Naomi took the news poorly, but took it. Like the newshound she was. "Do you know how he could have gotten tangled up in all of this?"

"Blackmail," Noda said. "Or worse."

"Does it jar anything loose?" I asked.

Lips pursed, Naomi shook her head.

I said, "Just prepare yourself, okay? We don't know which way this will go."

Naomi stood firm. "Someone's pulling my husband's strings. That's the only explanation."

A thread of an idea dangled at the back of my mind. I took a sip of the coffee. It was hot, bitter, and strong. Naomi threw out a few more questions. I let Noda handle them so I could pursue the elusive thread. The man of few words answered the distraught wife with clipped responses before shutting her down with a bulldog shrug. Great.

I closed my eyes to concentrate. The thread was coming.

Naomi turned to me. "Brodie, do you have any more information you could give me?"

I signaled for silence with a raised hand.

We've got a lead. We're heading to the Karuizawa area and a place called Tsumagoi, I'd told Tad.

That was it. Her husband *knew* we were going out to Mount Asama because I'd been foolish enough to tell him. As an informer, Tad made a more likely candidate than either the warehouse caretaker or the Komeki truck driver. My spirits sank at the discovery.

"Actually," I said, "I do. But you're not going to like this, either."

"I'm listening."

"Tad may have set us up for an ambush near Mount Asama. When we stopped for soba."

"Why? How?"

I linked it all up for her.

Naomi looked conflicted. "If what you say is true, wouldn't that suggest that . . . that . . . the leverage on Tad is even more persuasive than we thought?"

"Possibly."

Or, as Noda had said, worse.

Her confidence in her husband did not waver. "They forced him. He's not a very physical man. Whatever it is, I can forgive him when he tells me."

She smiled, relieved at the thought.

I met her smile with one of my own, weak but consoling. She latched on to it with a desperation that broke my heart. I couldn't blame her. Whoever the unseen puppetmaster was, he or she had cleverly played to Tad's weakness. Where they'd failed with the wife, they'd succeeded with the husband.

The only question was, how far had he fallen?

CHAPTER 71

WE barged in on Naomi's husband unannounced.

Tad smiled and waved from his bed, the top half angled up so he could sit with ease. Gliding in behind me, Noda slammed the door hard.

Tad's welcoming grin faltered. "Something wrong?"

"Narita Airport was a sham," I said. "And so is all this."

Naomi turned pale at my unexpected gambit. I felt terrible, but it had to be done. Simply requesting an explanation, as she had suggested, would not shake out the truth. The situation required more. On the return flight, Noda and I had decided against any advance warning. We needed Naomi to see her husband's reaction unfiltered. We needed her to pass judgment about his innocence or guilt in real time, with as little prejudice as possible.

Tad watched my expressive hand gestures with just the right amount of bewilderment for an innocent party. His performance was very believable—unless you knew he was a lawyer and could tap into his courtroom stagecraft.

"What are you talking about?" he said.

I told him how the fixer pointed us to the lobbyists and the lobbyists pointed us to him. "You're going to tell us everything or I sic Noda on you. For starters."

Tad stiffened, his face reddening with rage. "Are you threatening me?"

"If you don't come clean, yeah."

"About what? You got my name from a couple of lawyers you probably browbeat just like this. How do you know someone isn't trying to frame me?"

"You had to be there."

"Well, I wasn't. There or anywhere else in your fantasy."

Naomi looked in my direction, questions in her eyes.

"But—" I began, but never got the chance to finish. Tad ripped into me with a razor-sharp cross-examination.

"A couple of lawyers halfway around the world drop my name when they know my family's under attack, and you believe them? Over me? Over *us*, your clients?"

His disappointment in my betrayal could not have been plainer.

"I—"

"You had your say, Brodie. Now let me finish. You bring me a wild accusation and you offer it as proof? Our names are in all the papers. On the news. On the Net. It's a setup. Look at me. The kidnappers beat me to a pulp. Do you know how long I've been laid up in this place? I've counted every stain on the ceiling, every spot of mold. Do you know how ridiculous you sound?"

"Well, I—"

"I thought you were our friend. I thought you were working *for* us."

Noda said, "Both sons are dead. Daughter's the last one."

Tad stared at the chief detective. "So I kidnapped my own wife? Are you insane?"

I said, "That's not exactly—"

"First you, then your bloodhound. You're both out of your minds."

Throwing back his blankets, Tad slid from his perch and came at me. Noda leapt forward. His fist connected with Tad's jaw and the lawyer went down.

CHAPTER 72

NAOMI stared at us in disbelief. "I think both of you should leave."

He's not a very physical man.

She was sitting on the bed, with her husband's head cradled in her lap. She dabbed his face with a damp cloth.

"Noda pulled his punch, Naomi. The idea was to—"

"I don't want to *hear* it. Go. Now. Please."

We trailed out and stood in the hall. I had thought this case could drag me no lower, but I was wrong. It hauled me deeper still, then blew up in my face. What Tad said seemed plausible. And looked impossible to refute. Had the lobbyists played us after all? If so, how would I ever explain this to Ken when he came out of his coma? If he resurfaced at all.

Noda said, "Probably should have pulled the punch more."

"We may have overplayed our hand."

"You believe him?"

"In my gut, no," I said. "But what he told us makes me wonder. You?"

"Don't believe him."

"You got *anything* we can use?"

"No."

I was conflicted. My gut screamed guilty. And yet, for Naomi's sake, I wanted her husband to be innocent.

We were in limbo. We had the links in the chain. But Tad had been convincing. His words burned holes in our theory. He was smooth. He was also a lawyer. We needed more. If there was more to be had. The lobbyists' admission was not a smoking gun, so we'd stepped lightly around Naomi, dropping hints before trying to badger her husband into revealing the missing pieces. But Tad had stood his ground. And, as he'd pointed out, his condition spoke volumes in favor of his innocence.

My cell chirped with a call from our young partner. I hit connect. "Hi, Mari, what's up?"

"So while you two were flying back from Washington, I did what you asked. And you were right. I found something."

I knew it. "Great. Tell me. We need it now more than ever."

"I hacked Tad Sato's work email and saw a pair of client names that were way uncool. So I lined up some white-hat hacker friends and we cruised the data streams. We hit gold."

A pair of nurses scurried down the hall and ducked into Tad's room. Seconds later, a staff doctor strode by, harried but dignified. He, too, stepped into Tad's private chamber, sending a frosty glance our way.

"What exactly did you find?"

"All of the husband's income comes from sources on the outer reaches of the nuclear mafia. Distant but connected."

Still not a smoking gun, but closer. "When did he start working with these clients?"

"Since soon after they got married."

Naomi had begun the protest activities several years before they tied the knot. This would crush her.

"We dug up more dirt in his tax records. They file separately, you know."

"Didn't know that."

"I asked our accountant to look over the data. She said, 'Tell Brodie the income from the original clients was barely enough for a lawyer with the usual office expenses to live on. Ninety-two percent of his current income comes from the nuclear crowd, most of it in the form of recurring retainers.' "

"That's troubling."

Good for us. Bad for Naomi.

"The uncool clients came after. Started out way slow. Two the first year. Then three. Now's he's got twelve."

"As if someone were feeding him a calculated supply?"

"You'd know more about that than me, but the weird thing is they are all companies on the extreme outer ring of the nuclear mafia. Most people would not make the connection."

The timing and clustering of nuclear-related firms were far too prominent to be a coincidence. Since the Fukushima blowout, any close association with TEPCO or a firm affiliated with them carried a crippling stigma outside the pro-nuclear clique, especially since TEPCO continues to cover up radiation leakage and other mishaps even years later. And yet, curiously, Tad had not blinked at the potential disgrace or conflict of interest.

I asked for the rest of Tad's client list.

Mari shuffled some papers. "Same half dozen minor clients he had before his marriage, plus a couple more. None in nuclear.

"How much money are we currently talking about?"

Mari told me. It was a juicy figure, yet walked a fine line. Tad could live exceedingly well on it, and stash away a grand chunk of cash, but the total fell shy of living exceedingly well ever after. Rather, the sum seemed just enough to seduce an ambitious lawyer into seeking bigger scores.

Some very shrewd deliberations had been made, I decided.

I asked the clincher: "Is all your data from official sources?"

We *had* to get it right this time.

"After his emails, yeah."

Before I hung up, I asked our computer whiz for two more favors, then set the details in motion: she was to send the first one in fifteen minutes, after Noda and I grabbed another cup of coffee.

"Cool," Mari said, giggling over my initial request as I disconnected.

I filled in Noda on what he hadn't overheard and the chief detective cracked his knuckles.

After we'd fueled up on black gold, we charged back into Tad's room.

CHAPTER 73

ONCE more propped up on his bed, Tad held his wife's hand. Naomi was perched on the edge of the mattress, scrutinizing the screen of her cell phone, which she held in her free hand.

When we rejoined them, she thrust her mobile in my direction. "What's the meaning of this email from your office, Brodie?"

The first favor I'd requested of Mari.

"Do you recognize any of the names?" I asked.

"All of them, of course."

The weird thing is they are all companies on the extreme outer ring of the nuclear village. Most people would not make the connection.

But Naomi Nobuki—former television newscaster, journalist, and antinuclear-power activist—was not most people.

"A list of your husband's clients *after* you two got married."

Tad sneered. "Let me see that."

Turning whiter by degree, Naomi passed the phone to her spouse. He snatched at the device angrily, gave the screen a dismissive glance, and said, "Where did you get this?"

Wrong response, Tad.

His wife stared at him. "What do you mean? Aren't you going to deny it?"

Her husband grew indignant. "Why should I? There's nothing improper here."

Naomi turned paler still. "Nothing improper?"

"No. It's just business. I have to make a living and the offers came my way. They're minor players, Naomi."

"But, Tad . . ."

He took his wife's hand in both of his. His voice softened. "You're right. They're minor to *me* but maybe not you. I'm sorry. I've been naive. Stupid, even. And whoever's attacking us is using my mistake against us to frame me."

Naomi hesitated. I felt my jaw clench. We were on the verge of losing out to the silver-tongued lawyer a second time.

Then it hit me. I'd been bothered by the DC connection. Stockton had run the telephone search through his virtuoso software, but just because he was based in Washington did not explain why the link he uncovered should also be in the capital.

I said to Naomi, "Does Tad have access to your phone?"

"Of course."

"So he could have passed on the email you sent to the Nuclear Regulatory Commission to his Washington connection, who would know how to leak them to the feds. That leak put you in an extremely dangerous position. The DHS has extraconstitutional powers. When they discover a national security threat, real or potential, they can whisk the subject away for questioning. There's a good chance you would have disappeared into the post–nine-eleven system for months, if not years, had Stockton and I not been there. That would take out another Nobuki family member."

And the one the nuclear mafia would most like to see disappear.

"Absolute nonsense," her husband said. "Don't listen to him, Naomi. It's all fantasy."

Tad's influence over his wife was potent. Naomi was torn. Just as any investigator would be. Or any jury.

Nothing stuck to this guy.

At that moment, Naomi's, Noda's, and my mobiles began buzzing in unison.

The second favor.

We each turned to our cell phone as a text message from Mari scrolled down our screens.

> *You were right again.*
> *The Kyoto office has three*
> *support staff for four*
> *lawyers. What you wanted*
> *was in the private text*
> *messages of the newest*
> *staffer. Her name is Kako*
> *Abiko. They seem "close."*

Naomi spoke first. "Brodie, what does this mean?"

"Why don't you ask your husband?"

"Tad, do you know a Kako Abiko?"

Tad blanched. His courtroom face vanished.

Which said it all.

"Tad?" Naomi asked again.

Her husband only shook his head. He was scrambling to counter this latest revelation. He wouldn't speak until he could set a new defense in place.

"Brodie?"

"Ms. Abiko works for your father's lawyer. She's the newest hire."

"I don't understand," Naomi stammered.

"Your father's will has gone missing. Did you know that?"

"No. This is the first I'm hearing of it."

"Its disappearance puts the family money up for grabs. With all the deaths, and a lawyer in the family, it isn't hard to imagine who would get control of the money eventually. Especially if your father doesn't make it. In your grief, you and your mother would naturally turn to your husband, the lawyer, for advice on how to manage things. Then the rest is only a matter of time."

Naomi looked from me to her husband. It was of me she asked her next question. "Are you absolutely sure about this?"

"I asked Mari to look for any correspondence where there is talk between your husband and any of the staff about disposing of the will, and she found it . . . among other things."

Naomi disengaged her hand from her husband's and eased off the bed. "Another woman . . . is . . . is . . . bad enough, but the rest . . . does it mean what I think it means?"

She was unsteady on her feet. Noda and I rushed to her aid.

Tad said, "Naomi, it's not like that."

"It's exactly like that," I said, "and more. There was no puppetmaster. No blackmailer forcing you to turn against your family. It was only you."

"That's not true."

"But it is. We have your personal correspondence with the secretary conspiring to destroy the will. That says it all. *You* arranged the death of your brother-in-law in Napa. *You* put the sniper on the roof. *You* all but threw Akihiro and his fiancée off the temple balcony. You, and only you, hired the Steam Walker."

Naomi was shaking her head in denial. "Tad? Tell them there's been a mistake."

"It's *all* a mistake, Naomi. Someone very clever is framing me."

I shook my head. "You can either tell me what I need to know or—"

Tad rolled his eyes. "Here we go again. Or what, Brodie? You'll sic your bloodhound on me? You think I don't know how the system works. I'm a lawyer. This is Japan."

I exhaled noisily. "On these shores, we may not be able to make a strong enough case that you had your wife's brothers killed, but you did, didn't you?"

"Of course not."

"We have a solid chain linking you to the kill orders."

"All circumstantial nonsense."

"From you to the lobbyists to the fixer to the assassin. It will hold up in an American court."

Tad gave me a look of pity. "A bookie and two slimy lobbyists. People who leech off the system? Who buy and sell everything your country has to offer? Those kinds of witnesses don't play well in Japanese courts, and they are easy to paint black in your courts too."

"I never said he was a bookie."

"Yes, you did."

"He didn't," said Noda.

"He did," Tad insisted.

Naomi raised her hand to her mouth. For the first time, she was seeing her husband unfiltered.

I said, "Your plan was very clever, Tad. Once they converted you to the cause, you figured out a way to get the Nobuki family money *and* ingratiate yourself with the nuclear mafia. Disguised as an attack on the Nobukis, your plan would get you access to the family bank accounts and open the Big Energy floodgates for years to come."

"Nonsense."

Naomi's legs gave way. We caught her. Tremors shook her small frame.

"I never mentioned the bookie," I said again. "We know it. You know it. And most importantly, your wife knows it."

Tad shot Naomi a reproachful look, and the mask fell away. "You got it all wrong, Brodie. I married into a rich family that kept me from the money."

His wife's eyes dilated. "What are you saying?"

I stayed quiet.

Noda stayed quiet.

Tad's contempt soured the air. "Your father's been giving piles of money to your artist-dilettante older brother for years, and was supporting the younger one, too. Where was *our* money?"

Naomi stared. "Toru's career was finally going someplace, Tad. You know how hard he worked, and how hard it is for a sculptor to make it in Japan. He got his first big commissions only this year. And Akihiro was still in art school. Of course, my father was supporting him."

"Nothing was coming our way."

"We don't need it. I'm doing fine and so are you."

"We're not doing fine. Our lifestyle is below par. Our house is cramped. We're not making it and your father could have helped."

There it was. The venom behind the legal veneer. He wanted bigger and better, and both of them faster.

Naomi's legs collapsed under her.

Noda and I tightened our holds.

"Ge-ge-get me out of here," she said.

CHAPTER 74

AFTER our encounter with the Steam Walker on Mount Asama, Noda and I had developed three plans of attack, with probability ratings of slim, slimmer, and slimmest.

With a prey as crafty as the Walker, we knew we couldn't sit on our hands. Giving her too much slack would only encourage her—and get us killed.

Plan One was, sad to say, our best shot.

As soon as we were safely away from the poisonous gas, we had rushed in spotters from Brodie Security on the bullet train and set them up in rental cars at four points of the compass to watch for the Walker's descent.

She had to come off the mountain eventually. We knew she could camp out for days, but we expected her to emerge sooner rather than later. And she did, the next afternoon, while Noda and I were in Washington.

We prepared our spotters for an extended wait. Provisions included food, beverages, a portable heater, regular and night-vision binoculars, blankets, and a new sketch based on our mountaintop encounter worked up by the fourth spotter, who was also our in-house sketch artist. Our people were not to approach the Steam Walker alone, but tail her from a distance, switching off lead cars regularly, until they could mount a task force of no fewer than six operatives. We had no intention of losing another person to the assassin's formidable skills.

The spotters spent a night in their cars, wrapped in blankets to counter the winter chill. Late the next day, a group of senior citizens stumbled on a married couple trussed up and gaggled behind a ten-foot boulder. Both were roughly the Walker's size. They had been relieved of their outer garments three hours earlier, including a gray felt Tyrolean hat with a silver band. By the time the information filtered down to our staffers, the Walker was history. On debriefing, one of our spotters recalled seeing the Tyrolean hat on a male hiker, who wore the husband's blue wool pants and the wife's gray unisex mountaineer's shirt.

The killer had slipped away.

Our first plan collapsed.

Plan Two began an hour after Plan One washed out.

The same staffers dispersed across the region, going from house to house. They were seeking a photograph of Kiyomi Komeki, the fashion designer. We wanted to confirm one way or the other whether she could be the Steam Walker.

We knew the killer to be a woman, but we didn't have a positive ID.

Since current images of the publicity-shy couturier did not exist, we set our sights on a snapshot from her school days. A class photograph, maybe. Or a team picture. Or a causal moment with friends. School yearbooks were not an option since the practice did not exist in the area.

The major hurdle was that rural schools were collective. One school might serve a dozen villages and could be located anywhere within the region.

The staff canvassed the area without giving away our suspicions. Absenteeism among the working adults was high. Many of the farmers spent long hours out in the fields preparing for the next planting, or were away in the big cities for winter jobs. Still others worked on the other side of Mount Asama, in the resort town of Karuizawa, which meant long hours and a lengthy commute. A further complication was the natural reticence of the villagers. They were protective of their local hero. All were aware of her celebrity status, as well as her keen desire for privacy. Even though only a few had ever met Komeki, no one wanted to be the Judas who betrayed her.

It took our four staffers, working in pairs for their own safety, two and a half days to track down a local who possessed a fading snapshot of the fashion designer and was willing to share it. It took another day to negotiate the conditions. We would be allowed to look at the image, photograph it on a mobile phone for in-house use, but under no circumstances could we publish it or pass it along to anyone else, including the media or the authorities.

After clearing it with me, the Brodie Security staffers accepted the conditions, signed an informal memo agreeing to the terms, paid a "viewing fee," and then captured the image on their cell phone camera. The photo was creased and faded. It had been taken at a traditional neighborhood festival when Komeki was in junior high school. She wore a modest pink kimono and a tightly knotted red headband. The staffers spent an additional day hunting down two more locals who corroborated that the teenager in the picture was in fact the elusive designer's younger self.

Once authenticated, Noda and I received a digital copy. It was immediately clear that Kiyoshi Komeki was not the Steam Walker. Where the Walker had a longish, slender face and nose, Komeki's features leaned toward the classic round Japanese visage with padded cheeks and a broad nose.

Plan Two fell by the wayside.

All that remained was Plan Three—the slimmest of the slim.

Our Hail Mary pass.

On the off-chance that the Steam Walker might show up at Kiyomi Komeki's home, we had people watching the hermetic designer's Tokyo residence in the upscale Setagaya area.

Our reasoning was simple—and desperate. There was a strong connection between the two women that we'd never been able to clarify. They both grew up in the region. The Steam Walker wore Komeki garments. And the Walker's corporate entity had subcontracted Komeki Inc. to deliver victims to the Mount Asama area, although we could prove nothing. That was the extent of our knowledge. None of it was actionable.

The desperation had to do with the outstanding contract on Naomi. We'd caged Sato. He was in police custody, but the Walker didn't necessarily know that, and there was no way to cancel the contracts he'd put out. A search of his home and office turned up a throwaway phone with two untraceable numbers in the log—presumably those of the Steam Walker and her agent. Both led to burners long ago discarded.

We called on Stockton to work his software voodoo a second time, but his efforts led nowhere. Similar exertions by Mari and her hacker squad proved equally futile.

Time and events were working against us. Naomi was being kept under heavy guard with the rest of her family in Kyoto. As for me, we had to assume the Walker would prioritize my hit whether she'd be paid or not, since I could positively ID her and link her to the other murders.

We had no leads. My date for departure came and went, as did Jenny's birthday. I couldn't head back to San Francisco and risk bringing the Steam Walker with me, so I stayed in Tokyo. The surprise birthday party I'd arranged a month before went ahead without me. Jenny called me the same night to talk about the games and cake and presents she opened, and I promised more when I returned, but I could sense the hurt and the loneliness behind her words that I'd missed the festivities. I downed a couple extra beers that night.

Then, three days after the photo search went belly-up, the unthinkable happened.

The Steam Walker resurfaced.

CHAPTER 75

SETAGAYA DISTRICT, TOKYO, 10:30 P.M.

AT half past ten at night, the Steam Walker was spotted letting herself into Komeki's house with her own key.

The alert went out immediately. I swung into action. As did Noda and six Brodie Security operatives. I arrived in fifteen minutes, with my shadows. Noda was already there. Including the three lookouts stationed at the house, we mustered thirteen of our people on site within half an hour.

"Police coming?" I asked Noda.

The chief detective shrugged. "Bicycle cops, maybe."

"What's going on?"

"Jurisdictional problems."

"Great."

Tad had been taken into custody out at Narita, where Naomi's assault and kidnapping had occurred. The fashion designer's Tokyo residence was some fifty miles from the airport, in an entirely different jurisdiction. I shrugged it off. As Rie had pointed out, the Japanese police were thorough but slow. What she'd left unsaid was that their results were at best mixed when it came to complex crimes.

We gathered a block away. Our sentries had eyes-on from three rental units, each with a clear view of one of the three entrances: front, back, and west side. Everyone was in radio contact. As Brodie Security was a private firm, we couldn't officially arrest the Steam Walker, but that didn't mean we couldn't bundle her up and hand her over to the authorities. Preferably without casualties on either side.

"Anyone know if Komeki is inside?" I asked.

"She left at seven this morning and hasn't returned."

"Better we do this now, then, before she returns. It'll save us aggravation and maybe an official complaint and B and E charges."

"It's all illegal," someone said in my ear. "We move, we break half a dozen laws."

I looked toward Noda. "That many?"

He nodded.

"That ever stop anyone before?"

A chorus of no's resounded in my earpiece.

"Good enough for me," I said. "Let's do it."

We split up.

Our spotters came down from their nests and we put four people each on the front and back doors, then five of us hit the darkened side entrance the Steam Walker had used. Two kicks frayed the doorjamb, freeing the lock. There was no dead bolt or alarm system.

Our small group carried three guns and two knives. Only one of the guns was registered, which meant the other two and the knives would need to disappear if and when the cops appeared.

The interior of the house was pristine and immaculate, the perfect expression of what I'd come to call the "*sappari* look." The phrase captured a clean and refreshing feeling that the Japanese craved. In the designer's case, the look manifested itself in white walls, white carpets, and white marble in and around black and gray furniture, all of which was light and airy and, where applicable, tubular.

Every surface was spotless and gleaming. Every object was both of those as well as creaseless, flawless, and, irrespective of size, set parallel or aligned at right angles to every other object in the room. Every item from furniture to floor coverings to accessories to knickknacks was placed to within a millimeter of its life. Pillows rested on couches and chairs at right angles and were fully fluffed. Books stood straighter than soldiers. Surfaces were clean and uncluttered and polished. The kitchen carried over the white color scheme with white cabinets, white walls, and white marble on the floor and counters. All the appliances were white.

Chaos and dirt had been banished down to the level of the microbe. There were no dirty dishes, no stray hairs, no stray crumbs, no dust motes.

We cleared the rooms one at a time. Each was as pristine and immaculate as the last. Each showcased the same color scheme.

The Steam Walker was not in any of the rooms unless she'd camouflaged herself in white.

Then a voice in my ear said, "I'm in the basement. There's a passageway."

CHAPTER 76

TELL us," I said into my microphone.

"It's an underground corridor. Plaster walls. Linoleum floor. All in white. I don't know where it leads. I can take a look or wait."

"Wait," I said.

The four of us joined the detective in the basement. He pointed to a door opening onto a long dark hallway, and said he'd expected a closet on the other side.

"Did you turn on the light?" I asked.

"No. Used a flashlight."

"Good."

Simpler booby traps have been planted, but a surprise here seemed unlikely. We'd run a property check a few days earlier and Kiyomi Komeki was the owner of record. Not her company, not a fronting firm with an innocuous name. Which meant her public image was in play and needed to be maintained. There would be no rigging of the house with spyware or traps.

Still, there could be a hideaway built under the pretext of, say, an earthquake-proof bunker. One of us would have to clear the hall and investigate what was to be found at the other end. Since the case was mine and I knew the Steam Walker better than anyone else, I was up.

The detective said, "There's another door about thirty feet in."

I said, "Okay, I'll go first, followed by Noda. Wait until we give the all-clear."

I borrowed a flashlight and a gun. I scanned the first ten-foot stretch of corridor—floor, ceiling, and sides. I was looking for cameras, switches, indentations, or any other sign of an installation. I found nothing. There could be micro-optic cameras or laser alarms, but if we were dealing with security on that level of sophistication, there was nothing we could do. Besides, time was short. We needed to corner the Steam Walker while she was still on the premises. If she'd barricaded herself in an underground capsule, so much the better.

I advanced into the tunnel. Inside, the air was chilly and stale. I scanned the next ten-foot segment, then the last. Nothing and more nothing. We reached the door. Gun drawn, I crouched and, behind me, Noda did the same.

There was no lock on my side. Slowly, I turned the doorknob. I met no resistance. The door opened inward. My flashlight revealed another basement-like room. I scanned the space from the hall, keeping low. No Steam Walker. No stockpiling of supplies. No extreme fortification. This was no bunker.

There was a staircase leading up.

I touched no switches and no objects. I spied no booby traps. Once we cleared the room, we called for the others. Cautiously, I mounted the stairs, Noda right behind me. The stairwell was obstacle-free. At the top, I flashed a quick look at Noda, who nodded. His gun was drawn and ready. He took high, I took low.

Round Two.

I turned the knob. There was no resistance. I cracked open the door. A domestic setting. No Steam Walker. No occupants of any kind. In increments, I eased the door open. An empty hall. White and pristine. So much for hideaways and last-ditch stands.

We cleared the passage and the back of the house, then motioned the others to advance. We had a view of the backyard. Trees and shrubbery obscured the homes to the sides and rear. Straight ahead was the kitchen; to the right, the front of the house. While the others guarded our backs, Noda and I cleared the kitchen. Then we covered theirs as they inched through the front of the house: a bedroom, a bathroom, and a spacious family room with a picture window. We found ourselves gazing out onto an entirely different street.

We were in the home directly behind the fashion designer's main residence.

I said, "How about I look around the kitchen while the rest of you check the top floor?"

Everyone agreed.

Pristine and immaculate ruled the second home as well. The place was fully furnished but felt emptier. I strode back into the kitchen and yanked open the refrigerator door. Empty.

Into my mike, I said, "Someone check the bathrooms for supplies. Quick. Let me know what you find. Toothbrush. Medicine. Soap. All or none of the above."

"We're on it," one of the team said.

I opened the kitchen drawers. Then the cabinets. There were no pots or pans. There were no cooking utensils. There was silverware for four. There were place settings for four. All basic and serviceable in a pinch. I found dry condiments. Salt, pepper, basic spices. All open and partially used. I could find no wet seasonings or sauces: soy sauce, mayonnaise, dressings. Nothing that might spoil or sour or smell up the place. There was no cereal, flour, or rice. No dry foods to invite bugs.

When a meal was to be had, it was ordered or brought home, precooked.

"I'm in the bathroom," an op said. "First floor. There's only one. I see towels on the rack. Unused. No soap on the sink, liquid or bar. Medicine cabinet"—there was a pause—"empty."

None of the above.

"Kitchen's the same," I said.

This setup belonged to the fashion designer, not the Steam Walker. Other than the connecting passage, no stealth in any form was involved. For form's sake, the designer had stamped her imprint on the place, but this was a ghost house.

Noda strolled into the kitchen.

I looked at him. "Now we know how Komeki manages to avoid the paparazzi."

And how the Steam Walker had just avoided us. We'd mustered a small army, covered all the known exits, and had still been hung out to dry.

Plan Three had just gone up in smoke.

CHAPTER 77

I RETURNED to my hotel in a taxi, seated alongside my two Brodie Security minders.

I was fuming. We'd missed the Steam Walker yet again. First she had escaped by going into the volcano. I could accept that, given her background. Next, we missed her coming down off the mountain. Again, understandable. Mount Asama was her home ground, and the paths leading to and from the peak were numerous. The Walker could choose any combination of time and place to descend. And she had, with the addition of a stolen disguise.

But in an urban setting more our territory than hers, the Steam Walker had outfoxed us for the third time. *With thirteen of us on site.* We'd accomplished the near impossible and found her; we should not have lost her. Despite the lousy underground passage between houses. We were better than that.

I had no words for the turn of events. And neither did my cabmates. What I did have was a mandate to get back to my daughter. We'd been separated far too long. I'd missed her birthday. My absence had soured what should have been a perfect day. I heard the heartache in Jenny's voice during each of our now daily talks, even on the occasions when she wasn't asking me about my return. And I missed her tremendously.

I had vowed to keep a studied distance between my daughter and the Steam Walker, regardless of the consequences. But with the trained assassin's third escape, time was up. This could go on for months without a resolution. I needed to pass the torch to Brodie Security and get back home. Let them carry on the search. I'd take two operatives with me to San Francisco for protection. But only two. Not the six rotating guards I had in Tokyo. Which meant I'd have to curtail a lot of our normal activities.

Caution above all.

Especially where Jenny was concerned.

We had far too much proof that the Steam Walker could operate effectively overseas.

Rie was waiting for me in my room.

With our romance still a matter of discretion, I said goodbye to my watchers in the hallway. The room lights were on and I heard the loud splash of running bathwater. Rie had worked the swing shift and had probably only just arrived.

"I'm back," I said. "It was a complete bust."

"Brodie!"

My ears perked up. Her inflection was odd. Maybe because of the acoustics in the cavernous, marble-laden bathroom.

"Yeah, it's me," I said.

No response.

My spine tingled. My body tensed. Adrenaline kicked in.

My mind whirled. I juggled the pieces. Rie had called my name with a measure of excitement a new flame always finds flattering. But the last syllable had been clipped, the inflexion distorted. As if she'd spoken into her shoulder. Or had been distracted as she answered.

My next impression a half second later told me there was more.

Excitement was accurate, but there had been an unidentifiable edge to her voice. Three seconds in I knew it was the wrong kind of edge. Not one of exhilaration or endearment, but of agitation.

Swiftly, I backtracked to the door, dashed across the hall, and tapped on my shadows' door.

"Get in here, guys. Now. We might have a problem."

I was less than a hundred percent certain trouble had arrived, but better embarrassed now than regretful later.

I didn't wait for their response. Every second mattered. I left my door ajar, then in two bounds was standing alongside the bathroom door. Not directly in front. Alongside. Seven seconds had elapsed. Two each way to cross the hallway and return.

I tapped lightly on the door. "Everything okay in there?"

A half dozen innocent reasons could explain the rising pitch of Rie's one-word greeting. As she spoke, she could have slipped slightly on the marble floor. Or been moving around the room, in the middle of a chore. Or maybe she'd tested the bathwater and found it too hot. All three scenarios and more would account for the distortion.

But I still had no answer from her.

Nine seconds.

The water continued to slosh into the tub.

"Rie?"

The bathroom was luxurious and large and almost a labor to navigate. Television, phone, two sinks set in a long counter, a full-length lounge chair, and an oversized Japanese bath with jets and multicolored mood lights. Maybe she'd called my name while moving across the room to a distant corner.

Still no answer.

There could also be a half dozen less-than-innocent reasons.

Eleven seconds.

"Rie?"

I hesitated to enter in case it was a trap. I glanced over my shoulder at the front door. My guards hadn't come when called. What could they be doing? I called louder.

I scanned the room. Nothing was out of place. Rie's purse was on the table. Her jacket hung in the closet. I called one last time.

"Rie?"

Thirteen seconds.

"Come in."

I froze. Another terse answer. Which was not like her at all. The invitation to enter had been uttered quickly. And softly. In a decidedly feminine voice within the range of Rie's register.

Fifteen seconds.

I turned the doorknob. It wasn't locked. She *always* locked the door. But if she had planned to invite me in, she would leave it open.

Seventeen seconds.

The hair on the back of my neck bristled. This didn't *feel* right. Didn't *sound* right. Rie was usually light and playful. There was no reason to be stingy with her words.

Nineteen seconds.

In either case I had no choice but to enter. I cast a last glance toward the hall. My backup was otherwise occupied. Not encouraging.

I could hear the water cascading loudly into the tub. I opened the door and stepped into the bathroom.

The lights were bright.

The marble floors sparkled.

With my second step, I could see all. And was the recipient of a second greeting.

"Hello, Jim Brodie."

CHAPTER 78

ADRENALINE fired my veins. Every nerve of my body buzzed. I shifted automatically into a fighting stance. I was primed, but the scene before me trumped any play I might have made.

As always the Steam Walker was a step ahead.

The living legend faced me across two yards of gleaming marble. She'd slipped into men's attire yet again. No Tyrolean hat this time but a short-haired wig and makeup that accented her cheekbones and jaw and sabotaged her good looks. She was wearing one of the confrontational faces she wore before an attack. The one she wanted people to remember if they remembered anything at all. Using makeup was smart. Arriving as a man was smart. Both sexes noticed attractive women. Particularly in a nice hotel.

Seeing the Steam Walker in my private quarters had kicked up my heartbeat a couple of levels, but what my eyes alighted on the next instant started it thundering.

Behind the Steam Walker was Rie. Her ankles were bound. Her hands were secured at her back. She was also gagged and blindfolded and stood—precariously balanced—on a three-legged stool.

With a noose looped around her neck.

The Steam Walker had made an alteration to the hotel's first-class bathing area.

She had installed an oversize toggle hook in the ceiling. A simple matter of drilling a hole and inserting the straight end of the hooked bolt, with its spring-loaded wings folded. Once the wing end was in place on the other side of the ceiling, the wings sprang open, the toggle was tightened, and the spreading wings formed an inverted V to accept the weight of what was hung on the hook.

Which, in this case, was the rope around Rie's neck.

The rope rose straight up from behind Rie's head, passed through the hook, then came down at an oblique angle and was secured to the plumbing under the nearest sink. On the marble countertop next to the sink was an electric drill. Alongside the tool sat the Walker's baseball cap.

"You've been busy," I said through gritted teeth. "What do you want?"

The Steam Walker held one end of a second rope. "First, this."

My eyes traced the length of the new cord. The other end was affixed to a leg of the stool on which Rie teetered.

"I see it. So?"

The Steam Walker leaned left and looked around me. "I am sure you understand, Jim Brodie. But before we negotiate, I need the hall door closed. Come straight back, otherwise . . ."

She raised her end of the rope another few inches.

I didn't budge. I didn't want to take my eyes off Rie. I didn't want to leave her alone with a rope strung around her neck. I cast a backward look. Where were my watchers? How had they not responded to either of my calls?

"Your two lackeys will not be joining us," the Walker said.

"Sure they will. And that will put an end to this charade. It'll be three on one."

"The door, Jim Brodie. Do not test me."

I frowned, but didn't move.

The Walker shook her head sadly. "Stubborn to no good end. I have taken your men out of the game. They stepped into a roomful of gas. It is odorless and takes effect in thirty seconds. They will sleep for three hours and live to work another day. Just not tonight. One last time, the door, Jim Brodie."

I stepped away, crossed the room, and shut the door, the Walker's eyes crawling over my back.

"Now return to us, please," she called. "Hands loose and open. Pick up nothing."

"Let her go," I said, stalking back into the bathroom.

"A nice sentiment. Men should protect their women. *The world* should protect them."

Coming from someone with her history of childhood abuse, it was a potent comment.

"I couldn't agree more. And a rule I think you would follow."

"Rie Hoshino will not be hurt if you do exactly as I say."

Woman to woman that might be true.

"So let her go. This is between us."

"Do as I say and I won't hurt her."

"What do you have in mind?"

"You only need to let me kill you."

CHAPTER 79

"THAT'S not going to happen."

"Oh, but it is, Jim Brodie. And I will tell you why."

Raising her rope hand, she took up the slack.

My heart clenched.

She said, "I can see you understand."

I didn't reply.

The Steam Walker chuckled. "I will interpret your silence as a yes. But let me lay out the timetable so your comprehension is complete."

She paused for a comment.

I stayed silent.

"Very well," she said. "As soon as I pull this cord, Rie Hoshino's body will drop and she will begin to choke. The fall is not enough to snap her neck, but she will be unconscious in ten to twenty seconds. It could take three to five minutes for her to fully suffocate, but with each passing second the lack of oxygen will be devastating. Brain cells will start to die. She will be a vegetable long before strangulation is complete, and even should you manage to get past me in, say, a minute or two, which we both know is unlikely, a revived Rie Hoshino will not be the Rie Hoshino you know and love. Her mental faculties will be partially or fully impaired. Do you have the picture?"

I was quiet.

"I need an answer this time, Jim Brodie."

"I have the picture."

"Do you see why you will do exactly as I ask?"

"Yes."

"And why you *will* let me kill you?"

"You can try."

"If I start, I will finish. There is one possible way out for you."

"And what might that be?"

"I am going to beat you to within an inch of your life so you will *never* come after me again. Never. Neither you nor any of your people. At the point where you are near the end, I shall make a final decision on whether you live or die."

"And how will you do that?"

"It will depend on your cooperation and attitude. I will ask you some questions about your future pursuits. If your answers are to my liking, you might live."

The move was shrewd. Dangle a glimmer of hope and the victim will walk straight toward his own death, with an eye peeled toward salvation. I did not believe her for an instant.

I said, "How can I be sure you will let Rie go in case I don't make it?"

"Two reasons. First, because I am a professional and give you my word. Second, because I took great care to make sure your Rie Hoshino did not see my face. You may confirm this for yourself, if you wish."

"Rie, is that true?"

She could not see or talk but she could hear. She nodded, then tried to speak. Nothing but a string of muffled sounds emerged. But her tone was enough to clue me in to the Steam Walker's earlier gambit. Rie had called out the first time. Most likely, she'd already been gagged. The Walker had probably loosened the binding long enough for her captive to utter my name. One word. Rie had tried to warn me. That explained the rising inflection, clipped short as the Walker jammed the gag back home. In round two, the Steam Walker had simply imitated Rie's voice, keeping her words low and short to be safe.

The Walker ignored Rie's extracurricular effort. "Satisfied?"

The Steam Walker would be merciless with me but she held nothing against Rie. Rie *could* survive the encounter precisely because she would not witness what was to come next.

"Yes."

"Shall we begin?"

"Yes."

"Then kneel for me, Jim Brodie."

And I did.

CHAPTER 80

THE Steam Walker struck without warning.

She glanced casually over at Rie, and when I followed her gaze, she swung into action with a swift kick to my stomach. Caught off-guard, I doubled over. A jolt of pain rippled through my abdominal muscles but I sucked up the burn.

Slowly, I straightened.

In defiance.

Until I was once more kneeling fully upright. I locked eyes with my assailant. Behind her, Rie was still, her head cocked to catch the sounds of the scuffle, none of which would be new to her.

The Walker watched me with mild interest. "You're stronger than I imagined."

I didn't give her the satisfaction of an answer. She would pounce the moment the first word left my lips. Instead, I drew in my abdominals and tightened my muscles all the way around, digging in for the punishment to come. I lowered my eyes to the center of her body mass, giving me an even-handed view of all her limbs. I would know the instant one of them shifted. Or stiffened in preparation for the next assault. Which would, in turn, allow me a fraction of a second to brace myself.

The Walker continued to examine me. "You're a clever man, Jim Brodie," and as the last syllable left her lips she unleashed a second attack.

The same kick. To the same place. The *exact* same place.

I doubled over again. My head dipped. A white light flashed behind my eyes. I clamped them shut as my already injured abdominals throbbed. I waited for the torment to fade. Then I opened my eyes, raised my head, and straightened my back.

I returned to my original position.

I said nothing.

The Steam Walker smiled. "Very admirable. But useless."

Her leg whipped out, once more targeting the same location. She was intent on reaping the brutal toll repetitive blows could generate. But it was also third-time dumb. Which surprised me. I wasted no time in taking advantage of her blunder.

Sucking in my stomach, I absorbed the bone-jarring kick, distress rocking every nerve in my body. I collapsed forward and locked onto her outstretched leg before she could retract it. When she pulled away, I rode the withdrawal and hauled myself up.

I was back on my feet, with both hands gripping her leg. I raised the captured limb to waist height.

She hopped back to account for the movement. "You should not have done that, Jim Brodie." She pulled the rope taut.

I pretended to ignore the gesture.

"Down, please," she said.

I remained on my feet. I held on to the leg.

It was as if I had not inconvenienced her in the least. With impressive control, the Steam Walker took another hop. Sideways this time. In a precisely measured length. The stool skittered sideways with her. A muffled exclamation escaped Rie's lips as she scrambled to adjust her balance.

Not *third-time dumb*. The Walker was merely confident in wielding her advantage.

Without another word, I released the leg and dropped back down to my knees.

An uneasy silence hung in the air.

I sought a way to overcome the Steam Walker's trap. She stared down at me with the same composure I'd witnessed in our previous encounters. A slight haughtiness had crept into the expression. Its message: her next move would be vicious and vindictive.

I wasn't wrong.

My opponent lashed out with a kick to the side of my head. Reflexively, my arm rose up in defense but her foot plowed right into it and they both smashed into my temple. I sprawled across the floor. The Steam Walker had held nothing back. The full power of her strike released bolts of white light behind my eyes.

"Back to your position, Jim Brodie."

Behind closed eyes flashes of light exploded, each linked to a stabbing pain coursing through my system. I was dizzy and nauseated.

"Return, Jim Brodie, or else. I will not make my request a third time."

Rie picked up every sound. When the last kick had sent me reeling over the marble, a groan had escaped my lips of its own volition. Rie responded with a long, incoherent protest. It went unanswered.

I dragged myself back to my original location. My mind worked furiously. How could I take down the Walker without jeopardizing Rie's already precarious position? I racked my brain but found no way around what appeared to be a perfectly calculated setup. Systematically, the Walker was chipping away at my stamina, my core. I couldn't hold out forever.

The imperious look of a conqueror infused the Steam Walker's features. "Are we a little less full of ourself now, Jim Brodie?"

"I'm not sure that was ever the case," I said, which proved to be the wrong answer.

Her wrath unfurled itself in a cascade of blows. Stinging jabs. Hammer punches. Snap kicks. Then a knee to my face, which I avoided, but not fully, taking the brunt of the thrust on my ear.

The barrage was remorseless and kept me in a continual state of recoil. I covered myself as best I could, but without the ability to counterattack, there was little I could do. The Walker connected with a crushing kick to the ribs I hadn't seen coming, and I felt a rib crack. I grunted, smothering the hurt as best as I could.

The pounding continued. Ten, twenty, thirty strikes. Waves of pain rippled through my body, lapping into every corner. I blocked what I could but many got through. Close-fisted cracks and blistering kicks. An endless assault. From my paternal side, I'd inherited a high pain threshold, but the Steam Walker was making substantial inroads toward dismantling it.

Eventually I toppled over. The pummeling continued, so I took the only available choice. I curled up in a protective fetal position, my knees drawn in, my arms slung over my head.

The onslaught ceased.

Blood from my ear, nose, and a gash on my leg streaked the marble.

"Back to your position, Jim Brodie."

I shuddered, without rousing myself. I needed time to recover. Muster my strength. My thoughts. My last reserve. I scrambled for a way to circumvent the Walker's ploy, but it looked unbeatable. The minute I made a move, Rie would be hung. The Walker had only to wrench the stool out from under Rie and hold me at bay. I wondered if she'd learned this setup from the other Steam Walkers.

I couldn't last much longer. I had managed to stay conscious but was fading. Once I sank into darkness, all was lost. I no longer had illusions about her intended outcome for Rie or me. The Walker would not let a policewoman live, even if she was blindfolded.

An image of Jenny flickered through my thoughts. Someone would come forward to take care of her. Maybe the Rennas. She played well with their children, and Renna owed me. Less than a year ago, I had been counting on Bill Abers to fill the role if an emergency arose. My onetime shop assistant had practically been an uncle to Jenny. But those days were gone.

"Back to your position, Jim Brodie."

I lifted my head. I peered at my tormentor. I saw Rie's head poking over the Walker's shoulder. I opened my mouth to speak, then goose bumps flecked my arms and back. Not out of fear but because of what I'd just seen.

From this position, Rie and the Walker were aligned, with Rie two yards to the rear. The arrangement triggered a memory. About the unworkable. The impossible.

And yet the vision lingered.

"I expected more from you, Jim Brodie. If you can't rise, then it is over."

"I'm getting up," I said.

I struggled to my knees. The Steam Walker stood with her feet spread and aligned. I needed her to pull one leg back. But with the newfound arrogance her stance suggested, a shift seemed unlikely.

I fell forward.

The Walker laughed but did not stir. A glow of triumph infused her features. "I overestimated your skills," she said.

I started to rise again.

The Walker watched me with supreme satisfaction. I was on my knees, my hands on the floor to support my flagging bulk. I tried to straighten up, then fell forward a second time, my palms dropping back to the cool marble.

The Walker maintained her stance.

"We are almost finished here, Jim Brodie."

I drew myself up. My torso began to straighten. As I did so, I pulled one leg back farther, tucking the knee under. Behind my back, my foot came up on its toes. It arched. I made as if to stand again.

Then I exploded out of the crouch. I sprang off my back foot like a sprinter off a starting block. Only I surged upward more than forward, pushing with both hands as well as my feet. I leapt high. The move required height. I'd learned it in Bangkok five years ago at a Muay Thai training camp run by a friend, but I never imagined finding a practical use for the impressive but nearly impossible maneuver.

I was mistaken.

When events have taken you beyond the realm of the possible, avenues to the impossible open.

Then it happened.

As it always does when the adrenaline in my blood surges beyond a certain level. As they say it happens to a clutch ball player when he waits at the plate, hoping to connect with an unhittable pitch. Or when a wide receiver stretches his fingers out to reel in the unreachable catch. My awareness expanded. My senses kicked into overdrive. My eyes parsed movements in microseconds. I saw the action in a frame-by-frame sequence. Clearly delineated as I sailed through them—allowing me to sharpen my response.

The Steam Walker inched away. The slack in the rope increased. She dropped one foot back. I focused on the front leg, the thigh now slanting away in partial retreat. Believing me no longer a threat, the Walker felt no need to relinquish much ground. The rope still gave her the ultimate power over me. She raised it now in warning.

Adrenaline raged through my system. My body kept rising, propelled by strong, muscular legs. One of the side benefits of martial arts training.

The Steam Walker was puzzled. She couldn't see a strike forming. Neither my arms nor my legs were shifting into offense positions.

That was the beauty of the move. One of several.

My leap carried me higher. The moment came. My forward foot landed on her forward thigh. A second launch pad had been established. I pushed myself upward again. The knee of my opposite leg smashed into the middle of the Steam Walker's face. I heard cartilage crunch. My momentum hurdled me over her falling body.

I locked my eyes on Rie. I had planned to land on the edge of the stool but it was skirting away. The Steam Walker's reflexes were superb.

Even as she tumbled over backward, she wrenched the stool out from under Rie.

Rie's body was dropping.

The rope above her head snapped taut against the hook overhead.

Rie began to choke. A horrible gaggling sound escaped her lips. Her arms and legs churned against their restraints. I heard the crack of the Steam Walker's head on the unforgiving marble. In her vindictiveness, she had sacrificed the moment she needed to cushion her fall.

I plowed into Rie. Her body swung away from me. I found my footing and reached out. I wrapped my hands around her writhing form—and lifted. The rope slackened. Rie wheezed as she drew in fresh air. I shifted her sideways and disengaged the rope from the hook. Then I set my policewoman girlfriend down and ripped off the noose, the gag, the blindfold.

I glanced over at the Steam Walker.

She lay motionless on the white marble floor, a trickle of blood winding its way out from behind her head.

She was anything but pristine and immaculate.

EPILOGUE

THE SUN, THE MOON, THE TRUTH

THIS time the doctors persuaded me to stay. For fifteen days. I had two cracked ribs, a ringing in one ear, and countless bruises, to which they applied a glistening salve three times a day. Rie was a few rooms down, with a light rope burn and a sprained neck. But she was up and about and came to see me as often as she could.

Once I was released, we spent a weekend lingering in the restive waters of a secluded hot springs resort, then at long last I flew back to my daughter. Before I left, I broached the subject of latent psychological scars with Rie and she read me the Hoshino clan riot act about their being a law enforcement family, her being third-generation, and none of the men being as tough as she. I didn't bring it up a second time.

My return to San Francisco was joyous. Jenny leapt into my arms, hugged me, and refused to let go. I finally pried her loose with a promise of her favorite gelato. She upped the ante by asking permission to sleep in my bed. I accepted.

Knowing she'd stumbled onto a good thing, my daughter repeated the hugging act for ten days. By way of apology, I let her. And bought her gelato on each of those days as well. On the eleventh day, we rested.

The Steam Walker survived.

She regained consciousness the next day, and was transferred to a jail hospital. Arrest papers had been issued.

Kiyomi Komeki was questioned. The reclusive clothier had known the Steam Walker since grammar school. They were each other's oldest friend. The story spread by the Walker's abusive father when the teenage girl ran off into the hills was that she was staying with distant relatives.

Komeki never associated her classmate's disappearance with the legend of the Steam Walkers. It was easy enough to believe that a strong-willed girl would want to escape the cloistered village of their youth. By the time her friend was making a career of assassination, the mythic figure of a reemergent Steam Walker had shape-shifted into a man.

The pair was reunited in their late twenties, when the Walker showed up on Komeki's doorstep for a visit, as a small-time importer and exporter of furniture. Komeki was thrilled to offer her friend use of her transportation network, and to invite her childhood playmate into her home anytime she found herself in Tokyo.

Stunned by the news of her school chum's betrayal, Komeki supplied the Tokyo police with the Steam Walker's real name. When a detective dug into the Walker's past, they discovered she was an only child, her mother had died during an accidental spill on a staircase, and her father had disappeared one morning on the way to work and was never heard from again.

SAN FRANCISCO AND TOKYO

Ken Nobuki emerged from his coma six weeks after the shooting, healthy and cheerful, though with residual problems. His speech was ragged at first and he had trouble recalling certain words and parts of his life. Therapy brought mental and physical improvements, and doctors felt confident the setbacks would be overcome. Ken was itching to return to Japan and climb back behind his potter's wheel, but a clean bill of health was not immediately forthcoming.

Naomi, Mrs. Nobuki, and Shu flew to San Francisco to be with him. His wife and grandchild stayed two weeks, then returned to Japan for Shu's schooling. Before the eight-year-old left, he asked to visit his friends at the Napa County Sheriff Department. Mrs. Nobuki tried to talk her grandson out of the idea but soon found herself unable to refuse his animated and oft-repeated request.

So, on a crisp sunny Northern California afternoon in the opening days of February, I drove Ken's wife, daughter, and grandson out to Napa. Sheriff Nash and police sketch artist Cheré Copeland greeted the arrivals at the station steps as if they were royalty. Inside, a surprise party awaited Napa's star witness. Shu received a hero's welcome from the whole department and was presented with an official Napa Sheriff Department hat, scaled to size. After cake and ice cream, Shu was given a ride in the sheriff's personal patrol car, with escort vehicles front and rear.

The three-car procession drove at a regal pace into the city of Napa, where the mayor presented Shu with keys to city and county, followed by a case of "children's wine"—a dozen bottles of high-end grape juice with personalized labels from a famous local winery that read FROM THE CELLAR OF SHU NOBUKI. A case of the adult version was lavished on Mrs. Nobuki. I translated every word for the young star. Rare was the moment when a grin was not splitting his face from ear to ear. The whole affair brought tears to his grandmother's eyes on more than one occasion.

After Shu and Mrs. Nobuki flew home, Naomi found long-term accommodations near the hospital and visited every day. She talked to her father, read to him, brought him Japanese snacks, and sat quietly by his side. I stopped by often, at times bringing Jenny.

In the fifth week of Naomi's tenure, the baton was passed to Japanese doctors of the family's choosing, and Ken and his daughter boarded a plane for home.

I may have mopped up the mess, but I was far from satisfied.

We'd nailed Tad Sato. We'd nailed the Steam Walker. We'd nailed two Washington vermin.

Yet one of the guilty escaped without a scratch.

I had hoped to land a few blows on the overfed ogre that was the Japanese nuclear cartel. Instead, at the other end of the tunnel, I found a greedy husband who had succumbed to the oceans of money they circulated—as had the legions of politicians, bureaucrats, media bigwigs, and professors before him.

TEPCO and its cronies were guilty by association. Naomi, her family, and I handed down a private sentence against them, but the broader scope was an issue for the people of Japan to resolve, with Naomi and others like her leading the charge.

On my end, taking out a few lobbyists—locusts who gnaw away at the heart and soul of the American system—made for a respectable consolation prize, though it paled in comparison. About the time I'd resigned myself to a runner-up position, Naomi called. After an exchange of pleasantries, she said, "Brodie, do you know the expression 'Three things cannot be long hidden: the sun, the moon, the truth'?"

"Yes, I see it often, sometimes as an inscription on some Buddhist piece. What about it?"

"I'm back on the road with other activists. And it's coming, Brodie. I can feel it. We'll get there." She meant *to the truth.* "Despite the evil, the cronyism, the corruption. It's coming."

"Very glad to hear it," I said.

And in my mind's eye, I set the runner-up trophy aside.

SAN FRANCISCO

Tension electrified the room.

In Sarah's eyes was expectation of the highest order; in her husband's, apprehension of equal measure.

The three of us sat in the private viewing room at the back of my antiques shop. In chairs set around a low William and Mary table, with a Charles Burchfield watercolor watching benevolently over us, I spread out a velvet cloth on the table to protect the table's surface and brought out the Oribe tea bowls—not one, but two. After which, not one but two gasps escaped Sarah's lips.

She drank in the pair of bowls—the black-over-white one I had hand-carried from Kyoto, and Takahashi's "returnee," which had arrived last night and lived up to its billing as a minor masterpiece. A smile she could not suppress spread across Sarah's face.

"Oh, Brodie, this is the best. You're the best."

"So, the new one?" I asked.

It was in the classic green-and-white mode.

"Yes, if . . ."

She cast a deferential look toward Sean, who nodded without hesitation.

I said, "No pressure. I imagine I'll be able to find another buyer if you don't want it."

Which, of course, was a major understatement. The piece wouldn't last a week after I'd made a few calls, and Sarah knew it. The comment was mostly for her husband's benefit.

"I'm grateful you showed it to me first," she said. "This will be our collection's crowning piece. Are you sure it's okay, Sean? Moneywise?"

Our. I glanced over at her husband. He blushed.

"Yes, of course," he told his wife.

Sarah had tears in her eyes. She leaned over and hugged her husband, then excused herself to freshen up.

Sean watched his wife walk away, then glanced my way. The strife of our first meeting had melted away. Fortunately. I'd had my fill of contentious husbands.

"I haven't seen Sarah this happy in a long time," he said.

"You might have something there."

"Damn decent of you to give us first crack."

"My pleasure," I said. "The bowl's found a good home. Maybe a great one."

"I appreciate the heads-up, too."

I'd called Sean to explain that I had good news and a dilemma. I told him about the Takahashi bowl. When he asked if the other bowl was inferior, I said far from it. Both would make good acquisitions. Because of their different color schemes, some people would want the pair. Think classic Caddy versus classic Rolls. It depended on your preference. I could show Sarah the Caddy and closet the other piece. The Caddy fit her needs perfectly. It met his budget. Sarah would want it. She'd be happy. It would make a good addition to their collection. I could sell the Rolls in a flash to another client, so there was no pressure on them. But he should be forewarned. The local tea world was small. The likelihood that Sarah would run across the piece in a year or two or five was great. Then she would want to add a piece of the same level to her assemblage. I didn't know what to do. I liked Sarah. She was a favorite customer. But I would abide by Sean's decision, and keep it between us. "You," I'd said, "have to decide for the three of us." He opted to show Sarah both bowls.

Now Sean said, "I suppose I should be a wee bit jealous."

"Of what?"

"That you could make my wife so happy."

"It wasn't me. It was the bowl. Maybe you could be happy *with* her."

As the words left my lips, a soft finger plucked at my heart. My thoughts strayed to Mieko, my deceased wife, Jenny's mother. Not that I needed to summon her consciously. The physical connection we'd shared in this life had been severed, but her presence was strong and vivid whenever I reached for it.

Sean saw something in my expression he couldn't interpret, and he was shrewd enough to leave it be. "You're a good man, Brodie. No hard feelings?"

"None whatsoever."

He smiled and held out his hand. I shook it, then he walked away with a lighter step to meet his returning wife near the middle of the shop, where he slipped an arm around her waist, whispered in her ear, and kissed her cheek. She smiled and kissed him back.

Brodie: art dealer, widower, adviser. Father, boyfriend, second-generation PI, and now—apparently—marriage counselor.

Funny how that works.

ABOUT AUTHENTICITY

Here's what's true.

In Kyoto, the Kiyomizu-dera is a long-established Buddhist temple with roots dating back more than twelve hundred years. Those planning a visit will be well rewarded by approaching the temple complex from the Ninen-zaka and Sannen-zaka walkways, a pair of picturesque historical lanes.

The Arashiyama district on the outskirts of Kyoto does indeed have grand bamboo forests that are illuminated part of the year. Nearby are a number of restaurants, temples, and shops. However, some of the best treasures the area has to offer can be found on the other side of the river, and are easily explored by bicycle, which can be rented locally.

The information about cosplay, manga, and vocaloids is accurate. The Kyoto International Manga Museum is, in comparison to the city's twelve-hundred-year-old history, a recent addition, having been established in 2006 in a former elementary school in the center of town. The museum has become a must-see for both Japanese and international manga fans. While the collection contains a few English-language manga, the vast majority of the volumes are Japanese. That said, since manga comics are a highly visual form of expression, enthusiasts should be able to find some displays and books that appeal to their sensibilities. Items in the gift shop will most likely also keep them entertained.

Mount Asama, the resort town of Karuizawa, and the village of Kanbara are actual places. Mount Asama is a twenty-minute drive from the town of Karuizawa, or a good two and a half hours by car from Tokyo. The village of Kanbara was indeed buried after one of the volcano's most notorious eruptions. It has been rebuilt and there is a modest local museum with exhibits and artifacts.

The volcanic hinterland known as Onioshidashi ("What the Devil Pushed Out") sprawls across a portion of the volcano's flank. A section of the alien landscape has been "tamed" to accommodate visitors.

To this day, volcanic hotspots dot the Japanese countryside. A tour through certain regions will yield vents and other "holes" where steam and hot spring waters spew forth on a continuous basis. In some parts of the country, steam rises up along mountain roads, creating an eerie sense of stepping back through time.

The brief geological references about the formation of the Japanese archipelago are also accurate. Coincidentally, around the time I began writing this book, an underwater eruption in Japanese waters some six hundred miles south of Tokyo gave birth to a new island, which in its expansion eventually combined with a small speck of an island known as Nishinoshima, the name the fused landmass assumed. As of this writing, the slowly expanding island is approximately one square mile in size, with a plume of white smoke rising from its center.

The events of the disastrous earthquake and tsunami, as well as the resultant triple meltdown of the Fukushima nuclear power plant, happened. Anti-nuclear journalists and media personalities remain at risk. Despite scathing reports from the US Atomic Energy Commission, the Fukushima Nuclear Accident Independent Investigation Commission (sanctioned by the Japan's National Diet), and the UN's International Atomic Energy Agency (IAEA) that involved 182 experts from 41 countries, the nuclear industry's business practices do not seem to have progressed beyond cosmetic changes. Cynics have postulated that the Diet report was allowed to see print in order to throw some crumbs to outspoken critics in Japan and present the image of a self-reflective Japan overseas, while behind the scenes the industry is permitted, with the government's blessing, to carry on as usual.

Fortunately, other forces are on the move, so the last chapter in the drama has yet to be written. (I should like to add that determining the nuclear mafia's potential for violence is a chore I will leave to nonfiction writers. My exploration is fictitious, as is, of course, Dr. Ohashi and his think tank.)

On the art side, Furuta Oribe (born Furuta Shigenari, 1544–1615) was a tea ceremony master and samurai recognized in part for his patronage of the ceramic style known as Oribe, named in his honor. He was instrumental in offering a more flamboyant slant on Japanese tea ceremony utensils than that preferred by his contemporary, the legendary tea master Sen no Rikyu. At its best, Oribe ware can be profound.

Traditionally, as mentioned in these pages, Oribe ceramics have two color schemes—green and black. Classic as well as contemporary pieces reside in museum collections throughout the world. These include tea bowls, fan-shaped dishes with and without lids, square and asymmetrical dishes with and without handles, tea caddies, ewers, small food vessels, and more. The pieces of the early Oribe potters remain as fresh and stunning today as when they were first crafted some three or four hundred years ago.

The Japanese tea bowl, of which there are many styles, is a central piece in the tea ceremony; the points of appreciation mentioned by Brodie as he inspects the offerings of his fellow art dealer are accurate.

Heading stateside, the San Francisco City Hall and the Asian Art Museum face each other across a plaza in the Civic Center section of the city. The Napa County Sheriff's Department is headquartered in a building near the Napa Airport. The di Rosa preserve is a prominent art destination in the Napa Valley. A visit makes for a pleasant afternoon. The art is big and brassy, the galleries inspirational, and the grounds worth exploring.

The work of the fictional police artist is based on a lengthy session I had with an actual police officer and forensic artist with FBI and other training. She is mentioned in the acknowledgments. I sat through a full session in which I described an acquaintance as if I were a witness to a crime he had committed. Her accuracy was uncanny.

In Washington, DC, the Willard and all the landmarks do, of course, exist. Chinatown is there in name, if little else. The House & Hill pub is, for better or worse, fictitious.

The upscale izakaya Uoshin in the Shibuya district of Tokyo where Brodie and Rie meet for the first of two dinners also exists, as does the fugu restaurant, Miura-ya, in the Asakusa area across town. Regardless of the blowfish establishment, the selection of dishes Brodie partakes of is a meal I have sat down to—and lived through—numerous times. Knock on wood.

ACKNOWLEDGMENTS

As always, I owe a deep debt of gratitude to my publisher, Simon & Schuster, and my agent, Robert Gottlieb of Trident Media Agency. Both have offered insights and given support that make the Jim Brodie series possible and better. At Simon & Schuster, I am indebted to Jonathan Karp, Marysue Rucci, Richard Rhorer, Sarah Knight, Elina Vaysbeyn, Brit Hvide, Leah Johanson, Jill Su, and Kaitlin Olson. At Trident, to Erica Spellman-Silverman, Mark Gottlieb, and Adrienne Lombardo; and at Creative Artists Agency, to Brian Pike.

I wish to thank Christine Golez, retired police officer and detective of the Fairfield Police Department, who is currently employed part-time at the Suisun City PD. Christine combined her policing and artistic talents to become a top forensic artist. She was kind enough to take time out from her busy schedule to lead me through the intricacies of the procedure. Based on subsequent collars by her colleagues, the accuracy of her police composites is impressive.

Additional thanks are due to Dr. William Sherman for his medical guidance, and to Dr. Robert Shpall, and his wife Beverly, for the introduction and general medical advice; to Shuji Yoshida, a Japanese geology professor who studies volcanoes and natural disasters in Japan; to Japanese-to-English translator Gavin Frew for reading behind me, and to his wife, English-to-Japanese translator Fumiko Yokoyama, for overall support; to Shigeyoshi Suzuki and Marc Lancet for lending me works from their personal libraries for my research; to Mio Urata for introducing me to the restaurant Uoshin; to Patrick Sherriff, whose interview inadvertently spurred me on to write about Japan's triple disaster—3/11—several years earlier than planned; likewise to those readers who attended my book talks and asked cogent questions about the disaster, driving the point home; to Hajime Saito for assistance with the mountain climbing terminology and Ginny Tapley Takemori for the introduction; and to the ever-vigilant, eagle-eyed production staff at Simon & Schuster: Kathryn Higuchi, Anne Cherry, James Walsh, and Ellen Sasahara.

I am indebted to Anthony Franze—friend and fellow writer—for generously finding the time in his ever hectic schedule to show me the ins and outs of his city, Washington, DC. And thanks to his wife, Tracy, for allowing me to steal him away for lengthy periods of time. I owe an additional debt to Anthony and our fellow editor of *The Big Thrill*, Dawn Ius, for giving me some leeway during the more intensive periods of writing this book, when I disappeared offline for a few days at a stretch.

As before, I wish to thank all the booksellers throughout the United States and Canada for their continued support, some of whom are mentioned in the acknowledgments of *Tokyo Kill*. This time I would also like to give a special shout-out to Parisian bookseller Jérôme Toledano for his tireless support of the French editions of the Jim Brodie series, starting with *Japantown* and *Tokyo Kill*.

And last but never least, my undying gratitude once again to all my family and friends for backing me up on so many levels.

ABOUT THE AUTHOR

BARRY LANCET's *Japantown*, an international thriller, won the prestigious Barry Award for Best First Mystery Novel and was selected by both *Suspense Magazine* and mystery critic Oline Cogdill as one of the Best Debuts of the Year. His second book, *Tokyo Kill*, is a finalist for a Shamus Award for Best P.I. Novel of the Year. The third entry in the Jim Brodie series is *Pacific Burn*.

Lancet moved from California to Tokyo in his twenties, where he has lived for more than two decades. He spent twenty-five years working for one of the country's largest publishers, developing books on dozens of Japanese subjects from art to Zen—all in English and all distributed in the United States, Europe, and the rest of the world.

His unique position gave him access to many inner circles in cultural, business, and traditional fields most outsiders are never granted. Early in his tenure in the Japanese capital, he was hauled in by the police for a noncriminal infraction and interrogated for three hours, one of the most heated psychological encounters he had faced in Japan to that point. The run-in fascinated him and sparked the idea for a mystery-thriller series based on his growing number of unusual experiences in Japan.

Lancet is based in Japan but makes frequent trips to the States.

For more information, please visit http://barrylancet.com/ or look for Barry on Facebook and Twitter (@barrylancet).

Turn the page for an excerpt from Barry Lancet's next Jim Brodie adventure.

THE SPY ACROSS THE TABLE

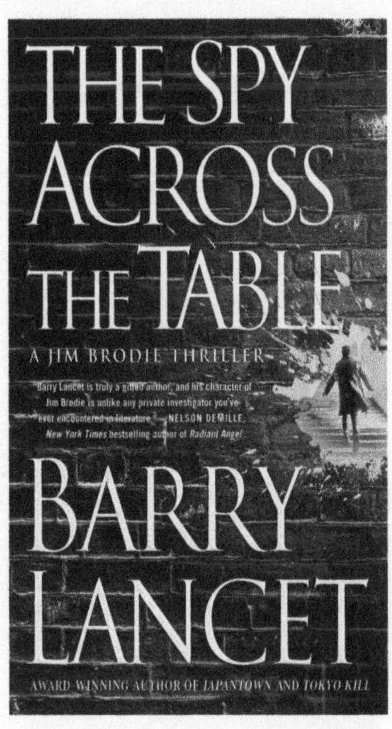

CHAPTER 1

DAY 1

SUNDAY, 3 P.M.

THE KENNEDY CENTER, WASHINGTON, D.C.

MIKEY was shot because he begged me for a favor and I complied.

My old college buddy and I stood in the wings of the Kennedy Center's Opera House theater, watching a Kabuki play unfold in front of a sold-out crowd. VIPs were abundant.

Mikey was starstruck. While everyone in the audience tracked the mesmerizing movements of the Japanese players in their colorful robes, Mikey focused on the bigger picture. Yes, he took in the artistry of the actors, but with their movements his expert eye cataloged the exquisite details of the backdrop, the exotic sweep of the pageantry, and how each played off the other.

"Her costume and makeup are perfect," Mikey said in a low voice. "Is that really a man under there?"

My friend's emerald-green eyes sparkled as he soaked up the spectacle. Onstage, snowflakes wafted down. A woman in an elaborately embroidered kimono cooed plaintively for her lover. The expression of emotional turmoil on her face was sublimely complex, half-hopeful even as it plunged toward despair.

"Yes," I said.

Early in seventeenth-century Japan, the shogun had famously banned women from the Kabuki stage. In times of peace, the elegantly clad females proved too much of a temptation for aristocratic samurai, who were expected to set an example for the common people by staking out society's moral high ground. Over time, the long-standing men-only policy evolved into a tradition, which persists to this day.

Mikey remained incredulous. "Are you absolutely sure?"

"I'm certain of it."

In compliance with the shogun's decree, Kabuki troupes wasted no time in seeking men with the prowess to play a woman. Costumes were upgraded. Makeup was subtly altered. Gestures demure and flirtatious were practiced endlessly. The illusion was refined, then perfected.

Talented male actors in female guise began to hold fans in rapt attention. As new stars were born, the Kabuki experience reached new heights. Women theatergoers modeled their wardrobes after what they saw onstage. Male patrons dreamed of finding equally refined lovers of the opposite sex.

Even today, Kabuki theatrics continued to win converts. Transfixed, Mikey was clearly another. Before him, an actor in snow-white makeup, coiffed wig, and ruby lips uttered a soft lament.

"What'd she say, Brodie?"

She. I told him.

"Brilliant," he whispered, scanning the gradation of light sweeping across the stage and the way the colors played off the falling snowflakes. "The mood of the lighting and even the set itself echoes her sentiment."

Michael C. Dillman was a production designer. He created sets for movies. Tonight he was a kid in a candy store. We'd run into each other at San Francisco State, where we shared the same artistic sensibilities. Mikey funneled his into set design. I channeled mine into a store selling Japanese art and antiquities out on Lombard, west of Van Ness Avenue.

"How is it you two never met?" I asked, a reference not to the "temptress" onstage but to Sayuri "Sharon" Tanaka.

My old college buddy blushed. "I . . . I just never found the time."

I smiled at his transparent evasion.

Mikey was shier than shy, even with two Oscar nominations and one win under his belt. Sharon Tanaka was a famed Japanese production designer and had been hired to create special backdrops for the *Kabuki at the Kennedy Center* show.

"Did I thank you for getting me in to see her, Brodie?"

Mikey was a longtime admirer of Sharon Tanaka's work.

"Yes. More times than I can count."

Sharon and I were friends and frequented some of the same art circles in Tokyo. When Mikey had heard she would be traveling to Washington with the Kabuki troupe, he'd asked me to arrange a meeting. I'd been honored to bring the talented pair together—a meeting of the minds long overdue, in my opinion.

"This is a dream. Thanks, man. I owe you."

"No, you don't," I said.

From under a disheveled bush of auburn hair, his eyes glowed with a gratefulness I found embarrassing. I looked away.

Mikey checked his watch. "Time to go see the grand lady. Thanks again, man."

"Stop saying that. Maybe one day you two can collaborate."

Mikey grew wistful at the thought. "That would be nice. Wish me luck."

"You don't need any. Just enjoy the get-together."

Turned out I was wrong.

He needed luck in the worst way—and didn't get it.

CHAPTER 2

THE muffled sound of a gunshot reached my ears during the fireworks scene, and momentarily my thoughts strayed from the spectacle before me to Mikey and Sharon.

Onstage, faux Roman candles shot glittering starbursts into the air. The bouquets of color enthralled onlookers, and temporarily deafened performers.

In the wings, the echo of gunfire alerted all who could decipher the backroom volley. Which turned out to be two wired-up Secret Service agents, and me. An American staffer from the running crew cocked her head at the distant pop, then dismissed it. The Japanese stagehands looked puzzled, as if considering the possibility of a rogue firework escaping the confines of its carton.

The Secret Service agents reacted instantly. Their presence confirmed the attendance of VIP heavyweights. With an event as rare as a Kabuki performance all the way from Tokyo, a heady cocktail of luminaries was guaranteed. No doubt a good sampling of senators and cabinet secretaries and ranking diplomats were in the theater. Rumors placed members of the White House family on hand as well.

The discharge had been partially muted either by distance or a closed door. Possibly both. The direction suggested the vicinity of the dressing rooms.

Where Mikey was meeting his idol.

There had to be dozens of people in the dressing area, including actors and staff preparing for the next play, but maybe I should wander back and check on my friends.

I cast a last glance at the actors onstage. The woman character, wrapped in kimonoed elegance, collapsed to her knees in slowly unfolding agony.

Her samurai lover raised his sword with justifiable fury, turning and twisting in hopes of striking a villain who, by pulling strings without showing himself, had snared the twosome in his web. They had set a trap and hoped he would appear, but to the end he outfoxed the star-crossed pair.

Saddened, defeated, and resigned, the couple froze, assuming a final dramatic pose. The moment was poignant. Into the stillness of the scene, a new round of fireworks released a climactic series of thunderclaps, sending out rivers of sparks arching over the heads of the doomed lovers. More than one jaw in the crowd slackened. More than one eye glistened.

On the heels of this fresh cascade came a second gunshot.

The dressing rooms it was.

I moved toward the rear, a nameless fear clawing at me.

Out front, the first of three mini-plays wound up. The gallery broke into a rousing applause. Cheers arose. I heard the rustle of the crowd rising to its feet for a standing ovation. But in the dim recesses of the box seats, I caught a parting glimpse of dignitaries being ushered from their privileged places by shadowy guards.

Near me, a Secret Service agent with a sharp nose and roving eyes spoke hurriedly into the microphone at his wrist, while his vigilant partner kept an eye toward the back. I slid past them. The second man called after me but I ignored him.

A third shot rang out.

I broke into a run, my insides swamped with a rising dread. Five seconds later, footsteps pounded the path in my wake. One of the agents, I guessed.

The changing area turned out to be a perplexing maze of narrow halls and unexpected turns. I'd heard about this. Temporary quarters had been erected for the flood of actors arriving from Tokyo.

No one was around, so I plunged into the network of plywood passageways. They were dark, the lighting high in the rafters overhead filtering down unevenly. A series of random turns brought me to a large communal area somewhere in the center of the makeshift paneled city—where I faced three routes, each winding away in a different direction.

I no longer heard footsteps behind me.

A band of Japanese staffers clustered in the center, falling silent when I appeared. These would be the wardrobe and makeup people from Japan, charged with maintaining the props and helping the actors with their costume changes.

The space overflowed with racks of sumptuous Kabuki robes against one wall, and spears and swords up against another. On a long table the coiffed wigs of Japanese aristocrats, samurai, and courtesans bristled with topknots for the men and colorful lacquered hair ornaments for the women.

"Where is Tanaka's room?" I asked the group.

They stared back at me without comprehension. What was I thinking? Few, if any, would speak English. Fewer still would speak firearms. Gun control was fiercely enforced in Japan, the guttural crack of a handgun as foreign to their ears as English.

"The set designer, Tanaka-san," I said in Japanese. "Where can I find her?"

Heads bobbed, then one staffer pointed to a murky hall. "Turn left at the end, then right at the second lane."

I nodded my thanks and charged back into the darkened maze. When I veered left at the junction, the shadows lengthened. Electric cords ran along the bottom edges of the makeshift walls, then slithered underneath and into individual quarters. Weak bands of light spilled from the gaps below doors.

I swung right in time to catch a light-skinned figure in a cap at the end of the hall slipping from a room and tucking a gun into a holster under a coat. Could have been a man or a woman with her hair tucked up.

"Hold up," I said loudly.

The shooter picked up speed and disappeared around a corner.

I raced after the fleeing form. My shout having caught the attention of actors readying for the next play, doors creaked open along the hall. Heads appeared.

"What's happened?" one of them asked.

I didn't stop to answer. As I charged past the open dressing room door from which the shadow had emerged, I glanced in. The acrid smell of cordite rolled over me, then the tangy copper scent of blood spilled.

There were two bodies in the unlit room.

No no no, I thought. *Not them. Don't let it be them.*

I dashed into the room and the forms clarified before me. It was my friends. Mikey and Sharon were sprawled across the floor, dark circles of blood pooling around them. I dropped to my knees.

This was bad. They didn't stir. And there was far, far too much blood.

Sharon had been shot twice in the chest. Mikey's wound was higher up, between the heart and the collarbone, as if he'd been in motion when the trigger had been pulled. Sharon had no pulse, but there was a faint beat at Mikey's neck.

I grabbed a towel off the dressing table and used it to stem his bleeding. Then I did the same for Sharon. Ghoul-like, cast members crept forward in the gloom and crowded around the entrance.

In the back of my head, a clock was ticking. The retreating figure was twelve seconds gone.

I laid crossed hands on Sharon's chest and began pumping. Quick chest compressions from the CPR playbook. Three, four, five times. I stopped and passed a hand under her nose. Nothing. I hammered home a second series, glancing up at the gathering in the doorway as I worked.

Twenty-five seconds gone.

"Any of you know CPR?" I said in Japanese.

"We do," a man at the back said. "I'm a doctor and my assistant is a nurse and physical therapist."

The medical personnel traveling with the troupe.

"Great," I said. "Can you take over? The man's got a pulse. The woman doesn't."

They jumped right in. The doctor took over the CPR, the nurse rushed to Mikey's side. I watched until I was sure the self-proclaimed medical staff knew what they were doing.

Thirty-five seconds gone.

"Anyone here speak English?" I asked, again in Japanese.

A young actor in the doorway said, "I do. I study UCLA two years."

"More than enough," I said, switching to English and enunciating clearly so he could catch the phrases he would need to use. I told him to run up front to the wings, ask for the first-aid station, and bring the defibrillator back here—the device that uses an electric shock to start the heart. At the same time, he should have someone call 911, the emergency number. After that, he needed to show someone else the location of the dressing room so the paramedics could be guided through the maze.

"Got all that?" I said.

"Yes."

"Good, then I'm off."

I dashed after the shadow, wondering if the fifty-five seconds I'd used to buy my friends a fighting chance had given the assassin enough time to escape.